THE THIRD PERIL

Best - J.P. Hoffman

What people are saying about The Third Peril

"The Third Peril is a novel that merges elements of historical fiction and contemporary suspense. In 1777, as he fought and suffered to win freedom for the fledgling nation of America, General George Washington received a divine revelation at Valley Forge: 'Three great perils will come upon this nation,' and 'The Third Peril will be the worst.' The first two great trials were destined to be the Revolutionary War and the Civil War; in the modern day, a terrible shadow looms. Influenced by a profound premonition, five-year-old Connor Hays, son of the Chief Economic Advisor to the President, warns that 'War is coming to America!' But will anyone listen to a child, let alone believe him? Re-examining the underpinnings of crises that can topple powerful nations, The Third Peril is a page-turner to the very end. Also highly recommended are author L. P. Hoffman's previous novels, 'The Canaan Creed' and 'Shadow of the Piper'."
–Midwest Book Review, June 2013, Small Press Bookwatch

"This book is a goose bump generator; exciting, intriguing, and foreseeing. The theme mirrors today's world conditions. This is Hoffman's third book. She has experienced the cultures of different countries. Her cultural and Washington insider experiences are reflected from unique viewpoints in her writing."
–Recommended and Reviewed in The Mindquest Review of Books by Lightwood Publishing

"THE THIRD PERIL by L.P. Hoffman is an intriguing tale with divine visitations that explores the line between belief and doubt amid the backdrop of politics. This is a novel for the thoughtful reader. The story is presented very well, and those readers interested in this type of book probably will not be able to wait to read the story. In that respect, well done. The story moves along well and is engrossing. The author has control of the subject matter and the exploration of religious topics is organic to the story rather than feeling inserted as a message. Good job! Overall, a story that will make the reader think and keep the reader entertained. Nice work."
–Writer's Digest Self-Published Competition, Judge's Commentary

"The author is a skillful writer who has crafted a fascinating novel. She created an intriguing premise and is adept in using the various novel-writing elements: characterization, dialogue, dramatic scenes, pacing, suspense, setting, and so on to maximum advantage. Her background lends itself to the plotline and helps the novel feel genuine. It's difficult to criticize the author's skill set, as her writing is definitely top-notch. The opening pages were compelling and well drawn, and the only (mild) detractors were the introduction of so many characters that it caused readers to wonder who to fall in love with. Generally, introductions are dispensable, but Ms. Hoffman's is stellar and essential to the novel, which is rare."
–Writer's Digest Self-Published Competition, Judge's Commentary

"The Third Peril is a heart-thumping book. I read L. P. Hoffman's books every second I can, including when I use the bathroom in the middle of the night!"
–Annette Hertzler, Annie's Gleanings

"Washington, DC, Florida, and a couple of small towns in North Dakota and Arizona; a little boy who's been diagnosed as schizophrenic, a teenager convicted of murdering his entire family, a troubled store owner, a presidential adviser whose marriage may be about to fall apart, and the President of the United States himself. How are all these places and persons linked? And how do they implicate the very future of the United States itself? Well, it's a mystery. . .the very sort of suspenseful mystery that only LP Hoffman can masterfully pull off. The Third Peril is Hoffman's third book and it delivers everything and more that made her first two books so successful: interesting characters, rich detail in locales, and above all, the role of faith and redemption in every life. Her characters and their families move through the stories with an uncanny authenticity. And that's even true when she writes about White House personalities and intrigue. This was a book that I had a hard time putting down even to go to bed. Alexander the Great himself would have difficulty untying the Gordian knot of this story before the end. I read 45 to 50 mystery novels a year, including long-established writers and new writers. Hoffman's books stand with the best of them. To even describe any of the story would be to give away too much, so I will simply say this is a must-read for fans of suspense, mystery, and even romance (real romance; no bodice ripping here!). Her earlier books were The Canaan Creed, and Shadow of the Piper." [Full Disclosure: I've known the author and her family for more than a decade.]
–Craig Manson, Former Assistant Secretary of the Interior

THE THIRD PERIL

Book One of the Trilogy by

L. P. Hoffman

www.hopespringsmedia.com

The Third Peril
By L. P. Hoffman

www.TheThirdPeril.com
www.LPHoffman.com

Published by Hope Springs Media.
www.hopespringsmedia.com
P.O. Box 11, Prospect, Virginia 23960-0011
Office: (434) 574-2031 Fax: (434) 574-2130

International Standard Book Number:
978-1-935375-04-3

Printed in the United States of America.

Cover and book design by Hope Springs Media and Exodus Design.
Original cover artwork by L. P. Hoffman.

Dedicated to:

God who is always faithful; to Paul, whose love is a blessing I count everyday; and to all who are thirsty in a dry and weary land.

Prologue

Valley Forge
December 1777

In the stillness of his room, General George Washington whispered, "Mercy. . . ."

The word dispatched upon the wind. "Have mercies upon us, Lord." Coals burning in the fireplace cast amber light upon his bowed head, yet even this could not take the chill from his troubled soul.

Beneath the wool coat of the fledgling nation's leader, Washington's flesh trembled. With hands clasped in earnest petition, he continued, "Sovereign Lord, I ask this not for myself, but for the men. Oh, the suffering." The general's voice trailed off with a moan of deep lament.

His thoughts turned to the bloodied feet, sunken eyes, and sallow skin of the soldiers, whose clothes and shoes were threadbare and tattered. Tragically, many had come through battles only to succumb to illness. Outside, the frigid wind whistled through the bare branches of the Pennsylvania oaks at Valley Forge.

Washington lifted his head and gazed beyond the wavy-glass window. Upon nearby hills, he could see the fire rings that dotted the encampment. The soldiers—mere shadowy forms—were huddled about the flames. Supplies had been sporadic at best. For weeks, the army had subsisted on fire cakes, a bland mixture of flour and water. The men's weakened bodies needed meat.

Washington's eyes filled with tears. God alone could know his brokenness for these soldiers, who had fought valiantly in worthy campaigns against the British. *Is this to be their reward?* he thought.

The general's fist curled in anger and frustration. He slammed it on the wooden table, and candle wax sputtered upon his papers. "How long, Lord?"

Without warning, a figure appeared at the far end of the room. His face flashed like lightning, and his eyes resembled flaming torches.

Washington recoiled when the angelic visitor reached out with a hand that shone like burnished bronze. "Fear not, Son of the Republic." His voice roared like a multitude, yet the words were strangely soothing. "I have come to testify of three great perils that shall come upon this land," he said. "The most fearful is the third."

A silence followed, so profound that the general fell mute.

"Look now and learn," the visitor beseeched. He raised his arms and an image materialized, shimmering as if it consisted of a thousand points of light. A picture formed.

Washington found himself gazing upon a moving map, his own eyes witnessing the battle through which the soldiers outside had just come. Then the picture moved to battles yet to come, reassuring the general that America's victory would be secured. The vision stilled and the image faded, leaving Washington feeling uplifted.

But then the mysterious visitor spoke again. "Son of the Republic, look and learn." Another vision formed: A storm cloud formed over Africa and quickly approached the great continent of America. It drifted over the map like a mist and seemed to hover over the southern portion of the United States. The general then found himself gazing on two armies bathed in sweltering summer heat. Soldiers dressed in uniforms of blue set themselves against soldiers clad in gray. The casualties and the suffering were massive.

Tears clouded the general's eyes as the angel traced the word UNION over the vision; then, in blood, he wrote, "Remember, you are brothers." When he was finished, the message melted together to form an American flag—slightly different from the one that Washington knew. The general watched with interest as the inhabitants dropped their weapons and, upon the smoldering ground of conflict, they united around the National Standard.

Washington felt weak now; his trembling turned into violent, convulsive shivers.

Again, the visitor extended a blazon hand and strengthened the general with a touch. "Son of the Republic, now the last great peril that shall befall your nation—look and learn."

He placed a trumpet to his mouth and blew three distinct blasts. A vision of a turning globe appeared. The angel reached into the apparition, taking water from the ocean and then sprinkling it upon select countries. A fearsome scene appeared.

From these nations, thick black smoke rose skyward and grew until it merged into a massive churning column with sinister fingers. When the dark haze cleared, the general could see hordes of armed men marching by land, sailing by sea, and flying upon the wind to America.

In that instant, George Washington perceived that he himself was there on the battlefield, watching; but, this war was different. The first attack was silent, yet insidious, like a deadly plague. The second attack took the country unaware. Instruments of war the general's eyes had never beheld assaulted the nation from all directions.

"The people of this land have forgotten the One who keeps them," the angel said as victory shouts echoed across the oceans.

"No!" Washington cried. Anguish broke his spirit, and yet his eyes could not look away.

"Tell them to remember. . . ."

"What will be the outcome?" General Washington demanded, but there was no answer, for the mysterious visitor had vanished.

Part 1
The Foreshadowing

O beautiful for spacious skies,
For amber waves of grain,
For purple mountain majesties
Above the fruited plain!

America! America!
God shed His grace on thee
And crown thy good with brotherhood
From sea to shining sea!

O beautiful for pilgrim feet
Whose stern impassion'd stress
A thoroughfare for freedom beat
Across the wilderness!

America! America!
God mend thine ev'ry flaw,
Confirm thy soul in self-control,

Thy liberty in law.
O beautiful for heroes prov'd
In liberating strife,
Who more than self their country lov'd,
And mercy more than life.

America! America!
May God thy gold refine
Till all success be nobleness,
And ev'ry gain divine.

O beautiful for patriot dream
That sees beyond the years
Thine alabaster cities gleam
Undimmed by human tears!

America! America!
God shed His grace on thee,
And crown thy good with brotherhood
From sea to shining sea!

Katharine Lee Bates

Chapter 1

Valley Forge

Saturday, June 23rd

Paige Hays squeezed her husband's hand as she gazed upon the quaint stone house famous for having been Washington's headquarters. "Somehow, I'd envisioned a bigger building," she said. "I mean, for a general destined to be the President of the United States."

"Yes, I would agree it's small by today's standards," Brody answered. "Though I doubt it bothered George Washington. From all accounts, he was a humble man."

"By today's standards," Paige added playfully. Her eyes were fixed upon the thick clouds building in the sky, where brilliant shafts of sunlight broke forth and fanned across Pennsylvania's bucolic landscape.

"Daddy, is this Valley Forge?"

"Yes, son." Brody stooped and tousled his five-year-old's unruly cowlick. "George Washington really slept here."

Paige smiled at her husband, but he had turned his attention to a historical marker. She watched Brody as he absently tapped a finger on the cleft of his chin and read.

Despite the premature graying of his light brown hair and the stress lines that marked his face, she still saw the same tall Yale graduate who had captured her heart so many years ago. These days, it was a rare sight to see Brody looking so relaxed.

Connor tugged his father's hand. "Let's go, Daddy. I wanna look inside."

"In a minute, son."

"The camera! I left it in the Land Rover!" Paige sprinted back down the trail toward the parking lot. She found the bag sandwiched between a cooler filled with picnic food and an assortment of Connor's toys. Paige plucked it up and jogged back to her family.

Brody was standing beside the front door of the stone house with his Blackberry in hand.

"For heaven's sake! One of these days, I'm going to throw that thing in the Potomac."

Her husband raised an eyebrow, but his focus remained on the device. "There's a law against destroying government property, you know." Brody finished punching out a quick email message. He slipped the PDA back into its holster and draped his arm across his wife's shoulder. "You should be grateful for such modern conveniences. This Blackberry allows me to enjoy these occasional excursions with my family."

"Where's Connor?" Paige's words came out calm, but her heart began to race.

"He's not with you?" Brody glanced about, cautioning his wife with a look. "Don't overreact."

Fear flashed through Paige's senses. Her throat

tightened. “Connor!” She spun around, her eyes keen for any sign of her child.

“He can’t be far,” Brody said.

Paige’s face reddened with anger. “How could you lose him? I was only gone a minute!” She jerked open the front door of Washington’s headquarters and called her son’s name again.

“I’m in here, Mom.”

Relief washed over Paige, but a sick feeling remained. Inside the building, she struggled to calm her nerves.

Brody’s strong arms encircled her from behind. “Honey, you’ve got to stop this,” he whispered. “You can’t go on like this. It’s tearing you up.”

Hot tears stung Paige’s eyes. “Are you asking me to forget?” She twisted from her husband’s embrace and searched his face. “Is that what you’re doing, Brody?”

Connor pulled on his mother’s arm and pointed toward a room located to the right of the entryway. “Mom, how come they got windows in the doors?”

Paige felt a rush of tenderness for her son and stroked his hair red, the same color as hers. “These are Plexiglas dividers. They’re used to keep people from going into these rooms.”

“How come?”

“The furniture is old and very fragile,” Brody explained. “They don’t want little kids poking around in there.”

Connor pushed on the Plexiglas as if testing its strength and left behind two faint handprints.

Paige’s mood lightened. She offered her husband a conciliatory smile as they lingered outside the office of the nation's first commander-in-chief. "It's almost like George Washington just stepped out for a moment." Paige pointed to his hat, which lay upon a desk strewn with books and papers. "Just think: in this room, Washington steered this great nation!" She glanced at her husband, considering the fact that Brody himself held a unique place in history as the chief economic advisor to the current president. Paige felt a swell of pride.

Connor dashed up a narrow flight of stairs, and the couple hurried after their young son.

Paige glanced around and, realizing they were alone, said, "I expected more tourists."

"The popularity of theme parks has its benefits." Brody leaned down and nuzzled his wife's ear.

A few yards away, Connor pressed his forehead against another Plexiglas partition. "I bet this is General Washington's bedroom."

Paige looked past her little boy "That's right, sweetheart." The room was small and modestly furnished. It had a four-poster bed, a woven rug, and a straight-back chair near the fireplace. Soft light spilled through the French pane window, illuminating the desk beneath it.

"But where did all the other army guys sleep?" the child asked.

Brody motioned toward the window as the sky outside darkened. "The soldiers stayed outside in tents. Some of the men camped on those hillsides."

Connor, having lost interest, turned his attention to three plastic army men that he had retrieved from his pocket.

Paige met Brody's eyes, and she shrugged. "Your son

has a longer attention span than most preschoolers." The sound of her husband's Blackberry trilled again, and Paige's heart sank. *Not today—not again!* She watched with disapproval as Brody scrolled through an electronic message, punched some numbers, and held the device to his ear.

"This is Hays. . . ." Gone in an instant was Brody's relaxed manner—in its place was a frown. "Yes, I understand. Listen, you're breaking up. I'll call you right back." He cast an apologetic look Paige's way.

She felt her teeth clench. "We've been planning this weekend for months!"

"We'll talk in a few minutes. Right now, I need to make this call." Brody descended the stairs.

Paige bit her lip and struggled to control her mounting frustration.

At her feet, Connor was making little noises like gunfire. "Sweetheart, are you ready to go?"

"No!" he protested. "I like it here. I want to stay for a little while!"

Anger percolated in Paige. *The whole day, ruined! No—this time I will not give in!* "Connor, I'll be right back," she said.

Outside, she found Brody pacing back and forth in front of the stone building, the Blackberry pressed against his ear. He was fully engaged in conversation, his mannerisms both animated and serious. A moment later, with shoulders slumped, her husband slid the device back in its holster and turned, surprised to see Paige leaning against the building.

She took one look at her husband's face and knew. "We're heading back to DC, aren't we?"

"I'll make it up to you, I promise."

As far as Paige was concerned, there was nothing more to say except, "I'll get Connor." Raindrops began to fall as she turned back to Washington's headquarters.

Brody caught up to his wife on the second floor. He reached for Paige, but her patience was dangerously thin. She brushed his hand away.

Connor was standing in front of the Plexiglas partition, staring into George Washington's bedroom as if mesmerized. Paige reached for her little boy's hand. "Sweetheart, Daddy's got work to do. I'm afraid that we have to go home."

The child poked his lip into a pout. "No fair! I want to spend a night at the hotel!"

"Some other time," Brody said. "Now, gather up your toys."

"Can't, 'cause I gave them to the giant man."

Paige's maternal antenna shot up. "What man?"

"He was really big and shiny," the boy said, making a sweeping motion. "He can walk through walls, too! But he's not a ghost. He's an angel."

"That's nonsense," Brody said impatiently. "Son, I don't have time for games."

The sound of enthusiastic footsteps rose from the stairwell, and the family turned to see an elderly man ascending. He paused atop the landing, ran a hand down his long white beard, and smiled. His pale blue eyes danced from Brody to Paige and then lit upon the boy, who was yanking insistently upon his father's sleeve.

"But it's true, Daddy," Connor insisted. "The angel asked me for some of my soldiers."

Brody flicked a self-conscious glance toward the visitor, who was now stooping to tie the laces of his hiking boots. The old man raised a bushy eyebrow and said, “When I was a kid, I gave a couple of my favorite marbles to an angel.” A puff of laughter blew through his downy beard. “Don’t you be thinking I lost my marbles, though, ’cause I offered ’em of my own free will!”

Paige studied the odd character, who wore baggy Bermuda shorts and an oversized Hawaiian shirt.

Connor stared at the traveler. “You look just like our yard gnome.”

The old man hooted with laughter as Paige offered an apologetic look.

Brody cleared his throat. “Yes, well. We’d better be going.”

A sudden clap of thunder shook the building, followed by buckets of rain that drummed on the ceiling overhead.

“That’s a curious sight!” The traveler nodded toward Washington’s bedroom window, where rain washed over the glass in glossy sheets. On the sill above the wax-laden desk were three plastic army men, positioned as if looking out upon the deluge.

“Those are Connor’s.” Paige shook her head in disbelief. “But that’s impossible!”

The elderly tourist walked over and inspected the Plexiglas partition. He scratched his head. “Well, there’s only one explanation. That angel must have had a good reason to put them there.”

Chapter 2

Washington, DC
Thursday, June 28th

Brody watched the president's helicopter bank right around the Washington Monument and head for the White House landing. On either side of the craft, two decoy helicopters split off and circled over the Mall until the commander-in-chief was safely on the ground.

On the South Lawn, the aircraft blades whined to a stop near the courtyard, where Brody and the usual entourage waited.

The helicopter's hatch opened, morphed into a staircase, and Thomas Atwood descended the steps. His salt-and-pepper hair glistened in the sun. He was only 44 years old when he was elected—one of the youngest US presidents on record. Atwood had aged visibly in the last few years. He looked more gaunt than lean, and his former youthful energy had flagged since taking office.

At the bottom of the steps, President Atwood saluted a marine and then made eye contact with his personal secretary, Jane Hennings.

"Welcome back, sir." With a stack of memos in hand, she moved forward briskly. "How was Camp David?"

"Not as restful as it should have been." The president's unibrow heaved in a scowl.

"Sir, I'm sorry that your sabbatical was cut short, but the Secretary of Agriculture felt it was important that you make a showing at this meeting." She consulted an oversized wristwatch and then added officiously, "I'm afraid we don't have much time; the event is nearly underway."

"You can be pretty bossy," Atwood quipped.

Jane looked stunned. "Sir, I assumed that's precisely why you hired me."

The president's thin lips twitched with a ghost of a smile.

Brody and Atwood shared a chuckle as Jane led the charge across the South Lawn like a long-necked swan with her gaggle. The president's personal secretary whisked them through the White House, below the south portico, and then out to his private driveway. There, a limousine sat idling, flanked just as the helicopter had been by two identical decoys.

Jane handed the president the stack of memos.

"How many are expected to attend this American Farm Bureau luncheon?" he asked.

"Around 500 invited guests. And I'm informed that the press has already swarmed L'Enfant Plaza Hotel."

"Another media circus," Atwood muttered, thumbing through the papers. "What's all this?"

"Brody Hays has put together a briefing for you, sir." Jane failed to mention that the chief economic advisor had been up all night working on them.

Atwood settled into the backseat of the limo and motioned to Brody. "Climb in, Hays. I don't see the sense of reading all this myself when the author is standing right in front of me! You can fill me in on the way."

Brody took a seat across from the president and waited patiently as he flipped through a series of photos. Brody knew the images of scorched earth, once fertile ground for dry land farmers.

Atwood seemed affected by the pictures. Finally, he looked up. "Give me the bad news first," he said, as they rolled down 17th Street.

"The Ag Department has a right to be worried, sir," Brody began. "We are heading into the second year of severe drought—well into the peak growing season, I might add. If this weather pattern continues, I'm afraid the long-term economic forecast will be less than favorable."

"That's all we need—another dust bowl!"

Brody looked down at his hands, conscious of the sweat that dampened his palms. He pondered the fragile economy, already weakened by the disasters that had plagued previous administrations. Now, the biggest suppliers of grain in the nation's heartland were withering away beneath a cloudless sky.

Up ahead, the streets cleared for the presidential motorcade, and people gathered for a glimpse of the nation's leader before he was spirited into the hotel parking garage.

"What's your advice, Brody?"

"Sir, I've outlined some economic strategies in the briefing—though these are only temporary measures designed to buy us some time for further analysis. Currently, I am weighing the cost of various options." Brody paused as the president drummed his fingers impatiently on the armrest. "To be concise, sir, I advise you to address the gravity of the situation, suggest an interim strategy, and pledge further attention to the matter."

Thomas Atwood raked his fingers over his silver temples. His mood grew pensive. "Are you a religious man, Hays?"

Brody shifted as the Secret Service detail opened the armored car door. "Not particularly, sir."

"If you were, I'd ask you to pray for rain." The president stepped from the limousine, leaving behind the photos of North Dakota's cracked and dusty landscape.

North Dakota

Wednesday, July 4th

It was going to be another scorcher, Nora Meyers had decided. The thermometer next to her door read 84 degrees, and it wasn't even 10:00 AM yet. *At least I'm on the shady side of Main Street*, she told herself.

Delmont's only police cruiser crept past with its flashers on, a signal that the parade was about to begin.

The mood was festive. *Rare these days*, Nora thought.

From somewhere out of view, the high school marching band started.

She straightened the red, white, and blue bandana that hid another one of her bad hair days. Nora smiled at a cluster of locals who strolled past and said, "There's room on my porch—the more the merrier!"

A small crowd soon joined her on the steps of the Bargain Bin, and they exchanged friendly banter as they waited for the parade.

"Here it comes! Here it comes!" A little girl pointed and sprang up and down. Other children appeared on cue.

"I'm gonna get the most candy," a round-faced boy boasted.

"Uh-uh!" a little girl challenged.

All heads turned to see an old Rambler station wagon rolling up the street on a set of bald tires. The car was a relic, pocked with rust and body putty. The fender was held in place by duct tape.

Children spilled into the street with their hands spread for offerings. The driver slowed the vehicle to a crawl and leaned his hoary head from the window. "Hi, folks!" A breeze caught his snow-white beard, and it fluttered like a flag.

"We want candy!" the round-faced boy croaked.

The man's cottony eyebrows shot up. "Afraid I don't have any."

The kid's chin jutted, and he eyed the driver skeptically. "Just what kind of a clown are you, anyway?"

The old man braked to a full stop and chuckled. "Been told I resembled a yard gnome, but this is the first time I've been called a clown!" He held up his index finger and said, "Hold on—think I got something you might be interested in." After rustling through a stack of boxes on the car seat, the traveler produced handfuls of little bright orange New Testaments. "The Gideons gave me a whole box of these."

The children snatched the Bibles as if they were priceless gems, and even a couple adults stepped forward to receive.

On the far end of Main Street, the band inched its way closer, but the elderly fellow didn't seem to notice. He hung his arm out the car window and motioned toward the porch. "Hey, which one of you is Nora?"

"I am," she said. "How do you know my name?"

His crystal-blue eyes glistened playfully. "I read it on the sign—NORA'S BARGAIN BIN." The stranger smiled. "Sure is a great town you folks got here. I do believe you've got the friendliest welcoming committee that I've ever run across."

"Then you're not part of the Fourth of July parade?" Nora asked.

"Parade?" The old man's eyes fixed upon his rearview mirror and widened as the band converged upon him. "Independence Day! I knew that!" He quickly dropped the car into gear. "Hey, Nora, I got my eye on that pretty Hawaiian shirt in your window display. I'd be grateful if you'd set it aside for me. I'll be back for it—you can count on that!"

The strange man drove away, leaving a cloud of blue smoke hanging in the air in front of a group of gangly, adolescent band members.

Nora clapped as the marching band shuffled in stride. Behind them, the baton twirlers kept time, except when they were chasing wayward spins. Proud parents shot video, and grandparents waved from lawn chairs. *The parade will soon be over*, Nora thought sadly. *This happy mood will wilt again under the cares and worries of shriveled crops and bills to pay*.

On the street, a warm gust of wind kicked up a pile of

gutter trash. A high-stepping red horse danced sideways and snorted at a paper bag that blew along the pavement. The rider, dressed as a decorated soldier, tried to calm his steed, but the American flag he was carrying flapped in the wind. Spooked, the horse reared back, shed his rider, and then galloped off.

Nora raced down the steps and bent over the man. “Are you okay?”

“I think so.” The soldier climbed to his feet, dusted off his pants, and stared at the American flag lying crumpled on the dusty asphalt. “She’s fallen to the ground,” he said. “The only proper thing to do now is burn it.”

Chapter 3

Washington, DC

Wednesday, July 4th

The White House security guard leaned down and peered through the window of Brody's BMW. "I was beginning to think you were staying all night again." The guard grinned. "Sometimes I think you keep a sleeping bag in the West Wing."

"That's not a bad idea," Brody said wearily. He had burned the midnight oil three times this week in a desperate attempt to come up with a stimulus plan for the flagging economy. Somewhere through the maze of red tape and beyond the ominous quagmire of indicators, Brody was determined to find that proverbial golden egg. But not tonight—tonight he had plans.

The guard punched in a code and the gate swung open. "Are you coming back to watch the fireworks this evening? I hear this year's display is choreographed to John Philip Sousa marching music."

"I'm sure it will be spectacular, but my wife has organized a small dinner party." Brody snapped his wrist over. "In fact, I'd better be on my way."

"Have a nice Fourth of July!"

"Thanks, Teddy, you too."

The fiasco at Valley Forge flashed through Brody's thoughts as he steered down Constitution Avenue. He had some patching up to do with his wife. Up ahead, a Metro Bus blocked the intersection, and commuters stacked up like dominoes. A bicyclist rolled past Brody's car and disappeared from view across the Roosevelt Bridge. Brody envied the cyclist and reminisced about the good old days when he used to ride his bike to work on the W&OD Trail. His finger rose to trace the small, jagged scar on his chin—a reminder of how fragile life could be. He had been lucky to get just a few stitches and a broken clavicle.

Paige had come undone. "You could have been killed!"

It had been an overreaction as far as Brody was concerned, but in Paige's mind a monster lurked behind every corner waiting to snatch away her loved ones. She had not been the same since Emily; even Connor's birth had not eased his wife's fears as he'd hoped. In some ways, having another child had only made things worse.

The traffic report indicated a snarl ahead on the toll road that led to the Northern Virginia suburbs, so Brody bailed out on the Georgetown Pike—his alternate route. It was far from an original thought. Brody fell behind a line of cars as they snaked down the tree-lined road, past old-money mansions and manicured estates.

As he neared the entrance of Great Falls Park, Brody felt a sudden wave of guilt and wondered what things might be like if he had turned down his DC position. *No,* he reasoned, *Paige and I made the decision as a couple. We were aware that the opportunity of working for the President of the United States came with sacrifices.* Still, they'd had no way of knowing what it would cost.

A BABY ON BOARD sign hung in the back window of a slow-moving minivan. In a sudden burst of impatience, Brody blasted his horn. A minute later, traffic slowed to a thirty-mile-per-hour crawl. The dashboard clock approached 6:30 PM. After several traffic light changes, Brody merged onto Route 7, and the traffic began to move nicely except for an SUV hogging the fast lane. He gripped the wheel of his BMW and surged on the commuter, coaxing him to move out of his way. This time, Brody was determined not to be late.

Virginia

Wednesday, July 4th

The classical station played softly on the kitchen radio as Paige arranged onion chutney, pickled garlic, cornichons, and Petrou olives on a large platter. In the center, she placed a roll of duck pâté and then sliced a baguette to garnish the edges.

"Smells great," Brody said, slipping through the kitchen door with a handful of letters in his hand. He tossed mail onto a built-in kitchen desk and then went to explore the pots simmering on the Viking stove. "What French culinary masterpiece are you working on tonight?" He lifted a copper lid and a mouthwatering aroma escaped.

"Normande sauce for the main course, with Scallopini

de Veau and veal tenderloin medallions." Paige wiped her hands on an apron and then handed her husband an unopened bottle of Burgundy and a corkscrew. "Any mail for me?"

"There's another letter from David. I was going to wait until after the dinner party to tell you."

Paige hurried over to her desk and shuffled through the pile until she found the one postmarked Arizona. The name on the return address was David Fillmore.

"Are you going to open it?" Brody asked, popping the cork. He set the wine on the counter to breathe and awaited her response. Paige chewed her lip.

"It's been two years," Brody said gently. "Maybe it's time to put your differences aside."

"Differences?" Paige shook her head and tossed the letter back into the pile.

Brody put his arms around his wife. "Honey, it was an accident."

In her head, Paige knew her husband was right, but this was a wound that would not heal. *How could it heal?*

Brody picked up the letter and handed it to her.

Reluctantly, Paige slid it open with a manicured nail and read. She felt her face grow hot. "David got married!"

"That's good news. It's about time someone came along to mellow your brother's wild tendencies."

She handed her husband a photograph. "I wouldn't count on it." It was a picture of David astride a motorcycle. Beside him was a petite Latina.

"Nice bike! The new bride isn't bad either." Brody tossed the photo on the counter. "So, what else does your brother have to say?"

"David opened a law practice in Arizona."

"Well, you have to admit, this is a start in the right direction."

A swirl of emotion engulfed Paige: doubt, anger, and, finally, the sting of rejection. "At least my brother could have had the decency to invite us to the wedding."

"Would you have gone?" Brody asked.

"That's not the point!" Paige turned back to her culinary tasks. "I'm not going to let this ruin my dinner party."

She loaded her arms with plates of pomegranate-garnished salad and pushed her way through the swinging door and into the dining room. The table had been set with hand-painted bone china and the family silver. Paige arranged the salads and then went to check on Connor.

She found him playing happily on the living room floor, nestled among their Federal-style furnishings. "It's almost bedtime."

"Can I sleep with my new toys?" He gathered his collection of battle figures into a bucket.

Paige scowled. "I don't think it would be a good idea."

Brody wandered into the living room with the plate of duck pâté. "What harm will it do if the boy sleeps with a few tin soldiers?"

With bucket in hand, they watched their son bolt up the curved staircase in his red-footed pajamas.

Paige shot Brody a look. "I still don't understand why you bought him both the Revolutionary and Civil War sets of soldiers from that antique store. They'll all just end up on the bottom of the toy box."

"The boy likes history, just like his dad."

The doorbell rang. Brody went to welcome the guests while Paige checked her makeup in a gilded mirror. She ran a finger around the liner that showcased her sea-foam eyes, pulled a runaway strand of red into her hair clip, and smoothed her silk dress.

"Darling! You look stunning!" Margaret Elliot rushed at her with arms outstretched. She pecked Paige's cheek and sniffed the air. "What is that divine aroma?"

"Maggie's been starving herself all day. I think she plans on eating a second helping of your famous crème brûlée."

"William!" Margaret squawked. Her husband, a short man with strings of hair plastered across a balding head, laughed.

Paige excused herself to tuck Connor into bed while Brody offered their guests refreshments. Upstairs, she found her child asleep, the soldiers scattered haphazardly upon his pillow. Connor had added a few green plastic army men to his collection. Paige kissed her finger and touched it to his forehead. *He's such a good boy—everything a mother could hope for.* Yet her heart still ached with a sense of loss and she felt selfish for it.

The doorbell rang again, and Paige returned to greet her other guests—her neighbors, Jim and Betsy Crew.

The dinner conversation was pleasant, except for Margaret bringing up a photograph that "she just happened to see" while in the kitchen. "Who is the nice-looking young man on the motorcycle? He looks delicious."

"He's my brother." Paige took a sip of wine and pressed a napkin to her lips.

"Really, darling, I didn't know you had a brother. He looks like such a rugged type, and you're so polished and proper." Margaret's heavily tweezed eyebrows rose like the Arc de Triomphe. "And who is the girl standing next to him?"

"David Fillmore is a sensitive subject," Brody interjected.

Paige smiled weakly at her husband, who had inadvertently fanned the flames of Margaret's nosy nature.

"Fillmore, you say?" Jim Crew stabbed a piece of veal with his fork. "Any relation to Steadman Fillmore, the publishing tycoon?"

"He was Paige and David's father," Brody said.

Jim Crew nearly choked on the piece of meat. "You're pulling my leg," he said. "Steadman Fillmore died twenty years ago, and he was ancient then!"

"I was sixteen years old. My brother was in kindergarten." Paige struggled to hide her annoyance. *Here goes,* she thought.

"We're sitting at the table with an heiress!" Jim, an investment banker, lifted his glass in a toast. "I would love to take a peek at your portfolio somc time."

"My husband is very good at what he does," Betsy chirped.

"I'm sure he is," Paige said, flashing a terse smile. "Dessert, anyone?"

Brody poured coffee from a silver setting while the guests lavished their hostess with praise for the gourmet meal. The night was winding down after another successful dinner party.

"Mom, I can't sleep." Connor shuffled toward the

dining room table in his footed pajamas. He held his bucket of soldiers.

"I'll tuck him in," Brody said, rising from his chair.

"Oh, please let him stay a few minutes!" Margaret said. "Whatcha got there, Connor?"

The boy's face lit up enthusiastically. "I'll show you." He climbed up on his mother's lap and dumped the bucket on the dining room table.

The guests seemed amused as they watched him line up each group of soldiers. Then Connor looked out across the table and said, "Ready?" They watched as the child knocked over the tin redcoats first, employing a spray of sound effects. Then he cheerfully said, "We beat these guys, you know." Next, Connor turned his attention to the Civil War pewter set. "Pow, pow. Boom, boom, pow." After knocking over all the soldiers, both Union and Confederate, the boy's face screwed into a frown. "A lot of people get killed in this war, but nobody really wins until the brothers put down their weapons."

"That's right, son." Brody puffed with pride.

Suddenly, the child rolled his tiny fists across his eyes and began to whimper.

"What's wrong, honey?" Paige circled her arms protectively around her son.

"The next war will be the worstest!"

"Must be talking about World War II," William Elliot speculated. He then took the opportunity to jab at Brody. "What are you doing teaching a five-year-old about war? SpongeBob would be more appropriate."

"Daddy, was war number two in America?" Connor

asked.

"No, son, it was in Europe and the Pacific." Brody stood and took the child from his mother's lap. "It's time for bed."

"But Daddy, the next war will be in America. That's what the angel said!"

"You must have been dreaming."

"Don't you believe me, Daddy?" Connor squirmed in his father's arms as he was carried back upstairs. "The angel told me it's true! Just like when the angel talked to me at Valley Forge! Remember?"

Paige tried to downplay Connor's strange proclamation, but worry needled her.

Margaret had other things on her mind. She tapped Paige's hand and leaned across the table. "So, tell me all about that rich brother of yours."

Chapter 4

Arizona
Monday, July 9th

David Fillmore opened his PO Box, reached inside, and thumbed quickly through the mail, mostly junk. There was no reply from Paige.

He had poured his heart out in his letter to his sister and tried to explain that things had changed—that he had changed. *Maybe forgiveness is too much to expect*. David crushed the junk mail, chucking it across the lobby and into a trash can.

Behind the service window of the tiny rural post office, the matron offered a toothy smile and hollered, "Have a nice day!"

David gave her a nod as the door close behind him.

Outside, two local kids were loitering near his motorcycle. A blond boy was running his fingers over the bike's black tank. He peered at David from beneath a shaggy ledge of bangs. "Dude, is this your ride?"

In answer to the question, David swung his leg over the seat.

"Sweet!" The kid gave a thumbs-up. "I've been telling my friend that the Triumph Rocket III Classic has one of the most powerful motors made. He doesn't believe me. That's right, isn't it?"

David snapped on his helmet. "I'll take your word for it." He turned the key and pushed the starter button. The engine rumbled to life.

The boy's button nose pinched into a scowl. "Man, you either don't know what you got, or you don't care!"

Probably the latter, David thought as his bike's wheels spun on the pavement and left behind a puff of white smoke. In the rearview mirror, the modest post office on the edge of town shrank to the size of a stamp and disappeared from sight. Highway 54 rolled ahead like the spine of a serpent, and David revved the Triumph's engine until it made a high whine. He picked up speed but couldn't escape from the heat that radiated from the engine and blacktop like from a brick oven.

David whooshed past an army of saguaros. *They look like weary soldiers*, he thought. *It might be easier to run straight into those massive, prickly arms than to find closure*. It was the silence that bruised David the most, those things that remained unspoken. He twisted the throttle until his fingers tingled.

David kept his eye on Eagle Pass, looming larger as he raced toward it. At the incline, he slowed just enough to keep his wheels from breaking loose and then leaned hard into the winding switchback curves that twisted skyward.

Just over the crest of the plateau, David rumbled into a pullout near a historic marker that chronicled Arizona's gold rush days. He climbed from his bike, removed his helmet, and brushed a tangle of damp dark hair from his forehead.

From the desert, a mournful cry arose—almost human—and David scanned the terrain for movement. His gaze froze on a coyote whose brown and silver fur was camouflaged among the outcroppings. The animal let out a series of excited yelps as it dug furiously. Suddenly, it sprang into the air and pounced on a rabbit.

There was a rhythm in the desert that put life in perspective. It was so unlike the ivy-laden walls of old money. Back east, the rules of conduct seemed sullied by tradition or driven by raw ambition.

No regrets, he told himself, as if the words could somehow make it true. There were plenty of regrets.

David slid a cell phone from his leather vest pocket. It barely registered three bars, but it was the best signal he could get in the middle of nowhere. He exhaled slowly and then dialed a Virginia number. As usual, it went to voicemail, and, as usual, David hung up and slid the phone back into his pocket.

He turned his thoughts back to the desert panorama. To the east, surrounded by federal public lands, sat a huge tract of private land owned by a rancher named Rupert Sims. Thousands of sheep once foraged these arid plains. It seemed like a miracle to David that any creature could survive in such a harsh environment.

David allowed his gaze to follow the razor wire that delineated the US-Mexican border to the south. Eight miles this side of the boundary, the highway gave way to a stretch of crumbling asphalt known as Arroyo Seco's Main Street.

The town had reached its peak during the gold rush days. Today, its wooden storefronts had seasoned to splintered gray ghosts with broken windows baffled by brittle yellowed newspaper. Some of the buildings sat empty; others warehoused dusty relics abandoned in the exodus.

Yet progress had left feeble marks on Arroyo Seco. David smiled when he thought of the town's only stoplight that dangled by a wire after being used for target practice for so many years. It didn't matter much anyway. According to Elita, the only traffic to come this way were the tumbleweeds that blew through town at a brisk clip.

There were two footpaths in Arroyo Seco that still hinted of life. The trail most worn led to a dive bar called the Watering Hole, a sundown gathering place for those either too hardy or too lazy to leave. The other path led to the General Store, where David lived with Elita in a tiny upstairs apartment. "Home." He said the word aloud because it sounded pleasant to his ears. It was something he hadn't been able to say for years.

David recalled the day he had rumbled into town on his Triumph with a duffel bag full of clothes and a proper wedding ring for his new bride. Some details were still fresh in David's mind, like the raucous music and laughter that spilled from the old-fashioned swinging doors of the Watering Hole. From the bar's deck, a man wearing a fishing cap hollered, "Hey, stranger, come tell us a story and I'll buy you a beer."

David had considered the invitation as he climbed from his bike. *Just one,* he thought; but then he flung the duffel over his shoulder and said, "Thanks. I'll pass."

The man with the fishing cap crossed the street, swirling what looked like a glass of milk in his left hand. "Not so fast, stranger! I made a bet with my friends over there." Fishing Cap tilted his head toward a couple of guys leaning against the outside wall of the Watering Hole. "You're the only one who can settle it for us."

David nodded at the men, a six-footer whose bald head glistened under the glow of a streetlamp and a skinny, slick-haired kid clad in desert camo. "What do you want to know?" Beneath the sun's glare, Fishing Cap looked older than he'd first appeared. *Mid-sixties,* David surmised.

"Are you running from the FBI, the IRS, or a bad relationship?" The man took a sip of milk and wiped his mouth. "Personally, my money's on the FBI."

David waited for the punch line, but Fishing Cap's face was serious. "What kind of question is that?"

"A logical one. Nobody comes to Arroyo Seco without a darned good reason!"

The General Store's screen door banged open, and a petite, long-haired Mexican beauty flew down the porch steps. David dropped his duffel as she leapt into his arms.

Fishing Cap's eyes were locked on Elita. He knocked back the last of his milk. "Take your money off the table, boys—we're all wrong!"

"Gordon Spitzer," Elita said, "I'd like you to meet my husband, David Fillmore."

"So this is the guy you told me about?" Spitzer pushed his fishing cap up and scratched his forehead. "I understand you two got hitched six weeks ago. What took you so long to get here?"

"I had some things to take care of," David said. *Rehab is nobody's business but mine,* he thought.

Spitzer stared at David's worn biker boots. "You sure don't look like an Eastern lawyer to me."

"Maybe that's because I'm an Arizona lawyer now." David grinned.

"You passed the State Bar!" Elita yipped and did a little victory dance.

Gordon Spitzer turned to go but then hesitated. He cast a sideways glance at David. "I've got a little compound a few miles from here. People around these parts call us the Civic Border Guard—or CBG for short. Stop by after you get settled and I'll give you a tour of the place."

Seven months had passed since then. To date, David still had not taken Spitzer up on his invitation. Now, standing on the top of Eagle Pass, he had a bird's-eye view of the CBG's compound. The place was once an old stucco mission, and it still looked like one with the exception of a barbed-wire perimeter and a metal Quonset hut filled with khaki-clad converts. *They're probably glassing me at this very moment,* David mused.

Elita believed the Civic Border Guard were just trying to help. "Illegal immigration is a very complex issue," she would say, gently reminding her lawyer husband that illegal immigration was, after all, against the law.

But there was another reason for David's reserve—one that he kept to himself. He didn't like the way that Gordon Spitzer looked at his wife.

Dusk was settling over the desert. Heat waves still shimmered from the porous soil, but soon the air would crisp with the evening chill. Overhead, a red-tailed hawk soared, its feathered wing tips spread like golden fingers. The sun sank lower, and a fan of amber light burst from over the horizon, making the skyline blaze with orange and crimson.

Emotion caught in David's throat. There was a subtle splendor here that could only be appreciated by the naked eye. No Harvard professor had ever come close to explaining the mark such a display of beauty left upon the human spirit. In all directions, the view faded in the soft light as if to disappear into some eternal vanishing point.

David fired up his motorcycle. Down below, roads were etched across the landscape like veins. There was a time not too long ago when he would have blindly followed them. But things had changed. Love found David when he wasn't looking. But it hadn't come without internal conflict.

"Elita," he said softly, "what did I get you into?"

Chapter 5

Washington, DC
Monday, July 9th

Behind his mahogany desk, Brody Hays stared at the latest economic projections—all portents of hard times. He could not help but wonder if he had climbed to the pinnacle of his career only to discover he was teetering on a house of cards.

Brody shook his head. "Not on my watch," he muttered, as if sheer will and determination could keep things standing.

There was a soft rap on his office door. Brody was tempted to tell whoever it was to go away, but the door opened and he launched to his feet to welcome the president. "Sir," he said, "please, come in."

Thomas Atwood dropped his thin frame into the chair and lifted a photo from the desktop. "That boy of yours must be, what, four or five?"

"Connor is five, sir."

"You're lucky to have such a fine-looking boy. Sometimes I regret not having a family." Atwood returned the photo to its place. "I just came from a meeting with the

Secretary of Agriculture, and I'm here to talk about increasing farm aid."

"Increased aid, sir? As you know, we have already reimbursed the farmers in the hardest hit areas for their crop losses. At this time, I'm not sure it would be fiscally prudent to—"

"It's simply not enough." The president scowled.

"I've been going over the most recent projections, sir." Brody swallowed. "And the economy is not responding to our stimulus. Tax revenues are down while government spending is up. To make matters worse, unemployment is up, and the Federal Reserve is concerned about inflation. I'm sure that you are aware that they are threatening to raise interest rates."

Atwood seemed to pale, emphasizing dark circles around his gray eyes.

Brody paused. "Are you all right, sir?"

"I haven't been sleeping well lately," the president explained as he stood and then moved toward the door. "Look, Hays, I hear what you're saying, but I'm concerned about the cost in human capital. People are suffering, and I am in a position to help. Have a proposal on my desk by tomorrow morning."

Atwood hesitated in the threshold and glanced back at Brody. "I received a letter from a woman in North Dakota a while back. Those folks could use a moral lift, so I've scheduled a trip to the heartland. I'd like you to accompany me."

"Of course, sir."

Alone again in his office, Brody thought about the overwhelming task at hand. A few silent minutes passed before he picked up the phone and dialed. "Paige, I won't be home for dinner. I have to work late again."

North Dakota

Tuesday, July 10th

From the window of the Bargain Bin, Nora Meyers could see a line of people all around the courthouse. A semi truck was parked in the east lot, its driver unloading cardboard boxes and stacking them like towers. Along with subsidies, the government was now supplementing food supplies.

"It will get better soon," Nora told herself. "All we need is a little rain." Sadly, such optimism was not shared by many in her tight-knit community. Two years of drought had nearly crippled the plains, and economic hardships soon resulted in business closures. No one dared to think what next year would be like if the heavens remained shut.

For the people of Delmont, the difference between hope and despair hinged upon the words of the weatherman, whose most recent report called for record heat and continued drought.

Nora opened a box of donated clothing and busied herself with the task of sorting. She brushed long bangs from her forehead and picked through a pile of threadbare and stained items. Nora noticed that even the quality of donations had sunk to an all-time low. She glanced again at the semi truck unloading supplies and thought, *I could be standing in that line*.

A small inheritance, along with her modest income, was the only thing that had kept Nora afloat—barely. This drafty brick edifice where she eked out her living had also seen its share of hard times. The building had once been a short-lived community vision called the Delmont Hotel. Back in the day, the town patriarchs had hoped that a first-class hotel would lure the railroad to town. The railroad never came and, like a jilted bride, the Delmont Hotel withered from neglect—that is, until Nora's aunt turned it into a colorful local hangout called Jem's Pancake Palace.

The faded sign still hung above the weathered porch, a memorial to Aunt Jem's hospitality. Over the years, though, buttermilk flapjacks and steaming crocks of maple syrup had been replaced with racks of used clothing and lollipop-fingered toys. A definite demotion, in Nora's opinion.

The screen door swung open, jarring Nora from her daydreams. "Hey, Ms. Meyers!" Lindsay Hall sauntered over with her toddler trailing at her sandaled feet.

"Hi, Lindsay girl." Nora, still kneeling at the cardboard box, threw open her arms. "Brooke, come give me a squeeze." The baby girl waddled over and dove into Nora's arms, giggling amidst a barrage of kisses.

The teenage mother glanced around. "Ya'll got anything new?" She rubbed a belly ring that was sandwiched between a skimpy halter top and a flowery skirt.

"Not much." Nora climbed to her feet as Brooke made a beeline for the toy box. "Oh, I almost forgot!" Nora dashed into the storage room and promptly returned with a colorful vest on a wire hanger.

Lindsay gasped, took the prize, and ran her hand over

the stitching. "I love it!"

"The moment I saw it, I knew it was meant for you!" Nora parked her hands on her hips and grinned. "Girl, you've got that Bohemian style."

"How much?"

"It's a gift."

Lindsay held the garment to her heart. Tears sprouted in her faun-brown eyes. "It's the best gift anyone's ever given me."

The words saddened Nora's heart. She opened her arms to embrace the young mother.

Lindsay had arrived in Delmont with a duffel in hand. Everything she owned was in that tattered bag. She was noticeably pregnant. Tongues had wagged in the small town when this child gave birth to her own child.

"Y'all have been so good to me." Lindsay's emotions floated to the surface. "I don't know how to thank you."

"Nonsense," Nora said with a flick of her wrist. "There's no need."

Lindsay stared intently at her.

"Do I have spinach in my teeth or something?"

"I was just wondering how old you are?"

"Lindsay! You're not supposed to ask a woman's age!" Nora shrugged and said, "What the heck—I'm 41."

"You could be very attractive if you did something with yourself." The teenage mom tapped her chin. "Y'all ever watch any of those makeover shows? It just so happens that I'm gifted in the areas of style."

"Really?" Nora looked up in surprise. "I didn't know that!"

"Someday I'll make a name for myself. You just wait and see." Lindsay worked her gum. "I could advise you on your wardrobe, too. Anything but those awful stretched-out t-shirts you're always wearing."

Nora slipped a freshly ironed blouse onto a hanger and pointed to a box. "That's wonderful, but right now you can sort that stack of children's clothes. Who knows, you might come across some outfits that would look cute on Brooke."

"Awesome!" The young mother dove into the box with enthusiasm and immediately pulled out a frilly frock. "What do you think?"

Nora glanced at the toddler, who was built square and sturdy like a little Mack Truck. "I think Brooke would look like a little princess in that!"

Lindsay set the item aside and continued sorting.

"Oh, yeah, I almost forgot," Nora said. "Today is a five-dollar-bag special."

Lindsay popped her gum. "I got my pride, you know. I ain't takin' any charity. I'll work for it. Tell ya what—this place could use a little of my artistic flair!"

Nora covered her mouth so the teenager wouldn't see her giggle. "Don't know how I managed before you came along."

The young mother slipped into the back room and returned with a Hawaiian shirt. "First, I'll start with a little splash of color on the walls. I'll need some tacks and a hammer."

"Not that shirt—I promised to hold it for someone." Nora thought about the odd little man who had blown through town on the Fourth of July. *Probably never see him again, but a promise is a promise.*

By noon, the Bargain Bin had seen a steady stream of customers, and Nora was glad for a lull. "Lunch is every man for himself!" Nora announced slipping into the kitchen to make herself a sandwich. She had just settled down at the Fifties-style table when the bell on the front door jingled and someone called her name. Nora recognized the voice of her dear friend Abigail. "I'm in here!"

Abigail appeared in the kitchen doorway wearing khaki Capris that made her short frame look even shorter. "What do you think of my new haircut?" She tousled highlighted blonde tufts. "You don't think it's too racy for a pastor's wife, do you?"

"It suits you." Nora nibbled on some ham and cheese. "Help yourself to the sandwich makings."

Abigail shook her head, poured herself some coffee, and plopped down at the table. "How's business?"

"Too good," Nora said softly. "I'm afraid a lot more people are thrift shopping these days."

Abigail blew steam from the mug. "Hey! Did you hear that the president is coming to North Dakota? It's in the paper. I read that Thomas Atwood had some family ties in this state—a brother and some grandparents."

"His brother passed away."

"Yeah, the article said he was tragically killed."

Nora stared at her sandwich. "I wrote the president a letter a few weeks ago—wanted to tell him how people are suffering around here."

"Really? Do you think he'll actually read it?"

Nora thought about another letter that she'd written long

ago but never sent. “I hope so.” She brushed crumbs from her fingers.

Abigail snapped her wrist over and checked her watch. “Look at the time! I’m supposed to be at the church to let Magna and Ava into the prayer room.”

“Where’s Pastor Henry?”

“You know my husband, always busy. Right now he’s on a prayer walk with Celeste.” Abigail sighed and rose to rinse her cup in the sink. “That woman is so amazing. She’s teaching a class on spiritual warfare. You really should come.”

As her friend turned to go, Nora detected sadness. She moved to her best friend’s side. “Abigail, is something wrong?”

“Don’t be silly.” The pastor’s wife forced as smile. “Are you coming to the worship service tomorrow?”

Nora seldom attended the Wednesday night meeting, yet something made her say, “I’ll be there.”

Chapter 6

Arizona

Wednesday, July 11th

David Fillmore sat in his makeshift office in the General Store's utility room and tried to concentrate on his work. It was a losing battle. The tapestry curtain that separated the storage room from the mercantile wasn't thick enough to muffle the noise of heavy foot traffic clomping across the old pine floor or the sound of the store's old-fashioned cash register chiming another sale.

David rubbed his temples and then positioned his fingers on the keyboard. *Just a few last-minute details,* he told himself. *Then, the affidavit of trust for the estate of Rupert Sims will be ready for signatures.* A mental image of the old rancher standing on the front porch of the General Store came to David's mind. Rupert resembled a caricature from a western greeting card with his bent straw hat, pearl button shirts, and wrangler jeans that hung loose over aged bones.

"So you're that lawyer fellow I've been hearin' 'bout?" Rupert had asked when they'd first met. He ran gnarled fingers over his leathered face. "Harvard, eh? Or do you boys pronounce it Haaavawd?" Rupert scrutinized David from beneath a wiry ledge of eyebrows. "What kind of a lawyer are you, anyway?"

David considered the question and then looked the ancient cowboy straight in the eye and said, "A reluctant one."

Rupert Sims had cackled with laughter. "I like you, kid! I got something I want you to do for me, a legal matter." He thrust forth a calloused hand, and they shook on it. "You've got a good, strong grip. I believe a fellow's handshake is as good as his word!"

The cowbell on the front door of the General Store clanged, jarring David's thoughts back to his cluttered desk.

A few seconds later, Elita slipped through the tapestry door curtains looking like an exotic gypsy in her white peasant blouse and festive cotton skirt. A smile played across her lips. "I wonder what my great-grandfather would have said if he knew his store would one day double as a law office."

"Is he the one who shot at lawyers?"

"No, that was my grandfather. Lucky for you he died young!"

"It sounds busy out front," David said, changing the subject.

"First week of the month is always busy." Elita mouthed the word "payday." "We're also getting a steady stream of campers—strange for the hot season."

David lowered his voice to a whisper. "Have those boys from the salt flats showed up trying to hawk their food stamps for beer money?"

"I married a cynic," Elita winked. "But a discerning one."

David pulled his young bride onto his lap and kissed her neck.

She flushed. "There's a woman asking for you."

"You're the only woman for me."

Elita untangled herself from his embrace. "I'm serious. Might be a new client."

She ran her fingers through her silky black hair, making David wish he could do the same.

The overhead pipes rattled and moaned. "I'd better meet her out front." David pushed himself up from his crude plywood desk, grabbed his suit jacket from a coat hook, and slipped it over his black t-shirt.

The couple moved through a maze of shelves stocked with groceries.

Elita stopped next to some wooden bins filled with penny candy and tugged on her husband's sleeve. "That's her." She pointed to a middle-aged woman who was waiting near the cash register. "She didn't give me her name, but I'm sure I've seen her before."

The potential client was staring into a glass display case. She turned toward David as he approached and said, "Mr. Fillmore, I presume?"

"That's right."

The woman tapped her finger on the display cabinet. "Is this authentic native jewelry?" She patted a massive squash blossom hanging from her neck. "I only ask because there are so many fakes these days."

David summoned patience. "The artisan is an old

Navajo woman who's been doing business here for generations. If that's why you came, my wife can tell you more."

"That won't be necessary. I was just curious." An awkward moment followed. "My name is Joanne Sims. I've come to discuss my father, Rupert." The woman was tall enough in her high-heel boots to look David square in the eye.

"Rupert's not. . . . I mean, is everything okay?"

"Dad is still with us," Joanne reassured him. "However, the doctor says that it might only be a matter of days."

Suddenly, a round woman wearing spandex and a tank top elbowed her way in the middle of their meeting to riffle through an old pickle barrel filled with sale items.

"Maybe we should continue this conversation in my office."

Joanne rolled her wrist over and checked her watch. "Mr. Fillmore, I'm in a hurry, so I'll come to the reason for my visit. I understand that my father has recently retained you." Without waiting for a response, she forged ahead. "I'm here to ask you to withdraw your services."

"Is there a problem?"

"I simply want to consolidate my father's legal matters where they've always been: under the trusted umbrella of Hartman and Hartman."

David noted that Joanne Sims had emphasized the word "trusted." In poker terms, it was a tell.

She opened a red leather briefcase, dug through its contents, and retrieved a checkbook. "You will be generously compensated for your trouble, and, of course, the retainer is yours to keep." Joanne clicked her pen and held it over a blank check. "Does $1,000 sound fair?"

"I'm sorry, Ms. Sims. I'm afraid I already shook on it."

Joanne's brow furrowed. "Excuse me?"

"Your father said a man's handshake is as good as his word," David explained. "We have an agreement."

Joanne puffed air. "Really, Mr. Fillmore!" She bit her lip and then continued with guarded words. "You strike me as an intelligent man. I'm sure you have observed that my father is. . . , well, let's just say he's eccentric."

True, David thought. *Rupert's instructions were unorthodox.*

"Look, this isn't personal," Joanne said. "It's just that Hartman and Hartman happens to understand my father's particular needs."

"Like I said, I can't help you." David's words were firm, but polite.

Joanne aimed her gaze down her sharp, pointy nose. "You can't, or you won't?" Her tone was clipped, like the sound of her boot heels as she moved toward the door.

Before leaving, she spun around and lobbed the last word. "Mr. Fillmore, my father can be very stubborn. I should warn you, it runs in the family."

North Dakota

Wednesday, July 11th

Sadness followed Nora all the way back to her little white house in the country, the kind of melancholy that had no reason. The mood stayed with her as she climbed the creaky steps past a splintered porch swing and into her modest home.

On the other side of the door, Nora knelt to greet a bouncing tangle of black and white fur. "Hey, Otis, how's my good buddy?" Nora took the shaggy mutt's head in her hands and gave his ears a tussle.

He shook free and flipped over on his back for a belly rub.

Nora laughed at his exaggerated leg twitching, but still the shadow of sadness remained. *Maybe church will lift my spirits*.

She glanced at the wall clock. It was 4:45 PM. *Just enough time to grab a bite*. Nora drifted through her living room, past early American furnishings and across a braided Ragg wool rug. The decorations were plain, even bordering on austere; yet, generations of joyful living had transpired behind these unpretentious walls, living that was real, deep, and full of faith. She could almost envision her mother sitting in the old Shaker rocking chair speaking words seasoned with wisdom.

"God is always welcome here," Eunice Meyers used to say. "But when that old devil puts on his god suit and comes knocking in all his finery—and don't you think he won't—then you'd better shut that door in a hurry!"

"How will you know it's the devil?" Nora asked.

Eunice Meyers's answer was always the same. "You'll never get fooled by a counterfeit if you study the real thing!"

Otis barked, coaxing Nora's thoughts back to the present. "Are you a hungry boy?"

He followed his owner into the kitchen and swept the floor with his wagging tail at the sound of the electric can opener. She set his bowl next to a water dish.

Nora opened her refrigerator and peered inside. There was a half-eaten bowl of oatmeal from breakfast, a few eggs, a small jug of milk, and some fruit. She grabbed an apple and dashed out the door. The Wednesday night worship service would be starting in forty minutes, and she lived a good twenty minutes from town.

As Nora drove down the country road, she reminisced about her friendship with Pastor Henry and Abigail. They had met shortly after Nora's mother passed away and the couple made a condolence call.

When the fog of grief finally lifted, Nora found her place among the family of believers at the Delmont Harvest Center.

Five years had passed since then. The little congregation had always felt like a church home until recently. Nora couldn't quite pinpoint the cause of her unease. From all appearances, church life was bustling. A wind of infectious enthusiasm had blown through the doors, and the pews were filling with new faces. "Revival is at hand!" Pastor Henry had announced last Sunday.

The words had caught in Nora's spirit. They still left her feeling conflicted and even a bit ashamed. *Revival is a good thing,* Nora told herself as she steered her Chevy through town and into the church parking lot.

In the sanctuary, the music team was tuning their instruments, and Abigail was busy setting Bibles in the pews. Her face lit up when she spotted Nora.

She rushed over, saying, "I'm so glad you came!"

"Where is everybody?"

Abigail motioned toward her husband's office and whispered, "Prayer meeting. Celeste and some of her intercessors came with a burden." The sound of muted sobs issued behind the closed door. "They're travailing in the Spirit," Abigail explained.

"Oh," Nora said, feeling awkward. "I'll make myself useful in the kitchen." She tackled dirty dishes that had been left in the sink and set up the coffee pot. Nora arranged a plate of cookies and nibbled on the broken pieces herself.

Before long, a fast-paced worship song thundered through the walls, and Nora hurried inside the sanctuary to take a seat. She nodded and waived at a few familiar faces: Freddie Ross, still wearing his Thriftway Grocers apron; and the Ramey family, who filled the back row with their brood of seven. Over on the far side of the room, Pops Turner leaned over a Bible marked with colorful sticky tabs.

The lively tempo of praise reached a crescendo, and the sanctuary doors flew open. Three women emerged, dancing barefoot and rattling tambourines over their heads. All eyes were upon the ladies as they moved, twisting, winding, and snaking their way up front.

Celeste was in the lead; her white hair swayed with the rhythm of her graceful gait. Trailing behind, protégées Magna and Ava flapped their gauzy arms like awkward goslings. The dance continued through the litany of praise songs. Others joined in until the music grew soft and reverent.

Pastor Henry stepped up to the podium, sporting the beginnings of a new goatee. He was a handsome man, in fine physical shape for his forty-some-odd years. The pastor lowered his crown of wavy brown hair and mouthed a silent prayer.

A few seconds passed. The congregation waited expectantly. With the Bible clasped firmly in hand, words began to rumble from the pastor's lips. "Beloved saints, our dear sister Celeste has sounded a spiritual alarm. The enemy of our soul is on the prowl!"

Henry motioned, and Celeste dutifully rose from her seat. "Come, sister. Share the burden that has been weighing heavily upon your heart."

Nora watched the woman as she moved to the platform. Celeste was a natural beauty whose premature white hair framed ethereal blue eyes and alabaster skin.

"Let's pray." Celeste drew in a deep, cleansing breath and continued. "Thank you, Heavenly Father, for choosing me to be your special messenger. I humbly accept this divine commission." She raised her hands toward the cathedral ceiling, but her eyes were on the congregation. "If you truly love the Lord, then stand with me!"

All across the sanctuary, people rose to their feet.

"Now lift your hands toward heaven!" Again, the woman's instructions were obeyed.

Nora remained in her seat. Something just didn't feel right about these Simon-says orders. *God knows I love Him,* she thought.

Celeste spread her arms like a grand bird of prey. "I had a vision of a beautiful crystal stream of light—power issuing from this very pulpit." She swept her long fingers toward the pastor. "This anointing was flowing from this mighty man of apostolic calling!"

The congregation was entranced.

The woman's countenance darkened and the air seemed to crackle with emotional energy.

"As I watched, the ground began to shake. A deep fissure was formed, and then a chasm swallowed that beautiful crystal stream!" She cried out, "There is sin in this camp—the sin of rebellion and of unbelief!"

Celeste's pale green eyes moved like a torch from face to face.

And then, to Nora's dismay, they froze upon her.

Chapter 7

Washington, DC
Friday, July 13th

Brody rapped his knuckles softly on the half-open door of the room adjacent to the Oval Office. "It's Hays," he said.

The door swung open to the owlish face of Jane Hennings, clad in tweed and sensible shoes.

"Mr. Hays, you're always the first one to arrive," the president's personal secretary said as he followed her into the Oval Office. "You shouldn't have to wait long."

Brody took a seat as Jane moved about the massive desk, straightening Atwood's papers and placing his morning schedule in the center.

"Oh, there's something I want to show you." Jane selected one of the memos and held it up.

"That's my briefing to the president about the World Fortress Institute," Brody said.

"I found a typo. Fortress is spelled with two s's, not one," she said officiously. "I thought you might have a word with your secretary."

"Mea culpa."

"Pardon me?"

"Mea culpa. Latin for 'my fault,'" Brody said. "I wrote the memo myself."

Jane's expression bore a strange resemblance to Brody's old Yale Professor for English Lit.

"Oh, well, I'm sure it was just an oversight." She returned the memo to the desk.

Chief of Staff Chip Skinner breezed into the office muttering something about last-minute schedule revisions. He spotted Brody and said, "Hays, you're up with the roosters. Or did you pull another all-nighter?"

Without waiting for a response, Skinner snapped his fingers in Jane's direction. "The 3:00 PM appointment with the Secretary of Agriculture has been shifted to tomorrow. Oh, yes, and the Speaker of the House requests five minutes of the president's time."

The chief of staff paused before heading out the door. "Hays, the president has a rigorous schedule, so I hope you'll move the meeting with the World Fortress Institute along at a brisk pace."

Jane slipped into her office to make the scheduling adjustments and returned a few minutes later.

The kitchen staff arrived with a silver coffee service and a plate of tea biscuits.

Brody started to rise when the president walked through the door, but Atwood motioned for him to remain seated and proceeded to go over the day's schedule with Jane.

With that out of the way, the president settled behind his desk and laced his fingers together. "Before we get started, Hays, I want point out that our Farm Aid media coverage has been favorable."

"I'm glad, sir."

"The oil and gas credits are still on the table, though," Atwood added. "Some of the folks at the Energy Department are spooked about the idea of tapping into our reserves."

The president directed his attention to the memo in front of him. "Let's see. . . ." After scanning the paper, he looked at his chief economic advisor and said, "World Fortress Institute. I'm all ears."

"They are a global organization whose primary aim is to ensure viable international trade."

"I've heard of them, but frankly my knowledge ends there."

"That's not surprising, sir. This group is relatively unknown, yet many of their board members are key players in international banking. After the World Fortress Institute helped to develop the new smart card technology, they shot through the global financial scene like a rocket. I have a feeling that we will be hearing their name a lot more."

"Do you have any idea what they want to discuss with me?"

"I believe they want to talk about the European Union's new resolution to make a transition to digital cash."

The president nodded thoughtfully. "The IMF and World Bank. . . , where do they stand on this?"

"In theory, they're behind the idea."

Atwood laid the stack of papers down and pressed the intercom on his desk. "Jane, you may send in my next appointment."

The president and his advisor rose as two men were

ushered into the Oval Office. A squat, dark-haired man with a square jaw thrust his hand into the president's and pumped vigorously. The second man, heavyset and a head taller than his colleague, stepped forward and made the introductions. "Mr. President, sir, my name is Walter Rutherford, and this is Jean Pierre."

Atwood directed the men to a cozy circle of chairs. "Gentlemen, what can I do for you?"

"That's what we find so refreshing about you, Mr. President," Rutherford said with a proper British accent. "You are quite direct and to the point."

Jean Pierre cleared his throat. "Sir, we are here to discuss your nation's goodwill." Perfect diction trilled from the man's heavy French tongue. "Mr. President, I'm sure that you are aware that in recent years the United States, shall we say, has suffered from a rather tarnished image within the international community." He flashed a micro-smile. "The World Fortress Institute may be able to help."

President Atwood's eyebrows rose slightly, and for an undetectable second he met Brody Hays's equally surprised gaze. "Please, go on."

"Europe is in the dawn of a new age," Rutherford cut in. "We are enjoying unparalleled economic cooperation among nations. It's really rather historic."

"My colleague is correct," Jean Pierre said, grabbing back the reigns of control. "Since Great Britain joined with the European Union, the response to our cashless incentives has been enthusiastic. More than a hundred countries have made inquiries." Pierre's fingers drummed his chin. "Everyone, it seems, is anxious to ride the crest of this unstoppable wave. That is"—he punctuated the moment with a pause—"almost everyone." The Frenchman cleared his throat and flashed another hint of a smile. "There is only one tiny obstacle to the universal success of this endeavor. In the world of free trade, your nation is a major player. Accordingly, all of the cooperative nations are watching and anxiously awaiting your response."

Thomas Atwood leaned back in his leather chair and closed his eyes. A protracted silence followed. A few moments later, he opened his eyes and peered at the visitors. "So you want the government of the United States to mandate the use of digital currency? No more cash?"

Heads nodded, and Rutherford spoke. "It's a rather simple transition from the convenience of debit and credit cards. The European market has adapted quite easily and with much success. The time is right for this win-win proposal. Your competitive edge on the international trade market would be assured. It may even recharge your flagging economy. But the real silver lining would be the global goodwill that would be generated by your cooperation."

"Your nation is halfway there," Pierre said as he pitched forward on the cushioned seat. "Research tells us that your military, government agencies, and welfare programs currently issue funds through a smart card. A growing percentage of your private citizens are already reaping the convenience of such technology."

"Yes, that's correct," Atwood said. "However, a significant segment of the population remains skeptical, citing privacy concerns."

Pierre tossed his head back and clicked his tongue.

"Mere details—easily worked out. I am sure that we can satisfactorily address these concerns at the upcoming International Economic Summit. I shall look forward to seeing you there."

"Gentlemen." The president stood and extended his hand. "I will study the issue and be in touch." Atwood walked the men to the office threshold, shook hands once more, and closed the door behind them.

He turned to his chief economic advisor. "Is it feasible, Brody?"

"Yes, sir—in theory. The idea is sold on the positives. No bad credit, no bad checks or overdrawn accounts. Cash robberies would be a thing of the past, along with counterfeit money, drug deals, and prostitution. The program also has potential when it comes to tracking terrorism and cutting off their funds. But for government, the most appealing thing behind the employment of smart card technology is that it would make tax evasion nearly impossible." Brody sunk his hands into the pocket of his black silk suit. "Of course, there would be new types of criminal activities to deal with: identity thefts, and the induced incentive to murder in order to acquire chips."

"Yes, we are an adaptable society," Atwood quipped. He poured himself a cup of coffee and handed one to his advisor.

"Thank you, sir." Brody took a sip.

"Okay," President Atwood said. "Let's hear the negatives."

"Aside from the problems associated with identity theft, you mentioned privacy concerns. With smart card technology, every personal transaction could be traced. The counter to this argument is that law-abiding citizens shouldn't care if they leave a paper trail." Brody sighed. "Still, the idea that someone knows every item that you purchase at a drugstore, or the movies you view, is disconcerting."

"Go on." The president swirled coffee in his cup.

"Well, sir, this is out of my area of expertise, but if the United States decides to climb aboard this money train, it would be wise to check the fine print on the ticket."

The president gave Brody a quizzical look.

"If a unilateral system of global currency was established, then international governing standards might soon follow."

"And. . . ?" Atwood pressed.

Brody replied cautiously. "There may be some issues of national sovereignty to consider."

Chapter 8

Arizona
Tuesday, July 17th

On the porch of the General Store, David inspected the old screen that was decorated with hundreds of collectible tin lapel pins. There were campaign slogan buttons that spanned decades displayed among faded flower power and yellow-smiley-face pins.

The screen on which the pins hung was remarkably intact considering its age and use. *Good thing,* he thought. *That stiff wire mesh is probably impossible to find these days*. The door itself was another story.

David knelt for a closer look. Some of the screws were missing from the hinges. The only things that kept it hanging were thick globs of petrified paint.

He stood, stretched, and pondered the task before him. The General Store was in need of repair, but it was a daunting chore. The whitewash on the porch frame had turned to powdery flakes on the sun-bleached wood. The walls had been plastered with a collage of road signs and vintage grocery posters. Even the windows were decorated with an eclectic mix of travel stickers.

It's like a virtual postcard of the past—a masterpiece of Americana, David thought. *Maybe some things are better left untouched.*

On the other side of the screen door, Elita appeared with a tray of refreshments. "I hope you're not getting any ideas about scraping off the family folk art."

David held the door open for his bride. "If I did, the whole building would probably fall over!"

Elita laughed. "Pretty smart for a gringo." She handed her husband a glass of lemonade and pointed to a rustic piece of barn wood. "See that sign?" AMERICAN TERRITORY was crudely chiseled on the slab. "That's where it all began. Legend has it that my great, great, great-grandfather nailed that up to cover a bullet hole left by a bandito."

"That reminds me," David said, downing his drink like it was a cold beer. "I could use some wood putty."

Elita leaned her petite frame against an antique Coke cooler. She was earthy and beautiful in her simple sundress and bare feet. David reached out and caressed the dark braid of hair that fell loosely across her shoulder. It felt like silk in his fingers. She looked at him with those warm, Hispanic eyes—those same eyes that had peered into his soul and coaxed him from the gutter.

David felt a surge of love so powerful it terrified him. He cupped Elita's face in his hands, kissed her tenderly on the lips, and felt her tremble.

She nestled her head against his chest and said, "I can hear your heart beating."

David ran his fingers down her spine. "What do you say

we close up shop for a while?"

Overhead, in the cloudless sky, a helicopter thrummed past. They watched as it circled back again.

"Way out here in the middle of nowhere, and we still can't get any privacy!" David complained.

"Third time this week they've flown over." Elita watched the aircraft with interest. "I wonder what the border patrol's up to?"

A rickety sedan with a tattered soft top turned onto Main Street. The relic rattled over some potholes and then lurched to a stop in front of the General Store.

David recognized the woman behind the wheel.

Miriam Baker lived in a weathered mobile home on the edge of town. During the winter months, she managed the Sunbird Oasis Campground, a seasonal city of retirees who rolled into town each winter to escape the cold.

In the passenger seat, a baby-faced man leaned toward the driver and punched the car horn. David nearly jumped out of his skin.

"That's Miriam's son, Benny," Elita explained. "He's just like a big kid—probably home for a visit from the state hospital."

Three short horn blasts followed before the car door creaked open and big Benny hoisted his ample girth from the passenger seat. "Hi, Lita!"

"Good to see you, Benny!"

His mother, a birdlike woman with a sagging thunderbird tattoo on her shoulder, laced a skinny arm around her man-child's elbow and accompanied him onto the porch.

"You got any Bazooka Bubble Gum?" Benny scratched

his massive belly that hung from the bottom of an undersized t-shirt.

"I keep a supply especially for you!" Elita followed her customers into the store.

The vintage motor oil thermometer that hung near the screen door registered 103 degrees in the shade. David lifted his ball cap, fanned his face, and yawned. *Whoever invented the siesta was inspired. The repairs can wait until tomorrow morning*, he thought as he gathered his tools.

The heat seemed to follow him inside, doing pirouettes beneath a squeaky ceiling fan.

The mother and man-child were taking up space at the lunch counter. Benny's cheeks puffed, and he blew a swelling pink bubble. Miriam, clutching a coffee mug in her veined hands, said, "I don't know what's goin' on. I rented eleven spaces last week, and this morning two more campers rolled in looking for hookups. I told 'em I'd have to charge double rates on account of the air conditioning 'n' all. It's crazy, if you ask me."

"Yeah, I've noticed it, too." Elita plopped a couple scoops of ice cream into the mixer and gave it a blast. She poured the shake into a thick mug, added a straw, and then set it on the counter in front of Benny.

"Folks must be crazy to come here this time of year," Miriam droned. "They're asking for a bad case of sunstroke, if you ask me."

Benny swallowed his gum, guzzled his shake, and moaned from the brain freeze.

The black resin desk phone trilled. "I'll get it!" David volunteered, moving to the nook behind the cash register and plucking the receiver from its cradle. “General Store.”

“Mr. Fillmore, please.”

The voice was vaguely familiar. “Speaking.”

“This is Doc Jansten.”

David gripped the phone. “Is it time?”

There was a brief pause on the other end of the line. “I’m afraid so.”

When David arrived at the Sims ranch, his elderly client was resting in his bed.

On the far side of the bedroom, Joanne was quietly conferring with the doctor.

Rupert’s face brightened when he saw David. He adjusted his oxygen cannula and pointed a shaky finger toward an outdated television set on wheels. “This is a classic scene coming up.” The old rancher was focused on an old episode of The Andy Griffith Show. He hooted with delight as bumbling Barney Fife caught another crook. “No, sir, they just don’t make ’em like that anymore.”

It seems odd that a dying man could be so lighthearted, David thought as the physician moved to his patient’s bedside. He opened his bag and produced a stethoscope. “Let’s have a listen.”

“I’ll spare ya the trouble, Doc—pretty sure I’m still alive.” The doctor was not amused.

“Dagnabbit!” Rupert sputtered as a special report interrupted the sitcom.

"The President of the United States declared the northern plains a disaster area because of an extended drought," the announcer said.

"If ya ask me, Thomas Atwood was the only decent one in the whole danged family. The rest of 'em were just a bunch of rotten bananas!"

Across the room, Joanne Sims pursed her lips in disapproval.

"You know the President of the United States?" David asked.

"Naw, but my sister-in-law up in North Dakota knew 'em all—God rest her soul." Rupert clicked off the TV and settled back against a mound of pillows. "Yup, when those Atwood boys were young, they used to spend summers on their grandparents' farm. She used to baby sit the younger one—a real hoodlum she said he was!" Rupert began to cough so hard that it sounded as if his lungs were shredding like tissue paper.

The doctor settled his patient with an inhaler, but the episode seemed to sap what little strength the old rancher had.

"Darlin', would you open the window?" Rupert asked.

Joanne Sims did as she was asked, and fresh air spilled into the room.

Her father breathed deep. "Always loved the smell of sage."

Outside, the sun was setting, spreading brilliant crimson hues across the sky.

The old man's breathing came quick and shallow, but Rupert seemed content as he took in the view. "Looks like blazing chariots might bust through the clouds any second.

Reminds me of another beautiful sunset." He motioned to a photograph on his bedside table. "That picture don't do it justice."

David lifted the black-and-white photo of a boy standing on a rock beside an ancient-looking man.

"Ugly little cuss, wasn't I?" The old rancher chortled. "Keep it—just a little something to remember this old coot."

"Who's the man standing beside you?"

Rupert didn't seem to hear the question. There was a faraway gleam in his eye. "I used to think that I could see forever from the top of that rock," he said, turning his face to the window. "Yes, sir, chariots of fire." The old man's chest rumbled as he struggled to catch his breath.

Joanne Sims stood a cool distance from her father, her arms crossed like body armor, and her brown, jaw-length hair casting sharp shadows across her features. Suddenly, her pale green eyes shifted to glare at her father's lawyer.

David slipped a hand in the pocket of his loose-fitting jeans and noted a spot of motorcycle chain oil on his t-shirt. *Ten minutes,* he chided himself. *That's all it would have taken to throw on a clean shirt and grab a jacket and tie.*

Rupert lifted a spotty, trembling hand and called out to his daughter. She moved to the bedside. The old man's languid gaze seemed to search her face. His gnarled fingers tightened around hers. "I have always loved you."

Joanne stiffened.

"Do you hear me, girl?" His words faded to whispered threads. Rupert loosened his grip.

A breeze blew softly through the room, and the spark in the old man's eyes faded away.

Doctor Jansten rushed forward with stethoscope in hand. He listened carefully, moved the amplifier, and listened again. Then he closed his patient's vacant eyes, cast a solemn look toward Joanne, and shook his head.

There was a look of peace upon the old man's face—a peace that David envied. For Rupert Sims, the work was indeed finished; something told David that for him, however, a struggle had just begun.

Part 2
The Preparation

O beautiful for halcyon skies,
For amber waves of grain,
For purple mountain majesties
Above the enameled plain!
America! America!
God shed His grace on thee,
Till souls wax fair as earth and air
And music-hearted sea!

O beautiful for pilgrim feet
Whose stern, impassioned stress
A thoroughfare for freedom beat
Across the wilderness!
America! America!
God shed His grace on thee,
Till paths be wrought through wilds of thought
By pilgrim foot and knee!

Katharine Lee Bates

Chapter 9

Washington, DC
Thursday, July 19th

Paige Hays was late as she hurried up the steps of Virginia's Loudoun County Library. It was not her fault; the line at Giant Food was long, and the girl at the register was a trainee. A couple of items had to be price-checked; then, to make matters worse, the person in front of Paige had had "insufficient funds."

Maybe Ms. Ruhauser will understand. But the truth was the woman was intimidating. Paige had recently watched the librarian flatten a shy mother with a Teutonic tongue-lashing. "I am here to inspire and educate, not to baby sit!"

In the children's section, Paige spotted Connor playing a video game at the media center and then turned to the woman behind the desk. "I'm so sorry to keep you waiting," she said breathlessly, "it's just that the grocery store was—"

Ms. Ruhauser held a fat finger to her lips to silence Paige. She peered over rhinestone-covered bifocals. "Please have a seat, Mrs. Hays." The command made Paige feel like she was back in grade school.

The librarian's small, slate eyes studied Paige.

"Believe me, it was unintentional."

Ms. Ruhauser's lips parted in an unexpected smile. "Don't give it another thought, Mrs. Hays." She leaned forward. "It works out better this way, because there's a matter I need to discuss with you."

"Oh?"

Ms. Ruhauser's square head bobbed above her muscular neck. "It's about Connor." She sucked in a sharp breath. "I'll get right to the point, Mrs. Hays. Your little boy is frightening the other children."

Paige was speechless. *Connor always plays well with other kids.*

"During story hour, he suddenly announced that a war would soon happen in our country. Connor insisted that it would be very scary and that people would die." Ms. Ruhauser's massive bosoms spilled across the desk as she leaned closer.

Almost subconsciously, Paige drew back in the chair.

"Connor claims that an angel from God told him this." The librarian curled her lip like she was detecting an unpleasant odor.

Paige felt heat pulsing through her temples.

"I'm sure it's nothing, really." Ruhauser's tone was placating. "Some young ones are naturally more sensitive than others. After our nation's last military campaign, some of the little ones needed counseling—you know, to express their fears."

Paige couldn't take much more. "Thanks. I'll talk to Connor." She pushed herself from the chair beside the desk.

Mrs. Ruhauser stood. "I do hope you understand that we simply can't have the other children exposed to this." She touched Paige's arm in a matronly fashion. "You and your husband are educated people. I'm sure that you will seek help before it's too late." The librarian lifted a newspaper from her desk and pointed to an article. "Other children aren't so fortunate, I'm afraid."

Paige read the headline. FLORIDA TEENAGER SENTENCED FOR THE MURDER OF HIS FAMILY.

Florida

Thursday, July 19th

It all seemed like a bad video game to Joel Sutherland as the van angled down the long driveway. In the distance, an institutional building jutted upward from a landfill. It resembled a drab castle, with eerie fingers of mist that swept across the Florida marsh.

The only thing missing is a moat, the fifteen-year-old mused. Nevertheless, the mesh-and-barbed-wire fence that circled the grounds told him it was no joke.

Joel still could not believe what his life had come to. This was to be his home until his eighteenth birthday. *The judge might as well have handed down a death sentence. It would have felt the same.*

Beside him, a square-built kid asked, "What are you in for?"

The fresh horrors of his past vexed Joel, bringing down an avalanche of raw emotion. "None of your business!" He regretted his response as soon as it burst forth, but it was too late.

The Sherman tank crossed his muscular arms and glared ominously.

Joel knew he had just made an enemy who could stomp his average-sized body to a bloody pulp. *Don't show fear,* he reminded himself, remembering the stories he'd heard about Waverly—stories that would turn a young man's hair white. The teenager set his face with a tough veneer, but beneath it, he was trembling. Inside, Joel was still just an average American boy.

The van slowed to a crawl, then braked to a stop, and the institution's big iron gates spread like arms to embrace its newest prisoners.

The place loomed like a monster, with small-eyed windows and gaping double doors that looked like a mouth with iron-clad teeth. They opened to swallow Joel's world.

Florida

Friday, July 20th

In the hall just outside of the reform school cafeteria, Joel stepped up to the end of the line and mumbled the numbers he had been assigned.

A short, squat woman looked up, half-bored, half-irritated. Her lazy eyes lit upon the digits stamped across Joel's overalls. "Didn't hear ya," she drawled.

"Nine, seven, six," the teenager repeated.

She cupped her ear and smirked like a lunchroom troll.

"What was that?"

He glared at the woman, and she yawned just to toy with the new resident.

A chorus of heckles and boos issued from behind. Joel felt his face flush with embarrassment. "Nine! Seven! Six!" He enunciated more clearly this time.

The troll smirked, batted fleshy eyelids, and called, "Next."

Joel grabbed a tray from a stack and fell into the monotone gray line with the other drones.

He scanned the room as he inched along. On the far side near the folded bleachers, his cellmate, Daryl Capps, sat alone, shoulders hunched, scrawny neck jutting forward, and food dangling from his fork. Even from a distance, he looked pathetic. Daryl's Coke-bottle glasses refracted prism colors upon a face that grew acne like a fertile garden. On the table before him, a Bible lay open.

Joel received two mounds of over-processed meat on mashed potatoes. He slipped into the first available space at a table and wedged himself between two kids' lively banter.

The teenager ate the tasteless meal quietly, absorbed in the cafeteria cacophony. Before long, the bell sounded and the "residents," as they were called, began to shuffle toward the door to deposit their trays.

A commotion arose from the back of the room, and Joel turned to see his cellmate smiling sheepishly as a pair of bigger boys fixed their hostile eyes upon him.

Capps tried unsuccessfully to maneuver around the bullies, but they refused to budge. "Hey, airhead, are you ignoring me? I asked you a question. How's God today?"

Daryl's response was too quiet to hear, but his tormentors exploded with laughter.

Joel recognized one of the troublemakers as the same Sherman tank with whom he had arrived at Waverly. Harley Boyd had wasted no time in finding a kindred soul named Gunner Hogan. In Joel's opinion, the two didn't have enough brain power to propel an ant's motorcycle around the inside of a Cheerio. Still, instinct warned him to tread lightly around the pair, who roamed the hallways like hungry sharks. Separate, they were dangerous; together, they were evil.

With sinewy muscles that twitched for action, Gunner leaned over Daryl Capps and glowered menacingly. "Hey, we're talking to you!"

Daryl scurried from under the giant's shadow, but Harley Boyd blocked his exit, spraying him with a burst of machine-gun laughter.

The scrawny teen looked desperate as Gunner Hogan closed in. "I don't want trouble," Daryl said. "I'd better go, or I'll be late for roll call."

"Oh, did you hear that Gunner?" Harley mocked. "Bible boy is worried about bein' late."

A group of kids walked past, casually observing the trouble, yet no one moved to intervene. "You can go just as soon as you answer my question!" Harley sneered.

"Yeah, answer the question, airhead."

Daryl clutched his Bible in his twig-like arms. "I forgot the question." Across the room, Daryl's eyes met his roommate's with a silent plea.

Joel looked away.

"Are you deaf? I asked you how God was?"

"He's fine."

"Does He ever talk about me?" Gunner's wide mouth spread into a Cheshire grin.

"He wants me to pray for you." Daryl began to stutter. "The B-B-Bible tells me to pray for everybody."

Gunner leaned close enough to blanket Capps with his steamy, putrid breath. Silence thickened the atmosphere.

Daryl's eyes blinked rapidly behind his thick lenses.

"So you think you're good enough to pray for me?" Gunner and Harley each grabbed an arm and hoisted Daryl headfirst into a plastic, muck-filled bin. "This is where you belong, 'cause you're nothin' but garbage." The bullies slapped each other on the back and sauntered out into the hallway, roaring with belly laughter.

Joel strode across the room as his roommate climbed from the trash bin. "You okay?"

Daryl groped through wet globs of food until he found his glasses. He did his best to wipe away the grease smears and then slid them on his face. "Thanks."

The word cut Joel like a knife. "I didn't do anything."

"You stayed," Daryl said before bolting through the cafeteria doors like a wounded antelope.

The warning roll call bell sounded, but Joel stood alone in the silence of the empty cafeteria. His mind replayed the moment when Daryl's eyes had met his from across the room—the moment when he had looked away.

On the floor, Daryl's Bible lay disheveled. Joel picked it up and glanced at the page to which it had fallen open. "Your sins are forgiven. . . ."

The last bell rang. Detention awaited Joel, but he didn't

care. In self-disgust, he slapped the book shut.

Forgiveness. Joel shook his head. *Too late for a loser like me*.

Chapter 10

North Dakota
Sunday, July 22nd

Nora walked along the road with a bag full of groceries and a burden of guilt. It was Sunday, and the faithful were ensconced in worship while she played hooky, passing the morning strolling up and down the aisles of the grocery store.

The truth was that Nora needed to clear her head. Over and over again, she told herself that she was just imagining Celeste's pointed stare.

As she stepped over clumps of dried weeds that grew down the middle of the county road, another possibility needled her. *Maybe that woman is right; maybe I am faithless.*

The midday sun was hostile overhead, and Nora was beginning to have misgivings about her decision to walk home. Oppressive heat radiated from the packed dirt beneath her feet. She stopped to roll up her jeans, hoisted the bag of groceries to her hip, and trudged on.

At least Otis doesn't seem to mind. Nora watched her little mutt kicking up clouds of silt against a pale backdrop of dwarfed wheat, all wilting in the breezeless air. Nora had never seen such dismal crops.

A quarter-mile down the road, she paused for a breather. *Should have brought a bottle of water,* she thought, trudging over the Delmont Canal Bridge. All that remained below was a trickle of water, not even enough to ration. The ditch rider had recently quit because of job stress, and the local irrigation district office had stopped taking calls. People were angry and scared.

Just beyond a spindly stand of corn, a blue house came into view. Nora could hear the sounds of children's laughter. The farm had once belonged to her great-uncle Irvin Meyers, a snarly beanpole of a man who kept to himself. After his death, the place was willed to Nora's mother. Now, it belonged to her.

On the far end of the scorched yard, the Tilden kids played in a pink plastic pool. They squealed with delight as they splashed about. The sight brought a smile to Nora's face.

Pepper Tilden appeared behind a screened door. She pushed it open and called to her oldest son, "Thaddeus, give Ms. Meyers a hand." The boy, a hefty, sun-freckled second grader, climbed obediently from the pool and slapped across the yard, muddying his feet.

"Thank you, Thad," Nora said, gratefully handing him the bag.

"Oh, wow!" the boy shrieked. "Fruit Loops and string cheese!"

Two-year-old Annabelle waddled toward the action, her waterlogged diaper leaving a trail behind.

"That pool sure looks inviting on a day like today." Nora wiped sweat from her brow.

Pepper shook her head. "Wouldn't recommend it. How 'bout a cold glass of iced tea instead?" She held the screen door open with one hand and rubbed her swollen belly with the other.

Nora guessed her neighbor was in her sixth month of pregnancy.

Inside, Pepper retrieved a plastic pitcher from the fridge and poured the tea into two Mason jars. She looked tired.

Nora was glad that she'd thought to include a jar of vitamins along with the groceries.

Pepper set the two Mason jars on the table and lowered herself into a chair. She took a sip.

They watched the children sprawled upon the cracked linoleum floor, searching the bags for treats.

A ray of afternoon sun peeked through the kitchen curtains and caught the sheen of tears in their mother's eyes.

"Pepper, what's wrong?"

"It's just. . . . We haven't paid you rent for the last three months."

Nora leaned forward and took Pepper's hand. "Listen to me. I'm not just your landlord; I'm your friend. You and Chuck didn't cause this drought. You're both good, hard-working people who've fallen on hard times—that's all."

Pepper's lip quivered. "Why is God doing this?"

Nora considered the question. "Maybe the Lord is allowing it for reasons that we can't understand."

"What do you mean by that?"

Nora swirled tea in her glass. "I asked the same question after my mom died. I couldn't understand why God would take her away and leave me feeling so alone. Then, when I least expected it, I got the answer on a bumper sticker of all things!"

"Well, don't keep me in suspense!" Pepper said. "What did it say?"

"It read something like this," Nora began. "'God will never be all you need, until God is all you've got.'"

Chapter 11

Florida

Sunday, July 22nd

It was quiet in the dorm room. Joel liked it that way. He was reclined across his bed with an open sci-fi novel on his lap, but he hadn't turned a page for over an hour. The teenager's thoughts were miles from this sterile room with its lag-bolted furnishings. In his mind's eye, Joel was back in Desoto, Florida, sitting in his bedroom and surrounded by familiar posters and childhood treasures. He imagined his favorite music cranked up and his mother's voice telling him to turn it down. A terminal sense of grief enveloped him. *Nothing can ever change what happened.*

"Whatcha reading?"

Joel shrugged and tossed the book aside as his roommate entered.

Daryl closed the door behind him and held up a box of chocolates. "Want one? My mom and dad brought 'em to me." He lifted a lid on the candy box, selected a nugget, and stuffed it in his mouth.

Joel watched his gangly roommate laboriously chew the

sticky mess. Daryl swallowed hard, his oversized Adam's apple shooting up and down like an elevator.

"There's more!" Daryl set the chocolates down and swung a plastic grocery bag that was dangling from his wrist. "You'll never guess what else my parents brought me."

"You're right," Joel said. "I never will."

"Corn nuts! Three flavors! Barbecue is my favorite, but the Ranch is pretty good, too." He offered to share, but Joel turned him down.

"Hey, how come I never see you in the visitor's lounge?"

Joel was silent.

"Do your folks live too far away?"

"Yeah, something like that."

Daryl tossed a handful of corn nuts in his mouth and plopped down on his bed. "Crunch, crunch, crunch." He studied Joel. "Crunch, crunch, crunch."

"Would you stop that noise?" Joel snapped. "It's annoying!"

"Sorry." Daryl set the bag aside, brushing salt from his fingers. "Want to know why I'm in here?"

"Not really." Joel reached for his novel and pretended to read.

Daryl was impervious to the brush-off. "I tried to kill a kid—he almost died, too." The boy paused to reflect. "His name is Ron Tuttle, and he was the captain of the football team—you know, one of those guys who always drives a new sports car 'cause he's got a rich dad. The girls went crazy over him."

Joel raised an eyebrow. "So you were jealous?"

"No," Daryl said with conviction. "Just about everybody else was, though." He paused and added, "I learned that after I shot him. A lot of kids—even some of his friends—told me that he deserved what he got." Daryl picked at a pimple on his chin. "That's sad, don't ya think?"

Joel didn't answer, but he was looking at his roommate now.

"I went over to my grandpa's house and snuck his pistol out of the bedroom closet. The next day I brought it to school and waited until lunchtime. I kept thinking how good it would feel to see Ron's scared face. It didn't feel good at all." A look of remorse spread across Daryl's acne-scarred features. "Ron yelled something—don't remember what—then he grabbed for the gun." Daryl's eyes blinked rapidly. "I guess I pulled the trigger. Anyway, he lived, but he's missing a spleen."

"Why did you shoot him?"

"I had my reasons," Daryl sniffed. "Did I tell you I once won the science fair for the whole school district?"

Joel shook his head.

"My parents bought me a new suit for the awards ceremony. My aunt and uncle drove over from Miami just to be there. I'll never forget the applause when I got up on stage to share my data on weather patterns." Daryl's smile suddenly vanished. "Then everybody started laughing."

"How come?" Joel swung his legs from the bed.

"Ron Tuttle had messed with my computer presentation and inserted a bunch of naked pictures of me in the locker room shower." Daryl's face reddened. He looked at the Bible lying open on his bedside table. "It was wrong to do what I did." He dumped some corn nuts into his hand. "Sure you don't want some?"

Joel threw himself back on his pillow and tried to block out his roommate's incessant crunching.

"So, what's your story?"

"You know what your problem is, Capps? You talk too much." Joel rolled himself from the cot as the bell signaled the end of afternoon break.

"What work detail are you in this semester?" Daryl asked as they made their way out the door.

"Laundry."

"I'm working in the kitchen. I had no idea so much preparation goes into cooking in a place like this." Daryl paused. "Sorry if I touched a nerve earlier."

"Don't worry about it."

"Hey, you wanna go to the church service with me?"

"No thanks." Joel shook his head, stepped onto the elevator, and breathed a sigh of relief when the doors slid shut.

In his mailbox, Joel found another postcard from New Orleans. It was the fourth to arrive since his incarceration. The teenager studied the colorful picture of the French Quarter row houses. His eyes traced every detail, searching the wrought-iron rails and window bars hoping to catch sight of a familiar face.

Just like the others—no signature. Joel turned the card over; nothing except his name and reform school address. He pondered the sharp, Gothic script. *Could it be?*

Joel slipped the mysterious postcard into his coverall pocket and headed for his room to hide it beneath his mattress along with the others.

He had hoped for time alone to try and make sense of things, but Daryl was sitting at the little metal dorm room desk, hunched over his open Bible.

Daryl seemed unusually preoccupied. His brow was creased, and his magnified eyes were blinking excessively behind thick lenses.

Joel plopped down on his bed. "How was church?"

"What?" Daryl looked up as if dazed. "Oh, it was nice. I wish you were there." With a thrust of his neck, he was back in the reading position.

Joel watched him curiously. "Is something wrong?"

Daryl's wiry frame tensed. "Why do you ask?" His eyes flicked briefly upward before returning to the scriptures.

Joel shrugged. "No reason, I guess."

"I was thinking—I mean—I was sorta wondering. . . ."

"That's easy for you to say!" Joel chuckled.

Daryl produced the expected laughter, but it fell flat. "I've been thinking about my family. I can't remember if I told Mom and Dad how much I love them and that I'm sorry that I put them through so much." He chewed his lip so hard he made it bleed. "I hope they know that I've found peace."

"Why don't you just let them know the next time you see them?"

Daryl's head bobbed up and down above his thin neck. "Tell them? Yes, good idea." He plucked his Bible from the desk and held it out. "I'd like you to have this."

Joel started to laugh, but caught himself when he saw the serious look on his roommate's face. "Are you giving up religion or something?"

"Oh, no!" Daryl's shook his head emphatically. "The Lord never gave up on me!"

This conversation is getting weird. "You carry that book with you all the time. It obviously means a lot to you." Joel shook his head. "No, I can't take it."

"It does mean a lot to me," Daryl agreed. "That's why I want you to have it."

Joel was suddenly out of patience. "Why are you talking this way?"

"No reason—just thinking." The skinny kid shrugged and flashed another sheepish grin. "Want a soda?" He sprang to his feet and jingled change in his coverall pockets.

"Yeah, sure." Joel waited until his roommate left and then retrieved the postcard for another look. *Could it be?* The teenager wanted to believe it was true.

In the hallway, someone ran past. Voices spoke in hurried tones, followed by more footsteps. Joel stepped to the door to see what the commotion was.

At the end of the corridor, near the stairwell, a crowd had gathered. One guard spoke sharply into his radio, while another ordered a loitering group of reform-school residents back to their dorms. A few yards away, the elevator doors opened, and Mr. Quill, Waverly's head administrator, stepped out. He pointed his face toward the stairwell and blew past Joel in hurried, jerky strides.

The group of banished boys ambled slowly back toward their rooms, pausing every so often to engage in hushed debates.

"Hey," Joel called, "what's going on?"

"Somebody just did the Bible nerd," one of the boys replied. "Bled him out by the soda machine."

Chapter 12

Arizona

Wednesday, July 25th

David Fillmore tugged at his starched dress shirt. “This truck is a sauna.” He slowed to turn onto the empty country road and ground the gears on the old Ford.

Elita was staring out the open window, her dark hair swirling in the air. “Kirby Hall was packed. There must have been three hundred people who came out to pay their respects to Rupert Sims.” She sighed wistfully. “Someday, when I die, I hope I’ve touched as many lives.”

“I know of at least one.” David reached over and stroked her olive cheek.

The corners of his wife’s mouth curled into a sublime smile. “Well, anyway, it was a nice service. Don’t you think?”

David offered a half-hearted nod and decided against telling Elita that he would have rather ridden to China on a seatless bicycle than attend the funeral. It didn’t help matters that Joanne Sims had glared at him throughout the rambling eulogy.

He loosened his tie and fiddled with the dashboard

controls. A blast of tepid air chortled through the air conditioner.

"Probably needs a charge of Freon," Elita said.

Nice, David thought. *A forty-minute drive in a blistering heat wave.*

Elita opened the glove box and dug around until she produced a small, folded towel and a couple clothes pins.

David watched his wife with growing interest.

She opened the water jug that they always carried and soaked the cloth.

"What are you up to?"

"You'll find out." Elita adjusted the truck's wind-wing until the warm breeze pummeled David, and then she secured the wet rag in front of it with clothespins. Immediately, the temperature in the cab seemed to drop. "I call this a poor man's swamp cooler!"

"You're amazing." He stole another look at his bride. *She has no idea how amazing!*

Suddenly, Elita pitched forward in the seat and squinted through the dirty windshield. "What's going on up ahead?"

On the right side of the road, nose down in a ravine, was a black van. Beside it, a Jeep was on its side, exposing the undercarriage and a spinning wheel.

"It must have just happened." David said, noting the cloud of dust that still hung in the air. He pulled onto the soft shoulder and grabbed his cell phone. "Great, no service!"

Elita hung her head from the truck window and yelled. "Anybody hurt?" A man on the far side of the Jeep was picking cactus from his sleeve. When he looked up, she gasped. "It's Gordon Spitzer!"

A commotion at the wrecked van drew their eyes. The side door slid open, and a brown-faced woman peered out. She spoke in hurried Spanish as the vehicle coughed up illegal immigrants like a rodeo clown car. Most of them dashed toward a thick patch of cholla, seeking refuge behind the spiny fingers.

The sound of a gunshot cracked across the landscape, halting the fugitives in their tracks. Spitzer fired another round from his Glock pistol and ordered them to return.

Elita pushed open the truck door and stepped onto the desert soil.

"Stand back!" Gordon Spitzer barked. "This is no place for a woman!"

David quickly joined his wife. "Do you smell that?" He sniffed the air. "Gasoline."

Spitzer instructed his prisoners to line up: four women, seven young bucks, and a shriveled old man with a straw cowboy hat. They raised their hands and did as they were told, but the old caballero poked a cigarette between his leathered lips and shuffled a good distance behind the others. He stopped, struck a wooden match on his belt buckle, and put the flame to his tobacco.

Elita reached for David's hand and whispered, "I've got a bad feeling."

Spitzer's face blazed with rage. "On the ground!"

The old man's jaundiced eyes stared from behind curls of smoke. In his fingers, the wooden match burned low. With great deliberation, he flicked it toward the overturned vehicle.

Flames sprouted instantly from the fuel-soaked soil.

Elita drew in a sharp breath and pointed toward the

Jeep. “Somebody’s in there!”

“Grab my motorcycle jacket!” David called and scrambled down the barrow pit.

When his wife returned a few seconds later, the flames were already licking at the undercarriage.

David tried to extinguish the fire with his leather jacket, but the saturated ground sprouted new flames.

“Get me outta here!”

In the distance, the faint sound of sirens could be heard, but there was no time to wait. David jumped onto the top side of the Jeep and tried to free the passenger. “The door is jammed!”

Inside, a wild-eyed man beat on the windshield.

“Cover your face!” David yelled. He lifted his boot heel and brought it down hard. Glass rained down in a thousand pieces.

“I think my ankle is busted.” The passenger’s bald head glistened with sweat. “The seatbelt—you gotta cut it off. There’s a knife in my boot. Maybe you can reach it.”

The victim grimaced as David worked a four-inch hunting blade from the man’s cowboy boot.

“Make it fast, man; it’s getting hot in here!” The flames were now lapping up the sides of the Jeep and blistering the paint.

Time seemed to slow as David sliced through the heavy nylon material.

“Okay,” David coughed as hot vapors assaulted his lungs.

The passenger squeezed his oversized torso through the compact window just ahead of a plume of toxic smoke.

"Jump!" Elita cried.

The large man landed alongside David and screamed in agony. A few yards away flames shot up from the Jeep with a roar.

Sirens wailed and stopped along the highway. Uniformed agents raced forward with extinguishers and quickly snuffed the inferno in a pillow of fire retardant.

"Thanks, buddy," the victim said as a medic rushed over. "I owe you one. My friends call me Tranch."

Suddenly, a ruckus broke out near the van. Heads turned, voices shouted. David launched to his feet and ran over to investigate.

Through a gap in the crowd of border patrol agents, he spotted Gordon Spitzer face down on the ground, wrists cuffed behind his back. "What's going on?" David asked.

"He was pistol-whipping that old Mexican," one of the agents volunteered.

"This is a heck of a way to thank me for doing your job! That piece 'a dried up leather's gonna think twice before pulling another stunt like that!" Spitzer squirmed in the dirt like a child having a tantrum. "What am I being charged with?"

"Assault." Two agents lifted Spitzer by his elbows and escorted him to a green-and-white Suburban. "Could somebody find my fishing cap?" Just before the door of the law enforcement unit shut, Spitzer locked eyes with David and said, "Hey, Fillmore! I could sure use a lawyer right about now!"

Florida

Friday, July 27th

The rumor crept down the hallways, bounced around the lunchroom, and built momentum. By the time it reached Joel Sutherland's ear, it had rolled over fifty tongues or more: Gunner Hogan and Harley Boyd were overheard bragging about the murder of Daryl Capps.

Now, seething with anger, Joel strode down the hallway with only one thing on his mind. "Justice!" He spit the word out with contempt. It was only a matter of time before the administration caught wind of the whisperings.

It was likely that Harley and Boyd would be processed through the system with nothing more than lockdown in maximum security. *That's too good for those animals,* Joel thought as he rounded the corner. In his hand, Joel gripped the iron pipe that he'd stolen from a plumber's salvage bin. Soon, very soon, he intended to settle the score.

Joel paused outside a closed door. On the other side he heard laughter, fueling his rage. The teenager's breathing quickened to shallow, rapid puffs. With his free hand, he turned the knob and felt it give. Joel kicked the door open and lunged inside, feeling bigger than life, as big as the imposing shadow he cast on the wall.

Stunned, Gunner and Harley cowered in surprise, ducking defensively against the iron blur of their attacker's weapon.

"This is for Daryl!" Joel screamed, clipping Boyd hard across the cheek.

Then, as if the blow had awakened a sleeping giant, Harley sprang to his feet. He caught the pipe in mid-swing and plucked it from his assailant's hand.

"Smash his head in!" Gunner Hogan shouted. In a flash, he was by his roommate's side. "Do it now!" The light from the desk lamp highlighted thick pockets of plaque upon his teeth. "Go ahead!"

Harley raised a hand to his swelling cheek. His eyes blazed with hatred. "You are gonna die, Sutherland," he snarled, "but I want to make it slow and painful."

The first blow hurt the most, cracking across Joel's skull like an explosion. He took it in utter silence, dropping to his knees at the feet of his attackers. A hailstorm of thunderous strikes ensued. *Weird,* he thought, aware of the pain, yet at the same time strangely detached.

Joel closed his eyes. The ringing in his ears grew louder, like steam hissing from a teakettle. It was the last sound Joel heard before he passed out.

Words wafted randomly through Joel's mind—unfamiliar, metallic voices. "Concussion . . . serious. . . ." As if engulfed in a thick fog, Joel struggled to find his way, making progress yet eerily frozen in place. "Lucky . . . could have died. . . ." Words came together to form fragmented, partial sentences. "Won't know . . . too soon. . . ." Then, as quickly as their meaning registered, they flew away.

Joel dreamed he was standing in his kitchen in suburban Desoto. *She was lying in a crimson pool. Her hand was as cold as the ring that adorned it. "Wake up," someone said.*

"Wake up!"

Joel's eyes opened wide with terror.

A man stood over him. "Calm down, son. We're here to help." Joel focused on the geometrically patterned tie that showed beneath his white coat. "I'm Doctor Lockhart. You've been out for a while."

Joel blinked, trying hard to make sense of his surroundings.

"I need to ask you a few questions. Some of them may seem lame, but just bear with me."

The teenager nodded. His mouth was as dry as burnt toast.

"What is your name?"

"Joel."

"What month is it?"

The boy thought for a second. "I don't know. July something."

The man seemed pleased. "Do you know where you are?"

"Waverly." He looked around. "But wait. . . . Am I in a hospital?"

"That's right. And your age?"

"Fifteen." Joel lifted his hand to touch his bandaged scalp. "My head hurts," he grimaced. "What happened?"

The doctor exchanged a look with the nurse. "You don't remember? Well, that's not unusual with head injuries." The doctor left Joel's bedside and moved just out of view. "He'll tire easily," he whispered. "Don't stay too long."

"Hi, Joel." The reform school's head administrator approached the bedside. "I'm glad you're doing better." Mr.

Quill smiled sympathetically. "So, you don't remember anything about how you got hurt."

It was more a statement than a question, so Joel didn't respond.

"Can you tell me what you do recall? Anything may be helpful."

The teenager searched his memory, trying hard to ignore the pounding in his head. Impressions vexed him—thoughts of his annoying yet likable roommate. "Daryl!" Joel sat upright in bed and collapsed again as a lightning bolt of pain shot through his temple.

"Demerol and a sedative." The doctor snapped his fingers to an attending nurse, and she shot out the door. "That's all for today. My patient needs to rest."

The administrator nodded and looked at Joel. "I'll be back when you're stronger."

The teenager lay in bed feeling detached and numb. *Stronger?* he thought bitterly as depression settled in. *For what?*

Chapter 13

Washington, DC
Monday, July 30th

A heat wave had settled over the nation's capital. Paige wilted in the steamy air as she walked across the church parking lot with Connor.

"Mom, look at all those ugly puppies!" he said, pointing toward the majestic roof of the Gothic cathedral.

Paige knelt beside her son and followed the line of his pudgy finger. "Oh, I see!" She laughed and playfully mussed his red hair. "Those are called gargoyles."

"I don't like them," he said firmly. "They look mean."

"They're just silly." Though in truth, Paige wasn't fond of them, either.

Shadowed by the massive building, they climbed the wide steps. At the top, Paige reached for the arched door, barely noticing its intricate ebony cherubs, carved by a masterful hand.

Anxiety mingled with foreboding moved within Paige as she recalled the days since Connor's strange declaration. "The angel said, 'A war is coming.' It is, Mom. It is!" Lately, her son's adamant belief had grown more insistent.

Inside the Apostle's Cathedral, the contrast from sun to mottled light was extreme. Paige stood for a moment until her eyes adjusted. A prism of stained-glass colors rained down upon the mother and son. She pondered the flags of every nation that hung from the ceiling between the Gothic arches.

They made their way across the mosaic floor and moved past marble columns. Up ahead, above the altar, was a statue of Jesus hanging in effigy.

"Does God live here?" Connor asked with childlike awe.

"Yes," Paige said reverently. "This is God's house." She led her son past rows of choir seats, beyond ornate wooden dividing screens.

It had been years since Paige had set foot in a church, and guilt nagged her as she paused outside the door marked REVEREND'S OFFICE. She rapped lightly and pushed it open.

"Come in, come in." A stork-like woman sitting behind a desk rose to gush over the boy. "You must be Connor. Aren't you a handsome little guy!" Long, secretarial fingers danced across his forehead and nose and landed on his chin with a playful jostle. "The reverend is expecting you both. He shouldn't be too long. Can I get you anything—coffee or soda?"

Paige accepted a cup of coffee but regretted it. The lukewarm fluid was bitter and hard to swallow.

An inner office door sprung open, and a large man stepped forward. He wore a white robe woven with gold damask impressions. Around his neck hung a wine-colored drape embroidered with silver symbols.

"Mom, is that God?" Connor whispered.

She set the Styrofoam cup on the end table and stood. "No, honey, but this man is a friend of God's."

"Mrs. Hays." The clergyman extended his hand. "I'm Reverend Salisbury." His head tilted toward the child, who was now peeking from behind his mother's skirt. "You must be the young man I've heard so much about." There was no response. "You have had some exciting things to talk about, haven't you, Connor? It is not every day I meet someone who speaks to angels. I'd love to hear all about it."

Connor lit up. "Okay, I'll tell you 'cause you believe in angels and God and stuff. Don't you?"

The reverend smiled and laid a hand upon the boy's head. "Of course, Connor. I believe in many things, like Sunday school, prayer, and even imagination." He led mother and son to his office and directed them to an oversized tapestry chair.

Connor perched himself on the edge of the seat, folded his arms, and crossed his legs like a serious little man.

The clergyman pulled another chair close and joined them. For an hour he spoke with the child, gently probing, asking open-ended questions, and listening as Connor described his experience with passion and intensity.

Paige felt strangely comforted as she watched the man share laughter and rapport with her son. Impressions of Christian goodwill stirred her heart, bringing a mixture of conviction and longing. These days, soccer, PTA, and lazy poolside afternoons loaded with water wings and flippers occupied her time. In her zeal to be a super-mom, Paige had neglected her child's religious upbringing. *Maybe all this angel talk was Connor's way of reaching for a sense of spiritual continuity.*

Reverend Salisbury rose to his feet. "I need to speak with your mother alone. My secretary has some great stories, and if you ask, I know she'll be glad to read one to you." He led Connor to the door and watched him skip across the room to the secretary's desk.

The clergyman turned his attention to Paige. "You have a very fine boy, Mrs. Hays." He gave her a lighthearted smile, but his eyes were somber.

"Thank you." Paige was suddenly aware that she was holding her breath.

"You were right to be concerned." Reverend Salisbury walked over to his desk and settled into his chair. He tapped the tips of his fingers together and waited for a response.

"Then you don't think he saw an angel?"

The clergyman raised his eyebrows. "Mrs. Hays, I'm sure that our church fathers had divine visitations. However, these were reserved for a special dispensation. There is little credible evidence to support the belief that such visitations still occur today."

Is that a look of pity on his face?

"I can understand your need to believe your child. It's only natural for a mother. However, in this case, a sound grasp of reality would serve you better."

Paige was stunned.

"There is no easy way to say this, Mrs. Hays. Connor truly believes that he has spoken with an angel, and, quite frankly, I find this disturbing. I suspect that your son may be in the early stages of a delusional form of mental illness. Of course, this is clearly out of my area of expertise—you understand."

Paige clutched her purse so hard her fingers went numb.

Reverend Salisbury stood and waited for Paige to do the same. "Might I suggest a referral? A member of our congregation happens to be a widely respected child psychiatrist."

The sentences flowed together and were lost on Paige. "Dr. Stanley Lavin . . . outstanding credentials . . . world-renowned . . . gifted diagnostician.

"Mrs. Hays?"

"Yes."

"Would you like me to phone Dr Lavin and see if he can work Connor into his schedule?"

She nodded.

Connor—mentally ill? The thought suddenly crashed upon Paige like a violent wave, and she felt her stomach turn.

Arizona

Thursday, August 2nd

In the dusky light, the desert glowed like a soft pink carpet that had been rolled out just for them. The air carried the sweet aroma of cactus flowers, and along the skyline, ocotillo branches waved their reedy arms in the breeze.

David took his wife's hand as they strolled.

"It'll be dark soon," Elita said, looking back from where they'd come. Their footprints were nearly hidden in the long shadows cast by evening light. "We'd better turn back before we lose our trail."

David leaned close to his wife, caught the faint smell of her jasmine perfume, and nuzzled her ear. "Do you know how much I love you?"

She answered with a kiss, and they lingered arm-in-arm beneath the moon.

Overhead, a streak of light blazed across the Prussian blue sky, and she responded with childlike delight. "That's the most spectacular shooting star I've ever seen!"

The couple searched the heavens for another but soon gave up.

Elita traced a jagged scar that ran along her husband's elbow. "Will you ever tell me what happened?"

"It's not important."

"Do you remember the day we met?"

"How could I forget? You were my angel." David felt his bride pull away. "Did I say something wrong?"

"No, it's just. . . ." Elita hesitated and then found the words. "It wasn't me who rescued you David; it was God."

"Well, then, he sure looks a lot like you," he teased.

"I'm serious! It's not like I make a habit of hanging around biker bars, and I wasn't supposed to even be in Tucson the day we met. I was only there because my supply truck broke down en route, and the driver called to ask me to drive to Tucson and pick up the perishables before they spoiled. Then, just as I was dashing out the door, a friend called. When she found out I was headed to Tucson, she asked me to check on her sick cousin who lived in a really bad part of town." Elita looked intently into her husband's face. "Don't you see? I almost said no. If I hadn't gone, we wouldn't be together."

"So, what are you saying? You think that God arranged our meeting?" It came out sounding cynical. Bathed in the faint glow of moonlight, David could see the hurt on Elita's face. "Sorry, I didn't mean to make light of your faith."

A long minute passed before she broke the gulf of silence. "Why is that so hard for you to believe?"

The question resurrected old wounds. David readied his tongue with the usual ivory tower rhetoric. *Intelligent design? Nothing more than a myth designed to placate the masses!* "I tried praying once," he said. "It didn't work."

Something rustled—an outline in the darkness.

Elita tugged on her husband's t-shirt. "What was that?"

"It's probably just a coyote." But David had the distinct feeling that they were being watched.

A twig snapped.

David's eyes strained to see a shadow creeping closer. *Definitely human.*

"Pare!"

"Que quieres?" Elita asked.

"Levanta las manos!"

"He wants us to raise our hands," Elita translated.

In the dim light, David could make out the lines of a gun. It was pointed at them. "What do you want with us?" He circled a protective arm around his wife.

"Fillmore, is that you?"

"Gordon!" Elita said. "I thought you were in jail."

"I'm out on bail, no thanks to that lawyer husband of yours!"

David shook his head. "Spitzer, as a witness I could not represent you."

"Spoken like a true lawyer!" Gordon sneered.

"What are you doing out here?" Elita asked.

"I was trying out my new heat-sensing equipment." Spitzer peered through his scope at David. "You'd be amazed at what I can see."

"Do you mind putting the gun down?"

Spitzer laughed and lowered his weapon as the couple turned back toward town.

"Be careful," Gordon called after them. "Strange things happen in the desert after the sun goes down."

Chapter 14

Florida

Monday, August 6th

Joel waited in Dr. Lockhart's office. The clock on the wall indicated that fifteen minutes had passed since an aide had escorted the teenager from his hospital room; it seemed like thirty. Anxiety about his return to Waverly nagged at Joel, but he focused on a renegade thread on the sleeve of his uniform, pulling it until it broke.

The door opened, and the doctor walked in. Mr. Quill and a woman Joel had never seen before followed behind.

"Good news! You're being released," Dr. Lockhart said, quickly adding, "from the hospital, anyway."

Joel eyed the woman, whose apple-red cheeks and upturned mouth reminded him of some *Wizard of Oz* character. She appeared to be enjoying herself, and he disliked her for it.

Mr. Quill held an unmarked cardboard box in his arms. He placed it on the floor and took a seat next to Joel. "Young man, your case has been the topic of some vigorous discussion. The circumstances surrounding your injuries are still being investigated." Mr. Quill faltered and cleared his throat. "I'll get right to the point, Joel. Your memory loss leaves us with only Hogan and Boyd's version of the incident that left you injured. This limits our disciplinary options. I do, however, want to reassure you about the investigation into Daryl Capps's death. We feel confident that Gunner and Hogan will both be charged. In the interim, however, your safety at Waverly has become an issue of concern."

Joel reacted with a yawn.

The administrator tapped his fingers on the arm of his chair. "This is Miss Toby of Heaven's Life Fellowship. They have generously agreed to admit you into their troubled youth program. We've arranged for your immediate transfer."

The woman sprang across the room with energetic steps and poked her lily hand toward the teenager. "I'm so pleased to meet you Joel! You're going to love the Redemption Shack—that's what we call our little youth facility. It will be a life-changing experience—trust me."

Joel didn't trust anyone, least of all this saccharine saint.

"Wait 'til you meet your new mentor, Clay Boggs. Have you heard of him?" she gushed. "He is a dynamic teacher, not to mention a sought-after youth rally speaker. He has three bestselling books out now."

Big deal, Joel thought.

"Good things are coming your way—just wait and see!" The woman seemed to quiver with excitement.

Is she for real?

"Well, what are we waiting for? Let's get started!" Miss Toby clapped her hands like a kindergarten teacher.

Mr. Quill lifted the box from the floor beside him and

offered it to Joel. "I've taken the liberty of gathering your things." He passed the carton to the teenager, along with an apologetic look. "I wish you the best, young man."

With the box in hand, Joel reluctantly followed Miss Toby to a waiting van.

On the way to the Redemption Shack, he sat quietly behind a wire mesh screen while the annoying woman jabbered nonstop about the benefits of their program.

Joel opened the box in his lap and peered inside: just a few books, a comb, a toothbrush—and Daryl Capps's Bible. He took it in hand, feeling a rush of emotion, and dropped it back in the box. The pages fell open; tucked inside were two new anonymous postcards from New Orleans. Their postmark indicated that these had arrived while he was still in the hospital. The other postcards, Joel figured, were still hidden under the mattress back at Waverly.

Miss Toby tapped the screen. "Did you hear me?" she asked. "I said we have wonderful counselors, fun youth activities, and a super-duper Phys Ed department. We believe that young people feel better when they stay in shape. Like I said, you're just going to love it!"

Joel stared out the window, wishing he could jettison himself from the speeding van. He looked again at the unsigned postcards, memorizing the touristy images of New Orleans on front and trying to draw meaning from the blocky note scribbled on the back. *THINKING OF YOU*. It was a mystery—a mystery Joel desperately needed to solve.

North Dakota

Tuesday, August 7th

It started with a box of canned goods and a note that Nora found on the porch of the Bargain Bin.

"God bless your kindness," the writer had scribbled. "Maybe this will help."

Nora turned the card over and looked at the stylized angel gracing its cover. It was puzzling, yet at the same time something stirred in her heart.

By noon, more food items had arrived. Most of the boxes were left discreetly on the porch, but a few were delivered in person. Millie Peterson brought in crates of fresh farm eggs and burlap bags chock full of dried beans. "The word is out about how you brought groceries to Chuck and Pepper Tilden even though they owe you back rent." The weathered ranch woman squeezed Nora's shoulder and said, "Darlin', you're a real saint, that's what you are."

The generosity of the community raised a lump in Nora's throat. People like the Petersons had been hit hard by the drought, and yet they shared what little they had.

By the middle of the week, Nora found herself looking at a growing mountain of food items, and she was more than overwhelmed.

She picked up the phone, dialed her church, and got the answering machine. "You've reached the Delmont Harvest Church. Leave a message and we'll get back to you. And have a blessed day."

"Pastor Henry," Nora spoke to the machine, "something amazing has been happening at the Bargain Bin. People are donating food and supplies for the local farmers. I was hoping you could round up a few church volunteers to help me sort things out." She hung up and got busy organizing stacks of groceries. Around 11:00 AM, Lindsay straggled in with her toddler.

The young mother's mouth fell open as she looked around. "Whoa! It's worse than I heard!" She set little Brooke down to play and parked her hands on her hips. "Okay, put me to work!"

"I'm not sure where to begin." Nora scratched her head. "Some of the donations included the names of people who could use a little help themselves. We need to start a list and then move the food items back to the storage room to sort."

They were discussing the details when blue-haired Gertie Bell clomped into the Bargain Bin with her wooden clogs. The stout Scandinavian grandma headed straight for the kitchen with her arms loaded with a basket of goodies. "I brought knoephla and some of my lefse bread because we'll need to keep up our strength!"

"We could use some muscle right now," Lindsay complained as she struggled with a heavy box. "I'm going to give myself a hernia!"

"Have no fear, ladies. J. J. O'Shay is here to serve!"

They turned to see a man standing near the front door with an impressive handlebar mustache. He flexed his sagging middle-aged bicep. "Heavy lifting and juggling are my specialties."

Nora smothered a smile. "Juggling? Oh my!"

"That's right. I'm recently retired after thirty years with the circus. Guess you could say that I'm a man of many talents!" Mr. O'Shay lifted his colorful hemp beanie and scratched a thinning crown. "I'm looking for work, and if I find any here—I'm leaving!" he said with a chuckle.

Lindsay giggled. "That's a good one!"

"I'm afraid that we are strictly volunteer-based," Nora said.

The man was undeterred. "Something sure smells delicious. What if I agreed to take my pay in food?"

"I suppose. . . ."

"My dear, you just got yourself a first-class helper!" J. J. rubbed his hands together and sniffed his way toward the kitchen. A minute later, with a clatter and a squawk, J. J. emerged ahead of Gertie, who was brandishing a wooden spoon like it was a war club.

"Who do you think you are?" the old woman squawked.

"Gertie, I'd like you to meet Mr. J. J. O'Shay," Nora interjected. "He's our newest volunteer."

"Just a big huckleberry, if you ask me!" The old woman's eyes flashed. "Big lug marched in, grabbed a mixing bowl out of the dish drainer, and helped himself to half my pot of knoephla!"

"Guilty as charged, madam," J. J. grinned sheepishly. "I simply lost all self-control when I smelled your heavenly cooking."

"All right, then," Gertie softened. "I'll fix you up a proper bowl, but only if you behave like a gentleman."

By early afternoon, the motley group had formed a plan. Nora organized the names of those in need; Gertie sorted canned goods from dry goods; Lindsay addressed cards, adding her own artistic flare; and J. J. loaded paper grocery bags and carried them out to his van for delivery.

A ministry was birthed. God was doing something extraordinary. There had been no praying and no committees—just willing hearts. The whole thing seemed to fall into place like it had been organized by heaven's CEO.

So many blessings, Nora thought, *including this unlikely work force: a teenaged single mom, a retired circus performer, and a blue-haired Scandinavian.*

Chapter 15

Washington, DC
Thursday, August 9th

Paige strolled along the shady pathway at the National Zoo, keeping a watchful eye on her son, who ran ahead with the boundless energy of all his five years. "Mom, I see the hippopasamas!" She laughed at the sight of her little boy jumping up and down in front of the massive creatures. For a moment, Paige could almost believe that everything was fine, but she knew it was not.

She paused upon the sun-mottled path as a sickening wave of helplessness threatened to undo her. Paige watched Connor carefully, as if trying to memorize every detail: a beautiful, red-haired child, with a freckled face and trusting eyes—eyes like Emily's. Tears clouded Paige's vision, and she angrily wiped them away. *This can't be happening. It isn't fair.*

She shifted the backpack that hung from her shoulder. It rattled, reminding her of the bottle of pills inside. The pharmacist had called them antipsychotic medication. The words had stunned her.

"I want to see the elephants!" Connor tugged on Paige's hand and led her around the bend as if she were the child. On the edge of a concrete pool, a mother elephant swayed next to her baby, her trunk falling in strokes across the young one's back.

Paige checked her watch. It was 11:45 AM. "Let's go meet Daddy."

Connor followed gladly, stopping periodically along the way to admire the animals and then running to keep up with his mother.

The Panda Café was already crowded with tourists, so Paige claimed a spot on the park bench. They settled back to wait for Brody. Half an hour later, Paige stepped in line and ordered a single-size pizza for her hungry son.

The cell phone rang, and Paige retrieved it from the bottom of her purse.

"Honey, I'm really sorry, but something has come up. I have to attend an important meeting and I just can't get away."

"This is more important!" Anger percolated within Paige from her disappointment. She handed Connor his pizza and pointed him to a picnic table.

"What did the doctor say?"

Paige's throat tightened. "Childhood schizophrenia."

"What? Listen, Paige, don't get yourself all worked up. We'll get a second opinion—okay?"

She held her breath.

"Honey, did you hear me?"

Paige struggled to hold herself together. "I'm here."

"Try not to worry. We'll talk more tonight," he said

before hanging up.

I can't do this, Paige thought, still clutching the phone in her hands. Never before had she felt so alone.

Washington, DC
Thursday, August 9th

Brody's thought were miles from the West Wing as key staff trickled into the room. A manila folder landed on the table in front of him, jarring him back from the troubles at home.

Spence Carlyle, the president's chief political advisor, peered at Brody over his bifocals. "Drought, pestilence, and famine don't hold a candle to a shaky economy when it comes to the reelection campaign," he said. "That's what I want to talk about."

Carlyle's rosebud lips and tiny ears looked misplaced on his square face. "From now until the election, we can all expect a sleepless ride on the old campaign trail." He pulled the others in with a glance. "This team must work as one organism. Are we on the same page here, people?"

Murmured affirmations rippled around the long table.

Brody slid the contents from the envelope. He could feel Spence Carlyle watching him, waiting for a reaction to the dismal press clippings: unemployment, falling stocks, and rising energy costs.

Carlyle circled the table and stood behind Brody. He pointed to a *New York Times* clipping that described Atwood's Farm Aid in a negative light. "I hear that a trip to North

Dakota has been scheduled. I don't think it would be prudent. The president's opponent and the press will play this up as nothing more than nostalgia at the taxpayer's expense!"

"This is about doing the right thing, not pandering to a fickle media," Brody said. "The Midwest drought has seriously impacted food supplies and has the potential to affect all Americans."

The chief political advisor's ears flamed red. "Hays, may I remind you of your title: chief economic advisor! You of all people should know that most elections hinge on the economy. Your job is to give sound advice, not to steer this administration into a political train wreck!"

The chief of staff jumped into the fray. "Brody, your economic intuition is usually on target. That's one of the qualities that got you noticed with this administration." Chip Skinner paused. "Consumer confidence is down. It's time to bring out the warm and fuzzy blankets. Am I being clear?"

Brody knew exactly what he meant.

"He's right!" Spence bellowed. "We need to get the taxpayers moving in the right direction. President Lyndon Johnson once said, 'In the end, the voters would paint their hind ends white and run with the antelope,' or something to that effect." The president's political advisor laughed, and the others joined in.

"I've got another meeting," Chip Skinner said, starting toward the door. He stopped and turned back. "I understand that you'll be accompanying the president to the G-20 Summit in Toronto. This might be a perfect opportunity to generate positive press."

"I'll do my best." Brody stared at the clippings on the

table, knowing full well that the president had his mind set on stopping in North Dakota after the summit.

Brody considered the massive task that had been set before him: shielding the president from the coming financial storm. He feared that the nation's economic woes were symptomatic of problems too deeply entrenched to gloss over with optimistic platitudes.

Chapter 16

Florida

Sunday, August 12th

"You gotta play the game," Joel's new roommate, Ricky Hernandez, advised. "It don't matter if you believe. Just learn to talk the talk and walk the walk. Boggs eats this stuff up!"

Joel stared at his "shack-mate," trying to decide what to make of him. Hernandez straightened his tie and modeled his best Sunday suit. "How do I look?"

"Fine," Joel said cautiously.

"You got a Bible?" Ricky pressed. "Take it with you. It'll make a good impression."

Joel had almost forgotten Daryl's old Bible that he'd tossed into the back of his bedside drawer. "Yeah, I've got one, but—"

"Trust me!" Ricky cut in. "Listen, man, I'm just trying to help you. If you want to rot in this place, that's your business, but I'll be getting out soon. I'm what you call "transformed"! In fact, Boggs has promised to tell that to the state board." Ricky blew on his knuckles and flashed a mischievous smirk.

"Get ready for inspection," one of the other boys alerted. They watched through the dorm's wire-meshed hallway window as the youth counselor approach with key in hand.

Clay Boggs unlocked the door and stepped briskly inside, followed by his aide, a Neanderthal named Schumer.

The counselor swept the room with a military gaze that seemed incongruent with his diamond-studded earring.

The man was an enigma to Joel, with his trendy acid-washed jeans and his funky tennis shoes. At first glance he appeared to be a gray-haired version of "one of the boys," but there was authoritarian blood coursing through his veins.

"Good morning, shack-mates." Boggs strolled through the dorm with his hands clasped casually behind his back.

"Peter." Clay snapped his fingers and pointed toward a bunk. "You can do a better job making that bed." The boy complied without protest.

The youth counselor stopped in front of Joel and looked intently at his newest resident. "You may not realize it now, but you were lucky to be accepted into this program. We change lives here at Heaven's Life Fellowship."

Joel stared at the pattern on the linoleum floor.

"We don't force our faith here, but we do promote biblical precepts that are vital for recovery."

What are precepts? Joel wondered but didn't ask.

Clay concluded his round with a couple of admonitions for better hygiene and then lined up the boys for inspection. "Shack-mates, we have a surprise for you this morning. Heaven's Life is presenting a special worship service."

The young men walked single file down a long corridor

behind Boggs, with Schumer the Neanderthal bringing up the rear. They moved along a hallway with couches, chairs, and brightly colored murals—a pathetic attempt to make the place look homey. To Joel, it was still just a prison, with thick metal doors, security locks, and wire-meshed windows.

The small group emerged from the building, passed through a fenced yard, and then stepped into a waiting van.

Schumer maneuvered the vehicle around a maze of buildings on the church's vast property. There was an amphitheater, mission center, a fully accredited Christian school, and a food bank. But the largest building was the Heaven's Life Church itself, a towering pinnacle of glass and steel.

The van turned into a concrete parking garage and ascended a series of ramps before coming to a stop on the rooftop.

The youth counselor jumped out and stretched his back. "Hold your heads high, men. Remember, you are Redemption Shack citizens!" Flanked by a group of trusted elite whom Clay Boggs called his chosen, the group was led across a glass-enclosed bridge, through a set of double doors, and into a special balcony reserved for the Redemption Shack.

Joel took a seat near the railing and looked down upon the church sanctuary. It was huge, bigger even than a stadium. Far below, the swelling congregation looked like swarming insects. Onstage, three massive grid screens, angled for maximum viewing capability, served as high-tech backdrops.

"We call this the bird cage," Ricky whispered, keeping one eye on his councilor. "I guess they stuck us up here in the nosebleed section 'cause they don't want us mixin' with those righteous tithers down there." He was snickering at his own cleverness when Clay cautioned him with a raised eyebrow. "I was just telling Joel about the espresso bars they have down there," Hernandez lied. He leaned toward Joel. "They've also got a gym and a Wednesday night aerobics class, too." He dropped his voice even lower. "Wish we could be up here when all those suburban housewives do their thing."

Canned music shook the auditorium. Musicians took their places on stage beneath a big screen, and then a clean-cut entertainer bounded onto the stage, followed by three high-stepping beauties.

Lively music filled the room, and the lead singer yelled, "Everybody, clap your hands!"

The crooners sang, "More power, more love!" The music director elevated the mood with audience participation. "Are you here to worship?"

The crowd responded. "Yes!"

"I said—are you here to WORSHIP?!"

The congregation shouted a resounding, "YES!!!"

Music blasted across the auditorium with electric energy, and song lyrics appeared on the overhead screen. The room rumbled.

Three lively songs later, the worship leader bowed his head, and the tempo softened from charged to contemplative.

Joel had never seen anything like it. He watched in awe as the people raised their hands. Some seemed to be crying, and a few sank to their knees. *They really seem to believe,* the teenager thought.

The man onstage uttered an emotional appeal. "Lord, we are grateful that you have found us pleasing in your sight.

Accordingly, you have blessed us with prosperity. Move our hearts to generously give as you have given." On stage, the trio of women trilled like songbirds as legions of ushers were dispatched to gather the offerings.

"Beloved," the worship director announced, "We have a wonderful blessing this morning. I know that our young people will be especially pleased. Please welcome the Christian rock band, Holy Phatt!"

Whistles and applause reverberated throughout the building as a brigade of black jackets and wild-haired young men appeared onstage.

Instruments shrieked, loud enough to rattle steel girders, and the lead singer crooned. Joel could not make out most of the words, but thought he heard the word "Jesus" bandied about a couple of times. The lead guitarist smoked, and the drummer was on fire.

It was just like attending a heavy-metal concert, minus the fists raised in the devil's salute. Joel felt both confused and strangely attracted by the glitter onstage.

When the song was over, Holy Phatt took their bows, awash with thunderous applause.

The pastor walked out dressed in a gray silk suit and Italian shoes. With open arms, he praised the band and then turned to the audience. "What talent!" he said, clapping as the musicians made their exit. "Holy Phatt will be performing in Tampa later this month. Check out their website and get your tickets early."

Ricky Hernandez whispered, "That's Pastor Cedric Holmes. He used to be some kind of motivational guru."

"Few are chosen!" Pastor Cedric began, "Yet many are

called." He began to pace across the stage. "Dear loved ones: There are those among us who have laid their lives down for this church. This is evidenced by their unquestioning obedience to leadership. Yes, the godly mantle of anointing falls on those who have the gift of service! Are you among the chosen?"

"I've heard this sermon before." Ricky sneered. "Must be gearing up for some kind of event and looking for free labor."

From the stage, Pastor Cedric invited the congregation to partake in an upcoming week-long seminar. "Christian counselors will be on hand to help you channel your gifts and talents into church service."

Ricky jabbed Joel in the ribs. "Told ya! You should hear the fundraiser sermon. That's one of his favorites."

As the service wound down, Joel's confusion turned to skepticism. There was more Hollywood glitter than true holiness, it seemed. Joel considered his old roommate, who had died for his faith, and something told him Daryl Capps would agree.

North Dakota

Sunday, August 12th

Nora arrived at the Delmont Harvest Center surprised to find the service already underway. She discretely slid into the back pew and checked her wristwatch. It wasn't quite 10:30 AM, yet worship was over.

Pastor Henry was immersed in his sermon and

preaching with gusto. "Some are called to be apostles; some are called to be prophets."

From the front row, Celeste delivered a breathy "Amen!" Magna and Ava echoed.

Nora chewed her lip and tried to push aside her misgivings about Celeste who claimed that she had been "sent" to the Delmont Harvest Church to impart wisdom.

The church bulletin directed Nora to the core of the message, and she did her best to follow along as Pastor Henry wrapped up his sermon. "Does anyone have a word from the Lord?"

Celeste rose and moved to the front. In her hand was a pale green pitcher of oil that she lifted for all to see. "Will you kneel before the Lord, Pastor Henry?"

"I will," he said, and when he obeyed, the woman trickled the contents of the pitcher upon his head.

The congregation seemed mesmerized by the ritual.

"Brother Henry, this day, among these witnesses, the Lord has endowed you with an apostolic anointing."

The pastor climbed to his feet as hushed whispers rippled among the congregation. "I am greatly humbled by this honor."

"Come!" Celeste called out. "All who desire a prophetic anointing come forth and receive!"

As people began to stream toward the altar, Nora gathered her Bible and slipped quietly from the sanctuary.

Abigail was standing alone in the church alcove. "My husband, an apostle! Isn't it wonderful?" Her face was serene, but her eyes told a different story.

"Yes," Nora said gently.

The door to the children's church opened, and the hallway flooded with happy noise.

"Why did church start early today?" Nora asked.

Abigail's brow creased. "Didn't you get an email notice? Henry moved the time back to 10:00 AM so the team could have more time to pray after the service."

Nora decided not to make an issue of it. "Hey, I need to pick up a copy of this month's cleaning schedule."

"Oh, dear," Abigail said, offering an apologetic smile. "I'm afraid that you're the only one scheduled to clean this month. I meant to tell you."

"What about Magna and Ava? I thought we were working together as a team?"

"They've been appointed as church intercessors. They just don't have time for cleaning."

"Appointed by whom?"

Abigail bristled defensively. "Celeste has a strong prophetic call."

"I see," Nora said, wishing that she didn't.

Chapter 17

Arizona
Tuesday, August 14th

"Rush hour in Kirby, Arizona," David chuckled as he idled behind a short string of cars. The traffic light changed to green. He let out the clutch, rolled the old Ford into the intersection, and quickly checked the address he'd scribbled on a piece of scratch paper: 206 CHULA LANE.

Paved streets, concrete sidewalks, and brightly colored houses with xeriscape yards—it was a far cry from the place he called home.

Arroyo Seco, David thought, *is more like a state of mind than a place.*

The law office of Hartman and Hartman was not hard to find. David parked and grabbed his briefcase.

He strolled down a walkway that ran between two gravel-bed cactus gardens.

At the door, David adjusted his tie and stepped inside to a blast of air conditioning.

A young receptionist looked up from a glass-top desk and asked, "Can I help you?"

"I'm David Fillmore."

She reached for the intercom button. "I'll inform Mr. Hartman that you have arrived."

David dropped into a leather chair and thumbed through a stack of magazines that were artfully displayed on the coffee table.

The receptionist rustled some papers. The phone rang, and the shrill whine of a fax came in as David drummed his fingers on the armrest.

"How do you do, Mr. Fillmore?" A compact man sporting a pencil-thin mustache positioned himself in front of the chair. "I'm Darrel Hartman. I hope you had a pleasant trip riding over on your Harley." The lawyer's voice was as smooth as butter.

The word *smarmy* came to David's mind. "I drive a Triumph, but today I borrowed my wife's pickup."

Hartman led him down a hallway toward some double-paneled doors and opened them. The conference room was spacious and decorated to impress with its Italian leather furnishings and built-in bookcases.

Joanne was seated at the far end of a long table.

David greeted her, and she reciprocated with a smug nod.

"Let's get down to business, shall we?" Hartman shuffled through a stack of papers and settled into a chair beside his client. "I've had a chance to go over the trust, and for the most part everything seems to be in order." He pulled a pair of readers from his shirt pocket and slid them on his nose. "There are, however, a few questions. . . ."

"Did you bring the box?" Joanne blurted.

Hartman touched his client's hand and said, "It's best if you let me handle this."

Joanne ignored her lawyer. Her slate eyes were locked on David. "I demand to see an itemized content list of the box before you mail it to my cousin."

"Your father sealed the carton himself and allocated it to his niece. I have no authority to open it."

Joanne's cheeks blazed red. "Nora Meyers doesn't deserve anything that belonged to my father's estate! She didn't even have the decency to attend the funeral!"

"Perhaps we should go over the document," Hartman interjected. "The bulk of Rupert Sims's estate goes to his daughter, Joanne. This includes land valuing upwards of eight million dollars."

"That's not the part that concerns me!" Joanne cut in.

Hartman leaned forward in his chair and laced his fingers together. "I believe Ms. Sims is referring to a tract of land on the northeast corner of the ranch that has been designated for"—the lawyer looked over his readers and continued—"special use."

David flipped through the pages of the trust, stopped on the section in question, and waited for the others to find their place.

Joanne's lawyer tapped his pen lightly on the table as he read. "I must say these are very interesting instructions, even for Rupert—don't you agree?"

David leaned back and folded his arms across his chest.

"I see that you've agreed to manage this property," Hartman said, peering over his glasses. "In all my years of practice, I've never known a trust attorney to be appointed as a successor trustee?"

"I advised Rupert against it," David said, "but he insisted."

"I see. . . ." Hartman ran a finger over his short-trimmed mustache and then he stood and said, "Mr. Fillmore, thanks for coming in."

Joanne's mouth gaped at her lawyer. "You've got to be kidding!" She scowled at David. "This isn't over, Fillmore. As far as I'm concerned, you took advantage of a feeble old man!"

Mr. Hartman accompanied David down the hallway, where he apologized for his client's outburst. "I'm sure we can clear up this misunderstanding," he said breathlessly. "All we need is some documentation—anything that will corroborate your claim that Rupert Sims was competent at the time the trust was drawn up." Hartman's eyebrows arched. "You do have something that will prove your claim, don't you?"

There was a bad feeling in the pit of David's stomach as he rattled down the highway in Elita's old Ford pickup. Maybe he had been careless regarding his client's mental state. But it was too late to change things now.

Arizona

Monday, August 20th

David checked the North Dakota phone number for Rupert Sims's niece and dialed. He listened to a couple rings before a woman picked up with a cheerful, "Hello."

"I'm trying to reach a Ms. Nora Meyers."

"Speaking."

David identified himself and told her that he was appointed executer for the estate of Rupert Sims.

There was a long pause. "Are you saying that Uncle Rupert passed away?"

The question took David by surprise. "I'm sorry; I assumed that you had been contacted by the family."

"Joanne and I were never close, but. . . ." Nora's voice was taut with emotion. "Was my uncle sick?"

"Yes, but I assure you that he passed away peacefully."

"I would have come if I had known he was ailing."

David shifted the receiver to his other ear. "Rupert set something aside for you. I mailed it to your work address: Nora's Bargain Bin, 102 Main Street, Delmont North Dakota." There was dead air on the line. "Ms. Meyers?"

"I'm still here."

"Your uncle sealed the box himself. You must have been very special to him." David offered his condolences and hung up, wondering why family relationships had to be so complex.

"There goes another one!" Elita pointed toward the window as an early model Winnebago cruised by. The motor home rocked over a couple of potholes and then stopped briefly at Main Street's broken stop light.

She emptied a roll of quarters into the cash register drawer. "Miriam Baker stopped by yesterday morning and bought a trunk full of paper goods. Her campground is being overrun with people. Poor woman said she nearly passed out from cleaning those restrooms in the heat."

In front of the General Store, the motor home's door swung open, and a couple of kids scrambled down the steps. A woman wearing Capris and a sleeveless shirt chased after them while her husband stayed behind to check under the Winnebago's hood.

"My curiosity is killing me," Elita said. "I'm just going to come right out and ask why all these folks are in town."

David made no attempt to talk her out of it; it was a futile exercise once she'd made up her mind.

The screen door banged open, and a bright-eyed boy blew into the room with his sister trailing behind. They spotted the lunch counter and raced for the same corner stool.

"I got it first!"

"Nah-ah! It's mine!" the girl insisted, trying to pry her brother's iron grip from the prize. When her efforts failed, she burst into tears. "Mom! Robert is being mean!"

Their mother appeared, looking weary. "Missy, dear," she sighed, "there are other stools." The woman's face brightened. "Maybe you'll find one that spins faster than your brother's." That did the trick.

"No fair!" Robert banged his small fist on the counter and folded his arms in a pout.

"Greetings from the great unwashed!" the Winnebago's driver called from the store's threshold. He lifted a Dodgers ball cap from a sandy mop of hair and strode across the floor to where the David and Elita stood.

"Randy Bales here!" he said, nodding toward the lunch counter. "That's my wife, Kay, and our kids, Missy and Robert."

"Welcome!" Elita said. "Where are you folks traveling

from?"

Randy locked his ball cap back on his head. "We hail from California—over near Lancaster."

"What brings you here?"

"Would you believe we heard about your world-famous malts?"

Elita parked her hands on her hips. "Nice try."

The traveler laughed. "All right, you got me! But, just so you don't think I'm all bull, we'll take three chocolate and one vanilla."

David accompanied his wife to the lunch counter and lined up some heavy glass tumblers next to the malt mixer.

"This is a great little town you've got here," Kay Bales said, keeping an eye on her kids.

Elita pulled two tubs of ice cream from the cooler. "We usually don't get much summer traffic." With scoop in hand, she turned to her customers. "Are you here on some kind of family reunion?"

Randy exchanged a fleeting look with his wife. "Yeah, I guess you could say that."

The lawyer in David kicked in, and he wondered what this guy was hiding.

The traveler looked around the room. "This store could be a movie set! I mean it! I feel like we've just stepped back in time."

"Say, do you good folks know of a place we can put down stakes for the night?" Randy's eyebrows arched hopefully. "The campground is full."

Before David could voice his protest, Elita invited the travelers to camp in the lot behind the store.

North Dakota

Wednesday, August 22nd

Nora tried to put her grief aside by throwing herself into her work, but her thoughts kept returning to Uncle Rupert. She wondered how her cousin, Joanne, had reacted when she found out her father had earmarked a box for her nemesis. *Not too well,* she imagined. It used to bother Nora that her only cousin didn't like her, until she realized that Joanne really didn't like anyone. *What a lonely person she must be.*

Nora wondered about the contents of the package that was being sent to her—probably photographs of the trips she and her mother had taken to Arizona. Such childhood mementos should be handed down to family. She wondered: *Who will treasure mine?*

On the desk, a new stack of mail needed Nora's attention, and she went to work. More names of families in need of help. Every empty cupboard tugged on Nora's heart. Times were getting tougher. The farmers were already harvesting their withered crops. The government farm subsidies had helped, but it wasn't enough to keep the rural farm supply store from closing. Rumors of impending foreclosure notices crept through Delmont and the mood around the community had become desperate.

Nora slipped open another envelope and found a sizable donation. Just when she feared the good folks of Delmont had reached their limits of giving, a new wave of generosity would roll in—sometimes in the form of money, other times with offerings of home-baked goods or prayers of encouragement.

Across the room, Gertie snapped a freshly ironed shirt and slid it on a hanger.

"I've been thinking of opening those rooms upstairs," Nora said. "They've been boarded up for years, but now it seems like a shame to waste all that space. If things keep getting worse, some people might need a place to stay."

"Great idea!" the blue-haired matron said. "Maybe after all these years this old hotel will finally have some guests!"

"It'll take a lot of work." Nora made a mental note of all the bedding and other supplies they'd need before they could open to the public, not to mention having to patch a leaky roof.

J. J. O'Shay ambled through the door whistling a happy tune. "Operation: Delivery complete!" He draped an arm over Gertie's shoulder and said, "I got the goods on you, grandma!"

The blue-haired matron scowled and said, "Only a big, dumb huckleberry would lend a fat ear to gossip!"

J. J. drew back in mock horror. "Whoa, granny! That look scares me, and I ain't scared of nothing!"

"Mind your manners!" she bellowed.

"Did you know that Gertie used to ride a chopped Harley to Sturgis every year?" J.J. blurted.

A mental image of the elderly woman sporting boots and black leather popped into Nora's mind. "Really?"

"What's so strange about that?" the old woman snorted. "Lots of people ride!"

Nora thought it best to change the subject. "It feels like fall is in the air. I wonder if we should make sure the old boiler is ready for the season."

"I'll go." J. J. laid the back of his hand to his forehead and sniffed for effect. He sauntered over to the basement door, threw it open, and, just before descending, said, "I know when I'm not wanted!"

A few minutes later, he was back. "We've got major problems with that old boiler."

The announcement stopped Nora cold. "Can it be fixed?"

J. J. scowled. "I can't say for sure, but it doesn't look good. There's a big crack in it and water all over the place down there." He shook his head. "Poor ol' boiler's gotta be fifty years old. Personally, I'm afraid she's dead."

"What do you think a new system would cost?"

O'Shay gave Nora a deadpan look. "You don't want to know."

Nora thought of all the people who would be let down if the place had to close. September was just around the corner.

Chapter 18

North Dakota
Monday, August 27th

Despite the boiler's tragic death, the volunteers at Nora's Bargain Bin carried on as though God was smiling on them. A steady trickle of relief packages streamed through the doors of the old building. The ministry was thriving.

In the kitchen, a kettle of Gertie's famous beef stew was simmering on the stove. The rich aroma went through the Bargain Bin like a goodwill ambassador. From upstairs, constant thwacks from a hammer and the whine of a Skilsaw could be heard thanks to a crew of out-of-work carpenters who were generously volunteering both their time and materials.

Our cup runneth over, Nora thought with a grateful heart; but the battle was far from over. Soon the air would turn frigid, and North Dakota's frosty chill would set in. Without a new boiler, the Bargain Bin would have to shut its doors. "Lord, we need a miracle," she whispered.

"Ho, ho, ho!" J. J. O'Shay bellowed. "The UPS truck brought you a present." He carried a medium-sized box around the other side of the checkout counter and set it down at Nora's feet. "Couldn't help noticing the package was sent all the way from Arizona."

J. J. offered his pocketknife and waited like a curious child as Nora opened the package.

Right on top was a photo that made her eyes tear up. "This is my late Uncle Rupert."

Gertie wandered in from the kitchen, coffee mug in hand. "He looks like a cowboy from one of those old spaghetti westerns," she said, leaning down for a better look.

J. J. lifted his beanie and scratched his thinning crown. "I don't see the family resemblance."

"Uncle Rupert was married to my mom's older sister."

"Oh, for heaven's sake, you don't mean Babs?" Gertie chortled. "We went to school together."

"Really? They had schools back then?" J. J. poked.

Gertie ignored him. "So this is the handsome rancher who stole Babs away from the promised land of North Dakota!" She shook her head. "I heard the poor thing died during childbirth."

"Sad, but true," Nora said, mining the box for other memories.

"Why would your uncle include a VHS tape?" J. J. asked, peering over her shoulder. "I don't think they even make machines that play them anymore."

Nora lifted the tape cassette from the box. FYI was scribbled on a plain white label on the front.

"What if this is one of those video wills?" Gertie blurted. "There's an old TV set in the back with a VHS player built in!"

J. J. took the hint and went to retrieve it.

A few minutes later, they were glued to the small screen, watching a recording of Rupert Sims sitting in his living room recliner.

Gertie clapped her mottled hands together. "This is so exiting—almost like watching one of my British mysteries!"

Uncle Rupert looks tired and shriveled with age, Nora thought, *but his face still has those same endearing laugh lines.*

The old rancher outlined his intentions to set aside a piece of his land "just as soon as I can find a good lawyer." A twinkle entered his eye. "Good thing I'm a man of faith!"

J. J. bellowed with laughter. "I like this guy."

"You're probably wondering why I'm rambling on," Sims continued. "I realized that some folks may think my wishes are a bit odd—some may question my mental faculties. So I made this little film to reassure everybody that I know exactly what I'm doing with my land."

Nora noted that the time and date stamped on the video indicated that it had been recorded over a year ago—probably around the time when his illness was first diagnosed.

They listened as Rupert Sims outlined his wishes. He ended by saying, "Nora, darlin', this brings me to why I'm sending this to you. Your old uncle Rupert has a favor to ask. I need you to slip this video in one of those overnight envelopes and ship it back to my lawyer. If you're watching this then I figure one has been in contact with you. Love ya, darlin'—always have. Don't be shedding any tears for me, little girl, 'cause I'm right where I want to be!"

Gertie grabbed a tissue and blew her nose with a honk.

"Would you like me to take it to the post office?"

Nora removed the VHS from the machine, still pondering her uncle's strange request. She scribbled a quick note to put with the tape and handed both to Gertie. "The lawyer's name is on the box. David Fillmore, I believe."

Next, Nora pulled a family Bible and an historic coffee table book from the box.

"Hey, can I see that?" J. J pointed to the coffee table book. "This is about the Delmont Hotel!" he said, thumbing through the glossy pages. "Wow, it was a real jewel back in the day."

Gertie grabbed a peek as she headed for the door. "The historical society would love to get their mitts on that." She cinched the belt on her alpaca sweater and announced that she was off to the post office.

"Wait a minute! Something's not quite right with this photograph." J. J.'s eyes widened. "I don't believe it!"

He handed the historic book to Nora. "Tell me what you see. Better yet, tell me what you *don't* see."

She stared at the image of the old hotel lobby. Nora gasped. "There used to be a fireplace over there!"

J. J. raced over to the wall in question and tapped it with his knuckles. He turned back wearing a grin. "I think we just found a solution to our heating woes—at least until we can raise money for a new boiler." He bounded up the stairs to speak with one of the carpenters.

Nora looked down at the family Bible, still in her hand. She opened it. Next to the names of relatives who had gone before her was an inscription ". . . the just shall live by faith. . . ."

Washington, DC

Tuesday, August 28th

At the top of the grand staircase, Brody Hays waited for the president and first lady. Beside him, Secretary of State Chase Radovich adjusted the bowtie on his tuxedo.

"How's Mrs. Hays?" he asked.

"Paige is home with our son, Connor."

The truth was that his wife had refused the invitation to the White House, saying, "Brody, your family needs you here—I need you!"

"Is the boy ill? Nothing serious I hope."

"No, Mr. Secretary," Brody said. "I'm sure that he'll be fine."

Chase Radovich cleared his throat. "So, the president asked you to attend the State Department dinner?" Without waiting for a reply, the secretary of state forged on. "It's prudent, I suppose. There are always economic implications."

An understatement. Brody kept the thought to himself.

The secretary of state's face lit up as the president and first lady arrived. "Madam, you look absolutely stunning this evening." She wore a royal blue gown with a deep scoop front. On her neck, a three-tiered diamond necklace glittered brilliantly next to her ivory skin. Chase extended his hand. When she offered hers, he kissed it.

"Thank you, Chase," Mrs. Atwood said, "but when are we going to get past all these stuffy formalities? Please, call me Heddy."

"With pleasure, my dear lady." He offered a sublime

smile before releasing her hand and turning his attention to the commander-in-chief. "Mr. President, we need to talk." There was a look of urgency on the secretary's face.

Thomas Atwood touched his wife's arm. "Heddy, darling, will you excuse us for a moment?" He waited as she sashayed past a flank of Secret Service and paused near a cornice to study a painting.

"What's on your mind?"

Even in a tuxedo, Chase Radovich looked somehow less than stately. He was an oddly built man with girth in all the wrong places, but his face was earnest, and beneath a full crop of sandy hair his eyes burned with intelligence. "Several things have come across my desk lately that have been a cause for concern," he began. "I wanted to give you a quick overview before the dinner this evening. Foremost is the APADS outbreak."

Atwood nodded. "Atypical Pulmonary Acute Distress Syndrome."

"The experts at USDA say we could have a major problem on our hands." Chase cleared his throat. "This outbreak doesn't appear to be species-specific. There have been documented cases from canines to humans, and there has been at least one confirmed case of cattle-to-human infection." He looked worried. "There is a very high mortality rate. It's really quite serious, and both the CDC and the World Health Organization are on it."

"Have they isolated a cause yet?"

The secretary of state shook his head. "No, but they are leaning toward the theory that it may be caused by some kind of toxic spore."

"Terrorism?"

"They haven't ruled that out, but it seems more likely that it may be related to something growing in the feed lots. The Canadian cattle industry is the hardest hit, losing nearly an eighth of their stock. This brings me to my point, sir. The USDA has stopped the importation of cattle from Canada, and the CDC is considering restrictions on human travel to the US from Canada as well." Chase shook his boxy head. "Needless to say, there is growing tension with our northern neighbor."

Thomas Atwood rubbed his chin as he pondered the situation and then signaled an aide standing nearby. "Get in touch with my national security advisor. Tell Marta I want to meet with her tomorrow in reference to the APADS situation in Canada."

The president turned to Brody. "The economic fallout for Canada could be staggering. I'll need a briefing. Don't be conservative on this one, Brody—I want a worst-case scenario."

"Yes, sir." Brody looked down past the rich red carpeting of the grand staircase. A Chopin tune played from the East Room below, where guests mingled and sipped wine before assembling for dinner.

Thomas Atwood and the first lady walked down the grand staircase, followed by the secretary of state and the president's chief economic advisor.

Chase Radovich prattled on as they descended. "I'm sure you are aware that the Canadian Prime Minister is attending the state dinner tonight." He cleared his throat. "I've been with Jacques Renoso all afternoon, and frankly, sir, he is not happy."

"That's understandable." The president glanced at Brody to emphasize their earlier conversation.

"There is one more matter." Radovich's lips tightened. "Yes, apparently the worldwide famine situation is reaching crisis proportions. The State Department has been receiving frantic calls to expedite foreign aid, but there has been some pushback from Agriculture. They claim our national surplus of grain is dangerously low because of the extended drought." He cleared his throat. "What with the recent farm subsidies and all, we are barely able to supply our own demand for grain. I thought you should be informed, just in case a foreign dignitary tries to extract a promise from you."

Brody felt a rush of sympathy for the president, whose tenure seemed burdened by crisis after crisis.

Outside the door of the East Room, Atwood paused to process the information. "Our nation's internal crisis is my first priority," he said, offering the first lady his arm.

Two staff members announced the arrival of the President of the United States. Beneath three Bohemian-cut glass chandeliers, aristocrats, in all their finery, applauded respectfully as the president and first lady entered. All eyes were watching as Washington's most celebrated couple moved across the classical room exchanging gracious greetings among a sea of pleasant faces—all pleasant, that is, except for Jacques Renoso. The Canadian Prime Minister stood with his arms folded rigidly, his face dark and brooding.

Washington, DC

Tuesday, August 28th

Paige watched her son with a mother's eye. He was racing Matchbox cars around the border of the Oriental rug, complete with sound effects. *If there is really something wrong with Connor, wouldn't I know?* Her thoughts drifted to the bottle of pills. The psychologists would say that she was in denial. *To heck with the psychologists!* Paige's heart won this round. *Next week*, she told herself, *a second opinion will confirm that the diagnosis was a mistake*.

"It's time for bed." Paige clapped her hands and then bent down and scooped Connor in her arms.

He rubbed his eyes with his fists. "I'm not tired, Mom."

The phone rang.

"Tell you what," Paige said as she set her son on his feet and patted his bottom, "You go brush your teeth, and I'll come read you a story."

Caller ID indicated her nosy friend was calling. Reluctantly, Paige picked it up on the last ring.

"I was just about to hang up," Margaret drawled. "Thought maybe you and Brody were out rubbing elbows with the rich and powerful."

"Just Brody. He's attending a State Department dinner." Paige regretted the words as soon as she spoke them.

"What? Why aren't you with him? Is anything wrong, dear?"

You'd be the last person I'd confide in, Paige thought. "I've been feeling a bit under the weather." The difficulties with Connor were a private family matter.

"I have just the thing for that—some immune system

booster tablets I picked up at the health food store. I'd be glad to run them over to you."

"No, really. Rest is all I need."

"Whatever you think is best." Margaret's tone was clipped.

After saying her goodbyes, Paige hurried upstairs to read a bedtime story to Connor.

He was sitting in his room, a mixture of army men and plastic farm animals strewn about. The child made a noise like an explosion and then grabbed some soldiers and moved them toward the animals, knocking them over one by one. Connor moved a plastic cow in his right hand. "Why do you want to hurt us?" In the left hand, he held a plastic army man. "So the people will get hungry." Then came the sound effects. "Pow!" The cow fell over.

Paige was shaken. "Put your toys away, now." She dropped to her knees and helped her son gather the figures into the bucket.

"I want you to read Clifford the Big Red Dog!"

"Good choice." Paige smiled, but her previous good feelings were now eclipsed by worry. She slipped Connor into his PJs, tucked him in bed, and began to read. A few pages later, he was fast asleep.

Paige kissed her child on the cheek. Then she gathered his bucket of soldiers and hid them on the top shelf of the hallway closet.

Chapter 19

Arizona

Saturday, September 1st

Dark clouds churned overhead, and David thought he detected the distant rumble of thunder. He stood on the sheltered porch of the General Store watching swollen raindrops falling upon the silt road only to vaporize in the heat.

It was the first good storm of the monsoon season, something Elita had been earnestly praying for. But now, as the weather rolled in, David felt no joy.

He looked down at the letter in his hand. It came as no surprise that Joanne Sims was attempting to break the trust agreement he had set up for her father. She was accusing David of knowingly, purposefully, and with self-interest manipulating the late Rupert Sims into a land agreement.

The whole thing was ridiculous considering that the trust provided only for the minimal legal stipends to carry out the duties involved in overseeing the land—barely enough money to pay the utilities in the tiny apartment over the store.

Still, the accusation bruised David's sense of integrity.

He tried not to think about the fact that a legal malpractice charge could end his career.

The screen door swung open. David discretely slid the letter into his jeans pocket as Elita joined him on the porch.

The raindrops had multiplied now, leaving mottled thumbprints in the dust. Elita moved close and nestled into the crook of David's arm. "I love the smell of ozone, don't you?" She took a deep breath and leaned her head upon her husband's chest.

"I love you more," he said softly.

The couple stood listening to the soft pattering of rain upon the porch. A chorus of thunder rumbled, shaking the ground beneath their feet. Suddenly, the sky opened like a floodgate and splashed upon the baked earth like a waterfall.

"Look!" Elita pointed toward the road. Through the steamy deluge, an old, battered station wagon emerged, fishtailing on the now-slippery clay road. They could barely make out the driver, who was obscured behind manically slapping windshield wipers.

A few moments later, the early model Rambler rolled up to the General Store, slid to a stop on bald tires, and then died with a sputter. The window cranked down, and an old man leaned out. "You folks open for business?"

"You bet we are!" Elita called and motioned to the visitor. "Better come in out of the weather."

"Hang on," David said. "I'll get an umbrella."

"That's okay, young fella, I love the rain." The visitor quickly rolled up his window, threw open the car door, and emerged. He stretched like he was warming up for an aerobics class and then opened his mouth and caught a couple raindrops on his tongue before bounding up the steps to the porch. There, he shook the drizzle from his long white beard like a wet dog.

Elita laughed with delight and said, “Welcome to Arroyo Seco!”

“Why, thank you, young lady,” the elderly gentleman returned.

David studied the stranger as he held open the door. “Your face looks familiar. Do I know you from somewhere?”

The old man considered the question. “That’s entirely possible, because I’ve definitely been somewhere! My friends call me Zeke.”

After introductions, Elita offered the visitor a complimentary glass of iced tea.

“My favorite thirst-quencher!” he said and followed the couple to the lunch counter.

“Hungry?” Elita asked as she set a tall glass in front of Zeke.

He shook his head. “Naw, I just polished off a can of Spam ’bout an hour ago.” The old man tapped his chest with his fist. “Actually, it’s not sittin’ too well.”

David watched the stranger gulp down his iced tea. “Where you headed, Zeke?”

“Right here!” He twirled the end of his long white beard. “Now, next week, that’s another story.”

“If you’re looking for the group of tourists,” Elita said, “they’re over at the Oasis Campground.”

Zeke shook his head. “I came for two reasons. To check out an old ghost town near here and to visit with the nice young couple who lives above a General Store.” He downed the rest of his iced tea and fixed his gaze on David. "There's something God wants you to do."

The couple exchanged a glance.

"Really? What's that?" David asked with a raised eyebrow.

"Got absolutely no idea!" Zeke smiled. "But I can tell you this much. You'll be vindicated from your present troubles."

"Everything is just fine around here." Elita looked at her husband. "Isn't it?"

David shook his head and slid the letter from his hip pocket. "I've been accused of legal malpractice." He handed her the summons. "The hearing is scheduled for a couple weeks from now."

Later that afternoon after the rain subsided, David drove Zeke to a hill on the edge of town. He pointed toward a castle knob of sandstone outcroppings. "That might be the place you were describing. You can just make out a few old structures over there."

He handed Zeke a pair of binoculars.

The old man squinted as he gazed through the lenses. "Yep, some of those buildings got a pretty good lean to 'em." He handed back the field glasses. "Who owns the land?"

"It's not for sale, if that's what you're asking."

Zeke looked amused. "Do I look like some real estate tycoon?"

David laughed. "It belonged to a client of mine, and it

was set aside for special use. I'm the trustee."

"Then it won't be trespassing if we go take a gander." The strange little man jumped out of the pickup and headed out across the terrain. "Come on," he beckoned.

David hurried to catch up as the old traveler hopped from one lichen-covered stone to the next.

"As I recall, there's a road here somewhere!" Zeke exclaimed, descending a stair-step ledge of rocks like an agile teenager.

Before David knew what was happening, they were halfway to the sandstone outcroppings. *This is crazy*, he thought, tugging at his sweat-drenched collar. David paused briefly under the spindly shade of a saguaro and shaded his eyes against the desert sun. "Wait up!" he yelled, pushing his limbs to catch up.

Up ahead, Zeke, in his oversized Hawaiian shirt and baggy shorts, stood out among the rocks. "This road hasn't been traveled in years; it's covered in yucca." The old man warned, "Watch the ruts. They're ankle-twisters."

"Maybe this wasn't such a good idea," David called out.

Zeke waited for the younger man to close the gap. "No worries. No worries." His pale-blue eyes glistened in the harsh light.

"It's dangerous to just take off across the desert, especially this time of year," David admonished. "We should have brought some water." He drew in a deep breath of hot air and felt droplets of sweat trickle down his chest.

Zeke placed his wrinkled hand on David's shoulder. "Pretty soon you'll be able to drink your fill of the sweetest water you've ever tasted."

David was mildly annoyed by the visitor's reckless optimism.

Just over a sandstone knob, they spotted the little piece of forgotten history. All that was left of the abandoned town were three old buildings. The taller one might have once been a town hall; now, it was listing heavily to one side. The first of the smaller buildings was sun-bleached and weather-beaten, but the doors and window frames were still intact. The last one, however, was nothing more than a wooden skeleton held together by rusty nails and dirt.

As they neared the ghost town, David searched the terrain for any sign of water. Any puddles left from the morning rain had evaporated. In the dry, unbearable heat, the vapor of hope vanished like a mirage. *This is not good,* he thought, doing a quick check of his cell phone. No service. A jackrabbit bolted from a tangle of tumbleweeds, startling David.

Zeke laughed with delight as he watched the little creature zigzag in front of them and shoot across the parched ground to an unknown destination.

Anger swelled in David's bosom—more toward himself than the old man. *What was I thinking?* A mild headache pulsed behind his temples—maybe the first effects of dehydration. They had told no one where they were going. Without water, they would never make it back.

At the ghost town, David located a rare patch of shade next to one of the structures and lowered his weary frame to think. No plan came to mind.

Zeke was whistling cheerfully and poking about for old relics, like a rusty iron rod that he pried from the dirt. The old man held the rod above his head and walked to the base of a sandstone hill, where he thrust the rod deep into the ground.

This man is eccentric, David thought. *Maybe crazy.*

"You goin' swimming, young man?" Zeke peeled off his shirt and unlaced his hiking boots.

The next thing David heard was the sound of water. He looked to see the most incredible sight his eyes had ever beheld. From the side of the hill where the iron rod was standing, water gurgled and burst forth like from a broken water main. David shot to his feet to witness the stream rushing headlong down the sloping hillside and into a sandstone basin.

"Last one in is a rotten egg." The old man stripped down to his boxers and made haste on bony legs. "Well? You comin' or not?" he called, sidestepping cactus and rocks.

David joined him, and the two grown men splashed around like a couple of little kids. "How did you know?"

"The town's name is Hope Springs." Zeke gave a little wink. "That's a pretty good clue, don't ya think?"

David cocked his head and looked curiously at the old man. "My wife has lived here all her life, and she's never met anyone who knew the name of this place."

"Sure she has—you both have." Zeke grinned, his white beard dripping water like honey. "A mutual friend of ours was born right here in Hope Springs. Yes, sir, this is where Rupert Sims got his start in life!"

Arizona

Sunday, September 2nd

From their upstairs apartment, David noted the empty space where the Rambler had been parked. "Zeke is gone."

"He must have left in the middle of the night," Elita said. "Maybe that's why the old man didn't want to sleep on the couch. He probably didn't want to disturb us." Elita lifted the framed photo and studied it with interest. "Honey, come look at this!"

"Rupert gave me that. It's a photo of him when he was a boy."

"Did you notice the guy standing beside him?"

"It's uncanny!" David said, leaning over picture. "Same full white beard, smiling eyes, and stature, but it can't possibly be Zeke. This photo was taken over sixty years ago!"

"Could be a relative," Elita speculated. "Maybe Zeke was also born in Hope Springs."

"We don't know anything about the man." David set the framed photograph back on the coffee table. "He's a mystery."

"Like somebody else I know." She sighed.

"Don't start that again. You know I love you—isn't that enough?"

"Is it wrong to want to know everything there is to know about the man I love?"

"Born in Connecticut, graduated from Harvard Law School. . . ."

"Those things are all public record!" There was a pleading look in his wife's eyes. "What about your family and your childhood? Everybody has stories and photos."

"Not all families are happy ones!" David said with an unintended tone.

After an awkward moment of silence, he moved to the dresser and retrieved a plastic folder from his sock drawer. "These are all the memories I took when I left home."

Elita quickly emptied the contents on the coffee table and deliberated over each photo like she was studying for an exam. "Grandparents?" She held out a snapshot of David sandwiched between a silver-haired couple.

"Mother and father," David said. "I was a menopause baby."

She smiled. "Wish that I could've had a chance to get to know them."

They would not have approved, David thought. Yet, as far as he was concerned, Elita was a class above them all.

His wife moved on to the next photo. "Were you an only child?"

"I have an older sister named Paige." David thumbed through the stack until he found a picture of her. "She was eight years old when I was born."

His wife's curiosity was primed.

David did his best to answer. "The family's home—more like an estate. The family's pet—a flat-faced Persian void of personality. Our family's lake house. . . ." David braced himself for the one question that he dreaded most.

"Who is this?" Elita held up a photograph of a tow-headed girl wearing a plaid pinafore. "What a beautiful child! Like a little china doll! Who is she?"

David didn't look at the photograph—he didn't need to. The image of Emily's angelic smile was branded on his heart.

She was holding the little toy Scottie that he had given her just a few days before she died.

Paige came to David's mind—the terminal sadness in his sister's eyes. "I need to get some air." He grabbed a set of keys from the table and then bounded down the steps of their apartment. Outside, David jumped on his Triumph, fired it up, and peeled away.

Chapter 20

Florida

Wednesday, September 5th

Clay Boggs leaned back in the overstuffed chair and studied Joel. The counselor rolled a small basketball around in his hands. "You've built an emotional prison." He lobbed the basketball across the room, and it swished through a hoop that hung from the door. "Brick by brick, you've constructed a wall." Boggs needled the teenager with his stare. "I'm going to find that cornerstone and bring the whole thing down."

"I told you, I didn't do it!" Joel returned. "Why won't anyone believe me?"

"A jury of twelve was convinced that you killed your family," Boggs said with a shrug. "You need to face the facts." The counselor offered a sympathetic look. "I'm here to help. Admitting your guilt is the first step to recovery." Clay Boggs opened a package of M&M's and offered to share.

Joel declined.

"Let's go over the facts." Clay consulted the clipboard on his lap. "Your letterman's jacket was found stuffed in the back of your bedroom closet. It was soaked in blood that forensics determined to be that of your mother, father, and sister." Boggs popped another M&M into his mouth. "Trust me; you will feel so much better when you get it off your chest. Don't you want to let the authorities know where you hid your sister's body so she can finally be laid to rest? What do you say, son?"

"Don't call me son!" Joel yelled.

Clay Boggs straightened in his chair and fixed his shiny brown eyes on the teenager. "Okay—let's talk about your father. What was your relationship with him like?"

Joel muttered under his breath.

"What was that?"

"You don't want to know!"

The counselor was like a hound on a fresh scent. "I'm sensing rage. Let's talk about your relationship with your father."

The teenager remained silent. His father, a retired colonel, was strict and sometimes unyielding.

"What about the last time you saw your old man?"

Joel thought about lying—telling Boggs that they hadn't argued that day. "Look, I loved my dad! If I hadn't been so stupid. . . ." He stopped himself.

"Go on!"

"He was upset about some bad grades. I just turned my back and walked out the door." *What if Dad and I hadn't fought? What if I hadn't driven around all night with the subwoofers cranked up? What if I had been there to protect my family?*

Boggs jotted some notes. "Let's talk about 29 Chipper Meadow Court."

The teenager chewed his lip. "I got home a little past midnight. There was an ambulance in the driveway and a bunch of cop cars. I asked what was going on and wanted to know where my parents were. When they wouldn't answer my questions, I ran inside." Joel's throat tightened. "That's when I saw her on the kitchen floor. I slipped in my mom's blood."

Clay Boggs pitched forward in his seat. "How did you feel when you realized what you had done?"

"Kiss off—I'm done with your psycho BS!"

The counselor popped a couple more M&M's into his mouth and shrugged. "Have it your way. We've got lots of time."

North Dakota

Thursday, September 6th

Nora headed to the Delmont Harvest Center early in the morning, hoping to do her chores in solitude.

Several cars were already in the parking lot, including Pastor Henry's late model Buick sedan and Celeste's yellow Mustang convertible.

The door was locked, so Nora rapped her knuckles on the solid wooden door. She waited a few minutes and then fumbled through her handbag for a spare key.

There was music playing softly in the sanctuary and a spattering of laughter issuing from Pastor Henry's office. *Ava and Magna and Celeste—the church prophetess and her newly appointed intercessors*, Nora figured.

She grabbed the cleaning supplies from the utility closet and got busy doing the worst job first—cleaning the bathroom. *Whatever you do, do it with all your might as unto the Lord!* Nora reminded herself that even such menial labor as scrubbing toilets could be an offering. She whistled softly through her teeth, working from room to room with diligence. In the kitchen, Nora tackled a sink full of dirty coffee mugs and a ripe garbage can before heading to the Sunday school classrooms. She vacuumed up pieces of construction paper and wiped little finger marks from the table before turning her attention her favorite room: the sanctuary. Nora rolled the vacuum cleaner into the large space and knelt to plug the cord into an outlet.

The double doors swung open, and Celeste swirled into the room, waving a tasseled shawl like butterfly wings.

Nora watched as the woman raised the shawl over her head and rolled her neck like an exotic dancer.

"Come! I bid you to come beneath the covering!" Celeste beckoned, and Pastor Henry entered the sanctuary like a man bewitched. She slid the shawl over his head and moved close to him.

Nora felt her cheeks blaze hot. She switched on the vacuum cleaner and turned away. Someone yelled her name, but Nora focused on the rug, where worshipers gathered every Sunday.

Suddenly, the pastor's feet were standing in front of her, and he yanked the plug from the wall. "I don't want you to get the wrong impression. Celeste was showing me how to use a tallith—it's a Jewish prayer shawl."

"I assure you, it's all very holy," Celeste purred. "I've

also promised to teach Abigail how to use one just as soon as she feels better."

Nora turned to Henry. "She's still sick?"

The pastor muttered something about making some phone calls and then spun on his heels and marched back to his office.

Celeste lingered, smiling her ethereal smile. "There is so much you need to learn about spiritual matters."

"If you'll excuse me, I've got work to do." Nora returned the plug to the outlet and the vacuum roared to life.

Chapter 21

Air Force One, following the G-20 Summit

Monday, September 10th

Air Force One banked south from Toronto and headed toward Minot, North Dakota. *Definitely not what Spence Carlyle had in mind,* Brody thought as he moved about the plane to stretch his legs.

Atwood was sitting in his personal office. He was leaning back in the desk chair and called to Brody as he passed by. "Hays, I'd like to speak with you."

For a few seconds, the commander-in-chief said nothing, just looked at Brody with tired eyes. Atwood took a deep breath and rubbed his face. "You think I did the right thing at the G-20 Summit?"

"I believe you did, Mr. President."

The stiff line of Atwood's shoulders softened, and he spread his hands upon the desk. "Of course, there's bound to be fallout."

"Yes, sir," Brody said, "but as you yourself said, the American people aren't ready to be told how they must transact their financial affairs. Someday social pressure may drive the demand for a reorganized monetary system, but we're not there yet."

Atwood looked at the stack of fresh press clippings that had just come in via satellite. "It seems I've become a nemesis in the eyes of the international community."

Hays considered his vicarious position among his West Wing peers. He nodded sympathetically and forced a reassuring smile. "Sir, there is a positive side. Your decisiveness on this issue has already earned you political capital with some voters."

Thomas Atwood tilted his head. "Go on."

The president's chief economic advisor read him the headlines from another AP story that had just hit the wire. "President Atwood makes a stand for democracy and personal American liberties."

This seemed to please the commander-in-chief. He leaned back in his chair and said, "Believe I'll rest a bit before we land in North Dakota."

Twenty minutes later, they landed at the Minot Air Force Base and were greeted by the usual dog and pony show. Across the tarmac, a band played marching tunes while North Dakota's dignitaries lined up among decorated military personnel.

Brody descended the plane a few steps behind Thomas Atwood and stood a respectable distance from the pomp.

The president seemed to draw energy from the crowd, pressing the flesh with ease, graciously enduring small talk, and lending a sympathetic ear to the state officials.

He and his entourage were transported to a luncheon given by the Minot Chamber of Commerce, where he gave a speech laced with data and projections that had been compiled by Brody. He ended his talk by saying, "When the breadbasket of our nation is empty, every citizen should be concerned. United, we will do what Americans have always done—we will persevere and overcome!"

The crowd responded with a standing ovation. The governor said a few words, and the Secret Service spirited the president and his entourage back to the air force base.

As they boarded a helicopter for a farm tour, Brody scanned more local media clips. ALMOST A NATIVE SON, one of the headlines read. Thomas Atwood had spent a few summers in North Dakota along with a kid brother—now deceased. People who knew the Atwood family had been interviewed, dredging up stories. The president's younger brother, Jimmy, had had a history littered with legal missteps. He was only twenty-seven years old when he lost his life at a train crossing, purportedly running from authorities. Atwood had never mentioned his brother. *No wonder,* Brody thought.

The military helicopter lifted off and breezed above miles of parched landscape. They flew along dry creek beds where cottonwoods reached out with dead, sun-bleached limbs.

"I've never seen it looking so bleak," Atwood said, directing Brody's attention to a train that rumbled over a trestle. "That's where my brother Jimmy died."

"Sir, I'm very sorry."

The sound of the military chopper absorbed the silence as the pilot navigated past farms with white picket fences and red barns that stood amidst the casualty of shriveled crops. It had the makings of a dust bowl.

The president motioned to a farm. "That place once belonged to my grandparents."

It was an obvious holdout against the commercial farms that had swallowed up most of the acreage in the surrounding area.

The pilot circled back to give the president another look. The house was modest and badly in need of a coat of paint, but the barn was massive and built to last.

"It looked a lot bigger when I was young," Atwood said. He directed the pilot's attention to a nearby town. "I'd like to make a brief stop in Delmont."

A Secret Service agent snapped forward in his seat. "This was not on the itinerary, sir. There has been no advance done."

Atwood dismissed the agent's concerns with a wave. "Relax! The fact that it's unscheduled means minimal risk of danger and no media hounds."

The helicopter angled closer, giving Brody a clear view of the small town. *Nothing special*, he thought. Delmont looked like a thousand other Midwest towns, with grid-like streets and shoebox homes.

The president indicated an old Victorian building that stood out of place among the mock storefronts of Main Street. "That's the place I'm looking for. Set it down as close as you can to the Delmont Hotel."

The pilot hovered over the building and set the craft down in a nearby vacant lot. The Secret Service detail spilled from the cab for a brief security sweep. They returned a few minutes later and gave the go-ahead.

Brody paused to read a sign that hung from the porch:

NORA'S BARGAIN BIN. "Sir, I'm afraid this is no longer a hotel."

"Hasn't been for years." President Atwood pulled a letter from the inside pocket of his jacket. "I came to speak with Nora Meyers, the person who wrote this."

Inside, the president locked eyes with a woman dressed in jeans and a sweatshirt. Her pleasant face froze in stunned disbelief as Atwood approached with arms extended.

Nora Meyers wiped her palm across the John Deere emblem on her shirt and held out her hand.

"We can do better than that!" The president gave her a warm embrace and said, "We're still friends, aren't we, Nora?"

The moment seemed surreal to Brody, who waited beside a rack of used clothing.

Near the back of the room stood a blue-haired woman and a tall man wearing a hemp beanie, their mouths gaping.

The president rested his hand on Nora's shoulder. "I was humbled by the letter you wrote and wanted to express my personal gratitude. Our country needs more people like you."

Her cheeks turned crimson.

"I'd love do some catching up, but, unfortunately, there's a schedule to keep." Atwood lingered a moment longer. "It was really good to see you again Nora."

The president seemed pensive as they headed back to Minot.

Back on Air Force One, Atwood retreated to his office. After giving orders not to be disturbed, he closed the door behind him.

North Dakota

Monday, September 10th

Nora's stomach ached as she drove to her farmhouse.

She had dashed out thc door, leaving Gertie and J. J. to take care of business. There was no other choice. The dam of her emotions had crested to the point of breaking.

Nora drove faster than usual. Otis hung his head from the Chevy's window, his furry spaniel ears flapping in the breeze like wings. Even this didn't raise a smile.

The president's visit had blindsided Nora, sending her memories spinning out of control. Thomas Atwood was a kind and stable soul—so unlike his wild younger brother.

In her mind's eye, she could still see Jimmy's dark, intense eyes and his cocksure manner. The day he died, Nora felt as though a part of her had perished with him.

She recalled that a blanket of new-fallen snow lay across the fields that day, sunlight glistening upon its surface. Overhead there were geese on the wing. She had waited for her love with giddy excitement, unaware that a few miles away Jimmy was gasping for his last breath. The impact of the train had ejected him from his vehicle, leaving his shoes on the floorboard. His pocket somehow still contained a small velvet box that held an engagement ring.

An investigation later determined that the ring had been stolen from a local jewelry store. When they laid Jimmy in the ground, the only thing that mattered was that she had been loved.

Nora pulled up to her farmhouse, and Otis spilled from

the car. He raced around the house barking like he was chasing an invisible cat.

Inside, Nora put the fire on under her teapot, went into her bedroom, and retrieved a Whitman's Sampler tin from the back of her closet shelf. Nora sat on the edge of her bed and went through the contents. There was a photo of Jimmy with wild hair falling across his forehead like James Dean. Nora ran a finger over the image and then lifted a small bouquet of dried flowers to her nose. The smell had long since vanished, but the memory was still alive. Jimmy had plucked them from a showcase garden in Delmont, laughing when the owner, old lady Tudor, had come blowing from her house in indignation.

Nora knew each love note by heart, but there was one letter that haunted her—one that she had written but never sent.

Nora thumbed through the envelopes and found the letter addressed to Thomas Atwood. Seeing him today filled her with regret and made her feel like such a coward.

The teakettle screeched in the kitchen.

Nora gathered her secrets back into the Whitman's Sampler tin and returned them to their hiding place.

Paris

Tuesday, September 11th

The Paris sky darkened and churned overhead as Jean Pierre strolled down the Boulevard Saint-Germain. He thought about the current American President, Thomas Atwood. His lip curled with contempt as he muttered the name. He hadn't liked the man during their White House meeting, and now he liked him even less.

Street venders scrambled to pack up their goods while tourists sipped French wine beneath café awnings. Pierre's half-mast gaze brushed over the visitors. Americans were easy to spot, with their fanny packs, tennis shoes, and loud voices. He made a clicking sound with his tongue as he moved past. It was a cynical expression, hinting at his deep contempt. These days, it came more frequently.

Rolling thunder growled overhead, and raindrops began to fall. From his satchel, Pierre produced a pocket umbrella and sprang it into action as people darted for the cover of storefront awnings.

Jean Pierre walked on through the downpour as the summer rain rinsed away the city's residue. He imagined it washing his beloved Paris of the defilement of foreigners, making her clean again. *How I wish it were so easy*, he thought.

At a newsstand, he put down a Euro and lifted the evening paper from a stack. Jean Pierre scanned the headlines: ISRAEL CLAIMS PEACE AGREEMENT IS BROKEN AFTER SUICIDE BOMBER KILLS FORTY PEOPLE IN CROWDED RESTAURANT.

Jean Pierre sniffed indifferently. His eyes locked on the caption he was looking for: THE UNITED STATES SNUBS THE EUROPEAN UNION'S CALL FOR MONETARY SOLIDARITY. The news was nothing new to him. With his own ears, Jean Pierre had listened as Thomas Atwood prattled on about being the leader of a democracy and representing his people. "Our Nation is not ready for the mandated use of smart cards," the

US President had stated.

"Rubbish," Jean Pierre muttered. "Self-serving imbeciles." He clicked his tongue and turned toward the river Seine, his anger following him. After years of planning, of building a fortress of political capital, so much was still riding on the cooperation of the Americans.

Rainwater cascaded from his umbrella, but Pierre walked unhurried, his mind turning angles and analyzing possibilities.

Jean Pierre stood firm. If the entire world was ready to lock arms in unity but America was unwilling, perhaps it was time to change the great nation's mind. His upper lip twitched at the idea.

As Jean Pierre crossed the stone bridge to the Île Saint-Louis, he felt invigorated, almost reborn. "Yes, perhaps it's time. . . ."

Chapter 22

Florida

Wednesday, September 12th

Joel couldn't believe his luck as he moved along the wooded area. He hadn't planned to escape, but the opportunity had been too good to pass up. Schumer had called in sick, so Clay Boggs had enlisted some extra help with KP duties—a decision that had turned out to be a mistake. One of the shack-mates left a burner glowing under a pan of grease. Fire had erupted. After a misguided attempt to put the flames out with water, the situation had quickly escalated.

"Nobody panic!" the counselor yelled. "I've called 911, and response units are on the way." Boggs quickly hustled his charges down the long corridor to the dormitory. "I'll be back," he said, locking the door as he left.

Within minutes, the sound of sirens screamed closer.

"Maybe the whole building will burn and we can be done with this place," one of the boys joked as a blur of yellow coats clamored past the wire-meshed windows.

"Be careful what you wish for." Joel pointed toward a ventilation grate in the ceiling. Faint strands of smoke curled downward into the room, soon followed by billowing puffs of gray.

Ricky Hernandez pounded the door with his fists. "Get us out of here!"

A couple of the boys lifted a metal chair and began to use it as a battering ram as black smoke began to fill the dormitory.

Clay Boggs unlocked the door, apologizing as the boys spilled into the hallway, gasping and choking for air.

At the end of the corridor, two more fire crews banged through the double metal doors loaded with hose and gear. "We need a medic to check these boys!" Clay called.

"Everybody outside!" A group of firemen rushed toward the kitchen with a hose and let loose the full force of its stream. Water and debris cascaded onto the floor.

"Sir, you need to vacate the premises," the captain ordered.

It was getting dark when the boys were escorted outside. Ricky Hernandez began to cough, and again Boggs yelled for a medic.

A new string of response units rolled through the yard's open gate. Firemen jumped from the trucks and rushed into the building. One dropped his jacket and mask at Joel's feet.

He had simply slipped them on and walked away. *Almost like it was meant to be,* Joel recalled.

Now on the run, Joel ducked behind a tree as a police car cruised past. He waited until it was clear and then ran until he dropped from exhaustion.

Joel lay in a field trying to catch his breath. Above him, the vast expanse of heaven shined. His skin tingled; his senses were sharp. *Keep going*, the teenager told himself. *By now, Boggs has discovered my absence and alerted the authorities.*

Leaving Florida

Thursday, September 13th

In the semi's rearview mirror, Joel watched the sun peeking over the horizon, feeling a measure of relief as he left Florida behind.

Each passing mile increased his odds, yet the danger still remained. By now, the police would have a description—it might even be wired to stations across the Eastern Seaboard.

"You want some coffee?" the truck driver asked.

Joel shook his head.

The man yawned, lifted his faded denim baseball cap, and fluffed a tangle of blond hair. He pointed a grease-stained finger toward a thermos on the truck's floorboard. "I could use a little shot of joe. Mind filling my cup?"

The teenager obliged.

The trucker took a gulp of warm coffee, shifting gears with his free hand. "You ain't said much since I picked you up last night. Where ya headed, anyway?"

The road hummed with traffic noise. A minute passed before the teenager answered. "No place in particular."

"I work the southern route, mostly. Sometimes I swear there's moss growing inside my air conditioning vents from all this danged humidity." The man swilled down more coffee. "There's a truck stop up ahead. I'll buy you some breakfast."

"That's not necessary," Joel mumbled.

"Oh, then I guess you're buying me breakfast?"

The teenager lowered his head and said nothing.

"That's what I thought." The driver grinned. "They make the best biscuits and sausage gravy at this place—just like my mama used to make. By the way, Roy's my name."

Joel responded with the first alias that came to mind. "Duke. My name is Duke."

The trucker raised an eyebrow. "Yeah? I had a dog with that name."

The scenery flew past, and Joel took in the Gulf of Mexico as it glistened in the golden morning light. "What's the next town?"

"We're skirting around Mobile, Alabama right now. That little diner I was telling you about is just this side of Biloxi."

New Orleans isn't far from there, Joel thought. *There's no sense in calling attention to my real destination.* "I'll be getting off in Biloxi."

"Suit yourself." Roy rummaged through a beat-up CD caddy. "I hope you don't mind music." He picked one titled "Down Home Country Gospel" and slid it into the player.

Joel found the twangy tunes annoying but was grateful that the driver didn't want to listen to the news.

They traveled the miles in comfortable silence until the semi's Jake brake rumbled and hissed.

"Here we are," Roy announced. "Biloxi Bill's Sourdough Grill."

Joel washed up in the bathroom and splashed water on

his sweat-stained face.

"Hope you don't mind—I took the liberty of ordering you the Traveler's Special! All the flapjacks and link sausages you can eat."

When the food came, Roy paused to say grace.

The teenager leaned over his plate like a prisoner and shoveled food into his mouth.

The trucker watched the boy sop up the last of his syrup with a wedge of pancake.

Roy set his fork down, reached into his hip pocket, and took out his wallet. "You got a place to stay?"

"Yeah, sure," Joel said.

Roy slipped two crisp fifty-dollar bills from his wallet and set them in front of the boy. "This may help."

"I can't take that." Joel felt his face redden.

"Listen," Roy said sternly. "I've got a son about your age, and if he was ever in your shoes. . . . Let me put it this way, I won't take no for an answer!"

"Thanks," Joel said as the trucker settled the bill. He stuck around long enough to wave as the semi pulled away from the restaurant. It was all he could do to show his gratitude.

Chapter 23

Arizona

Friday, September 14th

David stared at the legal papers spread across his desk. He had been up all night going over them, wracking his brain for a solid defense. David berated himself for being so careless, especially given his client's unusual directives.

Joanne Sims and her lawyer had built a compelling case. Most recently the family physician had agreed to testify to Rupert's incompetence during the time when the trust was drawn up.

By the end of the day, David would know whether he could still practice law. He was worried.

"I'm back!" Elita slipped through the curtained door to the storage room, her arms loaded with mail. "You got a package from someone in North Dakota." She placed it on the desk and handed her husband a stack of envelopes.

Still nothing from Paige. David lingered over a fat manila envelope from a Connecticut accounting firm that he slid into the pocket of his soft leather briefcase.

"You're wearing a watch," Elita said. "I didn't even

know you owned one."

"I only wear it when I have to be in court." David looked at the crystal face of the Rolex, a gift from his late father. "I need to get going!"

He gathered his papers and did a quick inventory.

"Are you sure you don't want me to go along?" Elita studied her husband's face as he straightened his tie.

David gave his wife a reassuring smile. "Somebody needs to run the store."

"Not the same," she protested. "You're my husband, and I want to be there for you."

"I need someone to open the mail."

"Wow!" Elita said with playful sarcasm. "Can I organize your desk, too?"

David cupped her face in his hands. "I need to do this myself."

"Talk to God," Elita called as her husband slipped through the back door. "He listens!"

David's Triumph was parked beneath the dappled light of a lattice arbor. Overhead, the remnants of a dead vine rustled in the hot desert breeze. He strapped his briefcase onto the bike. With his steel-toed boot, David gingerly rolled a toy dump truck away from the back wheel.

"That's my Tonka!" A little boy raced over, his chin jutting defiantly.

"Robert!" From beneath the camper awning, Kay Bales ejected herself from a lawn chair and wagged a finger at her son. "You leave that nice man alone."

The motor home's screen door swung open. Randy poked his head out and flapped a dish rag. "Howdy, neighbor!

You're dressed kind of fancy for a motorcycle ride, aren't ya?"

David buttoned his suit jacket and snapped his helmet. "Got that right. I'd rather wear leather." He fired the engine, waved goodbye, and rumbled down the alley beside the store.

The road to Phoenix was long and unbearably hot, but that was the least of David's worries. By the time he'd made his way through the city and pulled up to the State Bar Association building, his spirits were low. "God, if you're there, I could sure use a little help."

In the conference room, David was instructed to sit at a small table facing the bar committee.

The first witness called by the Arizona State Bar Committee was Doctor Jansten. "How long was Rupert Sims a patient of yours?"

"Twenty-five, maybe thirty years."

"What is your medical opinion regarding Mr. Sims's mental state at the time in question?"

"I believe he might have been in the early stages of dementia."

The committee lobbed more questions, each laying the groundwork for an ethics violation.

David braced himself when they called Joanne Sims to the chair.

She settled into the seat and was asked to express her concerns. "A few weeks before my father passed away, I went to see Mr. Fillmore and tried to explain how vulnerable my father was." Ms. Sims paused to dab at the corner of her eye with a tissue. "It wasn't until later that I realized why he refused to listen." She pointed her finger at her late father's lawyer. “Five thousand acres and a million dollars—that’s why!”

The committee took a short break to review David’s written statement and then regrouped with more questions, this time directed toward the accused.

“Mr. Fillmore, did you find any of your client’s requests unorthodox?”

“Yes, I did,” David said without hesitation. “It’s not every day I am asked to draw up a trust that will allocate land to be set aside for special use as articulated by my client.”

The committee chairman, a man with a face like a bulldog, rubbed his jowls. He thumbed through a copy of the trust. “More specifically, Rupert Sims instructed you to earmark a sizeable tract of land for, and I quote, ‘the people of faith.’” The chairman cleared his throat. “Mr. Fillmore, did you have any reservations about being named as conservator to this land and receiving monthly stipends?”

“I strongly advised my client against naming me as conservator, but he was adamant.”

An older woman on the committee peered threw her heavy framed glasses. “I note that a million dollars has been allocated for the upkeep of the land in question?”

David nodded. “More specifically, for taxes and the monthly trustee fee.”

The committeewoman removed her glasses and looked directly at the accused. “Exactly how much are your fees, Mr. Fillmore?”

“I am being paid $75 a month for managing this property according to my client’s instructions.” David opened his briefcase, produced the manila envelope, and offered the contents to the panel. "This should prove that I have no need for the money, or the land for that matter."

The committee thumbed through a deep stack of unredeemed checks. They drew their heads close, muttered together, and turned back to David.

"Mr. Fillmore," the chairman said, "the fact that you yourself are the beneficiary of a sizeable family trust fund does not negate your legal responsibility to your client. It is the opinion of this committee that your client showed diminished capacity prior to soliciting your services. His delusions are documented by his unusual instructions regarding the land in question. It is the belief of this committee that Rupert Sims's ability to make sound financial decisions or to appreciate the consequences of such decisions was impaired. Therefore—"

Suddenly, a commotion arose from the hallway.

Heads turned as the door opened and Elita burst through the threshold.

"Hope I'm not too late!" She held up a VHS cassette. "This is something you need to see!"

"This is highly inappropriate!" the chairman blustered.

"Sir, this VHS arrived in the mail today. It was recorded by Rupert Sims himself!" Elita boldly approached the committee. "Oh, I almost forgot the note from Nora Meyers!" She pulled a piece of stationary from her shoulder bag and read.

Dear Mr. Fillmore,

This recording was included in the box that you sent me. Uncle Rupert says that he made this recording just in case there was trouble regarding his will.

"This is some kind of trick!" Joanne Sims shrieked.

The chairman held up his hand in warning and took the VHS from Elita. "Let's hear what he had to say."

A clerk was dispatched to locate a VHS machine.

Elita smiled at her husband and took a seat on the other side of the room as a TV and VHS player were wheeled into the room on a cart.

The cassette was inserted. A dusting of snow fluttered across the screen, and then the Sims Ranch living room came into view. A date flashed in the corner of the screen. The video had been filmed almost a year before David met his client.

Rupert popped into the frame and sank into his favorite easy chair. He licked the tips of his fingers, smoothed his hair, and smiled for the camera. "I've been doing a lot of thinking since I found out I'm dying," he began. "There are a few arrangements I want to make before I leave this earth—just as soon as I can find a good lawyer. Good thing I'm a man of faith!"

The old man stared into the camera. "God's been mighty good to me, and I guess you could say this is my way of giving something back. This ain't a new dream of mine, neither. Setting aside a tract of land has been in my heart since I was a kid. Now, you may be tempted to think of this as some crazy notion, but I assure you I'm as sane as the rest of you—saner than some. The way I see it, a fellow has a right to do whatever he pleases with his own land."

Rupert leaned forward in his easy chair, his eyes sharp

and clear. "Joanne, I know you 'n' me ain't always seen eye t' eye on things, especially when it comes to my faith, but I'm asking you to respect my wishes on this. I'm leavin' you a wealthy woman, and I hope you can be content with that." Rupert blinked and wiped his eyes. "I've been praying for you, darlin'—praying that one of these days, you'll find real peace."

They waited while the committee quietly conferred with one another.

Finally, the chairman folded his hands on the table and said, "In determining the extent of the client's diminished capacity, the lawyer should consider and balance such factors as the client's ability to articulate the reasoning leading to a decision; the variability of the client's state of mind; the ability of the client to appreciate the consequences of a decision; the substantive fairness of a decision; and the consistency of a decision with the known long-term commitments and values of the client." He cleared his throat. "It is this committee's revised opinion that David Fillmore's client was in his right mind, and therefore the ethics charges are unfounded and the legal malpractice claim is dismissed."

Elita let out a hoot as her husband sat in stunned disbelief.

How did Rupert foresee trouble? What if Nora Meyers hadn't sent the package? What if Elita hadn't picked up the mail? David looked up. *Maybe God is listening!*

Chapter 24

North Dakota
Friday, September 14th

Nora set a basket of goodies on the floorboard of her Chevy and headed into town, praying as she drove. Abigail was still feeling under the weather; something just wasn't right.

Nora rolled her window down to enjoy the cool fall air as she steered down the street that led to her best friend's house. The track home yards were spotted with drought-baked grass, and the gardens were shriveled and dead due to Delmont's new water restrictions.

Pastor Henry and Abigail lived in a modest, ranch-style home with a one-car garage that had been converted to a family room. Nora pulled in their driveway behind Abigail's sedan.

The front door was ajar, so she leaned in and called out.

"In here." Abigail's voice issued from the den like a thin thread.

Nora found her dear friend sprawled in a recliner, bundled beneath a quilt.

"I was just reading about the president's visit. You never mentioned that your late boyfriend was his brother."

"It was a long time ago," Nora said with a shrug. "I brought you some of my strawberry rhubarb cobbler, and I stopped by the drugstore and picked up some magazines." She placed the items on the coffee table. "How are you feeling?"

Abigail's face was as pale as her blonde hair. "It's probably just a virus."

The television was on, but the volume was barely audible. Abigail struggled to adjust the recliner to a sitting position.

"Let me help." Nora fluffed the pillow behind her friend's head and was shocked to see patches of hair left behind. "Have you seen a doctor?"

"I'll be fine." Abigail flashed a stoic smile. "Everyone has been so kind. Magna and Ava have been doing all the cleaning and laundry, and Celeste stops by every day to fix me a cup of broth and anoint me with oil."

"Every day?"

"What's wrong with that?"

"I don't know Celeste very well, that's all." Nora bit her lip. *If I say nothing, I'll be a coward, but if I express my concerns. . . .*

"Henry tells me you're running a helps ministry out of the Bargain Bin," Abigail said.

"Yes. In fact, we've decided to have a community fundraiser so we can purchase a new boiler. It'll be fun! We're going to have face-painting and juggling—"

Abigail grabbed her friend's hand and squeezed it.

"Nora, I think you should know that my husband is very concerned about you."

"What do you mean?"

"The way you've recklessly forged ahead with your ministry. You don't have the blessing or the covering of the church. It's a matter of submission and obedience to leadership." Abigail gave Nora's hand another squeeze and then released it.

"Is Celeste concerned also?"

"I don't like your tone," Abigail bristled. "That woman is a saint. In fact, she and my husband have been praying for you!"

"Henry needs *you* by his side—not Celeste."

"I was told you might try something like this, but until this moment I didn't believe you were capable of making such vile insinuations!" Abigail pointed toward the door. "I think you should leave."

"Can't we talk about this?"

"Just go!"

Nora hurried to her car, feeling like she'd been punched in the gut. Her legs shook as she sat behind the wheel, struggling to pull herself together.

A few short months ago, church was a safe place where she belonged. Pastor Henry and Abigail were like family. *How could everything change so quickly?*

New Orleans
Friday, September 14th

The Greyhound bus traveled along the outskirts of New Orleans. Joel was fascinated by the colorful Cajun enclaves with their stilted claptrap shacks.

As they rolled into New Orleans, the city appeared to be like many others, with manicured homes, shopping malls, and parks. But the image changed as the bus moved through the older parts of town. Some neighborhoods resembled third world countries, with graffiti-marked walls and gutters littered with trash.

There was an air of heaviness in the atmosphere as Joel disembarked the bus in New Orleans's famous French Quarter. The teenager brushed his mood aside. He was on a mission to locate the places that were printed on the mysterious postcards.

Joel walked along the brick sidewalk, smelling the spicy scent of Creole cooking and magnolia blossoms. Above his head, verandas with lush hanging gardens graced his view.

A mule-drawn surrey loaded with tourists rattled down the cobblestone street as the teenager strolled past an outdoor café that trilled with jazz.

"Ohheee, now, dos da bes' mud bugs I eva di' tace," A fleshy-faced man bellowed. He leaned back in a wrought-iron chair and fondled his gelatinous belly.

A dark-complexioned woman caked with crimson rouge lifted a spoon. "Baby, try an oyster," she coaxed playfully. "Day good fo' what ails ya, now."

The man opened his mouth like a hungry shark and sucked the raw oyster from the spoon. Suddenly, his puffy eyes shifted to Joel. "Boo! Whachoo lookin' at, boy?"

The couple exploded with laughter as the teenager

crossed the street and hurried on his way. *Well, I don't have an appetite, now,* Joel thought as he scouted for a quiet place to count his money. After paying the bus fare, he had $68 and some change. Somehow, it would have to last.

Shadows lengthened on the sidewalks and streets. Colorful characters spilled from various doors and alleyways, their eyes roving with unrestrained appetites. Nightfall was announced by the sound of jazz, and Bourbon Street and the rest of the French Quarter revived with music and frolic.

"Hey, good-lookin'. How about a date?" A woman in steel-spiked heels beckoned the teenager with her long, blood-red nails. She snaked an orange-and-pink feather boa around his neck. *It reeks of whiskey,* Joel thought. He quickly distanced himself from her lascivious catcalls.

The teenager walked faster now, acutely aware of his predicament. *I need to find a safe place to hole up for the night, and the sooner the better.* Four blocks later, the revelry on Bourbon Street faded, and Joel felt like he could breathe again.

Two lovers kissed on the steps of a townhouse, tangled impassionedly as if they were the only two people in the world. Up the road, the clomp-clomp-clomp sound of shod hooves closed the gap. The mule-drawn surrey rolled past and turned sharply up an alleyway.

Joel followed it to a stable and lingered in the shadows, listening as the horseman slid a wooden gate open. "You done real well for us tonight, ol' girl," he said.

The mule whinnied, and Joel watched as her owner unfastened the harness and hung it on a hook. The animal was led into a roomy stall, where she lowered to the ground to roll in the dust and straw.

The teenager slipped into the stable and crouched behind a stack of straw bales as the horseman scooped oats into a pail and filled a fresh bucket of water.

Joel waited until the lights went out, the stable doors closed, and the padlock snapped in place. He settled against a bed of straw, listening to the mule crunching oats.

The big animal snorted and pawed the ground, as if to say she knew someone was there but didn't mind. In turn, the teenager felt oddly comforted by her presence.

He had survived today. Tomorrow would bring more challenges. *If I'm going to make it here*, Joel told himself, *I'll need to learn some street smarts*.

Chapter 25

Arizona
Saturday, September 15th

"Let's celebrate!" David said, lifting the picnic basket from the back his wife's old Ford pickup.

"This place is incredible!" Elita hurried to the side of the deep rock basin, kicked off her flip-flops, and dipped her toes into the swirling water. "It's the perfect temperature."

On the hill above the basin was the iron rod that Zeke had thrust into the sandy soil. David's mind tried to process the strangeness of that event as the indisputable evidence spilled across the terrace of windswept rocks and formed a network of pools. The fresh spring had also birthed an oasis, coaxing green vegetation from the desert's sun-cracked soil.

Clad in shorts and a halter top, Elita lowered herself into the deepest basin. "Come on." She splashed water at her husband, who was laying out beach towels on the warm sand.

"Lemonade?" David asked. He found the plastic jug in the picnic basket and poured them each a glass. "The heat is expected to be in the triple digits." He handed his wife the drinks, kicked off his shoes, and settled next to her.

"So, this was where Rupert Sims was born? It's strange that I never heard any of my relatives mention it." Elita raised her plastic tumbler in a toast. "Well, here's to Rupert's vision!" Their rims kissed, and they settled back to enjoy the peaceful morning.

David's fingers touched his wife's simple wedding band. "One of these days I'll take you shopping for a decent ring."

"This one's perfect!" She held up her hand to admire it.

"Do you ever wonder what it would be like to be rich?" David studied his wife's face. "Would you want a big house? To have servants?"

"What for?" she said with genuine surprise. "I've been blessed with good health, a beautiful place to live, and a husband who loves me. The way I see it, I'm already rich!"

"I've never known anyone like you," David said, pulling her close. They soaked in the moment, alone with saguaros that stood like salt pillars. Nothing stirred except heat waves undulating from the desert terrain. The hours floated past gently.

Suddenly, Elita sat forward and shaded her eyes against the bright sun. A large flock of scavenger birds were circling over a point in the desert. "Buzzards." She wrinkled her nose. "Nasty creatures!" Round and round the birds flew, until one flapped to the ground and the others followed.

Elita rose to her feet for a better view.

"It's probably just some poor jackrabbit," David said.

"I don't think so—there's something shiny down there." Elita grabbed a towel, snapped sand from it, and tied it around her waist. "We should check it out."

David gathered their gear and tossed it into the back of the truck.

Elita prayed in Spanish as the old truck made its way over the shallow washes toward the squabbling flock of birds. "Oh, sweet Jesus!" she cried as they spotted a tennis shoe.

"Wait here," David ordered, rushing over to shoo away the scavengers. He gasped. The bodies were unrecognizable, yet judging from their clothing, it was a man and a woman.

Elita screamed.

David spun around and saw her kneeling at the base of a bush.

"This baby's alive!" She scooped a limp child in her arms and ran for the truck. "We need to get to a hospital!"

David drove the backcountry roads like a maniac, bouncing over ruts and leaving a plume of dust in their wake.

The little boy was barely breathing. He was so weak he couldn't even drink water. All the way to Kirby, Elita dipped her finger to wet his mouth and soothed him in her native tongue.

At the emergency room, the child was whisked away, and David held his wife while tears streamed down her cheeks.

"Who is going to take care of him?" She looked pleadingly at her husband. "What about us? We could give him a home."

"That's not an option," David said.

Elita drew back and stared at her husband. "Don't you like kids?"

The emergency room entrance slid open, and a small group of border patrol agents walked in.

The woman at the desk nodded toward the couple.

"Mr. and Mrs. Fillmore?" The man in front introduced himself as Special Agent Willy Blake. "I'd like to get a statement from you."

"Did you find the bodies?" Elita's voice was edged with sorrow.

"They've been located from the air, and a recovery vehicle has been dispatched."

"What will happen to the little one now that his parents are gone?" Elita asked.

The agent turned the recorder off and slipped it back into his pocket. "In cases like this, the Mexican authorities locate relatives. As soon as the child is well enough, he'll be escorted back to his country."

"But what if they can't locate his family?" she pressed.

"Someone nearly always comes forward," the agent assured her.

"Are telling me this kind of tragedy occurs often?" David asked.

The border patrol captain nodded. "We're doing the best we can to stop human traffickers. Unfortunately, a few greedy coyotes always manage to slip past."

"It's such a senseless waste of life," David said. "There's got to be something more that we can do."

Chapter 26

Virginia
Monday, September 17th

Brody squeezed Paige's fingers as the pediatric psychiatrist studied Connor's medical records.

The physician rubbed his chin and leveled his gaze on the parents. "It's very rare for a child Connor's age to be diagnosed with schizophrenia. Although," he added, "there have been a few documented cases."

"Are you saying that my son may have been misdiagnosed?" Brody leaned forward with interest.

The doctor ran a finger around the collar of his white shirt. "I was merely speaking statistically. You see, little is known about this illness in very young children." He thumbed through Connor's records. "I see your son has been prescribed a powerful psycho pharmaceutical. How is he tolerating it?"

"I wanted to hear your opinion before I gave him a dose." Paige picked at her manicured nail. "Is this medicine dangerous?"

"There have been reported side effects." The pediatrician attempted a reassuring smile. "These drugs alter the brain chemistry, and in an undeveloped brain, we don't really know what the long-term effects are."

Brody could feel his wife staring at him as he studied the impressive collection of medical books that lined the shelves beside him.

"Honey, did you hear what the doctor said?" she asked.

"I heard." Brody abruptly stood and thanked the physician for his time.

"What's wrong with you?" Paige asked as she following her husband down the medical center corridor.

At the elevator, Brody punched the button. "What was the name of the first psychiatrist you took Connor to see?"

"Dr. Stanley Levine!" Paige snapped.

"That's what I thought." The elevator doors slid open and the couple stepped inside. "We're wasting our time consulting a novice. When you get home, give Connor his medicine," Brody ordered.

As they emerged into the medical center lobby, Paige demanded an explanation.

"Back in that office there were three books on the shelf about childhood schizophrenia," he said. "All of them were written by Dr. Stanley Levine."

Arizona

Monday, September 17th

"Business has been good this month," David said, emerging from the General Store's back room with an accounting sheet in hand.

He spotted his bride across the room, stocking canned goods and dusting the shelves. "Elita, did you hear me? We actually made a profit."

She shrugged but said nothing. His wife's brooding silence had been growing since they had rescued the child from the desert.

"What's wrong?" David asked. "That little boy didn't take a turn for the worse, did he?"

"His name is Juan, and he's going to be fine." Elita said. "In fact, you'll be relieved to know that they have sent him back to Mexico."

"What's that supposed to mean?"

"I always thought someday we would start a family. Why didn't you tell me that you didn't want children?" Elita's eyes filled with tears.

David reached for her, but she turned away.

A radio on the counter filled the silence between them. "A continued drought in the Midwest is expected to affect wheat prices; economy in crisis; Supreme Court upheld a ruling to omit the phrase, 'under God,' from the Pledge of Allegiance. . . ."

A string of sleigh bells jingled on the door of the General Store. Gordon stood in the threshold. He took one look at Elita and said, "Do I detect a blizzard on Bliss Creek? I guess this means the honeymoon is over."

As the amused grin spread across Gordon's face, David fought the urge to wipe it off. "What do you want?"

"I'd like to put a poster in your front window." Spitzer held up a small stack of flyers and handed one to David.

"Freedom Riders," he read. "Annual Cruise against

Illegal Immigration."

Gordon eyed David. "You may know some of these fellows. Who knows, you might even be inspired to join them."

David handed the flyer back. "I don't think so."

Spitzer's eyes narrowed. "By the way, I hear you've been thinking about placing jugs of water out in the desert for illegals."

"Might save some lives," David said.

Gordon laughed with a snort. "Don't waste your time! Any water you put out there will wind up spilling—if you know what I mean."

David felt his face flush with anger. "You have no right to interfere!"

"Listen, Fillmore, this may sound harsh, but the fear of death is a powerful deterrent." Gordon ran his tongue over his teeth. "You bleeding-heart liberals are all the same—you can't connect the dots! If you keep encouraging this behavior, the next family to die out there in the desert might just be on your head."

David grabbed a handful of Spitzer's shirt and drew back his fist.

"Stop it!" Elita shrieked, and her husband released Gordon.

"You got quite a temper, Fillmore." Spitzer straightened his collar. "One of these days, it might just get you into trouble."

Virginia

Monday, September 17th

A soft night breeze billowed through the bedroom sheers carrying the faint sounds of another vehicle. Paige stiffened under the comforter, straining her ear expectantly for the sound of a car door closing. She heard a group of teenagers bantering in the street. They soon said their goodbyes and sped away.

Paige looked at the clock; it was twenty past midnight. Just one hour earlier, her restless and combative child had finally collapsed in an exhausted heap. His mother had tucked him into bed and lingered there to stroke his fine red hair. She found a measure of comfort from the steady rhythm of Connor's breathing and the peaceful look upon his face as he slept.

Now, in the lonely master bedroom, she waited. Another car drove by and then another. Disappointment crested to frustration and resentment. Paige thumbed through a magazine without really seeing its pages.

Is that the sound of keys in the front door? Paige tilted her head to listen. *Yes, Brody's home*. She could hear him shuffling quietly in the entryway below, and for a moment Paige felt a rush of compassion for her husband. The feeling quickly dissipated. With each heavy footstep on the stairs, Paige's anger rose. She tossed the magazine to the floor.

Brody looked surprised as he pushed open the bedroom door. "Hi, honey." His tone was hushed. "I thought you would be asleep." He slipped the suit jacket from his shoulders and hung it up. "Sorry I'm so late. We've got a real quagmire with the economy right now and. . . ." The words trailed off when he looked at Paige's face. "How is Connor?"

"Are you really interested?"

Brody moved to the edge of the bed. "That's not fair. You know that we're in the reelection phase. We discussed the time commitment."

"What about the commitment to your family?" The words produced no satisfaction, only a look of hurt on her husband's face.

Paige began to cry.

Brody wrapped his arm around his wife. She struggled against his embrace for a few seconds and then gave in.

"We will get through this together—I promise," he said.

"Mom, I can't sleep."

The couple turned to see their young son standing in the doorway. The child's eyes darted about the room.

Brody knelt beside Connor. "Little boys need their rest. Would it help if I read you a story?"

"I don't want to go to bed, and you can't make me!" The child shrieked, bolting from the room and down the dark hallway.

Anxious looks passed between his parents as they moved about the house turning on lights. "Connor, this isn't funny," Paige admonished. "Come out now!"

In the den, Brody detected a faint giggle coming from behind the leather sofa and found Connor wedged between the couch and wall. "You heard your mother." Brody reached for his son, but the boy wiggled just out of reach. "This has gone far enough!" Brody pulled the sofa out from the wall and tried to retrieve his son, but Connor scurried out the other side and darted for the door.

Paige caught him and he clawed her like a tiger cub.

"Let me go!"

Brody strode across the room to restrain his son. "Stop it, Connor," he demanded. "Stop this behavior right now!"

Almost as if someone had flipped a switch, the child went limp in his father's arms, and he began to whimper.

Paige stood in the doorway, feeling the hardwood floor against her bare feet. A chill ran down her spine.

The boy began to quiver, mildly at first; then the shaking became violent, and his pathetic cries turned to sobs. A wet spot surfaced on the bottom of Connor's sleeper pajamas and then formed a pool on the floor.

Brody's expression held a mixture of horror and utter helplessness, and in that moment, Paige was terrified.

Chapter 27

New Orleans
Tuesday, September 18th

Joel sat on the curb in the French Quarter counting all the money he had left. He was hungry and discouraged. Last night he'd been rolled by a vagrant, who'd stolen everything but some quarters—barely enough for a cup of coffee. Somehow he'd have to come up with another plan.

Across the cobblestone road, the rich aroma of gumbo and fried bread enticed him. His mouth watered as he watched tourists lolling lazily at a sidewalk café. Half-eaten plates came and went, destined for the garbage bins. The idea of eating discarded food was repulsive, yet to Joel it had become a means of survival.

With the change rattling in his pockets, the teenager crossed the street and selected a seat at the café. After a few moments, a waiter approached.

Joel declined a menu and ordered coffee. "Cream and sugar, please."

The slick-haired waiter looked annoyed. "Maybe you'll be more comfortable sitting at the espresso bar?"

"I like it here."

The waiter snapped the order tablet shut and strutted away.

A few tables over was a gathering of raucous thirty-something adults who were sampling New Orleans cuisine and knocking back pitchers of beer.

Joel set his eye on more likely prospects: a family of four. He waited patiently as the exasperated parents tried to coax their finicky kids to eat. "Look at all the food on your plates," the mother nagged. "There are starving kids in Africa."

There's a starving kid right here, Joel thought as the waiter returned with his coffee.

The children's father threw up his arms. "Okay, have it your way—but I'm not buying you a snack when you get hungry!" The man snatched the check from the table and turned to his wife. "I'll settle the bill and meet you in the van."

In the flurry of the exodus, it was easy for Joel to grab some leftover food from a plate or two. He quickly loaded napkins and slid them discreetly into his pocket. No one seemed to notice or care. In a flash, Joel was back in his seat casually sipping hot coffee, the smell of food lingering deliciously upon his fingertips.

He left a meager tip and strolled through the streets until he found a little park with a bench. There, Joel devoured two half-eaten grilled cheese sandwiches and some cottage fries. He decided to save the rest for dinner.

Just beyond the park, a group of little girls from a nearby housing project jumped rope to the rhythm of a made-up song while Joel relaxed contentedly under the shade of an old magnolia tree.

"Hey, man, you on the wrong turf." The voice came from behind, low and threatening.

Joel had no intention of challenging the drug-crazed derelict. "No problem!" He crossed the street and picked up the pace. About five blocks from the French Quarter, Joel found himself in a questionable neighborhood. The odor of urine and decomposing food floated in the air as he walked beside weedy yards.

He nodded at a resident sitting on a porch.

"Git!" the woman hissed.

Joel turned the corner to circle back but stopped in his tracks.

Is that her? He watched a young woman walking barefoot, mincing with rows of bangles on her arms. *The hair is different,* he observed. It was bleached and twisted in messy knots.

She turned her face, and Joel's heart thundered with mixed emotion.

He called out as she climbed up the steps of a dilapidated row house, but the young woman disappeared through a red entryway.

Jade looked confused when she opened the door. Then the dullness in her eyes gave way to recognition. "Joel, I can't believe you're here!" The confusion returned. "But I thought—"

"That I was locked up?" Joel said. "I guess you could say that I got an early release." His sister's cheeks were sallow and sunken, making her look much older than twenty.

"Come in," she said, and her brother stepped into an apartment littered with items that wouldn't pass for trash at a yard sale.

Jade motioned to a threadbare couch and invited Joel to have a seat.

He pushed aside some magazines and dirty piles of sour clothes, some embarrassingly personal.

"I knew everything would work out." His sister was still smiling, but now there was tension around her mouth. Jade wrapped her knuckles on the wall behind her and yelled. "We've got company!"

She fumbled for a cigarette. "Did you like the postcards?" Jade touched a flame to her smoke and inhaled deeply.

"I still can't believe you're alive." Joel said as she watched him from behind a veil of smoke.

"Excuse me for a moment." She stubbed out her cigarette and headed toward a closed door. "Don't go away—I'll be right back."

Behind the thin wall, Joel could hear the low, angry voice of a man, followed by his sister pleading, "I promise he'll be no trouble. Please? I need it!"

The apartment grew quiet—too quiet. The minutes ticked past. Joel grew antsy and moved to the door. It was ajar, so he pushed it open.

Jade was sitting at the foot of a mattress on the floor, and a shirtless man was standing over her.

His upper body was tattooed with snakes that seemed to writhe when he turned toward the teenager. "So you're Jade's brother? You can call me Rommie. Suppose it wouldn't hurt nothin' if you bed down in the hallway for a few nights."

Joel's sister slumped back on the mattress, and she began to sway as if she was listening to music no one else could hear.

"It's all right now," Jade chanted, "all right now." Her eyes fluttered at half-mast for a split second before they rolled to white.

In Jade's arm, an empty syringe dangled below a blood-specked tourniquet.

North Dakota

Tuesday, September 18th

The September air felt crisp as Nora turned onto the open road in her Chevy.

"Look at that sky!" Lindsay looked up past the bugs on the windshield. "It's bluer than a robin's egg!"

Brooke, seated high up on her car seat, pointed a pudgy finger toward a farm and said, "Cow."

"That's right!" Lindsay clapped and tossed a smile Nora's way. "It was nice of you to let us tag along."

"I'm glad to have the company."

Lindsay unwrapped a stick of bubble gum and popped it in her mouth. "Did I ever tell y'all why I chose to come to North Dakota? My mama used to sing me an old Beatles song that went something like this: 'Somewhere in the hills of North Dakota there lived a man named Rocky Raccoon.' I forget the rest." The teenage mom worked her gum. "Mama quit singing after she took to the crack pipe—in fact, she pretty much quit being anything."

Instinct told Nora to tread lightly around this subject, and a comfortable silence settled over the car.

Lindsay whistled the Beatles' tune as the scenery rolled past. "This country sure is different than green ol' Arkansas. Can't see nothing there 'cause of all the trees." Lindsay blew a bubble that expanded until it popped. "These hills just seem to stretch on forever. A million miles of brown."

"You're looking at the effects of drought. Some of the old-timers are saying we are headed for another dust bowl, but with modern conservation practices I don't think it'll ever get to that point."

Lindsay's attention shifted to less weighty matters. "How far is it to Minot?"

"Almost eighty miles." Nora glanced at her passenger. "Do you have your list for the party store?"

"Yes'm." The teenager slipped a note from her pocket. "Face paint, streamers, balloons, sign board, and little prizes."

Little Brooke soon gave in to heavy eyelids. Lindsay slipped on her ear buds and settled back to listen to her iPod.

The miles flew past, and soon they were rolling into Minot. It had been a while since Nora had ventured to the North Dakota city that was now in the middle of an oil boom. It was a sharp contrast to the little vanishing farm towns like Delmont.

Still, not much had changed in Minot except for the prolific Discount Generals that had sprung up like weeds.

The Main Street was built wide enough to turn a large hay wagon around. Some of the brick storefronts still held advertising remnants from businesses long since gone, like the Northwest Piano Company.

Nora slowed her Chevy to a crawl at a corner where a white, federal-style building stood. There was a catch in her throat as she read the sign posted beside the door: FARLEY & HINES—ATTORNEYS AT LAW. *Some things don't change*, she thought.

They meandered through some backstreets and merged onto a well-traveled artery. A few miles past the old Soo Line Train Depot, Lindsay spotted the strip mall sandwiched between a Laundromat and a run-down motel.

Nora parked in the lot midway between the party store and a Chinese takeout restaurant and got herself gathered.

From the back of the Chevy, Brooke began to chatter. Lindsay unbuckled her daughter from the car seat, and they all headed for the store.

"Would y'all look at this place? I ain't never seen so many colors and shapes in all my life," Lindsay drawled. There were piñatas of Tinker Bell and SpongeBob; balloons in every size; flags and streamers; beads and bangles; and cake decorations.

"It's overwhelming," Nora said, staring at the selection of themed table settings.

From her seat in the shopping cart, Brooke spotted a pink wig. The toddler reached for it, working her pudgy fingers and swinging her plump legs. "Mommy! I want!"

"Let's see how it fits," Nora said and slipped the wig over the toddler's corn-silk hair.

"Looks like she's wearin' a big wad of cotton candy." Lindsay scrunched her nose.

Brooke patted the fluffy curls, and her little lips pursed

in a smile.

"Not another word—I'm going to buy it for her!" Next, Nora spoiled Brooke with a little pink purse and a Tinker Bell wand to match her hair. "I haven't had this much fun in years."

Lindsay found a face-painting kit on sale, and Nora threw in some cake decorations for Gertie and a black plastic derby for J. J.

Brooke began to fuss at the checkout counter, and Lindsay whispered, "I reckon it's her diaper."

"I'll meet you in the car." Nora settled the bill and made her way outside, pushing the loaded shopping cart.

She stopped in the parking lot and stared. *Is that Pastor Henry?*

From the motel next door she watched him climb into his car. She waved, but he didn't see her. *Probably making a charity call,* Nora told herself as he sped off.

Then, Celeste emerged from a motel room, fluffing her white hair with her long fingers.

The two women's eyes met.

A chill slithered down Nora's spine as she stood in the crosshairs of Celeste's stare.

Quickly, she threw the supplies into her trunk and jumped behind the wheel.

"Is everybody buckled?" From the rearview mirror, Nora could see the self-appointed prophetess watching as they pulled away.

I was right—Celeste is not who she appears to be. But such vindication felt shallow to Nora when she considered all the hearts that would be broken.

New Orleans

Wednesday, September 19th

Jade walked into her dingy living room and recoiled from a ray of morning light. "Rommie says you can't stay here anymore," she told her brother. "You have to go."

Joel offered no protest. The memories of the previous night were still fresh. He had barely slept, huddled in the hallway on cracked linoleum as cockroaches scurried about.

His sister and her keeper had given him a blanket that smelled of stale smoke. When sleep finally came, Joel dreamed of drunken men stumbling up and down the stairs and into his sister's apartment. *No*, he thought, *I don't want to stay another night in this hellhole*.

He looked at his sister curled up on the stained couch and felt a surge of pity. Jade's former healthy complexion had withered to gray. "I'll leave," he said softly, "but first, I need to know."

She stared blankly at the images flickering on her cheap television.

"Please," Joel said.

Jade pursed her lips "I don't want to talk about it. Anyway, Rommie will be back soon. You really shouldn't be here."

Joel blocked her view of the TV. "You killed our parents, didn't you?"

"What if I did? They were messing with both our lives!" She spread her fingers. "Look, everything turned out fine—even better than I thought it would! You're not in reform school anymore, and I'm free to do whatever I want."

The realization hit Joel like a missile. "You planned the whole thing?"

"I was a legal adult at the time, and you were only a minor. If they caught me, I'd go to prison for life. So I put on some of your clothes, and then I cut myself." Jade puffed at her own cleverness. "It worked! They all thought I was dead, too."

Joel shook his head in disbelief. "I don't even know who you are!"

Jade's face reddened, and she shot to her feet. "Yeah? Maybe you should ask yourself that same question!" She stomped into the bedroom and returned with a manila envelope. "They weren't even your real parents anyway!" She tossed the documents at his feet and dropped back on the sofa. "Where's Rommie? I need a fix!"

The television screen changed. "We interrupt this broadcast for a special report." The President of the United States was addressing the nation regarding farm aid.

Jade clicked manically through channels, only to find the same image of Thomas Atwood speaking from the White House Press Room.

Joel picked up the folder that lay at his feet and then walked out the door, leaving a piece of his heart behind.

Chapter 28

Washington, DC

Friday, September 21st

The Oval Office door was open. The president was standing near his desk gazing upward at a painting of George Washington.

Brody rapped softly on the doorjamb to announce his arrival.

Atwood turned his head and motioned toward the portrait. "An American icon," he said. "Sometimes we forget that he was just a man."

The president directed Brody to take a seat. "You're probably anxious to get home to your family, so I'll try to make it brief. Have you seen the recent editorials about the G-20 and my side trip to North Dakota?"

A few New York Times op-ed headlines sprang to Brody's thoughts: PRESIDENT'S DIPLOMATIC DEBACLE; FARM JUNKET FIASCO; ATWOOD PANDERS TO HIS ROOTS. Also still fresh in his mind was the tongue-lashing he'd received from Spence Carlyle.

"I want to hear your reaction."

Brody's neck felt hot, but he refrained from tugging on his collar. "I believe, in this case, it's prudent to balance the negative press with the favorable. The people directly affected by this drought have been encouraged by your responsiveness. If our farmers were to fold up shop, the long-range economic implications would be staggering. You have applied what I call 'psychological stimuli to a very bleak situation."

Atwood listened, his hands clasped on the desk in front of him. "'Psychological stimulus.' I like the sound of that. Go on."

Brody noticed the tremor in the president's hand and thought of the rumors of Parkinson's disease.

"Sir, the science of economics is complex. There are many factors to consider. Our nation's breadbasket has taken a hit, and our internal grain supply is dwindling. The economic scales of export embargos are staggering, and the. . . ." Brody stopped in mid-sentence and drew in a deep breath. "Mr. President, may I digress?"

Atwood nodded.

"There are many different factors that affect our economy. Fear is intangible, and yet, it can drive the stock market up or down."

"So you're saying that there are human factors to consider."

"Yes, sir, there are economic variables that can't be measured."

The president rose from his desk and began to pace. "Wisdom is shown to be right by the lives of those who follow it," he said softly.

"Excuse me?"

"It's from the Bible. Until now, I never knew what that particular passage meant." Atwood's gaze returned to the portrait. The tremor was more pronounced. "I've been having a reoccurring nightmare—almost every night."

"Sir, you've been under a lot of stress."

Atwood smiled, but his eyes were troubled. "Good night, Hays. Give my regards to your wife and son."

North Dakota
Saturday, September 22nd

The Bargain Bin had never looked so festive. Lindsay had transformed the walls with a pocketful of tacks and some colorful streamers.

"Where do you want the banner to hang?" J. J. hollered through the screen door. "Personally, I think it should be centered over the porch."

"I'll defer to you on that," Nora said, hurrying over to help Gertie with a tower of Tupperware.

"I made enough cinnamon lefse and fattigmann for an army," said Gertie.

"At least you didn't bring a pot of your cabbage soup," J. J. quipped from the porch. "No offense, but it stinks up the whole building."

"Oh, why don't you go join another circus?" Gertie bellowed. "But before you go, you can bring that big kettle of cabbage soup in from my car."

"What do y'all think?" Lindsay looked like an insect in

her lavender-striped leggings and butterfly wings.

"You look wonderful," Nora said.

"Not me, silly, the decorations!"

"It's all perfect!" Nora felt a swell of sentiment as baby Brooke toddled past wearing her rainbow wig. "Everything is going to be wonderful."

Gertie came out of the kitchen wiping her hands on her apron. "I've never seen so many pies and cakes! I think everyone in town baked something for this fundraiser."

The town's generosity had been overwhelming. The chamber of commerce had organized an art auction, and the mayor gave orders to cordon off the street in front of the old hotel. Many of the local businesses planned to close during the fundraiser.

"I painted numbers for the cakewalk on the blacktop," Lindsay announced. "It should wash off with a good rain."

Nora grimaced and tried to recall the last good rain Delmont had seen.

J. J. O'Shay hurried toward the kitchen, making funny faces as he delivered Gertie's cabbage stew. He returned with his best long-suffering look.

"Don't worry," Nora said with a wink. "We've also got plenty of hot dogs and chili."

"Time to get in touch with my inner clown!" J. J. said as he dragged his duffel to the bathroom. He emerged a few minutes later, complete with juggling pins and a bright orange nose that honked.

Within the hour, the street out front was clogged with locals wanting to be a part of the fundraiser. A cowboy poet arrived to recite a litany of farm-rangeland poems; some folk musicians took up residence on the porch and agreed to play for the cakewalk; and an artist donated three original paintings to auction.

Children squealed with delight as Lindsay painted fox and cat faces on their soft pink cheeks and people lined up for the cakewalk.

"Will you look at this?" Gertie said. "I think everybody in North Dakota turned out!"

This is much bigger than a fundraiser for the Bargain Bin's boiler, Nora told herself. *This is about a frightened community finding a way to come together and help their neighbors!*

The mayor interrupted the neighborhood chatter to auction off the paintings. "Who'll give me five hundred? Do I hear five hundred? Okay, how about six hundred? Got it! Now six-fifty—yep! How 'bout seven hundred, folks?"

Nora felt someone touch her shoulder, and she turned to see Pastor Henry.

"We need to talk."

"This isn't the best time," she said.

"What I have to say won't take long." His jaw was set with a hard edge. "Nora, I think it's best if you find another place to worship."

"What? The Delmont Harvest Center is my church home." Across the street, Nora spotted Celeste watching from the pastor's car.

"Maybe you don't understand what I'm saying," Henry snapped. "You are no longer welcome!"

Chapter 29

Paris

Monday, September 24th

Ensconced in a velvet chair, Jean Pierre took a sip of brandy and let his gaze float about the Parisian apartment. All around, mahogany paneling featured inlaid wood vines that were carved to look as if they were climbing toward the leaded glass windows. Pierre's eyes followed those lines up the spiral staircase. Maurine would be descending soon. Would she detect the nervousness he felt? Would she know that he felt mildly nauseous? His lover had a way of seeing right through him.

In the center of the room, a soft gas flame flickered in the fireplace, not for warmth but for effect on the warm summer night. Its light danced softly in Jean Pierre's brandy snifter. He swirled the amber liquid, mesmerized. His thoughts, dark and purposeful, struggled to grasp the enormity of the impending situation.

Beside him, lace curtains undulated and parted with a breeze, showing French doors that opened onto a small iron veranda. A puff of fresh air carried with it the moist and mildly pungent smell of the Seine River. Jean Pierre set his drink down and rose to pull the curtains back. The view was unparalleled: Notre Dame, in all its glory! The crest of the evening had descended; now, the lights of the great cathedral cast upward shadows, beautiful yet haunting.

Jean Pierre glanced over his shoulder at the grandfather clock and turned to pace nervously on the room's massive Persian rug. "Details, details," he muttered. It was the little things that worried him.

"Talking to yourself, my love?" Maurine Velar filled the room with her stunning presence as she descended the spiral stairs. Her body moved with graceful ease beneath a shimmering gown.

Jean Pierre watched as Maurine paused to check her makeup in a gilded mirror. She ran her hand through waves of silver hair and touched her moistened lips. She seemed to sense her lover's interest and turned to him, smiling coyly. Maurine looked beautiful in the warm, forgiving glow of her Parisian apartment. Her violet eyes shined as if the stage lights she loved so much had never dimmed.

Maurine moved to Jean Pierre's side and ran her delicate fingers across his neck, purring as they danced playfully down his spine.

He brushed aside her overture and offered her a glass of brandy instead.

She took it in hand and lowered herself into a chair. "Do you think they will all come?"

Jean Pierre gripped the curtains and again peered into the darkness. With a little help, the streetlights had conveniently stopped working a few hours earlier, cloaking the address in a shadowy blanket. "Yes, I believe they will."

A limousine slowed to a crawl and stopped in front of the blue double doors. Its occupants emerged, and the vehicle discreetly rolled away.

First to arrive was Jacques Renoso, Canada's Prime Minister. Others soon followed in the same clandestine fashion.

Maurine, a sparkling hostess, rose to the occasion like fine effervescent champagne. She threw open the cabinet of her exquisite built-in bar and sashayed about the room filling drinks while the heads of state exchanged solemn looks above social niceties.

The mood was heavy but charged with energy. Invitations had been carefully considered. Only a few G-20 elites had been included; four leaders arrived to speak personally for their nations: France, Canada, Germany, and China. The rest—Japan, Italy, Russia, and the United Kingdom—had sent trusted envoys to represent their interests. Conspicuously absent was a representative from the United States.

"Ladies and gentlemen," Jean Pierre said, raising his brandy glass in salute, "I am so pleased that you have come." A hush fell over the room as the host thrust his glass high into the air. "In the spirit of cooperation—here's to global unity!" After an echo of hearty hails, Jean Pierre squared his shoulders and launched into his well-rehearsed speech. "My dear fellows, the international community stands at a crossroads," he proclaimed. "To the right, we face the shackles of a self-serving superpower. To the left, we face a defining moment, not only for the financial integrity of our own nations, but for the future of the world. Are we to hang our heads in defeat while our own people suffer monetary stagnation? What about our children? When will such arrogance end?"

Heads bobbed, and throaty affirmations rolled through the coalition. "The Americans must be humbled!" the German Chancellor exclaimed.

Crystal glasses kissed in the muted light. The sentiment was unanimous.

Chapter 30

Virginia

Wednesday, September 26th

The George Washington Parkway was bottlenecked with traffic up ahead. Brody Hays slowed his BMW to a crawl and looked at his watch. "I'll never make it!"

He punched Paige's cell number and listened to it ring. When she didn't pick up, he left a hasty voicemail message. "Honey, I'm caught in some kind of rubberneck delay on the GW Parkway. Go ahead and eat without me, and I'll meet you and Connor at the movie theater."

Twenty-five minutes later, he rolled slowly past flashing lights where traffic cops directed motorists around a disabled car. There were no apparent injuries, only a distraught-looking woman standing beside a station wagon full of children.

Brody thought about his own son's struggles. The doctor had reassured Paige that Connor would acclimate to the medication, and they had been encouraged by some measured progress. Tonight the Hays family planned an evening out—the first in a long time.

Traffic finally began to move. Brody accelerated to cruising speed as the cell phone rang. He punched the receiver. "Yes."

"Hays, this is James."

"What's up?" Brody asked with a sense of foreboding. James Galloway, one of his team of economic advisors, never called during off hours unless it was important.

"Something strange is happening with the big-volume traders in the Asian markets. It appears several European traders are dumping huge amounts of US currency on the market. The dollar seems to be losing ground rapidly and severely."

"How much?"

"Ten cents against the Euro." James waited as Brody mulled the information over. Brody steered around a lawn care truck. "Let's keep an eye on it and see what happens when the US markets open tomorrow. Thanks, James. I appreciate the heads-up."

The Leesburg Pike was jammed light-to-light with commuters. Brody used the time to pry his anxious thoughts away from work. *My family needs me, and for now, that's all that matters.*

Brody arrived at the Regal Cinema just in time for the previews of coming attractions. He bought a ticket for an animated film called *Kangaroo Alley*, grabbed a bag of popcorn and a soda, and set out to find his family.

An usher hurried past Brody as he approached Theater Seven. He followed the young man inside, where a commotion had disrupted the movie. Over the buzz of whispers, Brody detected Connor's shrill voice.

"I did see an angel—I did!" the child screamed. "He said a war is coming!"

Brody's heart sank as the lights came on, illuminating Connor in the glow. The wide-eyed boy stood just below the big screen, imploring the audience like a miniature prophet. Behind him, an animated cartoon played on.

Paige moved closer, but Connor dodged away and shouted, "You don't believe me, either!"

Brody could see the humiliation upon his wife's face. He strode quickly toward his son. "Connor, stop this behavior!"

The boy raced for the theater door, where an usher grabbed him.

Brody scooped the flailing child into his arms and whisked him into the hallway.

Paige joined her husband, and the parents rushed their screaming boy past gawking faces at the snack counter. Someone held the door open, and the couple fled into the parking lot.

In his car, Brody held Connor until the boy's muscles relaxed and the shrieks subsided. "We'll have to get your car later," he said.

Paige, gulping back sobs, nodded.

At home, Brody gave Connor a mild sedative prescribed by the psychiatrist. After it took effect, he carried his son to his bedroom and tucked him in.

He returned to the living room to find Paige staring out the window at a neighbor's neatly landscaped front yard. In her hands, she held a half-finished glass of wine.

"I think I'll have a glass, too," Brody said. "You

shouldn't drink alone."

Paige seemed to find his words amusing. She laughed aloud and downed her wine.

"We'll get through this." Brody touched his wife's shoulder; she recoiled. "It's just going to take time for Connor to adjust, that's all."

"That's all?" Page said sarcastically. "I'm losing another child, one piece at a time." Tears rolled down her cheeks.

"Don't be ridiculous." The moment he opened his mouth, Brody knew it was a mistake.

Anger and hurt flashed in Paige's green eyes. She launched from her chair, hurried up the stairs to their bedroom, and slammed the door.

Brody sat alone in the impeccable formal living room surrounded by trophies of his success: opulent furniture and expensive knickknacks displayed beside personal photographs with presidents and heads of state. In the lengthening shadows of the evening, it all meant nothing.

Washington D.C.

Thursday, September 27th

Brody arrived at the West Wing to find the staff in the middle of a hair-on-fire drill. The hallway in front of the Roosevelt Room buzzed with scintillating speculation.

Standing a few yards away, the president's chief of staff was talking into his Blackberry. Chip Skinner spotted Brody, pointed toward the Roosevelt Room, and mouthed the word, "Meeting."

"What's up?" Brody asked as he settled into a seat at the long mahogany table. Several staffers flicked a nervous gaze toward Spence Carlyle. The president's chief political advisor was leaning back in his chair, staring up at the ceiling. His eyes were angry and his mouth tight.

Brody recognized the look, not uncommon in Washington's fast lane. *Someone*, he thought, *is about to be thrown under the proverbial bus*.

James Galloway, the youngest member of his team of economic advisors, picked nervously at his fingers as the chief of staff breezed into the room.

"Ladies and gentlemen, we have a potential crisis on our hands." Chip Skinner dropped into his seat and shuffled through a stack of papers. "A major divestiture by foreign investors is occurring in the US. Markets are dropping, and the numbers are significant." Skinner's slate-gray eyes locked on Brody. "Mr. Hays, this would be a good time to explain why you chose to keep this from us."

"I've been monitoring movement in the European currency markets, and I've asked for an evaluation of the economic triggers." Brody took a moment to choose his words. "Investment hiccups are not uncommon; therefore, I felt it was prudent to analyze the situation before I raised an alarm."

"Let's talk about the evaluation you asked for." Spence Carlyle held up a CIA report. "Mr. Galloway brought it to my attention. Frankly, Hays, your lack of diligence concerns me."

Brody glanced at his assistant, who was staring at a hangnail. "May I see that?"

Carlyle tossed the report across the table and glowered

as the president's chief economic advisor skimmed its pages.

"This is the first time I've seen this document." Hays shook his head in disbelief. "The CIA actually postulates that we are experiencing economic backlash from the position taken by the US at the G-20 Economic Summit."

Chip Skinner thrust himself from his chair and began to pace the room. "Our skittish institutional investors are already nervous. Now the Federal Reserve is calling an emergency meeting to see if they can head off a spike in interest rates. We may have to exercise our option to temporarily shut down the markets."

"This is totally insane!" Brody exclaimed. "I can't believe the foreign investors would jeopardize millions for spite."

Spence Carlyle unleashed his disdain. "Maybe if you had foreseen such a reaction, we could have taken steps to avoid it!"

Beside Brody, young James Galloway was playing with his tie and avoiding eye contact.

I've been sandbagged, he thought.

Washington, DC

Thursday, September 27th

Paige pulled up in front of the Old Ebbitt Grill feeling a little guilty about leaving Connor with a babysitter.

"It'll do you good to get out of the house," Brody had said.

She knew he was right.

Paige stepped from the Land Rover, handed her keys to the restaurant's valet, and went inside.

Old Ebbitt Grill was bustling with DC's evening crowd. Paige smoothed her sleeveless satin dress and looked around as she waited for the host's attention. Soft light glowed upon the backdrop of cherry-wood paneling, providing a rich atmosphere for the capital's movers and shakers. Paige recognized a few.

"Can I help you?"

"I'm meeting my husband here." Paige absently ran a finger around her gold-braided necklace. "I believe the reservation should be under Brody Hays."

The host scanned the list. His eyebrows arched. "Yes, of course, Mrs. Hays. I'm afraid your husband hasn't arrived yet, but others from the White House party have already been seated."

White House party? Paige thought as she followed the maître d' to the old section of the grill. Brody hadn't mentioned others when he'd phoned with the suggestion of dinner in the city.

Paige spotted Vincent Demarco of Congressional Affairs. He was flirting with a young intern. Across the table, Irene Moyer, the White House Press Secretary, was speaking officiously into her cell phone.

Vincent rose as she approached. "Paige, you look stunning! Come have a seat and let me introduce you!"

Irene looked down her bifocals, offered Paige a condescending nod, and turned back to her cell phone conversation.

"Can you believe this gorgeous creature is married to

Brody?" Vincent said with a wink. "Lynette Green, this is Paige Hays."

"I'm so glad to meet you!" the young woman said. Her bright, eager face reminded Paige of her own college years and the youthful idealism that had once motivated her.

Paige offered a handshake.

"Darling!" Irene cut in. "Nice of you to join us. How are you holding up?"

Paige stared at Irene, not knowing how to respond. *Did Brody confide our struggles with Connor?*

"Your husband asked me to let you know that he's running a bit late." The formidable woman's mouth screwed into a frown. "But, of course, *you* understand, don't you, dear?"

Paige sensed a cryptic message, but decided not to take the bait. If something was wrong, she preferred to hear it from Brody.

"Do you work in DC?" the young intern chirped as if sensing the awkwardness of the moment.

"No, I work in Northern Virginia," Paige said, grateful for the diversion.

"Really, darling?" Irene's voice was buttery smooth. "You're working?"

Paige felt her face flush and hoped it didn't show.

"What do you do?" Lynette pressed.

"Right now, I'm a fulltime mother. But one day I hope to resume my legal career."

Irene took a sip from her Manhattan. "I didn't know you worked with the legal profession."

Paige met the woman's gaze. "Harvard Law School."

Irene almost choked on her drink.

"Sorry I'm late." Brody leaned over his wife, kissed her cheek, and settled into the chair beside her. He looked exhausted.

Across the table, everyone studied their menus. Paige studied her husband. She leaned close and asked, "What's wrong?"

Brody stiffened. "Nothing I can't handle."

Irene Moyer's cell phone trilled again. "The New York Times!" she said loudly as she took the call. "What? AP has picked up the story?" Irene rubbed her forehead. "Okay, we'll get to work." The White House Press Secretary punched the end key and jutted her chin toward Brody. "It looks like you'll be splashed all over the news by tomorrow morning."

Silence settled over the table.

"It's probably nothing more than the media's election-cycle feeding frenzy," Vincent said. "I'm sure this will blow over."

"I'll have the prime rib." Brody handed his menu to the waiter and smiled at his wife. "What looks good to you?"

A few feet away, Irene sprang into action. "The best strategy is to cover this whole event with numbers—economic figures and projections."

Brody seemed annoyed. "I believe this can keep until after dinner."

Irene's lips shrank into a pout. "Fine." She snapped open her menu.

Brody rested his hand on Paige's shoulder. "Don't worry about a thing."

The food came, and Vincent and his date rattled on

about trivial matters, but the mood around the table remained tenuous.

On the sidewalk in front of the Old Ebbitt Grill, the group parted company. Brody lingered beside his wife as she handed the valet her parking stub.

Paige curled her fingers around Brody's coat sleeve. "Why didn't you tell me there were problems at work?"

He didn't answer.

The valet arrived with the Land Rover.

"Don't wait up." Brody brushed a kiss across her cheek.

Paige drove the winding roads of the GW Parkway with a sense of grief. Brody had shut her out again.

As Paige merged onto the beltway, her mind turned again to Connor. *What if there was another episode like the one at the movie theater?* She had forgotten to call home and check. Anxiety rode home with her, and by the time Paige pulled into her driveway, her imagination was turning cartwheels. She raced through the door feeling like the worst mother on the planet.

Inside, all was quiet except for the soothing sound of Mrs. Alcorn's voice. Paige was stunned to see Connor lying contentedly upon the woman's plump lap as she read from a book.

Paige approached gingerly, afraid to disturb the moment.

Mrs. Alcorn looked up. "Oh, my dear, is it that time already?"

Connor slid from the babysitter's soft lap and skipped across the rug and into his mother's open arms. "Hi, Mom," he said happily. "Look what Mrs. Alcorn gave me." Connor proudly displayed a plastic, glow-in-the-dark cross that hung from a string around his neck.

"That's nice." Paige kissed the boy's cheek and gave him a hug. Over his shoulder, she looked at Mrs. Alcorn. "Was there any trouble?"

"Heavens, no! We had fun, didn't we, Connor?"

"And he took his medication without giving you a hard time?" Paige pressed.

Mrs. Alcorn looked blank and then seemed to pale. "Oh, my dear! I forgot to give him the pills." She launched her round body from the chair in a fluster. "I am so forgetful these days. I hope I haven't messed things up!"

"Don't worry about a thing, Mrs. Alcorn," Paige said reassuringly. She handed the elderly woman a check and walked her to the door. "Thank you so much."

"Any time, dear. You have such a delightful child. Bye-bye, Connor," the kindly neighbor called as she left.

In the kitchen, Paige grabbed the prescription from the cabinet above the sink, carried it into the living room, and stood for a moment, watching her son.

Connor, surrounded by an array of broken crayons, was working hard on a mountain scene. He selected blue for the sky, yellow for the flowers, and green for the grass. In itself, there was nothing spectacular about his actions; lately, though, angry black and purple scribbles had been his colors of choice.

Paige looked at the bottle in her hand and bit her lip. "Connor. It's time to take your medicine."

Chapter 31

Virginia

Sunday, September 30th

Paige rose early on Sunday morning. She tiptoed to her walk-in closet and slipped into the clothes that she had laid out the night before: black slacks and a lavender silk blouse.

Brody stirred as she retrieved her handbag from the dressing table. She waited for her husband to settle back into a sound sleep before leaving.

It felt wrong sneaking out, but Brody would not understand her need. Church was just a waste of time as far as he was concerned. Paige backed the Land Rover from the garage, rationalizing that it would take too much energy to explain her feelings. *It would probably end in a fight anyway.*

As Paige meandered down the Georgetown Pike, she tried to remember how to pray. *Our God, who is in heaven. . . , or was it Father?* It had been so long she wasn't sure.

Now on the Capital Beltway, Paige backed off on the throttle as she took Exit 43. The early morning light played soft upon the trees along the George Washington Memorial Parkway. She opened a window and let the brisk fall air blow across her face.

Traffic was light as usual on a Sunday morning in the Metro area, yet a few hours from now things would be different. The Smithsonian museums would open, and the late season tourists would swarm the nation's capital.

Across the Key Bridge, Paige turned onto Wisconsin Avenue and found a parking space a few blocks from the church. She locked the car, inhaling deeply, and began to walk. She moved briskly past some weekend dog walkers as if trying to outpace her troubled thoughts.

Paige's gaze rose above the angular row of buildings to trace the gray, Gothic arches of the Apostle's Cathedral. She paused to check her watch before slipping through the massive doors.

Right on time, Paige thought as she settled into a pew near the back and watched people file past dressed in finery. She recognized a few faces: a local news anchorman, the mayor of DC, and the secretary of state, who was flanked by a security detail.

A hidden pipe organist played a fugue that echoed like a delicate symphony across mosaic tiles and grandiose marble pillars.

Up front, an altar boy lit candles while a deacon waved a brass canister, releasing ribbons of smoke. The room filled with the aroma of incense. Finally, the organist played the invocation tune, rousing the congregation to their feet.

Paige found comfort in the communal liturgy and the worship-prompted memories of her family's biannual pilgrimage to church—Christmas and Easter. She looked upward at the Michelangelo-style murals that graced the ceiling. Angels riding the crests of clouds and dancing among bolts of lightning served to remind worshipers that they were under the watchful eye of God. With all her heart, Paige needed to believe that.

They sang a few songs from the hymn book, and then a deaconess dressed in a white linen robe approached the pulpit. She bowed her head and opened a large Bible. "The scripture reading for today is from the Book of Revelation, Chapter 2, Verse 17. 'Anyone with ears to hear must listen to the Spirit and understand what he is saying to the churches.'"

Reverend Salisbury waited for the woman to descend before taking his place at the pulpit. "You may all be seated." He waited for the congregation to settle as instructed.

"We are all brothers called to love and accept one another," he began. "Our differences make us unique; our beliefs define us."

He implored the congregation with an earnest look. "And yet, there is a monster among us! This enemy is called intolerance! Beloved, there are many paths to God. Why must we stand in judgment? We must resist the mythical God of vengeance and embrace diversity!"

The reverend smiled sublimely. "Simply put, God is a creative consciousness, a regenerative force of nature. This revelation liberates us from the archaic notion of judgment and frees us to embrace our individuality."

Paige shifted on the hard wooden pew. Something about the message made her uneasy. She didn't like thinking about God as an impersonal force of nature. Wasn't he supposed to be personal and benevolent?

The sermon wound down with an announcement of an

upcoming seminar on environmental Christian consciousness. Reverend Salisbury invited the congregation to attend. Then he summoned a young family to the altar.

The clergyman spread the arms of his robe like the wings of an angel. "Ladies and gentlemen, you are called to witness a joyous occasion!" He took a fussing infant in his arms. "Let us join with John and Bev Howe to celebrate the baptism of their daughter, Christina."

The parents' faces were aglow with pride as Reverend Salisbury smiled down upon their offspring and carried her to the baptism fount. There, he uttered a prayer and sprinkled the child with water.

Memories of another time rolled in like a dense fog, and Paige dropped her head into her hands. Gone forever was the opportunity to hear those words of blessing spoken over Emily.

The service ended. People began to leave, but Paige remained in the pew to ponder the artwork that adorned the walls. *Did these artists personally witness angels, or were they deluded, too?*

Her gaze was drawn to the inlaid statue of Jesus as he hung upon a wooden cross. The reverend had called God a "force of nature." The description reminded Paige of *Star Wars* and left her feeling cold. She had hoped to find comfort from a personal, loving God.

In the cavernous sanctuary, Paige's heart was breaking. There could be no greater pain than to lose a child—but two? Emily's death had come suddenly and violently; now, Connor was slowly slipping away. *Maybe the Reverend is right, and God is nothing more than a big, impersonal force.*

Paige reached for her handbag and saw a Bible lying open on the pew. Her eyes fell upon the words, "He will feed his flock like a shepherd. He will carry the lambs in his arms, holding them close to his heart. He will gently lead the mother sheep with her young." Mascara bled onto Paige's silk blouse, but the tears she shed were not from sorrow. *Are these the words of a God who doesn't care?*

Arizona

Sunday, September 30th

The desert sun had barely risen when David was awakened by someone banging on the door of the General Store.

Beside him in the big brass bed, Elita arched her back and opened her eyes. "What's going on?" she asked as David moved to the window to raise the blind.

"Campers," he said, glancing up and down the street to see a caravan of motor homes, fifth-wheel trailers, and pop-up campers.

Elita joined her husband at the window. "I recognize some of their faces. They've been staying over at the Oasis." She threw open the closet, tossed David a pair of jeans, and slipped a dress from a hanger.

Downstairs, David turned on the lights while his wife flipped the OPEN sign in the General Store window and unlocked the door.

Most of the crowd was clustered on the porch.

"Good morning, folks," Elita called as she opened for

business. “You traveling back home today?”

An older gentleman stepped forward and said, “I’m Jim, and this is my better half, Bonnie.” He draped his arm around a tiny woman with silver, spiked hair. “We’re looking for a new place to camp.”

“What’s wrong with the Oasis?” David inquired.

The man seemed surprised. “You haven’t heard about Miriam Baker? I just assumed in a town this size. . . .”

Elita’s brow creased. “What’s wrong with Miriam?”

“Poor woman collapsed yesterday and was taken to the hospital over in Bixby.” The little woman with the spiked hair patted Elita’s arm. “Don’t worry, honey, the good Lord answered our prayers. We got word this morning that Ms. Baker is going to be just fine!”

“She just needed some rest,” Jim said, “which brings me back to the reason for this visit.”

“You’d hardly know we’re here,” Bonnie chirped.

David couldn’t believe what they were asking. “There must be a couple dozen campers out there.”

“We have twenty-nine families represented here,” Jim volunteered. “Thirty if you include the one already staying in your back lot.”

“It’s out of the question. We don’t even have the resources to handle the campers.”

The gentleman was not put off. “We anticipated such a response, so we’ve all agreed to run generators for power.”

Elita gave her husband a *why not* shrug, but David stood firm.

“There are other logistical challenges. Water and sewer, for instance.”

"What if we agree to haul our water from Bixby and dump our tanks there, too?" Bonnie lobbied.

A cluster of other travelers echoed their agreement.

"Bixby has a few campgrounds that would be more accommodating. I don't understand why you want to stay in Arroyo Seco."

There was a long pause before Bonnie spoke. "We just adore this little town. It's a special place."

Suddenly, David felt like he was being played. "What's going on here?"

Elita glared at her husband. "You don't have to be rude."

Jim looked around the group and pointed to a rough-looking black man who was leaning against the wall. "Raymond, we'll start with you. Tell this nice young couple your story."

The man jingled change in his baggy slacks. "I come here because of the dreams. It's hard to explain the whole thing without sounding like I'm touched in the head. I knew deep down in my soul that I was supposed to find this place, so that's just what I done."

"I had visions of a map!" A young mother shifted her baby to the other arm. "Just as clear as can be," she said. "I saw an angel put his finger right on this town."

Next, a woman with a battle-weary face told a similar story. "I prayed for months that God would take me out of an abusive relationship. I read the Bible every day, hoping for a sign, and then one day I opened a travel book and saw a picture of your little General Store. That same day, I opened my Bible to a scripture about the springs in the desert, and everything just seemed to click."

"We could go on, but all the stories are similar," Bonnie said.

"So you're telling me that none of you had ever met before coming here?" David raised a skeptical eyebrow.

"Incredible, isn't it?" Bonnie said.

Unlikely, David thought. "Why here?"

"We can't answer that." Jim shook his head. "I guess it wouldn't be faith if we knew all the whys and hows and whatnots."

David watched his wife admiring the stranger's baby. "That still doesn't change the fact that we're not set up as campground."

"What about Rupert's vision?" Elita asked as she took the infant in her arms. "Hope Springs has plenty of running water and lots of space."

"No electricity," David argued.

"If there's water and a hill, my husband can generate electricity," Bonnie volunteered. "He's a retired engineer."

"I know a thing or two about hydroelectric plants," Jim explained. "Not quite as simple as my wife makes it sound, but with the right equipment, it is possible."

The whole conversation seemed surreal to David. *Is this the manifest vision of Rupert Sims?*

A few feet away, Elita cradled the baby to her breast and gave her husband a pleading look. "It all seems to fit."

"Aside from a few scrub pines, there's no shade," David mumbled.

A young man with a mullet jumped into the debate. "If we can get our hands on some building supplies, I can put up a pavilion."

Brakes squealed on Main Street, and heads turned as a long flatbed truck came to a stop behind a parked camper. A short, squat character emerged, bounding onto the porch and through the door. “Hey, y’all!” he said adjusting a toothpick in his lips. “Anybody know where I can pitch a tent around here?”

“God provides!” Bonnie exclaimed joyfully. She pointed to the flatbed truck that was loaded with lumber and roofing materials.

Chapter 32

Quebec, Canada
Sunday, September 30th

In the walled city of Quebec, Jean Pierre watched from the tavern's shuttered window. Outside, five men and two women emerged from nearby hotels and quaint bed and breakfasts. They walked quietly under the cover of darkness, pulling up coat collars and wrapping wooly scarves tightly against the chilly northern air.

Like the spokes of a wheel, the group converged from different directions, moving with purpose toward a common destination in the city's historic district. The hour was late and the streets silent except for an occasional insomniac or secret lover skirting the faint glow of the old-fashioned streetlamps.

The tavern doors opened for each guest respectively and quickly closed behind. Most moved toward the heat radiating from a wood-burning stove in the corner to warm themselves. None spoke as they waited. The mood was tense and their faces solemn.

When the last of the party arrived, they were all ushered into a back room. The group seated themselves around a long, benched table as a cuckoo clock announced the eleventh hour.

Jean Pierre slapped his palms on the head of the table and looked into the faces of each man and woman—some young, others seasoned with age. "Ladies and gentlemen," he began, "before we proceed, I must remind you of the gravity of our task and the need for the utmost discretion."

The group responded with nods and affirmations.

"The hour is late, in more ways than one," Jean Pierre said gravely. "Let us begin."

Each man and woman produced a memory card and laid it on the table.

The Frenchman gathered up the offerings and slid them into a secret pocket in the lining of his coat. "I trust these contain all the information we asked for?"

"Yes," an older man with a heavy German accent assured him. "All our people are in place. The targets have been carefully analyzed. We don't foresee any problems."

"Au contraire! You must plan for all contingencies," Jean Pierre admonished. "Anticipate the unexpected. For your sake and for the world's welfare, it is vital that everything be in perfect order."

He looked around the table. "This will be the last of these meetings. It is much too risky. If the information gathered is indeed complete, you will not be contacted again."

Jean Pierre rose from the bench and slid his hand into a heavy wool coat. "I remind you one last time that the stakes are very high. Our future, possibly even our very existence, is perched at the edge of this precipice."

Chapter 33

North Dakota

Monday, October 1st

Nora found Lindsay and baby Brooke on the porch when she arrived in the morning. She knelt beside the young mother and toddler, who were huddled beneath an old bedspread they'd found among some donations. "What are you doing here?"

Lindsay looked up and shivered. "I had no place else to go."

"What about your room at the Delmont Apartments?" Nora reached out to help the teenage mom to her feet.

"They asked me to leave." Lindsay blinked back tears. "I can't blame them, really. They already let me stay three weeks without paying rent."

Nora unlocked the door to the Bargain Bin and directed mother and child to a loveseat next to an electric heater.

"Hey, when did they finish working on the fireplace?" Lindsay asked.

"Yesterday. And it's a good thing, too, because it's starting to get chilly."

"Tell me about it!" Lindsay said, rubbing her toddler's pudgy arms.

Nora scrunched up some newspaper, arranged a stack of wood on top, and lit it with a long-necked lighter. "You could have told me that you needed a place to stay."

"Reckon I just didn't want to be a bother."

"You know how much I care about you and Brooke!" Nora parked her hands on her hips. "I have plenty of room at the farm. You're both coming home with me, and I won't take no for an answer!"

"Okay, but just until I can get back on my feet," Lindsay agreed. "I ain't takin' no free ride. I'll work for my keep."

Nora fluffed her straight, brown hair and said, "As a matter of fact, I've been thinking about getting that makeover you've been taking about."

"Are you serious?" Lindsay launched to her feet like a rocket. "I know just what to do. First a body perm and then some warm highlights! I'm gonna bring out the brown in your eyes with some gray eye shadow, and then—"

"Whoa, let's not overdo things!"

"You won't be sorry," Lindsay told her. "Someday when I'm a famous hair designer, you can tell folks that you were my first customer."

Nora watched Brooke playing with her doll in the orange glow of the fireplace and thought about others who were going through tough times. At least a dozen new names had been added to the helps list this week alone.

Gertie arrived mid-morning with some sausage-filled rolls and a kettle of potato stew. Five minutes later, she emerged from the kitchen with a coffee cup and her blue eyes flashing. "You call this coffee? It looks more like dishwater to me!" She turned back, muttering something about making a fresh pot.

Brooke scattered toys around the floor while her young mother searched through racks of clothing and prattled on about the latest hairstyles.

The room warmed by fire, along with the homey scent of baked goods, transported Nora back to a time when her own family was alive.

J. J. O'Shay straggled in for a late lunch, and they all broke bread together.

Nora found herself whistling a cheerful tune while she worked and thanking God for all her blessings—Gertie, Lindsay, Brooke, and J. J. included.

New Orleans

Monday, October 1st

There was a cry in the streets of New Orleans. "Par-tay like there's no tomorrow!"

The nation's economy is tanking, but yeah—let's dance! Joel thought as he watched the sidewalk jazz band whip the crowd into a native frenzy.

Nothing makes sense anymore, the teenager thought as he read the legal documents his sister had tossed him. They were in an envelope from the law office of Farley & Hines in Minot, North Dakota.

Joel slid the adoption papers back into his backpack. *Is everything a lie?* he wondered with a heavy heart.

Down the road, someone pushed a fire hydrant over, and crack house children spilled from their hovels to splash about in the spray. The sun was hot and the air muggy. Beads of sweat formed on the teenager's face, and he wiped them away.

Plate glass shattered across the street, and Joel watched jagged shards disintegrate into a thousand pieces on the sidewalk.

A gang of looters entered a store and tossed goods to their accomplices while the street musicians played on.

The crowd seemed to multiply by the minute. Before long, hookers trolled half-naked while addicts groveled and voodoo kings patrolled the French Quarter in a victory strut.

Joel lowered his weary frame to the curb and wept. Since the murder of his parents, it was the first time the teenager had really let himself cry.

A painted mime approached to mock his tears, but Joel was too numb to care.

A few yards away, an ancient man stood watching, his bony limbs protruding from khaki shorts and an oversized Hawaiian shirt. The stranger acknowledged Joel with a nod. "It's hard to believe that full-grown humans can act this way."

There was something different about him, something Joel couldn't put his finger on.

"Mind if I take a load off my pegs?" the old man asked, sitting down beside the teenager to watch the debauchery. "Makes me think of a herd of sheep—poor shortsighted critters have been known to follow the others right off a cliff. I'm Zeke. What's your name, kid?"

"Joel," the teenager said, silently berating himself for

forgetting to use an alias.

"There was a prophet with that name once. Come to think of it, the Book of Joel describes some very interesting times—kinda like these." Zeke twirled the end of his long white beard, rose to his feet, and stretched. "Well, I suppose it's time to head on down the road."

A cluster of transvestites minced past, trailing ostrich feathers, and Joel shot to his feet. "Hey, mister! Can I get a lift?"

"Where're you headed, kid?"

"North Dakota."

"No foolin'?" The old man grinned. "Well, it just so happens. . . ."

Chapter 34

Washington, DC

Monday, October 1st

Brody Hays stared at a stack of newspapers on his desk—all bad press for the administration, all mentioning him by name.

With his free hand, Brody rubbed at a pounding headache in his temple. His heart sank as he listened to the voice on the other end of the receiver. The news was ominous. Institutional investors were beginning to dump stock, and the decline showed no signs of slowing.

Brody swallowed hard. "Okay, thanks. I want an hourly report." He hung up and riffled through his desk for some aspirin. In the next room, he could hear young James Galloway shuffling papers, and he wondered how long it would take the office mole to run to Spence Carlyle with another report.

The intercom on his desk rang, sending a lightning spasm of pain through Brody's head. "Federal Reserve on line three," his secretary announced.

Brody punched the line. "Yes, Marvin, I heard. . . ." He

let out a weary sigh. "We've got major problems."

At the stock market's closing bell, gloomy staffers milled about like undertakers waiting for the corpse.

In his office, Brody scrambled to pull together a report. With focused urgency, he lined up key players for an emergency meeting with the president. Within the hour, flanked by two economic analysts and a representative from the Federal Reserve, Brody headed for the Oval Office.

Jane Hennings, the president's personal secretary, met him in the hallway. "Mr. Hays, the president would like to see you alone before the meeting."

Brody squared his shoulders and followed her through the door of the Oval Office. Atwood was sitting at his desk, looking pale and somehow smaller. He motioned for Brody to approach while Jane slipped past and closed the door behind him.

Brody respectfully acknowledged his commander-in-chief.

"Have a seat." Thomas Atwood wasted no effort on political demeanor. He looked as worried as the rest. "There's a lot to do, Hays, so I'll get right to the point." The president tapped a pen on the desk and fixed a pointed gaze on Brody. "Spence Carlyle strongly recommends that I ask for your resignation."

"I understand, sir. I will tender it immediately." Brody felt an unexpected flood of relief as the words left his mouth. *It's over,* he thought.

"Not so fast, Hays." Atwood slapped his hands upon the desktop. "I won't accept your resignation. I won't have you abandoning ship on me now!"

"But sir, I thought—"

"I know the election is just around the corner, but that doesn't mean I'm ready to jump through every hoop Spence sets before me."

Atwood stood and began to pace about the Oval Office. "There's a quote by Abraham Lincoln that keeps coming to mind these days. 'I've been driven to my knees many times by the overwhelming conviction that I have nowhere else to go.'" The president reflected for a moment. "I need to follow my conscience and stand behind the position I took at the economic summit. I still believe it was the proper course."

"Yes, sir," Brody agreed as Thomas Atwood returned to his chair.

The president's fingers twitched on the armrest. "Those European scoundrels have got me over a barrel. Unless things turn around fast, my bid for reelection is over. I might as well go out with integrity." He rubbed his bloodshot eyes. "They've waged economic war on us—that's what this whole situation amounts to!"

"Sir, I think you need to tell the American people what you just told me."

"You mean address the nation?"

"Yes, Mr. President, as soon as possible. If Europe's recent actions are seen as an act of economic aggression against our country, the people may rally behind you."

"It's worth a shot." The president seemed encouraged.

He punched the intercom and asked Jane to have the kitchen send down some coffee before returning to the business at hand. "Hays, I want you to put together some talking points while I air this idea out with the rest of the staff."

"Consider it done, sir."

By primetime, the media had gathered to await the president's statement.

Brody went over the notes for the teleprompter and made a few simple revisions.

Thomas Atwood stood behind the podium that bore the presidential seal. A media aide stepped forward to powder the shine on his forehead and brush color into his ashen cheeks. He waved her off.

Spence Carlyle leaned against a wall in the back of the room, his arms folded across his chest. The president had ignored his advice to fire Brody and had instead appointed his personal nemesis to a special taskforce. Needless to say, the chief political advisor did not look happy.

Irene Moyer went over a few last-minute press details before stepping aside as the president took a sip of water and looked at the camera.

The room grew still, like the calm before a storm. The green light flashed.

Thomas Atwood faced the media with focus and poise. "I have called this press conference to speak candidly to the citizens of our great nation." The president paused, his silence encapsulating the seriousness of his task. "Our nation's economy has suffered a major setback from a catastrophic drop in the stock markets. A dramatic decline in the value of the US dollar triggered this event.

"As President of the United States, I am determined to do everything within my power to bring swift resolution to this matter. In order to circumvent further economic damage caused by panic, I have, under the 1933 Securities Act, suspended trading in the stock markets until further notice. I will not rest until we have adequately addressed this crisis."

The president faltered momentarily and then pressed on. "My fellow Americans, the events surrounding this crisis appear to be a well-planned act of economic aggression against our nation. This signals a much deeper problem of malice.

"In an unprecedented move of hostility, European investors have attempted to topple the economic stability of the United States of America by selling off their investments in the US dollar in the world currency markets. The evidence is indisputable."

Atwood paused as the gravity of these words reached the ears of millions of Americans. "I am calling on every American to be strong. Together, we must take a stand against this economic tyranny. I am confident that, as one nation under God, we will overcome this crisis, just as our forefathers met the challenges of their time."

The president kept his gaze steady until the camera was turned off; then, his shoulders slumped, and Jane rushed forward to help him from the room.

In the Oval Office, Brody and other key staff joined the president to watch the network news coverage. In a few minutes, they would know how it had all played out. Talking heads from all political bents would be analyzing the president's words and molding public opinion.

Scary, but true, Brody thought.

Unexpectedly, the chairman of the joint chiefs of staff arrived in the Oval Office. He approached the president with an urgent stride. General Teasdale halted before his commander-in-chief for a military salute.

Atwood studied his face and said, "Clarence, you look like you've just buried your best friend. Was my speech that bad?"

"Sir, we appear to have another crisis. China is positioning to invade Taiwan. The defense secretary has been briefed and is on his way back to Washington now."

"How serious?" Atwood asked.

"This has the potential to become very serious," the general responded.

"What about diplomatic efforts?"

"The secretary of state is already working on it, to no avail." Deep furrows formed on Teasdale's brow. "Sir, it might take a show of force to stave off this one."

As the president processed the information, Spence Carlyle turned to one of his aides and authorized a media leak. "This couldn't have come at a better time," he whispered. His eyes were pinned on Brody. "This is just what we need to take the media focus off the economic mess."

A few yards away, the general pressed the president for a plan of action.

"Call up the National Security Council to get their advice," Atwood said. "Have the Pacific fleet on standby. We may need to do a little saber-rattling in the Formosa Strait."

Chapter 35

Great River Road

Monday, October 1st

"Ever been up Great River Road?" Zeke asked as the Rambler station wagon sputtered and coughed.

Joel shot a look at the old man as they headed north. "I don't think so."

"Don't think so? You're in for a real treat, kid!"

Still on the outskirts of New Orleans, traffic slowed to a bumper-to-bumper crawl.

"Everybody's always trying so hard to get somewhere," the old man said philosophically. "I'm content to be right here."

Joel was staring at the Rambler's gas gauge. "You're almost out of gas. There's a station up ahead."

"Don't trust everything your eyes tell you, kid." Zeke gave the dashboard an affectionate pat. "She gets great gas mileage."

Someone blasted a car horn. Angry mouths gnashed in frustration, and an impatient motorist drove up on a sidewalk to avoid the bottleneck.

"Yup, like I said, everybody's in a hurry." Zeke whistled softly through his teeth.

"Mind if I turn on the radio?"

"Suit yourself, kid."

Joel turned the retro knob until he found a station.

"Faith is the substance of things unseen, the evidence of things hoped for. . . ."

He tried another.

"The nation's economic future is uncertain in the wake of. . . ."

The teenager gave up on radio and turned it off. "I think you need to get your antenna replaced."

"Really? It suits me fine except for all that news."

"So why are you going to North Dakota?" Joel asked.

"Didn't have anything better to do." The old man grinned. "Besides, I promised a woman up there in God's country that I'd be back to settle up on some business. I gave her my word, so I aim to keep it."

Joel leaned back for the ride, grateful for every mile that carried him farther from Florida.

"Whenever you get hungry, there's a cooler in the back loaded with bagels, cream cheese, and orange soda. Oh, yeah, if you have a hankering for protein, there's a bag of teriyaki jerky in the glove box—no MSG."

The teenager rummaged behind the driver's seat and came up with a small cooler. He popped the top on the soda and gulped down half a can.

"Don't be shy—there's plenty more where that came from."

Joel found a plastic knife in the bottom of the cooler and

spread a healthy dollop of cream cheese on a bagel. He offered to make one for Zeke.

"Naw." The old man rubbed his belly. "I'm watching my girlish figure."

The teenager ate his snack like a hungry pup and washed it down with the rest of his soda. "It'll be faster if you take the interstate," Joel said as they neared an on-ramp.

"I'm not in any hurry. Are you, kid?" Zeke's fuzzy eyebrows arched. "Besides, haven't you heard? Friends don't let friends drive interstates! We'll just meander up the Great River Road until we turn onto another. I figure we'll get there when we arrive."

The traffic opened up, and Zeke pushed on the throttle and loped the old wagon up to a brisk forty-five miles per hour. "Now this is more like it," he said, rolling down the window.

Joel caught glimpses of the mighty river through the dense stand of trees. Before long, the view opened up to the nation's largest waterway. A blue heron flapped its graceful wings, and Joel watched it glide along the glassy surface and settle in a grassy swamp.

"The Ojibwa Indians named it the Misi-ziibi, meaning 'Great River,'" Zeke said. "The name stuck."

Joel fell into a brooding silence as they traveled. Behind him was a past he wanted to forget. Before him was an uncertain future.

The sun had set when Zeke left the main road and drove past a sign. "Welcome to New Roads, Louisiana." The old man motored through the small town and pulled up outside a narrow stick building.

The name MABEL MAY'S was painted on a weathered sign illuminated by a naked light bulb.

"I can smell Creole shrimp gumbo ten miles away," Zeke said and hopped from the car like a child.

He beckoned to the teenager.

"I'm not very hungry," Joel said, sinking his hands into the empty pockets of his jeans. "I'll wait in the car."

"Nonsense! You haven't lived 'til you've tasted this heavenly cuisine." Zeke's white beard swayed in the sultry breeze, and he wagged his finger. "I'm warning you, kid—I got money, and I know how to use it!"

A couple of black men loitered near the door, eyeballing the travelers as they approached.

"Evening, fellas." One stared, and the other just shifted a toothpick in his mouth.

"Talkative bunch," Zeke said as they stepped inside. The place was narrow like a train car, with a long counter down the middle and a tiny fry kitchen off to one side.

Zeke slapped his hand on the counter and hollered Mabel May's name.

A woman with a colorful orange-and-purple scarf poked her head from the small steamy kitchen. "Well, I'll be a river boat captain!"

Mabel May was a huge woman with skin the color of rich coffee beans. She leaned her massive bosoms across the counter and squeezed both of Zeke's hands in hers. "Honey darlin', you've just blessed this ol' fluffy woman's evenin'!"

"Told you I'd be back to collect that second helping of shrimp Creole you promised."

Mabel May summoned a lanky patron with a crisp snap

of her fingers. "Hey, Jamal, be a darlin' and run the kitchen for a spell."

The man jumped up, lifted a gated section of the countertop, and traded places with the cook.

Mabel May swallowed Zeke with a hug. "We've got some catchin' up to do. Tell ya what—it's a nice, warm evenin', so I'll grab your plates and meet you and your young friend out back."

Behind the restaurant, the old man and teenager settled at a picnic table and listened to the bullfrogs croak. Joel spotted a bat swooping past a yard light.

The back door of the diner opened and Mabel May filled the threshold with her girth. She waddled across the lawn carrying steaming bowls of shrimp Creole.

Mabel May set the meals in front of her guests and plopped down on the bench beside Joel. The wood creaked under her weight. Her smiling, almond eyes shifted to the teenager, and proper introductions were exchanged.

Joel turned his sights on the heaping bowl in front of him. He shoveled a spoonful into his mouth before realizing the old man's head was bowed in prayer.

"Dear Lord, thank you for the hands that prepared this meal." Zeke opened his eye to peek at Joel. "Bless this food and all that is within us! Amen."

Mabel May pulled a wad of napkins from her sleeve and handed them to her guests. "Remember that grandbaby of mine?"

"How's little Leesha doing?" Zeke asked, mopping a dribble of sauce from his beard.

The proud grandma patted a popsicle-stick cross that

was tied around her neck with colorful yarn. “She made this ’specially for her nana.”

Zeke admired the necklace. “You may be raising a future artist.”

His words brought a contented smile to Mabel May’s face. “You remember what you said about faith? Well, it’s true. If you got the real thing, just a little itty bit will do. A lot can happen if we just trust the good Lord and wait on him to work things out.”

Joel scraped up the remains of his meal and listened as the cook prattled on.

“I seen some miracles since you was last here,” Mabel May told Zeke. “Leesha’s mama put herself through rehab. That’s right, my daughter has sworn off crack. She’s goin’ to church and learning to be a certified nurse’s aide!”

“Praise the Lord!” the old man hollered.

All this God talk was making Joel uncomfortable. He thanked Mabel May for the meal, mumbled something about being tired, and wandered back toward the Rambler.

“Don’t roll your sleepin’ bags out on the grass,” Mabel May warned, “’cause the chiggers’ll eat you alive!”

Virginia

Tuesday, October 2nd

It was 2:45 AM when Brody arrived home. He found Paige asleep in a den chair. Connor was lying in her arms, his mouth agape and drooling.

Brody looked at his wife with a mixture of love and regret. Part of him wanted to wake her with an embrace, but he dreaded the confrontation that was sure to follow.

The quick message that he'd left on the answering machine left him feeling hollow. Brody longed to tell Paige that he loved her. Most of all, he needed reassurance that she still loved him.

Lately, Paige had brushed aside all his efforts, calling them leftovers or empty placations. *Who can blame her?* Brody thought. *At the end of each day, there's little left to give.*

He reached out and tenderly touched his wife's cheek.

Paige opened her eyes and frowned.

"I'm sorry about everything, honey. It's just. . . . There's a lot going on right now."

Brody waited for a response from his wife, but her lips pressed together in silence. She turned her face toward the wall.

In a gesture of defeat, Brody raised his hands and let them drop at his side. "It's been a long day," he said, trudging up the stairs toward the bedroom.

"I'm taking Connor off the medication," Paige announced. Her tone was defiant.

Brody turned on the stairs. "Just like that?" He felt his jaw clench. "Have you forgotten that Connor is my son, too? I forbid you to tamper with his medication!"

Paige wiggled carefully from under their sleeping boy and padded to the bottom of the steps. "You *forbid* me?"

"That's right," Brody challenged. "Where's your medical degree?"

"I may not be a doctor, but I *am* a mother. The side effects are worse than the illness!" she challenged back.

Brody turned away.

Chapter 36

Great River Road
Tuesday, October 2nd

The bottoms of his shoes were slick with blood, and he fell. His mother lay near the kitchen table, her hands shredded with defensive wounds. He scrambled to his feet and saw the knife in the sink. Without thinking, he turned on the faucet as his mother's lifeless eyes looked on.

"Wake up, kid, you're having a nightmare!" Zeke rapped on the window of the station wagon, yanked open the car door and leaned inside. "Besides, you gotta take a gander at this beautiful sunrise. You'll kick yourself in the pants if you miss it."

Joel's heart was still thumping from the dream when he climbed from the car and followed the line of the old man's finger. Brilliant hues of crimson, orange, and purple fanned the horizon.

Zeke stood, casting a sublime look toward the heavens. When the colors faded, he patted his chest and said, "Gets to me every time!"

In the morning light things looked different. Zeke and

Joel watched a flock of ducks land upon the water behind Mabel May's restaurant.

Something isn't right, the teenager thought. And then he realized what it was. "When did we cross the Mississippi?"

"We didn't."

"Quit messin' with me! Last night, the river was on our right; now it's on our left."

Zeke held up a finger. "Ah, but remember, things aren't always what they appear to be!" He flashed a mischievous smile. "You're lookin' at a big puddle that was left behind when the grand old river changed course. This is called the False River."

"Hotcakes on the grill!" Mabel May yelled through the screened-in porch.

"There's two kinds of people—the quick and the hungry!" Zeke said as he hurried to the diner for breakfast.

Mabel May was humming an old-time spiritual. "Mornin', campers! I figured you'd be up with the sun, so I came in early." The woman's kind eyes danced with joy as she placed the flapjacks and a jug of warm maple syrup on the counter.

This time, Joel waited for the prayer before drowning his pancakes in syrup.

After breakfast, Mabel May wrapped the travelers in her ample embrace and sent them on their way with full bellies.

Zeke burst into song as they drove north along the Mississippi.

Ol' man river—
Dat ol' man river,
He mus' know sumpin',

But don't say nuthin',
He jes keeps rollin'–
He jes keeps rollin' along!

The old man drummed his fingers on the wheel and glanced at his passenger. "Come on, let's have a sing-along!"

Joel shook his head and stared at the open road. He was beginning to wonder if it had been a mistake to hitch a ride with this strange, ancient man.

North Dakota

Tuesday, October 2nd

Nora's tidy little farmhouse had come unraveled. Toys were strewn about and clothes were heaped on the floor below the washing machine. Yet Nora had never felt happier.

From the bathroom, she could hear Brooke from the next room giggling at cartoons—sounds almost swallowed by the classic rock station that Lindsay had cranked up, saying, "Music helps me get in touch with my creative side."

The chemical odor of perm still hung in the air, and Nora's scalp burned slightly as Lindsay leaned in, scissors snipping.

Nora tried to sneak a peek in the bathroom mirror but was scolded.

"You'll see soon enough!" The young mother riffled through clutter and found a little round brush. Lindsay, armed with a blow dryer, sang along to Van Morrison's "Brown Eyed Girl."

Nora's heart skipped a beat. It had been years since

she'd heard that song, and it took her back to the time when her lost love sang it to her. "You will always be my brown-eyed girl," Jimmy used to say.

"How come you never had kids of your own?" Lindsay asked as she worked.

Nora changed the subject. "You're very talented at working with hair."

"Yeah, all's I need is five grand for beauty school."

"You're young. I'm sure you'll find a way."

"Almost done!" Lindsay announced.

Piles of snipped hair lay on the bathroom floor. Nora raised a nervous hand to her head. "It feels so much lighter."

"Trust me. You're gonna love it!" Lindsay made some last-minute touches with the straightening iron, rubbed a dab of hair product between her hands, and ran her fingers through Nora's hair. "Okay, get ready to be dazzled."

Nora turned to the mirror and blinked in disbelief.

"What do you think?"

A short, wavy style framed Nora's face. Subtle highlights warmed her mousy hair and brought out her brown eyes. "Is that really me in the mirror?"

"You look at least ten years younger," Lindsay puffed. "Are you sure I can't add a touch of foundation?"

Nora shook her head and repeated herself when Lindsay tried to coax her with some mascara.

After a quick lesson on styling, Lindsay announced that she was going to the living room to catch up on her favorite soap opera.

Nora shook out the towel that covered her shoulders and grabbed a broom and swept up hair clippings. She pushed the counter clutter into the trash bin and glanced at her watch. "Gertie agreed to open the Bargain Bin today, but I don't want to take advantage. We really should be heading into town soon!"

Lindsay was looking out the picture window when Nora breezed in to grab her coat. "That guy is delivering another truckload of wood. You don't even own a woodstove."

"Chuck and Pepper Tilden are tenants who have fallen on hard times. This is their way of paying rent," Nora explained. "Besides, we can always use firewood over at the Bargain Bin."

Lindsay plopped down on the couch. "Would it bother you if Brooke and I hung out here today?"

"Aren't you feeling well?"

The teenager stretched and yawned. "I just need a break, that's all."

"Okay." Nora searched for her car keys and found them under a stack of magazines. "It would be a good time to work on your mountain of laundry. I'll pick up another bottle of detergent in town."

"Could you bring home some more soda and chips?" Lindsay called as Nora slipped out the door.

Chapter 37

Virginia
Tuesday, October 2nd

Paige stared at the TV as the same headline news stories recycled again. The Taiwanese crisis had now become the lead story, but the exodus of foreign investors from US markets was still being assessed by the media's panel of experts. An interview with Chief Economic Advisor Brody Hays was replayed over and over.

Seeing her husband on television only salted Paige's wounds, especially since their early morning argument. "You always shut me out!" What she'd meant to say was, "I want to be a part of your world, and I need you to be a part of mine." Brody had walked out the door without a response.

Now, Paige watched her husband deflect reporters' questions, showing them the same stony face he had used on her.

She scrolled through the channels and stopped on an old movie network. *Gone with the Wind* was showing.

"What shall I do?" Scarlett O'Hara whined.

Rhett Butler's famous response followed. "Frankly, my

dear, I don't give a damn."

The sentiment was familiar to Paige. *Gone is hope, and peace is as elusive as the wind.*

The phone rang on the table beside the couch, and Paige looked at the caller ID. It was Brody.

She let the telephone ring until the answering machine picked up.

"Honey, listen, I'm sorry about this morning. We'll talk."

The obligatory phone call was no longer enough to hold their tattered marriage together.

Her thoughts turned to her son, who would be waking soon from his late morning nap. She moved to the kitchen to prepare him a peanut butter sandwich and a glass of milk. Paige headed upstairs to check on him.

The racecar bed was empty, and his favorite blanket lay crumpled on the floor.

Remain calm, Paige told herself as she searched the house. *It's not the first time Connor has hidden himself, especially after his morning dose of medication.* She looked everywhere a five-year-old could hide—except the basement.

Quickly, Paige descended the carpeted stairs, calling out. The sliding glass door in their walk-out basement was open. A tingle of fear crept across her flesh.

"Time for lunch!" Paige's eyes scanned the woods behind their house. "Connor!" Paige yelled, anxiety giving way to full-blown panic.

Somewhere in the neighborhood, a lawnmower rumbled; a squirrel chattered. There was no response from her son.

Maternal instinct took over as Paige's mind raced through all the potential dangers. She thought of the Potomac River, just a half-mile away. Propelling her legs over fallen branches and weeds, Paige crossed a small creek, sliding on the mud, and then made her way down the trail that joined with an old dirt road leading to the Potomac River. "Please, Lord, please."

Blood coursed through her veins as Paige slowed to speak with some dog walkers. "Have you seen a little boy?" They shook their heads, and she sprinted past them.

The picnic site near the river was empty, and Paige felt mildly relieved. It wasn't the first time she had overreacted.

Connor is probably swinging at the neighborhood playground. Maybe he's back at the house wondering where his lunch is. Her thoughts brought little comfort.

Then, something near the river's edge caught Paige's eye. It was one of Connor's sandals. In the next moment, she was standing over them, not knowing how she got there. Emily's face flashed before her eyes, her hair tangled in moss, her skin blue and cold.

Paige's knees gave out, and she wailed, "Not again!"

"Don't cry, Mom." A tiny hand touched her shoulder.

Like a miracle, Connor was in her arms, bringing forth a rush of sweet relief. "Why did you come down to the river when you know how much it scares me?" Paige sobbed.

"I don't know." The boy's lip quivered. "I'm sorry, Mom. I don't want to be bad anymore."

She stroked his red hair. "It's okay, sweetheart. I'm going to help you."

A plan began to form. In Paige's mind, she no longer had a choice.

Great River Road

Tuesday, October 2nd

Zeke parked the old Rambler on the St. Francisville Auto Ferry and emerged to revel in the misty morning beauty. Joel stayed in the car as the slow-moving platform inched its way across the river. He was nursing a bad mood.

The old man, on the other hand, had acquainted himself with most of the passengers. By the time the ferry docked on the other side, Zeke knew each by name, and they parted like old friends.

North of St. Francisville, Zeke asked, "Ever tried catfish, hushpuppies, and fried dill pickles?"

Joel shook his head and waited for the punch line.

"It's settled!" The old man slapped a hand on the steering wheel. "'Cause you can't roll through Natchez without a nibble."

Joel shrugged. "I'm just along for the ride."

After having crossed into the State of Mississippi, Highway 61 veered away from the river. The Rambler loped over farmland and through patches of timber stands and then skirted along the edge of a national forest.

As they neared Natchez, Zeke started humming the tune for "Ol' Man River," and Joel came close to yelling at him to stop. Then, a breathtaking view of the grand Mississippi opened up, complete with barges and river boats.

The restaurant, called the Paddle Wheel, was nestled in a touristy area of Natchez near a wide expanse of river. The building was rustic, and the interior was more of the same, with shiplap siding and cypress flooring.

A young hostess escorted the travelers to a heavy wooden table with blocky seats and handed them a brown-paper menu.

"Catfish, hushpuppies, and fried dill pickles?" Joel looked up from the menu. "That's all they have in this place?"

"What can I say?" The old man grinned. "A winning combination is hard to beat."

The waitress arrived with two mason jars of sweet tea, and Zeke ordered the River Boat Special, which was one of everything on the menu.

The teenager stared at the crude timber rafters while the old man reminisced about the first time he'd ever come through Natchez.

The catfish and fried pickles came on tin platters and the hushpuppies in a cast iron skillet that the waitress tossed before placing on the table.

Joel casually studied the mysterious little man as he ate. *Who is he? Where is he from?* The teenager's curiosity was tempered by his own secrets. *Don't ask, don't tell,* he decided.

"What do you think about the fried pickles?"

Joel took another bite. "Not bad." To his surprise, he meant it.

When the meal was over, the old man paid the bill, leaving a generous tip, and they returned to the car feeling full and sleepy.

Zeke looked skyward at the dark clouds that roiled overhead. "Looks like a storm is brewing."

Forty minutes later the rain was falling hard and the Rambler had slowed to a crawl, its windshield wipers slapping wildly. “Makes me think of Noah,” Zeke said, squinting through the deluge.

“Maybe we should pull over?” Joel suggested.

“Great idea!” the old man said as the tires sliced through a deep puddle. “We’d better head for higher ground, because these storms have been known to make the river swell.”

Just over a series of hills they spotted a pullout and parked beside a driverless Mercedes sedan.

“Hope you brought along some reading material,” the old man said.

Joel considered the Bible given to him by Daryl Capps that was still in his backpack. “I don’t read much.”

“Think I’ll just close my eyes ’til the storm blows over.” Zeke settled back on his seat, unruffled by waves of rolling thunder. Before long, the old man began to snore, fluttering strands of long white beard with each breath.

Joel tried to take a nap, but his legs twitched from pent-up energy. Raindrops slithered down the windshield, and the teenager watched their tracks. *I’m bored,* he thought, and he began to imagine sounds, intermittent pounding followed by muffled yells. After a few moments, Joel rolled the car window down and cocked his ear to listen more carefully.

The noises were coming from the abandoned Mercedes. “Zeke, wake up!”

The old man sat upright. “What’d’ya say?”

“Do you hear that?” There was a definite banging sound coming from the car.

Zeke stepped out into the storm. “What we have here is a divine appointment!”

Pummeled by sheets of rain, the travelers circled the

Mercedes.

The old man leaned his ear to the trunk and knocked. "Hello! Anybody home?"

Someone pounded back from the inside.

The Mercedes's doors were unlocked. The teenager located the release button and, like a jack-in-the-box, a man popped from the trunk. His hands were bound with a belt, and his mouth was covered with duct tape.

Zeke quickly removed the restraints.

The man thanked him. "I was beginning to think I'd never get out!"

"Mister, those are some nasty bruises on your face," Zeke noted.

"I stopped to help some young motorists. When I leaned over to have a look at their motor, I was hit from behind." He reached to the back of his head, withdrawing a bloodied hand.

"That's quite a goose egg you got there." Zeke helped the victim from the trunk and over to the Rambler.

"They took my wallet and my cell phone. My name is Robert Heinz. Could you call my wife? She'll be worried."

"I don't own a cell phone," Zeke said, "but I'm sure somebody over in Vicksburg will give her a jingle."

Zeke drove faster than usual, even in the rain. Winding up the Great River Road, he made cheerful small talk with their newest passenger. "So what brought you out and about today?"

"I'm a shipping consultant," the man drawled. "I was called out to advise some clients along the Mississippi River. Everybody's nervous about this economic mess. Did you know that 60% of our grain exports travel down the

Mississippi?" The victim's words came out slightly slurred. "What is happening to our country?" He touched his head wound and cringed.

"Only God can answer that question. Hang on partner!" The old man slowed as they passed a City of Vicksburg sign. He spotted a hospital marker and tossed a quick look in Joel's direction. "Make sure our new friend stays awake."

"So, do you have any kids, Mr. Heinz?" Joel asked.

A weak smile formed on the man's face. "Two daughters. The youngest is in college. Danced at my firstborn's wedding last year. I'm going to be a grandpa." Robert's eyes fluttered like they were about to close. "I'm feeling tired."

"When's the baby due?" Joel blurted.

The victim seemed dazed.

The Rambler circled an institutional building and lurched to a stop in front of the emergency room.

The teenager dove from the passenger seat, burst through the automatic doors, and yelled for help.

They stayed just long enough to hear a good report.

"Mr. Heinz was fortunate that you came along when you did," the doctor told Zeke. He pointed to a policeman who was standing nearby. "We notified the authorities about the assault, and this officer would like a word with you."

Joel's heart rate picked up as the man stepped forward to take a statement from Zeke. "Is there a number where you can be reached?" the officer asked when he was finished.

"Afraid not," Zeke said. "Don't own a phone and the car's my only residence."

The policeman's brows kissed in a scowl, and his eyes

moved from the old man to the teenager.

Joel sunk his sweaty palms into his jean pockets and shook his head.

The officer settled for the old man's license plate number and then sent the travelers on their way.

"Race you to the elevator!" Zeke challenged the teenager.

Joel won and was just about to punch the button when the doors sliced open and a woman with a fur coat stepped out. She stared at the old man clad in his Hawaiian shirt and oversized shorts; then her gaze landed on Joel. "Are you the two angels who saved my husband?"

"Naw, God's the only one who's in the business of saving. We just happened to show up," Zeke said.

"Well, you're fabulous to do what you did, and I want to show my appreciation!" The woman snapped open her pocketbook, produced a credit card, and pressed it into the old man's palm. "This is a Best Motorway Guest Pass. I'm Gloria Heinz, and my father owns the franchise."

"Actually, I'm into camping." Zeke grinned. "Still working on my Boy Scout merit badge!"

The joke flew right over the woman's head. She flicked her wrist. "I don't care what you do with the pass. Give it away if you like." Mrs. Heinz said as she sashayed through the doors marked INTENSIVE CARE.

Before leaving town, Zeke took a detour through the Vicksburg National Military Park. "Since we're in the neighborhood, we might as well poke around."

They walked along a trail in the southern corner of the park, stopping to read the historic markers. "Vicksburg was once a center of commerce and agriculture, and a strategic Confederate stronghold during the Civil War," the sign read.

Zeke pointed out the river's sharp bend. "A few years after the war ended the Mississippi changed course and turned away from Vicksburg. The town hasn't been the same ever since."

A few droplets of rain began to fall. Another line of clouds were forming, so they decided to press on.

By late afternoon, the sun came out and they rode in silence until Joel could take it no more. He tried the radio again—nothing but gospel and news.

"How's your gas supply?" The teenager asked when they passed another gas station.

"Still half full." The old man grinned.

Skirting around Memphis, Tennessee, Joel spotted a Best Motorway Motel and suggested they stop for the night.

"Now why would we do that when we can camp out under the stars?"

Zeke drove through a maze of city streets and popped onto a back road. Fifteen miles north of Memphis, he turned into a campground. "Did I mention that I just got a couple brand new sleeping bags that need breaking in?"

Joel started a fire, and the old man rustled around in the back of the Rambler and came up with a couple beach chairs and a small tent.

They roasted brauts on some willow sticks and sipped coffee from tin cups as the sun went down. The evening passed like the gentle river beside which they traveled.

"Nothing like roughing it, eh, kid? What do you say we stay here a couple a' nights?" Zeke cracked open a box of

Hostess Ding Dongs for dessert.

Joel looked up at the clear night sky. "There must be a billion stars up there."

"God knows exactly how many there are." Zeke brushed crumbs from his fingers. "It says in the Book of Isaiah that he has called each star by name, and not one is missing!"

"You really believe that?"

"Yup." The old man poured another cup of coffee into his tin mug. "What about you?"

Joel shrugged. "If I were God, I'd destroy this whole messed-up world and start over again." He jabbed a stick at the fire, sending embers airborne.

"It may come to that someday," Zeke said, "but in the meantime, I'm sure glad you're not God. He's mighty patient, and you never know—hard times might just change folks for the better!"

Soon, quiet hour settled over the campers as an owl hooted from a treetop. A toddler fussed somewhere, and the sound of snoring issued from a nearby tent.

Joel lay in his sleeping bag, gazing up at the stars of heaven. He wondered if God also knew his name.

Chapter 38

Virginia

Wednesday, October 3rd

Paige glanced over her shoulder and smiled at her little son, who was bouncing with excitement in his car seat. He had his father's smile. "It won't be much longer, sweetheart. We're almost there."

Her heart ached at the thought of causing her husband pain. Paige reminded herself that she had no other option. *Connor's future is at stake—maybe even his life*.

She turned on the radio, hoping for a diversion but finding only bad news. "The situation in the Formosa Strait is escalating. . . ." Paige switched it off, preferring silence.

The narrow road wound through a tunnel of trees, inching closer to the highway. The view opened up to rolling hills and hunt-country farms. She drove past the tiny village of Paris, Virginia, and its quaint, historic bed and breakfast. Just last year, Brody had surprised her on their anniversary with a weekend at the Ashby Inn.

"You're the love of my life," he'd told her as they watched the sunset over the Blue Ridge foothills.

Paige pushed on the throttle. The road wound toward the Big Meadows Lodge. The leaves were just beginning to turn, promising a spectacular fall showing. It seemed to Paige that winter had already come to her soul. She felt cold and stripped, like a naked tree shivering against a slate sky.

"I see it!" Connor pitched forward in his car seat and pointed. "I see the big cabin!"

"Honey, it's called a lodge," Paige explained. "That means we'll have to share it with other people." A disappointed look crossed her little boy's face, so she quickly added, "But we'll have our own room."

Connor looked thoughtful. "Is Daddy going to meet us here?"

Paige opted not to respond as they pulled up in front of the office.

She released Connor from his car seat. "Last one inside is a rotten egg!"

As they waited at the front desk, Paige casually observed her son. It had been almost a full day since she had weaned Connor from his medication. Except for a small facial tremor, he seemed normal.

"Reservation for two?" the desk clerk asked.

"Yes." Paige paid him with cash and glanced at the wall clock behind the desk.

Unless Brody is working late again, he will be heading home in a few hours. Sadness engulfed Paige at the thought of her husband wandering the empty house, only to discover the note that she had placed upon his pillow.

Arizona

Wednesday, October 3rd

The road to Hope Springs had been beaten down by the steady flow of traffic. Almost overnight, a village on wheels had sprung up beneath a soft cloud of dust.

"Everybody in Arroyo Seco is talking about it." Elita swept a pile into a dustbin. "I heard the pavilion is nearly finished." She cocked her head toward her husband, who was busy checking the inventory for reorder.

David nodded, but the whole thing still made him uneasy. *Who are these people, anyway?*

The Bales family barreled through the front door, filling the atmosphere with their usual family chaos. "We're moving over to Hope Springs with the rest of the great unwashed." Randy slapped a thank-you card on the counter. "There's a check enclosed to cover our expenses"

Elita wandered over. "Is it true they're putting in some kind of fancy water system at Hope Springs?"

"Yeah, they got the idea from studying the way they conserve water over in the desert of Oman." Randy anchored his cap on his head. "I volunteered to help."

Kay Bales motioned for her kids, who came forward with a colorful crayon masterpiece. "Missy and Robert made this for you," she said as they presented the artwork to Elita.

"I drew the picture!" Robert blurted. "All Missy did was color it."

"Uh-uh!" The girl bristled. "Liar, liar, pants on fire!"

Elita admired the primitive artwork. "It's absolutely

beautiful!"

"That's you." The boy pointed to a smiling stick-figure woman with long black hair and a colorful skirt.

"Me?" Elita looked puzzled. "But why is there a baby in my arms?"

Robert scowled at his sister and said, "I told you not to put a baby in the picture!"

"I thought you'd be a really nice mommy," Missy said, sticking her tongue out at her brother.

Elita's eyes misted. "That's one of the sweetest things anyone has ever said to me. I'm going to find a very special place to hang this." She turned away and hurried up the stairs to the apartment.

The Bales family scrambled out the door and into their motor home, leaving David alone in the General Store.

All was quiet, except for the hum of the ice cream cooler, the squeak of the ceiling fan, and the sound of Elita weeping overhead.

Chapter 39

Washington, DC
Wednesday, October 3rd

Brody rubbed his throbbing temples as he shuffled a mountain of data on his desk.

"You look terrible." Atwood stood in the doorway of Brody's office.

"I'm fine, sir."

The president wasn't convinced. "You know what they say, Hays—the difference between hope and despair is a good night's sleep. Maybe you should go home and get some rest."

"Sir, with all due respect. . . ."

Atwood held up his hand. "Not another word, Hays. The media is foaming at the mouth over the China and Taiwan crisis, so you have a golden opportunity to grab some rest. Go home, Hays. That's an order."

"Thank you, sir," Brody called as the president ambled away. After tending to a few last minute details, he did as he had been told.

Pain hammered in Brody's skull as he jockeyed with the other commuters on the beltway, but he did his best to ignore it. Paige would be surprised to see him, and he was bound and determined to make the most of the evening. Maybe tonight they could finally sit and talk things over.

On the radio, WTOP kicked in with their traffic report. A crash on the toll road had snarled things up ahead, so Brody bailed off on the Georgetown Pike, maneuvering over hilly roads past rolling estates and towering mansions. Brody's thoughts were on his marriage and his strategy to set things right. After a quick stop at a grocery store for a colorful bouquet of flowers, Brody steered into his quiet suburban neighborhood.

The garage was empty when Brody rolled inside. *Paige and Connor are probably at the grocery store,* he thought.

Brody tossed the newspaper on the entryway table. In the kitchen, he laid the bouquet of flowers near the sink and poured himself a tall glass of sweet tea.

The house was still. Brody settled back in his recliner to unwind.

Minutes ticked by. The shadows lengthened, and before long, Brody began to feel antsy.

He punched the speed dial on his Blackberry and waited for Paige to answer her cell phone. Her voicemail kicked in. "Honey, I'm home early," he said. "Where are you?"

Brody wandered over to the front window and waited. Finally, he climbed the stairs to hang his coat. Brody emptied his pockets and placed loose change on the butler at the end of the king-size bed. That's when he saw the letter lying on his pillow.

"I've taken Connor away for awhile. I believe it is in our son's best interests. Please, try to understand."

Brody read the words again and crushed the paper in his hand.

Great River Road
Thursday, October 4th

Joel awoke in the campground to find a little girl peering down at him.

"It's alive!" she shrieked, jumping back in mock horror as the teenager sputtered in surprise and scrambled from his sleeping bag.

The child wrinkled her nose. "Eww, you sleep in your clothes? Bet you're stinky!"

"Morning, kid!" Zeke, hunched over the campfire, waved his tongs. "I see you've met Jeannie!"

"I'm her mama, Martinique!" A woman sitting in one of their camp chairs flashed a wide, toothy smile. "Hope y'all don't mind. Mr. Zeke was kind enough to invite us over for some breakfast."

Joel was just about to respond when the girl poked an electronic game in his face. "Wanna play? Bet I can beat ya."

"Come and get it!" Zeke hollered, just in time to rescue Joel.

They gathered around the picnic table for link sausages and scrambled eggs.

Martinique volunteered to say grace, and her daughter clasped her hands in prayer. "Dear Lord, thank you for this meal that we're about to share, and especially for letting us run into Zeke and Joel. Amen."

When did the old man stop for breakfast supplies? Joel wondered. He was just about to ask when little Jeannie bragged, “We get to stay in a real motel tonight—with a TV and everything!”

Martinique’s eyes welled with tears. “You don’t know what this means to me. Now I’ll have a place to stay while I look for work.”

Joel had been looking forward to a hot shower and a bed. He shot Zeke a disapproving look but then spotted some purple bruises on the young mother’s arm and cheek. The teenager hung his head.

After saying goodbye to their guests, Zeke and Joel packed up camp and wandered over for a quick look at a swampy inlet.

Joel studied the oddly shaped trees that grew from the brackish water and tapered skyward.

“Those bad boys are called bald cypress,” Zeke volunteered. “Some can live up to a thousand years.”

It’s hard to believe anything could survive that long in this rotten world, Joel thought bitterly.

“There’s a scripture passage that compares God’s people to trees planted by a river. Makes me think of bald cypress.”

“Why are you always quoting the Bible?”

The old man’s bushy eyebrows shot up. “Doesn’t everybody?”

“No!”

“Well, then,” Zeke said with a wink, “some folks just don’t know what they’re missing!”

Chapter 40

Washington, DC

Thursday, October 4th

Brody had checked Paige's email, Facespace page, and their joint banking account before heading to work. There were no clues as to his family's whereabouts.

He punched a number into his cell and listened as it rang. A woman with a pleasant voice answered.

"General Store, Elita speaking."

Brody introduced himself and quickly added, "Congratulations on your marriage."

"I can't wait to meet you and Paige!" his new sister-in-law said.

So she isn't headed there, Brody thought. *Another dead end.*

"Hang on; David wants to talk to you."

"Hey, bro, it's been a long time."

"Too long." Brody took in a lungful of air. "I'm trying to find Paige and Connor. I was hoping that you might know where they are."

"Whoa! What's going on?"

"She's left me, David." There was a pause before his brother-in-law spoke.

"Do you mind if I ask why?"

"It's complicated." Brody swallowed hard. "Do you think she may have gone up to Finger Lakes?"

"It's doubtful."

Brody moved his blackberry to the other ear. "David, I want you to know that I never blamed you for what happened there." The statement was met with silence. "I'm pulling up to the White House security gate. If you hear from Paige, would you give me a call?"

In the West Wing, Chip Skinner had called another urgent staff meeting. Everyone had been summoned to the Situation Room, known among the White House personnel as "the woodshed."

Brody slipped past a handful of NSC officers loitering in the hallway. He took a seat at the long table and looked around at the paneled whisper walls and six flat screens for video conferencing.

The Situation Room began to fill as more staffers arrived. Finally, Chip Skinner stepped inside and announced the president's arrival.

Everyone stood as Thomas Atwood, General Teasdale, the national security chief, and the joint chiefs of staff took their places at the table.

Atwood motioned for everyone to be seated. "Let's get right down to the business." The president laced his fingers together in an attempt to hide the tremor in his hand and then nodded to an NSC officer poised at a computer terminal.

All six flat screens promptly flickered on, showcasing a

map of the Pacific.

General Teasdale cleared his gravely throat. "Ladies and gentlemen, after exhaustive diplomatic efforts, the situation between China and Taiwan has remained unresolved. As a result, further measures are necessary. Our Pacific fleet has been deployed to the Formosa Strait as a warning to these nations." The general paused for effect. "Russia has agreed to stand with us, and their warships have also been dispatched."

The staff was given a strict admonition to treat the matter with discretion. As far as the media was concerned, this was to be nothing more than a peacekeeping operation.

After the meeting was dismissed, the president asked Brody to remain behind for a private word.

"I'd like to run something past you," he began when they were alone in the room. The president gathered his thoughts and then said, "What I'm about to share with you may sound odd, so I'm asking you to keep it just between us."

"Of course, sir, you have my word."

Atwood nodded. "Hays, do you recall me mentioning a reoccurring dream? It was more like a nightmare, actually."

"Yes." Brody tried not to appear surprised. "Sir, I'm hardly qualified—"

"I realize this isn't part of your job description, Hays." The president's tone carried a ring of desperation.

"I'm listening, sir."

"Do you believe in prophecy?"

Brody was considering his response when they were interrupted by a rap on the door. The chief of staff strode back into the Situation Room along with Spence Carlyle.

Atwood was visibly annoyed.

"Sir, we need to talk." The president's political advisor looked down his nose at Brody and added, "It's of a personal nature."

"Hays can stay right where he is," Atwood snapped.

"Very well." Carlyle chewed his lip. "A damaging story has just surfaced."

"Cut to the chase, Carlyle!"

"I believe you are acquainted with a woman named Nora Meyers."

The president nodded. "She was a close friend to my late brother."

"A tabloid journal has acquired a letter penned by Ms. Meyers, and it is addressed to you by name. It was purportedly written many years ago, yet never sent." Spence Carlyle pulled a paper from his breast pocket. "I have a copy."

He slipped on his readers and began:

> Dear Tom,
>
> This is the most difficult letter I've ever had to write. Shame and regret have been my constant companions since that night. No one is to blame for what happened. We were both overcome with sorrow over our mutual loss, and we found comfort in each other's arms. It doesn't make it right. It was a moment of weakness that would best be forgotten, except for one thing—I am with child.
>
> After months of soul-searching, I have decided to place my baby in a loving home. I've found a measure of peace knowing this child will be raised

with the nurture of a complete family.

Tom, you are a good man, and I hope and pray that this knowledge will not bring you pain.

Nora

They waited for the president's response. The room grew still—quiet enough to hear the sound of breathing. Atwood's stare was distant, and his face was pale.

Carlyle cleared his throat. "Sir, I recommend a swift campaign to discredit this woman. We can chalk it all up to dirty campaigning."

The president shook his head. "Get Nora Meyers on the phone."

"But sir," the president's political advisor said, "this response would send the wrong message and give the whole story credibility!"

"Find her number, ASAP!"

Spence Carlyle promptly left to do as he was told.

From the threshold of the Situation Room, Chip Skinner cast a worried look back before he closed the door behind him.

The president began to shake so violently that Brody reached out to steady him. "Are you all right, sir?"

There was a strange look in Atwood's eyes. "No, Hays. I am not all right!"

North Dakota
Thursday, October 4th

Nora looked up from the Bargain Bin's front desk as the postman came through the door and dropped a bundle on the counter. He hesitated before leaving. "You did something different with your hair! It suits you."

She blushed and busied herself with the mail. Aside from the usual junk mail, there were letters and cards from people as far away as Minot.

Gertie poked her head in from the storage room. "Where is J. J.? I could use some muscle back here."

"He's out making deliveries," Nora returned. "When Lindsay gets here, we'll all pitch in."

"That girl is always flitting about!" Gertie huffed, wandering over to help sort the mail.

"Well bless my socks!" The old woman pulled a twenty-dollar bill from one of the envelopes. "Another cash donation for the new heating unit."

Nora found more among the stacks of cards. "This renews my faith," she said, wiping a tear from her eye.

"Faith?" Gertie shook her head, "I used to go to a big church—nice new building, filled with Bible studies and programs. I attended them all, but there was one thing lacking."

"What was that?"

"God," the old woman snorted cynically.

"That's not fair!" Nora responded. "You can't speak for the whole congregation. Only God can look into a person's heart."

"You're right," Gertie conceded. "Still, it took those folks six whole months before they even realized that I wasn't sitting in the pews anymore."

"There are a lot of good churches in this world, but you won't find perfect people in any of them." Nora considered her own struggles with the Delmont Harvest Center. "We are all works in progress."

J. J. O'Shay burst through the front door, belting out a song. "The hills are alive with the sound of music!"

"Heaven help us!" Gertie yelped. "What's got you feelin' so froggy?"

"Do I need a reason?" He came around the counter, planted a kiss on the old woman's cheek, and gave Nora a squeeze. "Hey, what were Lindsay and her kid doing down at the bus station?" he asked. "Are they going somewhere?"

"I don't think so," Nora said.

The phone rang, and Gertie snatched it up. "Bargain Bin. Yeah, she's right here."

Nora took the receiver and listened to the man on the other end. Her mind was slow to process what he was saying, but then it hit her like a bomb. "No comment!" She slammed the receiver in its cradle and tried to stand, but her legs felt rubbery.

J. J. and Gertie rallied to her side. "What's wrong? What happened?" Their words sounded brassy.

Beads of cold sweat glistened on Nora's skin, and she grew faint. "I don't feel too good. I need to go home." She hurried out to her car.

At the farm, Nora went straight to her bedroom and scattered the contents of the Whitman's Sampler tin upon her bed. She searched frantically for the letter, but, just as she had feared, it was gone. *Lindsay probably sold it to a tabloid for beauty school tuition!*

"Oh, God!" Nora cried when she thought about what the president must be going through. *He doesn't deserve this*.

Otis jumped up and licked tears from Nora's face. Emotions swirled in her head like a tempest. *My shame is exposed to the whole world!* And then, the worst fear surfaced. *What if the media finds my son?* The normal life she'd hoped to give him would be over.

The phone rang. Nora let the answering machine pick up.

"White House calling. . . ."

She bolted into the next room and snatched the receiver from the cradle.

"I am trying to reach a Ms. Nora Meyers," the voice on the other end said.

"Speaking."

"Please hold for the President of the United States."

Nora's heart thundered in her chest as he came on the line. "Tom—you've got to believe me, I never meant for this to happen."

"Just tell me: is it true?" Atwood asked.

"You had just announced a run for state office when I found out that I was pregnant." Nora rubbed her forehead and sobbed, "I'm so sorry. I should have told you when he was born. I just never found the courage."

"We have a son?" There was a moment of silence. "Did you hold him?"

Tears rolled down Nora's cheeks. "He was a perfect baby."

"Where is he now?"

"I only know that he was adopted by a couple in Minot."

"A military family?"

Nora did not like where this was going. "Promise me you won't try to find him!"

"It may be out of my hands, Nora. There are disclosure laws."

Nora clutched the phone tight. *This isn't happening*.

"I'll keep you informed. In the meantime, try not to worry," Atwood said before hanging up.

The telephone rang again. This time it was Gertie. Her voice was urgent. "The media buzzards have landed. I just ran off a crowd of reporters. Heads up—there's a fleet of vehicles loaded with TV cameras, and they are heading your way!"

Nora grabbed her keys and the dog. They fled in the Chevy. She drove without a plan and found herself turning down a country road that she hadn't traveled in years.

Over some grassy hills and nestled low in a valley, an old stone barn came into view. Once used by a cattle ranch, the BLM had absorbed the property; now, its existence was known only to an occasional arrowhead hunter or to teenagers seeking a party haven.

Otis jumped from the car just as soon as the door opened. He bounced among the sagebrush sniffing for horned toads.

Nora approached the barn but stopped short of the door. She closed her eyes and let her recollections carry her back in time. It was here that Jimmy Atwood had taken her into his sinewy arms and asked her to be his bride. A precious memory now tainted by regrets.

Wind whistled briskly across the October sky, and Nora realized that she hadn't brought a jacket. She settled with her back against the building's sun-warmed cornerstone and began to pray. "God, help my child, wherever he may be."

Chapter 41

Virginia
Thursday, October 4th

The trail to Lewis Falls was steep and rocky, but Paige and Connor took it slowly, pausing to study the shelf lichen on a hollow stump.

Overhead, the turning leaves shimmered beneath a brilliant October sky. It was a beautiful, sunny afternoon—perfect weather for a hike.

"Be careful," Paige admonished as the boy rushed over to a big boulder and scaled its smooth surface with ease.

Connor had actually slept through the night, which meant that Paige had as well. She felt encouraged enough to dump the bottle of pills down the toilet.

"Come on, Mom, let's be mountain climbers!"

She opted instead to rest on a fallen log while Connor slid from the boulder and hurried on ahead.

"Honey, come back here!" Paige pushed her tired legs onward. It was her first hike to Lewis Falls, but the people at the lodge had told her it was safe. *Good thing*, she thought as Connor disappeared from view.

Past a marker and across a shallow creek, Paige tried to keep her anxiety in check as she scanned the terrain for her child.

A few steps later, Paige caught sight of Connor sitting on the stone wall of an overlook. She settled beside him, inhaled a lungful of misty air, and watched the waterfall spraying the rocks down below.

Lewis Falls was smaller than she had envisioned but still not disappointing. Paige laid her hand upon her son's shoulder and smiled. In that moment, life was good.

"We'd better hurry back to the lodge now, Mom."

"But we just got here."

"It's gonna rain—lightning and thunder, too!" Connor shimmied from the ledge and tugged on his mother's hand. "Come on, we'd better go."

Paige shook her head. "I looked at the weather report. It's going to be sunny all day."

Connor shook his head. "We're gonna get wet—you'll see." The words had barely left his mouth when a sudden breeze kicked up, tussling the boy's hair.

Overhead, a tiny cloud formed. It seemed to grow and thicken by the second. Suddenly, a bolt of lightning flashed above the canyon, followed by a crack of thunder.

"How did you know?"

"Cause the angel told me!" Connor called as he started down the trail.

Drops of rain mottled their path—rain that had not been forecast. *Could it really be true?* Paige asked herself. It was an incredible notion, yet now, beneath this unexpected deluge, it was the only explanation that seemed to fit.

Great River Road
Thursday, October 4th

When they passed through New Madrid, Missouri, Zeke told an interesting tale. "Back in the eighteen hundreds, a major earthquake rocked this town. Witnesses swear that the Mississippi River ran backwards for several hours."

Joel snorted. "Yeah, and I'm Robin Hood!"

"I'm not joking, kid. Just goes to show that some things are out of our control."

Further up the road, the travelers passed through some bottom farmland. Joel spotted a team of horses pulling a plow across a field. It was a throwback to another time. Dense stands of trees tinseled with Spanish moss hid the river from view, but every so often Joel would catch a glimpse of the muddy waters—a river that had once run backwards.

"Next stop, Hannibal, Missouri," Zeke announced. "Ever heard of Mark Twain?"

"He wrote Huckleberry Finn," Joel said, drawing on his English Lit lessons.

"That's right, kid. Samuel Clemens was his real name. He was born just a few miles up the road."

The old man practically idled down Main Street, pointing out the town's brick and stone facades and explaining that these were unchanged since the days when the famous author had lived there.

"Mark Twain had a unique way of seeing things," Zeke said. "He believed that clothes make a man because naked people have little or no influence on society. It's hard to argue with logic like that!"

They passed through Hannibal without stopping, which seemed odd to Joel. Zeke seemed in an uncharacteristic hurry to get somewhere. The travelers continued north past long shadows. The air grew frosty enough to produce a few snowflakes as the Rambler motored through the dusky countryside.

They made it to Le Claire, Iowa, just in time to see the old-fashioned streetlights flicker on. A fine powdering of snow dusted the village, making it look as cozy as a winter greeting card.

Zeke knew exactly where he was headed. He zigged and zagged through a series of backstreets, braking to a stop in front of an old Victorian house.

"Kid, you're about to meet Bella Louise Lancaster, one of the most beautiful women on the planet!" Zeke fluffed his beard, straightened his collar, dove into the back seat of the Rambler, and came up with a heart-shaped box of chocolates.

They hadn't gone five steps up the walkway when the front door flew open and a figure stepped beneath a wash of porch light.

Joel drew back in horror as the woman peered at the men through one good eye. Her face was hideously disfigured.

"Zeke, is that you?"

The old man hurried up the steps and spun her around in a joyful dance. When the reunion wound down, Zeke made introductions.

Bella Louise extended a shriveled stub with only the remnants of a thumb and finger. "It's a pleasure to meet you."

"Same." He took her hand reluctantly, lowering his gaze to see ten perfect toenails painted the color of lilac.

"It happened when I was eight years old," Bella Louise explained without a hint of bitterness. "I was in a house fire." She smiled. "Most people are too polite to ask, but I find it breaks the ice."

"Oh," Joel muttered. "That must have been awful."

"Adversity either makes us bitter or better," she returned.

"You're lookin' at the tractor pull champion of Le Claire—seven years straight!" Zeke's eyes twinkled. "Bella Louise is a legend around these parts."

She waved off the praise. "Don't listen to a word he says."

Zeke slipped the box of chocolates from his jacket. "I brought you a little something sweet."

"You shouldn't have!" Bella Louise giggled like a school girl. "But I'm glad you did!" She invited her guests inside and offered them beds for the night.

Bella Louise adjusted the wig that sat crooked on her head and passed around the box of chocolates.

Joel looked around at the beautifully decorated living room while Zeke and his old friend brought each other up to speed.

The more Bella Louise talked, the more she puzzled the teenager. She had a passion for opera and also for tractors. Bella Louise was an avid outdoorsman who had once shot and skinned a bear, yet her home was filled with feminine finery and lace. She played classical violin for town concerts, but in her spare time, Bella Louise was a referee at the local boxing club.

Zeke gazed at the woman as if smitten by her beauty. "You haven't changed a bit."

"I was going to say the same about you. How many years has it been?" she asked.

"I'd get out my calculator out, but the batteries are dead."

"Remember the county fair?" Bella Louise asked.

"How could I forget?" the old man hooted. "It rained so hard my cotton candy melted right in my hand!"

"I'm going to go get my photo album. I'll be right back."

Zeke jabbed the teenager. "Isn't she the prettiest little thing you ever laid eyes on?"

"I don't think you should make fun of her!" Joel scowled.

"What are you talking about?"

"Those hideous scars."

"Oh, is that all?" Zeke seemed relieved. "Listen, kid, you gotta learn to look at the heart if you want to see true beauty."

Bella Louise returned with a stack of scrapbooks, and the old friends drifted down memory lane. She looked up, catching Joel in a protracted yawn. "Poor boy, you must be exhausted! Where are my manners? There's a guestroom upstairs with two single beds. I'd be honored if you and Zeke would be my guests." Bella Louise's scarred lips stretched into a smile. "You can stay as long as you like!"

Zeke looked at his traveling companion. "What do ya say, kid? Let's stick around here a few days and knock off some of that road dust."

Arizona

Thursday, October 4th

David stood in the middle of Main Street weighted down by guilt—both past and present. He had ruined his sister's life, and there was nothing he could do that would make things right. Now, his wife wanted children, yet that was the one thing he was unwilling to give her.

Elita was inconsolable in her grief for the babies she would never hold.

Across the street, music and laughter pulsed like sonar from the Watering Hole Bar, and David's mouth felt dry. He took a step in the wrong direction but stopped when his ear detected the unmistakable sound of Harleys. A large group of bikers rolled around the bend and rumbled slowly down Arroyo Seco's primary artery, US flags fluttering from their handlebars. The Freedom Riders had arrived.

David stepped aside and held his hand out in the biker's salute. More than fifty riders had come for a week-long show of strength along the border. Some of the bikers looked familiar as they rumbled past. Most continued on through town looking for Arroyo Seco's only motel, a flea trap known as the Tumbleweed Inn.

A few Harleys braked to a stop in front of the Watering Hole. David kept his eye on one in particular, a squat, stocky man who wore a frayed Levi's vest with a map of Texas stitched across the back. The biker peeled off his helmet, ran a gloved hand over his long, braided hair, and looked around.

David grinned as their eyes met.

"Well, I'll be darned! Fillmore, I can't believe it!" The biker rocked his Harley onto the kickstand and wagged his beefy face. "I heard you had yourself a rough ride over in Tucson!"

"You haven't changed much, Hugo," David said. "You're still wearing that same dirty vest."

"Careful now, it was a gift from dear old Mom." Deep, throaty laughter burst from the biker's weathered lips. "There's a nasty rumor flying around. Word is you got hitched." Hugo gripped David's shoulder and ushered him into the bar. "First one's on me!"

David settled onto a barstool and didn't protest when his old friend ordered a couple shots of tequila with beer chasers.

"How are things going?" Hugo asked.

My career is going nowhere, my marriage is in trouble, my family won't speak to me, and I'm about to fall off the wagon. . . . "Fine," David said.

The bartender set two shot glasses beside a couple foamy mugs of pale ale.

"Remember when we rode from LA to New Orleans? Man, that was some party!" Hugo lifted the shot. "To wild times on the open road!"

The open road. David stared at the glass, feeling the lure of his past. *Go home and work things out,* he told himself.

Someone tapped David's shoulder, and he turned to see Gordon Spitzer swirling a half-empty glass of milk in his hand.

The head of the CBG was staring at the shot glass of tequila in front of David. "I didn't know you were a drinker.

Next round's on me."

"I'll pass." David's instinct told him to keep a watchful eye on Gordon's reflection in the mirror behind the bar.

"Anybody ever tell you you're rude, Fillmore?" Spitzer's face twisted in rage. "In fact, you're nothing but an arrogant Eastern highbrow." Gordon slammed his milk on the bar and spun David around for a sucker punch. The fight was on.

Spitzer launched himself at David, pounding his face with the visceral frenzy of a man half his age.

David got in a few good shots before he was bent over with a kidney punch. In the next moment, he was slammed to the floor military style and then hailed with steel-toed boots.

From the corner of a swelling eye, David caught sight of Tranch reaching in to restrain his boss.

Hugo misread the action and bellowed, "Ain't no fair fight now!" The stout biker clipped Tranch with a left hook. Glasses shattered, chairs and tables toppled, and blood and sweat flew.

The bartender shouted a warning and fired a round of bullets into the ceiling, stopping the fight as quickly as it had begun.

David climbed to his feet, brushed floor grime from his bloody knuckles, and headed for the door with wounded pride.

Gordon Spitzer followed him to the threshold. "This isn't over, Fillmore!"

David checked his pocket for his motorcycle keys and cell phone. Ignoring the hail of mocking laughter, he limped around the back of the General Store and mounted his bike with a grimace. David's ribs ached as he revved up the Triumph. He spit blood from his mouth and drove into the night.

At a rest stop, David looked at the man in the mirror. He was a mess—swollen eye, split lip, and blood-caked mouth. *What would Elita say if she saw me now?* The temptation to drive north was great, yet the thought of causing his bride any more heartache restrained him.

David splashed cold water on his face and made a decision to tell his wife everything.

He returned to his bike and headed back toward home, hoping it wasn't too late to make his marriage work.

It was well after midnight when David rolled up to the General Store. Elita rushed onto the porch looking frantic. There were dark circles under her eyes, and her hair had been scraped into a hasty ponytail. "Where have you been?"

"I'm sorry," he said. "I just needed to clear my head."

"David, there's trouble."

Two uniformed men walked through the door of the General Store. One flashed a sheriff's badge. "David Fillmore," he said, pulling a pair of handcuffs from his belt, "I'm placing you under arrest for assault and battery."

"You can't be serious! I was on the worse end of that fight—just ask anybody."

The sheriff slapped on the cuffs. "You can give your statement down at the station. The cruiser is parked out back."

"It's Gordon—he was taken to the hospital over in Bixby with a skull fracture." Elita blinked back tears. "David, he says you attacked him."

Chapter 42

Arizona
Friday, October 5th

In a jail cell in Bixby, Arizona, David waited for Elita to post bail. There was nothing he could do but lie on the cot and stare at ceiling art left by former inmates.

From the next cell, a man studied him. "What did they arrest you for, drugs or something?" He scratched at his pockmarked face and waited for an answer.

"Or something." David returned his attention to the renderings on the ceiling. Some were cartoonish; others reflected real artistic talent. *Hopefully, I won't be around long enough to make a contribution*. The thought was shattered by a commotion a few cells down.

David sprang to his feet and listened, but the caustic words were spoken in Spanish. A young Mexican, his eyes bulging with rage, lunged at his cellmate and pounded him with a fury.

The jailer blew past, his keys jingling. "Okay, fun's over!" The cell door swung open, and several guards pried the men apart and yanked the younger one into the corridor.

Then, to David's surprise, they shoved the red-faced kid into his cell.

"Ya got a roommate, Fillmore. His name is Alberto."

"Wait a minute!"

"What do you think this is—a luxury hotel?" The jailer hooked the ring of keys back onto his belt, adding, "Don't worry, he'll be sent back to Mexico just as soon as the immigration facility processes him. Besides, the kid's got no beef with you. It's that coyote over there he blames for dropping his family members out into the desert to die."

"Are you talking about that couple found near Arroyo Seco? My wife and I were the ones who discovered them," David said.

Alberto's eyes widened, indicating he understood some of what was said. He rattled off more Spanish.

The jailer looked at David. "Alberto wants to know if you found a little boy, too."

"That's right."

The illegal immigrant spoke again.

Mr. Jingles laughed. "He thinks that you were sent by God!" The jailer swung the bars shut and swaggered away.

The morning passed slowly for David, who grew annoyed by Alberto's frustrated attempts to communicate.

"Muy importante por los Estados Unidos!" The words were packaged a hundred different ways, but the language barrier remained.

After lunch, Elita arrived with bail, and while they waited for the paperwork, David asked her to have a word with Alberto.

When the visit was over, she seemed troubled, but said

nothing as they were escorted to a room where a lawyer waited.

Jerry Beakman of the Schuster Law Firm introduced himself to David, running through his educational degrees like he was reading his résumé. "Okay, tell me about the assault."

"The last time I saw Spitzer, he had just kicked my. . . ." David paused. "He was fine."

Beakman scratched some notes on a legal tablet. "Where did this altercation take place? Were there any witnesses?"

"The Watering Hole. There are a number of people who can confirm the story." David gave his wife an apologetic look. "I wasn't drinking."

Elita sat quietly twirling the gold wedding band on her finger.

"We'll go over all the details tomorrow at our next meeting." The lawyer tossed the pad in his briefcase and stood. "Right now, let's get you out of here."

"Things will be different, I promise." David said as they walked to the jailhouse parking lot.

He climbed behind the wheel of the truck and took Elita's hand in his.

She squeezed his fingers. "We'll talk about that later. Right now, I need to tell you what Alberto shared."

David listened as an incredible story unfolded. "Are you sure that's what he said?"

"Positive—and I believed him, too," she pointed toward a country road that led to the border patrol station.

A lingering plume of dust hung in the air behind them as

David sped down a long stretch of border road that paralleled the ten-foot fence. He slowed as they approached a fenced-in yard filled with jeeps, motorcycles, and some ATVs.

They spilled out of the truck and hurried up the slab sidewalk to the border patrol's prefab headquarters. Inside, the air-conditioned room was utilitarian: dull white walls illuminated by florescent lights and windows tempered by aluminum blinds.

A man was sprawled behind a metal desk. He pushed up the brim of his green cap and asked, "Can I help ya?"

"We have some information," Elita announced. "It is a matter of national security."

The border agent leaned forward, resting his elbows on the desktop. "Is that right?" He instructed the couple to take a seat.

Elita repeated the story told to her by the young detainee. "Alberto says that some kind of military group is making arrangements to slip across this section of the border sometime soon."

"Can you elaborate?"

"We didn't get any more details." Elita's face brightened. "But he thought that some of them spoke German."

"Hmm." The border agent's eyebrows rose and fell. "Anyone care for coffee?"

Both David and Elita declined but waited while the government employee poured one for himself.

"German, you say?" He blew steam from his cup and shook his head. "From time to time, we hear of a few religious extremists trying to slip into the country, but this one's new to me," he chuckled. "Tell me more about this informant of yours."

"If you don't believe my wife," David said, "then I suggest you drive over to the county jail and take a statement from the young man yourself."

"There's a code of silence among the illegal community. I would be the last person that kid would open up to." The agent studied the young couple for a moment. "So, why did he talk to you?"

Elita explained about the recent deaths in the desert and about the rescued child. "The young man in question is a relative," she added.

The agent scratched his forehead. "How did you happen to be chatting with this kid over at the county jail?"

"My husband shared a cell with him."

"Hmm." The border agent repeated. He drummed his fingers on the desk then rose dismissively. "Tell you what, folks. I'll look into it."

Heat waves rose from the baked, sandy soil as David and Elita left the building and walked back to the truck.

"I don't think he took us seriously," Elita said as they drove away.

Silence filled the cab of the truck as they traveled back to town. Troubled thoughts roiled in David, and by the time they arrived at the General Store, he had pushed his pride aside.

David grabbed his motorcycle keys. "There's something I need to do." He kissed his worried wife and dashed out the door.

North Dakota

Friday, October 5th

It did not take long for the media to swoop in like vultures. TV crews and newspaper reporters were camped outside, leaving Nora no option other than to hide behind drawn curtains. Nora felt like a prisoner in her own home. Even a peek outside would incite a feeding frenzy, while inside the phone trilled incessantly, forcing her to turn off the ringer and screen her calls by sight.

Otis paced near the door and whined. He hadn't been out since they woke up a few hours ago. Nora stooped to stroke his shaggy head. "I'm sorry, boy, but I can't take you for a walk today."

The phone's caller ID lit up again. It was the Bargain Bin, so she answered.

"I'm coming over," J. J. O'Shay announced. "You need anything?"

"Some eggs and a small bag of dog food."

"You got it. And I'll even throw in some breakfast sandwiches." J. J. paused. "How're ya holding up?"

"It's like a carnival," Nora sighed. *More like a freak show*.

"Yeah, well, maybe I can give 'em something to talk about," J. J. chuckled.

What does he mean? She was too drained to ask.

There was a knock on the door. "Go away!"

"It's Abigail."

Nora opened the door a crack so her old friend could

squeeze through amidst a lightning storm of camera flashes.

"I wasn't sure you'd let me in after the way I treated you. I've been a terrible friend." The apology came with a hug.

In the kitchen, Nora poured a couple mugs of coffee and settled at the table, noticing that her old friend had lost more weight since their last meeting.

"You could have confided in me," Abigail said. "I would never pass judgment."

"It was too painful to talk about." Nora lowered her gaze and scratched at a smudge on her kitchen table. "I've hurt so many people. How can I live with that now?"

"Do you love God?"

The question startled Nora. "Of course I do."

"Well, then, remember what the good book says," Abigail said gently. "All things work together for the good of those who love God and are called according to his purpose."

Nora sighed. "I trust God. It's me I'm not so sure about."

"That's where the Lord wants all of us to be. 'Not I, but Christ. . . .'" Abigail clutched her mug until her knuckles turned white. There was a long silence. It broke when Abigail blurted out, "Henry has left me!"

The abruptness of the announcement left Nora speechless.

Her friend continued through heavy sobs. "Henry emptied out our savings account and took off in the night with Celeste. You were right to try and warn me. How could I be so blind?"

Nora opened her arms to Abigail, and they wept

together.

There was a knock on the back door.

It was J. J. O'Shay with a duffle slung over his shoulder. He held up a bag full of breakfast sandwiches that he tossed on the kitchen counter and pulled one out. "Man, you picked a great day to play hooky. That motel just delivered all those donated beds, and we've been lugging them upstairs all morning!" He unwrapped the sandwich and loaded his mouth.

"How's your TV reception out here?" J. J. asked between bites. "There's a news conference in a few minutes."

Abigail made her way to the back door. "I'll be praying," she whispered.

"Me, too," Nora said as her old friend ventured out to brave the media gauntlet.

J. J. busied himself in the living room flipping through TV channels. The talking heads were abuzz with speculation. Most believed that the president would deny all allegations that he had fathered an illegitimate child.

Cameras shifted to a podium in the White House Briefing Room. "Ladies and gentlemen, the President of the United States."

Thomas Atwood looked straight ahead, his face somber. "I have asked you here today to address recent allegations regarding my past." The president paused and clutched the side of the podium. "It is true that I am acquainted with Nora Meyers. We met almost seventeen years ago—before I met my wife. It is true that we had a brief relationship."

Reporters' hands went up, and the president pointed to a woman wearing a gabardine suit.

"Mr. President, are you saying that these allegations are

true?"

"The paternity in this case is being investigated. However, I have verified that the letter in question was indeed written by Ms. Meyers. I have always known her to be an honest person. I see no reason to doubt her."

Hands shot up again.

Atwood gave the nod to a gentleman wearing a pink tie. "When did you learn of the existence of a love child?"

"At the same time you did," the president said calmly.

"Is it true that your brother was barely in the grave when you slept with his fiancé?"

Atwood's face reddened. "I loved my brother very much, as did Ms. Meyers. We were both devastated when he was killed." He held up his hand. "That's all I have to say."

Nora moaned and turned off the set.

J. J. rose from the couch and grabbed his duffel. "I didn't vote for that dude, but he just earned my respect."

He disappeared into the bathroom and emerged a few minutes later wearing a clown costume.

"What are you doing?" Nora asked as he headed for the front door with juggling pins in hand.

"Those media peeps came for a show, and I aim to please."

Later that evening when Nora was alone, she watched J. J. on the evening news, along with a few unflattering shots the cameras had caught of her.

The major networks were having a field day. The story of the president's love child had even dwarfed the trouble that was brewing in the Formosa Strait. It was tabloid journalism at its worst.

Nora numbly searched for a bright side. *As bad as things are,* she told herself, *others are suffering, too. Like Abigail, whose husband has left her for another woman.* She uttered a simple prayer for her friend and for the Delmont Harvest Center's tiny congregation.

The phone blinked, signaling another incoming call. It was the White House. "Please hold for the President of the United States," a monotone voice said.

"Nora, the investigation has uncovered some disturbing developments, and I'm afraid it's been leaked to the press. I wanted you to hear it before it hits the air."

She felt her blood run cold. Nora held the receiver so tight that her fingers went numb. "What is it?"

"Our son was convicted of murdering his adoptive family. His name is Joel Sutherland. He was serving a sentence at a juvenile detention facility in Florida but was recently transferred to a church-run program. He escaped from there, and his whereabouts are unknown."

The words sent a shockwave down Nora's spine.

"Some postcards were hidden under his mattress," President Atwood continued. "The FBI has reason to believe that Joel might have gone to New Orleans."

Nora hung up feeling like she had been shot—yet even a mortal wound could never hurt this much.

Arizona

Friday, October 5th

Maybe this isn't a good idea, David thought as he

slowed the motorcycle to a crawl near the gate. The last person on the planet that he wanted to see was Gordon Spitzer, but something much bigger than his personal feelings compelled him.

The head of the CBG has probably been glassing me for the last mile or so, David figured, *maybe even bracing for a violent confrontation*.

He dismounted, pushed the gate open, and rolled on through.

A group of civic guards had gathered under the old mission's portico, and a few more trickled from the building as he leaned the Triumph onto its kickstand.

The reception was just as he'd anticipated: cold and cautious. David spotted Gordon Spitzer standing in the compound's threshold. A white gauze bandage was visible beneath his fishing cap.

"If you know what's good for you, Fillmore, you'll turn around and hop back on that bike of yours!"

"I need to talk to you."

"Whatever it is, tell it to my lawyer!" Gordon's hand rested on a holster that hung from his leg. Tranch and a few other border militia members flanked their leader.

"Get off my property!" Spitzer shouted.

"This isn't about our personal differences."

Gordon drew his pistol and fired a bullet into the soil at David's feet. "That's a warning, Fillmore, just in case you didn't hear me the first time. Leave!"

David stood his ground.

Spitzer aimed the gun. His finger twitched on the trigger. "Don't say I didn't warn you."

Suddenly, Tranch shoved the gun aside, sending a bullet rocketing into the desert. “Leave him alone, boss. He don’t want no trouble.”

David seized the opportunity to state his case. “I have some information pertaining to border security. There’s talk of trouble.”

Gordon chewed on the words for a few seconds; then, he snapped his fingers and ordered one of his men to frisk David. “You’ve got ten minutes, Fillmore.”

David passed a troop of hostile recruits and followed Spitzer inside to a large room that was used as a fellowship hall, with a podium and a big screen TV.

Gordon settled himself at the head of a folding table and invited David to join him. Across the room, Tranch stood vigil. “What’s on your mind?”

David told him the story. He held nothing back.

Spitzer scratched the bandage on his head. “Did he mention how many there were?”

“No, only that they were foreign,” David said. “The border patrol isn’t taking this seriously. Maybe they’re right.”

The head of the CBG’s lip curled in a sneer. “How do I know this isn’t some kind of setup?”

“It’s no secret that I don’t like you, Spitzer. In fact, I’d love to wipe that smirk off your face,” David said. “But this isn’t about us. If covert activity is afoot, we should lay our personal differences aside.”

Spitzer leaned back until his metal chair creaked. “Maybe you’re not the coward I took you for.” He stood and motioned for David to follow.

They walked through a short maze of halls and stopped

at a door marked War Room. Gordon unlocked it with a key that hung from a chain around his neck and pushed the door open. "After you."

The space was filled with high-tech equipment, shelves lined with night vision apparatus, thermal sensors, security cameras, listening devices, and radios. "State of the art surveillance, made available through the generous donations of concerned Americans." Gordon punched an intercom button near the door. "Core staff meeting in the war room!" Before ringing off he added, "And bring me a tall glass of milk."

Gordon lingered near a row of computer monitors, all rotating through digital images of the desert. "We've scanned in over three thousand faces of known terrorists and drug runners. Our facial recognition software is pretty remarkable. In fact," Spitzer puffed, "this organization has assisted the US Border Patrol in intercepting some dangerous illegals—including several known Islamic extremists!"

Other guards began to trickle into the room, and Gordon turned his attention to a keyboard. A monitor screen showed sound waves and fuzzy static. Unintelligible phrases crackled—voices speaking clear, guttural German. Then they faded again to static.

"Didn't know what to make of it," Spitzer said, "but in light of what you just told me. . . ."

He turned to the group and clapped his hands together. "People we've got work to do!" He took a swig of milk that left behind a foamy mustache. "We appear to be up against some kind of special ops. The question we need to ask ourselves is: What are they after?"

Ideas flew around the table—some laughable. Foreign competition to the Mexican drug cartels; spies wanting to study the high-tech equipment used by the border patrol; a band of political refugees seeking to assimilate into American society.

"Worst-case scenario," Gordon said, "let's assume that these are enemy combatants who want to strike a blow to our country. What are their possible objectives in choosing this particular stretch of border?"

"Maybe our water supply," David said, considering the possibility. "That would make Salt River Project a target, or possibly even the Glen Canyon Dam."

Gordon wiped the liquid mustache from his lip. "Fillmore, those biker buddies of yours are gathering tomorrow morning to talk about the freedom ride," he said. "I want you to rally the troops."

Chapter 43

Great River Road

Friday, October 5th

Autumn had turned blustery. Fine flakes of snow spiraled toward the Rambler's windshield, reminding Joel of *Star Trek*'s warp speed.

"Feel free to crank up the heat," Zeke said. "No sense being uncomfortable."

Joel fiddled with the controls until he felt a swell of warmth at his feet. "You think it's going to freeze tonight?" He kept his eye on a large gaggle of Canada geese near the river, their downy feathers fluffed against the frigid north wind.

"No worries!" Zeke replied. "We'll be stopping off near Winona to visit an old buddy. His name is Leroy Lumpkin. Bet you can't say that three times fast!"

"Do you have friends all over the country?"

"Yup, and my newest one is sitting next to me!"

The teenager cast a skeptical look at the driver. "For all you know, I'm a murderer."

Zeke kept his eye on the road, but a subtle smile formed

on his lips. "Are you?"

"No."

The old man's smile blossomed into a grin. "I didn't think so."

As they crossed into Minnesota, rays of sunlight broke through the clouds, casting a sharp reflection of fall foliage on the river's glassy water.

The Rambler rolled past a well-tended farmhouse adorned with bric-a-brac. In the front yard a large sign had been erected that said PRAY FOR AMERICA.

"Not a bad idea if you ask me," Zeke said as the car puttered slowly up the Great River Road.

Traveling with this old man is like riding in a covered wagon. The teenager yawned and glanced at the gas gauge. *Still half full*. He yawned again and drifted off to sleep.

Joel awoke to a finger in his ribs.

"Wake up, kid! You gotta see the Sugar Loaf." The old man pointed to a massive rock that jutted from a bluff.

The teenager rubbed his neck and wondered how long he'd been asleep.

"This is quite a village," Zeke said. "Between wheat, lumber, steamboats, and railroad freight, Winona once had more money than they knew what to do with. So they gussied up the place. You'll know exactly what I mean when you see all the fancy architecture."

The teenager was impressed. Some of the buildings looked like they would be more at home in Paris or Rome than in an obscure Minnesota town. A massive Catholic church, its towers capped by conical roofs, resembled a castle. The Winona County Courthouse was an equally impressive brownstone with arched windows and buttresses.

"Does your friend live on a street like this?" Joel asked as the car meandered through tree-lined avenues with stately homes.

"Better!" Zeke waved his hand toward a bridge. "He lives on Latsch Island. Look, a sea monster!" Zeke hollered as they crossed over.

Joel pitched forward and then frowned. "That's just an old section of railroad trestle sticking up out of the water."

"Had you going, though," the old man snickered.

Joel shook his head. "You're crazy."

"I resemble that!"

Crossing over to Latsch Island was like passing into another world. They went by a well-kept marina with buildings to match, but as they drove farther along the shoreline many of the buildings morphed into funky floating shacks. The farther they traveled, the more interesting the boathouses became.

"Leroy lives on the other side of the island," Zeke said as he turned down a swampy road. The Rambler ground over a series of deep ruts before popping onto a road near the shoreline. There were boathouses made of cedar shingles and shaped like domes; boathouses clapped together with recycled material; and cheerful boathouses decorated with bright, artistic flair. A couple of residents gave the travelers a friendly wave as they drove past.

Joel shook his head. "I can't believe people actually live here."

"They don't look dead to me!" Zeke returned with a wink and smile. "Most of these folks go south during winter, but there's a few who stay on, like Leroy Lumpkin." He rolled to a stop beside a two-story boathouse shanty with a wraparound deck.

"You'll get a kick out of Leroy. Funniest guy you'll ever meet. Got no sense of humor, though."

Joel followed the old man to a porch cluttered with bait boxes, rubber boots, boat parts, and even a spare tire.

Zeke rapped his knuckles on a door thickened by layers of weather-crackled blue paint.

"Over here!"

The travelers turned their ears toward the woods just across the road.

"Watch this," Zeke whispered. "Leroy Lumpkin, come out of those woods and show me the whites of your eyes!"

A man wearing greasy clothes and a stained shirt appeared at the edge of a stand of willows. He strode across the road spreading his eyelids with his fingers. "Happy now?" he asked, eyes bulging.

Joel laughed.

Leroy glared. "What's so funny, boy?"

"See what I mean about the sense of humor?" Zeke chuckled. "Leroy, I'd like to introduce you to my young friend, Joel."

The man slipped off his Scotch cap and scratched a bushy mop of hair. "Pleased to make your acquaintance." He anchored the cap down so far that his red ears stuck straight out. "I got a problem back over there."

"We'll be glad to lend a hand," Zeke said.

"I don't need your hand, but I could sure use a little help," Leroy muttered as they followed him into the woods.

He pointed to a tangle of fishing net. Trapped by its strings, a bald eagle struggled in vain to free herself. "She's got herself in a heck of a bind," Mr. Lumpkin said. "The more she fights it, the worse it gets."

Joel dropped to his knees and leaned in for a better look. "Awesome! I've never seen a bald eagle this close before!"

"Move in a little closer, boy, and she'll give you a nose job." Leroy tossed the teenager a golf club cover and donned a thick pair of leather gloves.

"What's this for?"

"First thing we need to do is cover her eyes so she don't try to fight us." The boatman grabbed the bird's beak and held her in place while the teenager slipped the leather sock over her eyes.

Joel could feel the eagle's muscles tense as the netting was cut away. Her heart pulsed beneath his fingers.

"Okay, boy, remove the hood and stand back."

Joel was fascinated by the massive bird of prey.

Though free to go, she lingered for a moment, her black, shiny eyes watching the men. Then, the eagle opened her impressive wings, flapped, and was airborne. They admired her until she flew out of sight.

"Got a fresh pot of beans on the stove—been simmering since yesterday." Leroy lumbered off toward his boathouse, his baggy corduroy pants tucked into rubber boots.

"Beans are Leroy's specialty," Zeke said as they turned toward the boathouse. "You'll know what I mean when you get inside."

The place smelled of damp wood, smoke, and something else. "Do I smell propane?" Joel said.

Zeke smiled and jabbed Leroy's elbow. "The kid thinks you got a gas leak."

Leroy responded with a deadpan look. "A farting horse will never tire; a farting man is one to hire! That's what my daddy used to say."

The teenager laughed.

Leroy scowled. "You disrespecting my daddy?"

"No, sorry," the teenager said, glancing around the boathouse. It was small but homey in a primitive sort of way. In the corner near the door, a tiny wooden staircase angled sharply to the second floor. *Probably a bedroom*, Joel thought. Most of the furnishings were moth-eaten or broken down, with the exception of a platform rocker upholstered in brown and orange plaid. This well-kept piece of furniture sat beneath some raw pine shelves that housed a large collection of books—not the paperback variety but hardbound leather books, the kind one would expect to find in a gentleman's library.

On a potbellied stove near the kitchen, Leroy lifted the lid from a cast-iron skillet and stirred the beans. "Can you smell that blackstrap molasses?" He jerked open a compact fridge. "Don't have no beer. Those days are long gone, and I can't say that I miss 'em, either. How 'bout some milk?" He held up a plastic jug with solid, floating chunks.

"I'll take water," Joel said.

Leroy rummaged through a sink full of dirty dishes, found a glass, and gave it a quick rinse. "Pardon the mess—it's the maid's day off."

"Is Ms. Wigglesworth still cleaning houses?" Zeke interjected as their host rattled through a drawer and produced some clean spoons. "Poor dear must be pushing a hundred."

"Am I in the Twilight Zone?" Joel blurted.

"No, boy, you're at Latsch Island!" Leroy shook his head. "Students today just ain't taught their geography."

Leroy instructed the guests to have a seat at the kitchen table and bowed his head. "Dear God, thanks for the grub."

Zeke shoveled a spoonful of beans into his mouth and savored them. "Best beans I've ever tasted!" He chased it down with some water.

Joel poked at the food in his bowl, listening to the old friends reminisce. They'd met nearly thirty years earlier when Leroy's world was crumbling. "It was a particularly bad year, that was," the old fisherman said, rubbing his chin stubble. "The wife left me, and my dog got run over. She was a good dog, too. A month later, my bait and tackle shop burned to the ground, and I didn't have any insurance. I was thinking of packin' it all in, and then this old coot here came strolling into my life." He cocked an eye toward Zeke. "You left before I got a chance to thank you for steering me toward that job at the marina."

"No need. Every good and perfect gift comes from above." Zeke polished off the last of his beans.

Joel put his bowl in the crowded sink and plopped down on the seedy couch to watch a primitive television set that was playing quietly in the corner.

"I heard that some weather's movin' down from up north. Might get dicey," Leroy said. "You're welcome to stay all day. Heck, you can even stay all night. I've got a couple mats you can roll out on the floor."

Zeke looked at his traveling companion. "What do you

say, kid?"

Near the old couch, a rustling sound caught Joel's attention. A whiskered nose and two beady eyes peeked out from a pile of trash. "A rat!"

"That's just Ron—a little river rodent who visits me sometimes," Leroy explained. "He don't eat much."

"I vote we push on," Joel said.

"Suit yourselves," Leroy shrugged. "But at least let me build you some sardine sandwiches."

Zeke volunteered to help, and the two men bantered back and forth about their culinary expertise.

Joel turned his attention back to *The Price is Right*. "We interrupt this program for a special report: President Atwood admitted to fathering a love child."

Annoyed, Joel turned off the television.

Chapter 44

Arizona

Saturday, October 6th

David found the Freedom Riders congregating in the parking lot of the Tumbleweed Inn. The roads into Arroyo Seco were clogged with a steady flow of new bikers, most likely weekenders from the greater Phoenix area.

He parked beside a cluster of silver-haired riders and spotted Hugo.

"Good to see you, buddy!" His old friend approached and slapped a gloved hand on David's shoulder. "I heard you were hauled in the other night by some po-pos." Hugo shook his head. "I knew that loudmouthed idiot was trouble! I should have put his lights out for good!"

"You're the one who fractured Gordon Spitzer's skull?"

"Hey, man, I'll square things. I ain't gonna let you take the rap for what I done."

"Listen," David said, "I need to speak to the road captain."

"You're lookin' at him!" Hugo puffed.

David quickly briefed him on the situation that might be

brewing across the border.

The biker ran his hands over his loose braid. “So, you’re asking me to organize volunteers to defend the border against some foreign agents who are planning to sneak over here?”

David nodded and assured his old friend that all the gear would be supplied—tents, sleeping bags, food, water, and base radios.

“A lot of these bikers have concealed carry permits,” Hugo volunteered.

“It shouldn’t come to that,” David said. “If any activity is detected, the border patrol will be called in.”

Hugo kicked at a piece of trash with the toe of his Dingo boot. He looked at David with a wry grin. “Whatever you need, you got it, buddy. We’ll be ready to roll!”

Virginia

Saturday, October 6th

Paige dreamed of Emily, her blonde hair being tussled softy by the lakeside breeze. She kissed her daughter’s cheek, but it was cold. She dropped to the sandy soil and stared in disbelief at the lifeless body of her child. Emily opened her crystal eyes and said, “Mom, please tell Uncle David not to be sad anymore.”

Paige opened her eyes. It took her a moment to remember that she was at the Big Meadows Lodge. *I must have fallen asleep in the chair*. She watched Connor a few feet away as he tossed beneath a tangle of bedding. He muttered something unintelligible before settling again into slumber. A sudden surge of sadness engulfed Paige as she thought about what she had lost—including her brother, David.

The bedside clock indicated that it was 10:45 PM. In Arizona, it was a few hours earlier. Paige reached for her cell phone. The low battery light was blinking, so she put it on the charger and decided to call her brother from the lodge phone. Paige dialed David's number. It rang six times and went to voicemail.

"David, it's me. I've been thinking a lot about you and our relationship." Paige took a deep breath and continued. "Emily's death was an accident. It wasn't your fault. I just wanted you to know that." The words released an unexpected flood of peace. "I love you," she said before hanging up.

Part 3
The Third Peril

O beautiful for glory-tale
Of liberating strife,
When once and twice, for man's avail,
Men lavished precious life!
America! America!
God shed His grace on thee
Till selfish gain no longer stain,
The banner of the free!

O beautiful for patriot dream
That sees beyond the years
Thine alabaster cities gleam
Undimmed by human tears!
America! America!
God shed His grace on thee
Till nobler men keep once again
Thy whiter jubilee!

Katharine Lee Bates

Chapter 45

Paris

Sunday, October 7th

Jean Pierre rose before sunrise. Lately, sleep had been elusive. *If all goes well, things will soon be different,* he told himself. *I shall rest easy, like a little child.*

Maurine shifted beneath satin sheets as Jean Pierre quietly slipped on his robe. He kissed her. "Slumber on, my love."

Downstairs, he paced the room. There was no need for coffee; Jean Pierre's mind was racing with anxious thoughts. *Sunday, October 7th. A fitting day to remind the United States that she is vulnerable—that she must cooperate in order to survive!* He poured himself a glass of sherry to calm his nerves.

In the stillness of the pre-dawn shadows, Jean Pierre ran a nervous finger around the rim of his glass as his small, dark eyes flicked from the lighted silhouette of Notre Dame to its reflection in the Seine River. Each long minute passed with mounting expectation. The pendulum rhythm of a stylized grandfather clock marked the passage of time; the seconds turned to minutes that seemed like hours.

Morning would soon break over the magnificent French city, spilling light and life to its streets. But, in another part of the world, darkness would be more profound.

Jean Pierre thought of how well the plan had come together so far. China had been brilliant, playing their part with excellence. The trap had been set. A US Navy battle group had been sent toward their destiny in the Formosa Strait. With the military divided, on American soil there would be a coordinated series of attacks designed to bring the great nation to her knees. Jean Pierre took mental inventory; all the key players, stationed throughout the country, awaited the signal to move. Their tasks were to be specific, and their implementation was to be swift.

Jean Pierre pondered, *What thoughts will pass through the mind of the US President at the precise moment he learns of the invasion? Will he feel the rumble beneath his feet as the explosion rocks the East Coast?*

Beads of perspiration sprouted on Jean Pierre's forehead, and he mopped them with a handkerchief from his robe pocket. Absently, he swirled the liquor in his glass. Their greatest advantage, the element of surprise, still held risks. *So much can still go wrong*. It was a tormenting thought.

Jean Pierre clicked his tongue anxiously and swallowed the last of his sherry.

Chapter 46

Arizona

Sunday, October 7th

Perched high atop the Eagle Pass outlook, David glanced at his watch a little after midnight, and there was still no sign of trouble. He lifted his night-vision binoculars and scanned each of the strategic posts.

Along the border, the Freedom Riders had been dispatched to establish a formidable wall of motorcycles. The bikers, gathered in clusters, were like leather-clad troops.

A few miles to the north, nestled near some sandstone outcroppings, was the tiny community of Hope Springs—where David had asked Elita to wait. The place had morphed into a trailer town, with rows of awnings adorned with tube lights and paper lanterns. Its residents had gathered at the pavilion to pray. Elita was likely among them.

The two-way radio crackled beside him, reminding David of the ham radio operator on standby in the makeshift village. He turned his mind back to the duties at hand.

To the south of Eagle Pass, the CBG's compound stood like a fortress illuminated by floodlights. Khaki-clad figures moved about swiftly beneath the light. David watched the chain-link gates part as a caravan of jeeps rolled onto the road.

He turned his sights on the desert, sweeping the countryside for any sign of movement. Somewhere among the brush, electronic ears and infrared cameras had been set up by Gordon Spitzer and his recruits.

David settled back upon the rocky ledge to wait—all night if necessary. He had his sleeping bag, water, and a sandwich he'd made in haste. The only thing missing was Elita's embrace. He decided to send her a text message reminding her of his love. David fished his cell phone from his jacket pocket and was surprised to find he had a voicemail. The number indicated it was from some place in Virginia. David retrieved the voicemail and heard his sister speaking words that he had longed to hear. "Emily's death was an accident. It wasn't your fault."

He listened to the message again, just to convince himself this was not a dream. *She forgives me!* Relief flooded his soul. David replayed the message once more, just to hear it again, and then he remembered his brother-in-law worrying about Paige's whereabouts.

After banging out a quick text message giving Brody the phone number from where Paige had called, David nestled back into the cleft of a rock and sent a love note to Elita. All seemed calm. The minutes passed beneath the stars, and the night was chilly.

Around 12:30 AM, a shot rang out, and David sprang to his feet. He glassed the countryside with his night vision field glasses and spotted a flurry of activity along the border.

Motorcycle headlights came on like a wall of fire, and their motors rumbled to life.

Another gunshot cracked through the desert, and David's eye locked on two men moving swiftly on foot. The suspects resembled glowing embers through the night vision lenses as they scrambled over the rough terrain. They seemed to be moving in a straight line, so David glassed ahead. A few miles to the north a vehicle was parked on a dirt road, its engine warmed and ready to take them away.

David passed the information to the ham radio operator, along with approximate coordinates. "Relay to Gordon Spitzer and the border patrol."

Down along the border, the Freedom Riders scuffled with a couple different suspects.

Further north, Spitzer's men moved out to position themselves for an ambush, and the operatives were apprehended as they approached the waiting vehicle.

In the black sky, a border patrol helicopter circled Arroyo Seco and zeroed in on the Civic Border Guard's conquest. More response teams arrived, and the desert was soon lit up like Las Vegas.

North Dakota

Sunday, October 7th

"Are you sure there is a road out there?" Joel leaned over the dash and strained to see. Sheets of water had rendered the headlights nearly useless, and the moonless night didn't help matters.

A gale rocked the Rambler, and waves lapped over the causeway, tumbling debris onto their path.

"They don't call this Devils Lake for nothing," Zeke said as the tires ground slowly over the bramble. "There's a town on the other side with the same name. Figure we'll find us a motel and stop for the night. I don't know about you, but it's late, and I'm ready to put my head under my wing."

Up ahead, a small log had washed across the road. Joel volunteered to move it. He jumped from the vehicle and picked his way carefully over the slick mud. The lake surged, lapping at Joel's tennis shoes. Though battered by wind, the teenager managed to drag the waterlogged wood to the side.

When he climbed back into Rambler, Joel was chilled to the bone. "Maybe this isn't such a good idea." He shivered and rubbed his hands in front of the heater vent.

"I hear ya, kid!" the old man sympathized. "But I think we're entered, now!"

The farther they drove along the narrow causeway, the worse it got. The road was covered with a few inches of water now. The windshield wipers slapped overtime, yet barely kept up with the wind spray. Only the rock berms on either side of the causeway assured them that they weren't driving straight into the lake.

Zeke let out a hoot as the Rambler bucked over small branches. "It's a rodeo!"

Joel clutched the dash and squinted to see through the deluge. "We must be close to shore. I think I see a light!"

Suddenly, the Rambler coughed and died with a shudder.

Zeke turned the key. The engine started, sputtered

briefly, and stopped. Again he tried—nothing. The old man looked quizzically at the dash, twirling the tip of his beard. "Fine time to run out of gas."

"No way!" Joel exploded.

Another gust pummeled the car, and cold air whistled through breaches in the window seals.

Zeke drummed his fingers on the steering wheel. Then, his hoary eyebrows rose, and he leaned over the seat and reached into the back of the Rambler.

The teenager watched him rummage through a paper grocery bag.

The old man pulled out an eight-hour emergency candle and a book of matches. "This'll help keep you warm while I'm gone."

"Wait a minute!" Joel protested. "If anybody's going for help it should be me. I'm in better shape."

"I believe I've just been insulted!" Zeke quipped. "Look, kid, you need to stay here and flash the headlights if another motorist happens by. We don't want to be a road hazard out here." The old man slipped on a rain parka and zipped it up to his nose. "I'll be back before you know it."

The car door sprang open, and frigid air plunged inside. "Keep a candle burning while I'm gone, kid."

The teenager watched Zeke trucking up the causeway like he was impervious to the gale-force winds and spray. Finally, the old man faded into the darkness.

Joel struck a match and set the candle on the Rambler's dashboard. Alone, he felt as restless as the wind.

In the glove box, Joel found a box of petrified Good & Plenty candy, a toy soldier, a pair of thermal mittens, and some sunglasses with one lens missing.

He popped the stale licorice candy into his mouth and thought about home and the love he'd known there. *Why didn't Mom and Dad tell me that I was adopted?* The knowledge would not have changed his feelings for his parents. He had always known their love was genuine.

He slipped the documents from the manila envelope for another look. Baby boy Meyers, born in Minot, North Dakota, on November 2nd. *Nearly sixteen years ago.* Joel's curiosity gave way to questions. *Is my birth mother alive? Still living in North Dakota? Does she want to be found? What about my birth father?*

In the faint flicker of candlelight, the teenager tried to process it all.

The time was marked by the growing smudge of candle soot that spread on the windshield. Joel grew uneasy. *Zeke should be back by now,* he thought. *What if he never returns?*

The wind screamed over the station wagon like a banshee. White-capped waves crashed over the road hard enough to send small rocks from the berms tumbling.

Joel picked nervously at a hangnail before grabbing for the Bible in his backpack—anything to calm his nerves.

In the flickering light, he opened the book. ". . . a strong wind had risen, and they were fighting heavy waves." The teenager shook his head at the irony of the words. He continued reading. "Jesus came toward them walking on the water. . . . In their fear they cried out, 'It is a ghost!' But Jesus spoke to them at once. 'Don't be afraid,' he said, 'Take courage. I am here!'"

Eerie coincidence—nothing more, Joel thought. He

slapped the book shut, switched on the headlights, and gasped.

In a wash of white light, the old man was walking toward him, water lapping at his feet, his white beard whipping in the wind, and his parka fluttering like a robe. He looked like Jesus walking on the water!

Joel's heart boomed like a kettledrum as he launched from the Rambler and ran to greet Zeke. "Man, am I glad to see you!"

"I'm glad to be seen!" The old man raised a full gas can like a trophy. "Good news. There's a National Guard training center just up the road. Nicest folks you'd ever want to meet. They said we could bunk there for the night."

Joel volunteered to fill the gas tank while Zeke took his place behind the wheel and turned the key. The Rambler fired up on the third try, and they were back in business.

It was just over a mile and a half to Camp Grafton. When they rolled to a stop beside the guard shack, Joel was ready to call it a night.

A young man in fatigues leaned from the window and smiled. "That didn't take long. Let me give you directions to our guest accommodations." The telephone was ringing in the guard shack. "Excuse me, sir, I'll be right with you."

When the soldier returned, his demeanor was changed. "I need to see some valid ID."

Zeke popped the button on his glove box and pulled out a driver's license. The guard checked the likeness with a flashlight and then pointed the beam at the teenager.

Joel shrugged and shook his head.

"You look familiar," the soldier said. He let his light

linger a few seconds more on the boy's face before turning his attention back to the old man.

"Sir, I'm afraid we've just been put on active alert, so I can't let you pass since the boy has no valid ID. You'll find accommodations over in the town of Devils Lake."

"What's going on?" Zeke asked.

"The Minot Air Force Base has just been bombed. The power grid near the northern border had been compromised, and there have been reports of ground fighting," the young soldier said and then promptly returned to his post.

Chapter 47

Virginia
Sunday, October 7th

Brody awoke to his government Blackberry ringing. The digital clock beside his bed read 3:55 AM. *Who would be calling at this hour?* He switched on the lamp and scrambled for his phone before remembering that Paige was not beside him to be bothered by the ringing.

"Hays," he said, but heard only an automated message.

"This is the White House Emergency Notification System. At 3:45 AM, Eastern Daylight Time, the US was attacked along the northern border. All essential personnel are to bring their go kits and proceed with their immediate family to the Site C Hangar at Dulles International Airport for immediate transport to Site C for continuity of government operations. This is not a drill."

Brody was stunned. He had been through training programs for such a contingency but never thought he would face an actual event. He hurried to the closet, found his go kit in the back, and hastily threw on his clothes.

His personal cell phone lay on his bedside table, and

Brody checked it hoping for a message from his wife. There was none.

The floor beneath his feet shuddered, and Brody's gaze shifted to a crystal glass of water sitting on the table. Its liquid was trembling, forming concentric rings. "What in the heck is going on?" he said aloud. He grabbed his things and hurried out the door.

Brody tried his wife's cell phone once more. It went straight to voicemail. "Call me," he said, leaving a hasty message. He backed out of the driveway and raced toward Dulles International Airport.

There, he was briefed by national security personnel and then whisked to a waiting helicopter. Details were sketchy at best, but one thing was certain: *In a few hours, America will awaken to a nation in crisis.*

The helicopter crested a rise, and the Thunder Ridge facility came into view. The craft hovered over the heliport and began the descent.

Down below, squired beneath a granite mountain, all the king's horses and all the king's men will try and put their broken country together again, Brody thought.

Soldiers with glow wands directed the helicopter as it settled onto the concrete pad. The pilot cut the engine, and the blades wound down. Brody still could not wrap his brain around the events of the last few hours, but he knew for sure that the United States was under attack.

Brody waited as the president's staff and their immediate families disembarked the military helicopter. He trailed behind a mother trying to sooth a fussy child, and his anxious thoughts turned to Paige and Connor. Brody's stomach churned with worry.

"Can you believe this place?" Spence Carlyle said, rubbing his arms vigorously in the chilly night. "I've heard all about Thunder Ridge, but until now, I've never laid eyes on it. The place is a virtual fortress carved deep inside a granite mountain."

"Kind of like a school field trip, huh, Carlyle?" Brody quipped and walked over to join a group milling near a double metal door that was large enough to accommodate a semi-trailer truck.

Brody slipped his cell phone from its holster and again tried to contact Paige. All circuits were busy.

Electronic security doors parted to a large lobby. A team was waiting there with clipboards and scanners in hand. They bore the emblems of the Department of Homeland Security.

"Welcome." A man wearing a black suit and tie stepped forward, and the process of screening began. Key personnel were asked for PIV II cards, and their family members were checked for clearance.

After the security issues were complete, Janet Gates of Homeland Security addressed the crowd. "Ladies and gentlemen, this is a day we hoped would never come." Her voice wavered, and she paused briefly before continuing. "I will be facilitating your orientation to the Thunder Ridge facility. If you have any questions, please don't hesitate to ask." Janet spun on her heals and led the charge down a long, gray corridor and through another set of security doors.

The group was given a tour of the sleeping quarters, a hospital, and the dining and recreation areas. "This will be your home until further notice, but don't expect to get much rest," she warned. "There is work to be done."

Spence Carlyle raised his hand. "What about food and water?"

"This classified facility is designed to provide a safe base for government operations. We are equipped with a vast reservoir of drinking and cooling water, not to mention a sewage and water treatment plant. Thunder Ridge also houses a power plant, emergency broadcast system, radio station, and state-of-the-art telecommunications and information technology. Food has been stockpiled for just such a contingency."

Brody looked back toward the doors. *Out there*, he thought, *my family will not be so fortunate*.

North Dakota

Sunday, October 7th

The explosion knocked Nora from her bed. She clambered to her feet, feeling disoriented. The outside wall of her bedroom was completely gone, and in its place was a massive fireball. The heat was unbearable. The smell of fuel permeated the air.

With Otis at her heels, Nora felt her way through what remained of her house.

She felt a rush of cold air and moved toward it instinctively, fleeing into the frigid North Dakota night.

Outside, Nora saw what was left of a fighter jet. One wing was broken and dripping fuel. The nose and other wing were embedded in the house. Nora stood in her bare feet shivering as she watched her family farmhouse being incinerated.

There hadn't been time to grab a robe. It was below freezing, but Nora told herself that emergency response units would arrive soon. *A horrible accident,* she thought, feeling a rush of grief for the pilot who had just lost his life.

Suddenly, two more fighters streaked across the sky, banking sharply and firing into the darkness. A third plane cart wheeled out of the sky and burst into flames when it hit the ground.

Nora ran to the edge of her field but realized there was nothing she could do. It was eerie listening to the crackle of twisted metal and the soft roar of burning jet fuel.

The neighboring farms were dark—no yard lights. *The power must be out*, Nora thought. *Yet, surely, others have been awakened by these explosions and called for help.*

New fires began springing up across the plains. Whittaker's barn was first. Nora's heart sank in the cold, brittle air. Just over the hill, at Ingram's feedlot, she could hear the bellows of hundreds of cattle.

Is this a nightmare? Barns, haystacks, silos, and gas tanks ignited like torches. "Oh, God!" Nora cried, still not comprehending what she was seeing. *This can't be happening!*

The crack of gunfire echoed in the distance. *Definitely a shotgun*, Nora thought. Then she heard the unmistakable staccato of machine gun fire.

A chill snaked down Nora's spine. She rubbed her arms 'til they tingled, suddenly aware that her shivering had turned violent. *The Chevy!* It had not been hit when the fighter crashed, and the keys were always in it. Nora and her little dog sought shelter behind the wheel and started the engine for some heat. From there, she watched her world burn down.

Otis barked.

Someone emerged from the shadows, calling Nora's name.

She rolled down the window and yelled, "Over here!"

Her neighbor, Pepper, rushed over with her two young children in tow. "I'm so relieved to see you! When I saw your house on fire we practically ran all the way here!"

"Why didn't you drive?" Nora asked as Pepper and her brood settled inside the car. "Where is Chuck?"

"He took the truck a while ago. A group of local farmers are rounding up more volunteers. Oh, Nora," she lamented, "they told him to bring all his guns and ammunition."

"Don't cry, Mom," little Thaddeus said. "I'll protect you."

"I don't know what's going on," Pepper said as a new volley of gunfire punched through the heartland. Suddenly, she pitched forward in the passenger seat and clutched her pregnant abdomen. "Oh, no! Not now, please, not now!"

"What's wrong? Are you in labor?" Without waiting for the answer, Nora put the car in gear and pulled onto the road.

"Don't think I can make it to a hospital," Pepper grimaced. "The pains are coming quickly."

Nora pressed the gas pedal and fishtailed down the country road. "I'll take you to the Bargain Bin. It's safer there!" She rattled over the rural dirt road, apologizing for every pothole and rut.

Halfway to town, it began to snow. Huge flakes fell like

paratroopers, and Nora hoped it might help quench some of the fires. Deep inside, she had her doubts. The North Dakota skyline glowed with orange flames—destruction was all around.

Pepper moaned and shifted as another contraction came.

"How many minutes apart?" Nora asked.

"I'm not really sure. Five minutes, maybe."

"We can do this," Nora said with forced calm. She hoped Pepper couldn't see the panic in her eyes. *I can't do this,* she thought, knowing that this baby would come whether she was up to the task or not.

On the edge of town, Nora's heart sank. Thick black smoke issued from the space where the granary had once stood. The whole block was devastated. The Laundromat and adjacent car lot across the street looked like a scrap metal yard.

Pepper clutched her belly and yelped in pain. "I think this is it!"

Nora was relieved to see that the Bargain Bin was still intact. She braked hard and jumped from the Chevy to help Pepper up the steps.

Nora handed Thaddeus her keychain and told him which key would unlock the door. Then she helped her neighbor from the car.

Pepper bent over with a grimace on the porch. "The baby's coming!"

"Just a few more feet!"

There was no time to fetch a doctor and no time for boiling water. James Tilden slid red-faced into the world on a braided rug just inside the room. He coughed, sputtered, and loudly protested his unorthodox arrival with a healthy set of lungs.

Nora built a fire and settled the other children to bed on a thick pile of vintage coats.

Too exhausted to sleep, she sat in a rocker, listening to the contented sound of the newborn suckling. She wondered, *What kind of world will he grow up in?*

Chapter 48

Virginia

Sunday, October 7th

Paige lay in bed thinking about her husband. Before dawn's first light she had made up her mind to return home and work things out.

Connor was no longer combative or rebellious, and his eating habits had returned to normal—all evidence to support her unilateral decision to take him off the medication. *Still, convincing Brody won't be easy,* she reminded herself.

Someone yelled, and from the hallway the sound of footsteps issued forth. Paige pulled on her cotton robe and opened the door to see a family standing with their luggage.

"Excuse me, but could you keep it down?" Paige glanced over her shoulder at Connor, lying in a tangle of bedding. She turned back to the hall with a conciliatory smile. "My little boy is still sleeping."

The man's mouth fell open. "Lady, you've got to be kidding! Our nation is under attack, and you're worried about your kid's sleep?" He hoisted a bag in each hand and herded his wife and kids down the corridor.

Paige called the switchboard. It rang and rang. She threw on her clothes and roused Connor. "Get up, honey. You can sleep in the car."

Connor sat up. "Are we going to see Daddy?"

"Yes," Paige said, quickly helping her son into a pair of sweats and a t-shirt. She packed their things.

There was chaos in the lobby—people everywhere, some pushing and raising their voices, others standing like pale corpses on a pilgrimage to the checkout counter.

"Can you tell me what has happened?" Paige asked a man beside her.

He mumbled something under his breath and tried to make a call on his cell phone.

A woman with an owlish face heard the question. "We've been attacked! The Newport News naval base is completely wiped out, I hear."

"Our Pacific fleet was hit, too." The man next to Paige had given up on his cell phone. "It appears they were ambushed by our allies in the Formosa Straight!"

"There's something going on along the Mexican border, but those reports are sketchy," the owlish woman said.

"See, Mom, I told you there would be a war," Connor said matter-of-factly.

Paige tried to remain calm, but panic set in. She decided to leave and send the lodge money later. "Listen, honey, we have snacks in the car. I think we should skip breakfast and go see Daddy right now."

Fifteen minutes later, they were inching down a winding road behind a bottleneck of other frantic drivers. Paige turned on the Land Rover's radio and flipped through static channels. Finally, she picked up the ghost of a news station. ". . . invasion over the Canadian border . . . fires, damage, and casualties. . . ." In the shadow of the mountain, the radio signal went fuzzy and was lost.

Paige glanced in the rearview mirror as cars stacked up behind her. Ahead, it was worse. There was no place to go.

She fumbled through her purse and grabbed the cell phone. For the first time in days, she dialed Brody's number. The call failed. She tried again with the same result.

The traffic went from a crawl to a complete stop. At this rate, they would never descend from the mountain. "Dear God," Paige prayed, "please help us."

North Dakota
Sunday, October 7th

In the cold October morning, Nora summoned her courage and drove to her farm to assess the damage. She looked upon the blackened remains of her smoldering home with stunned disbelief.

The jet fuel had incinerated everything, even melting the kitchen appliances. The plane was unrecognizable except for a few pieces that had scattered in the yard from impact. An emblem on the body of the fighter identified it as Royal Canadian Air Force. *Aren't they our allies?*

Before heading back to the Bargain Bin, Nora stopped by the Tilden's place to gather a few things for Pepper and the kids. Chuck had still not come home, so Nora left him a note telling him where his wife and children were. She didn't mention the new baby—that was Pepper's happy news to share.

Nora climbed back into the Chevy and took the long road back to town.

Smoke hung over scorched and smoldering fields. Yesterday's drought-stressed crops had flashed like a match set to tinder. Over and over again, the same scene played out; silos and barns were reduced to charred skeletons. *Who would do such a thing?*

Up ahead near Ingram's feedlot, the carcass of a cow lay across the road. There was room to go around, but Nora slowed to a stop and rolled down the window. The place was too quiet.

Several cowboys stood near the stock pens, their faces grave.

Nora called to them. "Can I help?"

"Lady, nobody can help." The elder man pushed the brim of his hat up. "Every last animal here has been poisoned."

"No!" Nora gasped.

He pointed to a black cloud on the horizon. "Looks like they took out the oil refinery, too."

All the way back to the Bargain Bin, Nora prayed for mercy.

Pepper was waiting for her when she walked through the door. "Did you see Chuck?"

"He's probably still busy helping out," Nora said, opting not to worry the new mother with the chilling details.

Pepper cradled her newborn and turned her worried eyes toward the window as a convoy of National Guard units drove past.

"I'm sure glad we've got this fireplace to keep us warm. I hear the whole power grid is down—no telling when they'll be able to get the juice flowing again." Nora poked at the coals, stacked some more logs on the fire, and went to make herself useful in the kitchen.

Gertie was making biscuits and praising the benefits of cooking with natural gas.

Nora lifted the lid on a massive pot that was simmering on the stove. "That's quite a batch of chicken noodle soup!"

"Mark my word," Gertie predicted. "By noon, this place will be overrun with folks." She was right. Some arrived hungry. Others came for warmth and comfort.

The local hardware store owner donated several boxes of supplies: utility masks for the smoke, candles, kerosene lanterns, batteries, and a hand-powered emergency radio. "I'm spreading the word," he announced. "Nora's Bargain Bin is the new community center!"

The radio was put to immediate use. The crowd gathered to listen to the report.

The naval base at Newport News has been destroyed. The Pacific Fleet was ambushed in the Formosa Straight. Massive casualties are feared. Along the northern border, the power grid has been sabotaged. Minot's air force base has been attacked. Grain, stockyards, and oil supplies were sabotaged.

The information was still spotty, but one thing was clear: the United States of America had been attacked on multiple fronts. Some operatives had been apprehended along the Mexican border, where another attack was thwarted. It was still unclear who was responsible.

J. J. O'Shay walked through the door. His eyes searched the crowd and stopped on Nora. "I need to talk to you alone," he said, mouthing the word, "alone."

She followed him to the storage room. "What's this about?"

He closed the door behind them and handed her a newspaper. "I picked this up at the grocery store last night."

Nora read the headlines and moaned. PRESIDENT'S LOVE CHILD WANTED FOR MURDER.

O'Shay put his big hand on Nora's shoulder. "Nice-looking boy. His name is Joel Sutherland."

The article featured a high school yearbook photograph. She couldn't take her eyes off of the image.

There was a knock on the storage room door. "Not a good time!" J. J. warned, but Gertie pushed her way inside.

"There's a customer who's come to claim a Hawaiian shirt. He says that he put it on layaway last summer." The blue-haired woman rolled her eyes. "Heck of a time to be shopping if you ask me!"

"It's okay." Nora found the shirt easily at the end of a storage rack and was passing it off to Gertie when the old man appeared behind her.

"There's the shirt of my dreams! I knew you wouldn't forget!"

Nora smiled politely. "I wasn't sure you'd come back."

"Always keep my word!" The bearded man approached and thrust out his hand. "Don't believe I properly introduced myself when I rolled through town last Fourth of July. The name is Zeke." He shook vigorously and then motioned over his shoulder. "And this here is my young traveling companion, Joel. You might be able to help the kid out. He's trying to find a relative who lives somewhere around these parts."

Nora froze as the teenager moved across the threshold. *He has my eyes and his father's nose.* She found herself across the room, carried by emotion. It felt like a dream. "Your search is over. I'm the one you're looking for."

Joel stared at Nora as though he was trying to process the words and their meaning.

She handed him the newspaper and waited anxiously as he scanned the article.

Finally, Joel looked up. His face was pale. "You're Nora Meyers? Is this really true?"

Her head was spinning. "Yes. I'm your birth mother, and Thomas Atwood is your father."

The teenager leaned against the wall. After a long minute, he asked, "Why did you give me up?"

"I wanted you to have a normal life. All these years I imagined you playing football, hanging out with friends." Nora choked on the words. "If I'd only known. . . ."

"What—that I would turn out to be a murderer?" Joel shot her a caustic look. "You think I killed my parents?"

Nora searched his eyes and shook her head. "No," she said, but he turned away.

"What's the use?" Joel jerked open the storage room door and made his way into the thrift shop, calling for Zeke.

"If you're lookin' for the old man who brought you, he's gone," Gertie called from the cash register. "He insisted on giving us twenty dollars for that shirt and didn't even want a receipt."

"That's just great! What am I going to do now?" Joel said staring out thc window. His eyes widened as a local sheriff pulled up in front of the Bargain Bin and then climbed from his cruiser.

Nora's heart sank as the lawman came through the door, but he looked right through her son. "I understand that Mrs. Chuck Tilden is staying here."

Pepper clutched the newborn babe to her breast with trembling hands. "Have you found my husband?"

The sheriff removed his hat and looked at her with sad eyes. "There was an explosion at the granary last night, and we have reason to believe. . . ."

The new mother let out a wail, and Gertie rushed over to take the infant from her arms.

"Chuck never got to see the baby!" Pepper sobbed as Nora came to her side.

Little Thaddeus Tilden collapsed on the floor and began to cry.

Joel stepped forward, gingerly placed a hand on the third-grader's shoulder, and knelt beside him. "I know how you feel. I lost my parents, too."

Chapter 49

Virginia
Sunday, October 7th

In the War Room at Thunder Ridge, Brody Hays sat with the president's cabinet members and key military personnel. It felt like a morose gathering of pallbearers at a funeral.

All eyes turned to the satellite images that flashed upon a large screen. The Navy base at Norfolk, Virginia, and much of the Hampton Roads area had been leveled.

General Teasdale stood below the screen with a laser pointer. "We have analyzed before and after images of the naval base. The explosion originated from this point—a disabled Russian missile submarine that had been escorted into port yesterday for emergency repairs." He indicated the spot with his pointer. "As you can see, the surface blast decimated the area. We anticipate mass casualties within a several mile radius of ground zero. The radiation hazards for fallout downwind of the blast are still being evaluated."

President Atwood slammed his fist on the conference table.

Beside him, the Secretary of Homeland Security tugged on the collar of his white shirt.

The door opened, and the national security advisor entered. Marta Bergen wasted no time on formalities. "These facts have just come in, sir." She handed the commander-in-chief a memo and then proceeded to read her own. "At approximately 3:45 AM, Eastern Daylight Time, on October 7th, a major power grid failure was reported. This outage affected the Midwest region and corresponding areas of Canada. Minutes later, a group of bombers crossed the northern border. A series of targets were struck, including granaries, refineries, and pipelines. These attacks were reported all across the heartland and continued as far south as Nebraska. Several operatives have been apprehended; they were suspected of poisoning stockyards throughout the region."

"I recommend that we mobilize ground units to perform additional sweeps," General Teasdale interjected.

"This appears to be a well-organized attack on our nation's infrastructure," the president said. "What about civilian casualties?"

Marta Bergen shook her head. "Undetermined at this time, sir."

"Two of our air bases were hit in the northern region, rendering our nuclear missile system inoperable," General Teasdale explained. "Several fighters managed to scramble from the Minot Air Force Base. Three invading planes were downed—F-18s from the Royal Canadian Air Force."

Atwood closed his eyes. "And the Pacific Fleet?"

"Two ships sent out distress signals: the USS La Jolla

and the USS Sampson." Teasdale lowered his head. "The carrier battle group was hit hard. I'm afraid there are reports of mass casualties."

"Eighteen thousand lives, or more!" the president snapped.

"It appears that our navy was lured into an ambush by our allies," Marta Bergen added. "Sir, we need to consider the possibility that this attack was coordinated multi-nationally."

"We know that Canada, Russia, and most likely China are involved. Do you think there are others?" Atwood asked.

Nathan Kooper, head of the NSA, leaned forward. "I'd like to address that possibility. During the late evening hours, we picked up a lot of suspicious cell phone chatter. Of particular interest was some unusual cell phone traffic in German and French. Our analysts are currently working on this, and we should be able to provide more information within the hour."

The president looked at Brody. "What if the mass stock divesture was the first phase in a larger plan of attack?"

News feeds began to flood the screen. The camera's eye showed oil refineries all across the northern US burning out of control, issuing huge plumes of black smoke. Pockets of smoldering earth marked spots where granaries had been, and feedlots were littered with thousands of carcasses.

Thomas Atwood processed the information in silence and then stood abruptly. "I want a statement prepared. The American people must be reassured that their government is operational."

As the crowd filed from the War Room, the president pulled his chief economic advisor aside. "I hear your wife and son are missing."

Brody thought about the text message that David had sent. "They are, or at least they were somewhere in Shenandoah."

Atwood's eyebrows rose. "That's not far from here."

"That's correct, sir, but the roads are impassable and cell phone service is jammed. I have not been able to reach them."

"You'll be no good to me if your mind is elsewhere, Hays," the president said. "Use our resources and get your family here."

Virginia

Sunday, October 7th

Paige listened to the rapid beeping of her cell phone. All circuits busy. She tossed the phone on the car seat beside her and stifled the urge to scream. Interstate 66 had become one long parking lot, a host to travelers desperate to contact loved ones. Local cell towers were overwhelmed.

A car horn honked. Paige jumped and craned her neck. She saw nothing but traffic that hadn't moved for over an hour. *At least we made it off the mountain.*

Paige kept an anxious eye upon the Land Rover's gas gauge. There was less than a quarter of a tank left.

She grabbed her cell phone and again tried Brody's number, to no avail.

Another chorus of horns blared. Paige put her hands over her ears and tried to think, but nothing came to mind. She attempted prayer, but the words came out wrong. *Why is this happening?*

People began to emerge from their cars to stretch and mill about.

A commotion erupted behind the Land Rover. Paige adjusted her mirror for a discreet look. Two women nearly came to blows beside a rusty Ford Ranger. One, wearing jeans and a baggy t-shirt, shoved the other, who was dressed in a tailored business suit. The businesswoman opened her mouth and spewed a volcano of profanities.

Paige glanced at Connor, coloring intently in the back seat. He didn't seem to notice.

The woman wearing jeans marched over to a sedan, reached inside for the keys, and lobbed them through the air, laughing as the businesswoman scrambled to fetch them.

One by one, frustrated travelers came unraveled. *Things are getting dangerous!*

A few cars ahead, a young man wearing a hoodie climbed on the roof of his Jeep to survey I-66. Paige lowered her window and called out, "What do you see?"

"Nothing's moving." He hopped down and approached the Land Rover. "Hey, lady, you got anything to eat or drink in there?"

Paige replied with a fib. "No." There were only two juice boxes left and even less to eat—a half-eaten box of animal crackers and a granola bar.

The air outside carried an October chill, yet Paige noticed pinprick beads of sweat glistening on the young man's face. "Are you all right?" she asked.

"I've got diabetes. I'm feeling hypoglycemic."

Paige retrieved a box of juice from the glove box and handed it to the young man with an apologetic shrug. "Sorry

I wasn't straight with you, but my son and I have to ration what we have."

He gulped down the juice and turned desperate eyes to the road. "Thanks," he said, crushing the empty juice box and returning to his car.

Paige turned on the radio and perused the stations for news. Accounts of the attacks flooded the airwaves—US Navy casualties, massive losses to granaries, livestock, and oil refineries—but the reports gave no indication that help was coming her way.

This is worse than a bad dream—it's a nightmare! Grocery stores all across the country were being pillaged, and supply trucks could not get through.

The shrill whine of a motor caught Paige's attention. From her side mirror, she watched a motorcycle wind like a serpent through the traffic jam. It shot the gaps with ease and found no resistance until it passed the Land Rover.

Suddenly, there was a clatter, and the biker was taken down by the kid in the hoodie. Fists flailed; in the end, the young man in the hoodie roared off on the motorcycle.

Paige gripped the steering wheel and began to tremble.

A little hand touched her shoulder. "Don't worry, Mom. The angel said we'll be okay."

The shadows lengthened. Some of the motorists were abandoning their cars and setting out on foot. It would be dark in about three hours, and it was doubtful they could find shelter. *It's out of my control,* Paige told herself. There was nothing left to do but cling to the faithful words of her child.

Paige rubbed her hands together and started the engine to let the heater cycle again. The dashboard flashed a low fuel warning.

Their food and drink was nearly gone. Connor was napping now, but he would be hungry when he awoke. *What then?* she thought.

The Land Rover's engine died with a shudder and a gasp.

Paige opened the suitcase and layered its contents over her sleeping boy. *Survival is no longer just a theme on TV,* she thought.

Arizona

Sunday, October 7th

David unlocked the General Store, held the door open for Elita, and followed her inside. She reached for the sign in the window, but he grabbed his wife's hand. "Leave the Closed sign right where it is today." David pulled her close enough to feel her beating heart and kissed her silken hair. He lifted his bride and carried her up the stairs to their apartment.

The afternoon sun streamed softly through their window sheers and fell across Elita's olive skin. Her eyes glistened with flecks of gold.

"You have never looked more beautiful than you do right now." David kissed her gently and felt her open up to him.

They expressed their love without a word, melting into each other's arms until time suspended and their souls became one.

In the afterglow, David stroked Elita's warm, satin skin. "There was a time when the love in your eyes frightened me," he said.

"Why?"

"I didn't believe that I could ever deserve such love."

"Love is like the mystery of God's grace. None of us can ever earn it." Elita placed her hand over her husband's heart. "David, you promised no more secrets," she said. "I want to know what hurt you bad enough to make you want to run all those years."

He stared at the ceiling. "Do you remember the photograph you asked about?"

"The pretty little girl?"

"That's my niece, Emily." David paused. "She was three years old when I caused her death."

Elita sat up and pulled the covers around her. "What happened?"

"We were at my family's summer lake house. I was trying out my new Jet Ski. Emily wanted to go for a ride, but my sister Paige said no." David closed his eyes. "I gave my sister a hard time—ribbed her about being overprotective. She finally relented." He grew quiet.

Elita curled her fingers around her husband's. "I'm listening."

"There was a speedboat full of teenagers; they just appeared out of nowhere! The next thing I remember was coming up out of the water holding my niece and some fishermen helping us into their boat."

David's face dropped into his hands. "I had to give Emily's body to her mother."

The couple held each other as tears flowed.

Outside, the nation is in chaos, David thought as he held his bride. *In here, all that matters is this love.*

Chapter 50

Virginia

Sunday, October 7th

On the helipad at Thunder Ridge, a Huey sat fueled and ready to fly. Nearby, a small troop of soldiers huddled together. The mission to rescue Paige and Connor, dubbed Operation: Driftwood, had been treated like a special ops assignment.

Brody's stomach churned as he watched the skyline for the arrival of a Black Hawk from a nearby base. He checked his watch—thirty minutes to go. He'd been told that the mission was risky; the masses of stranded and frightened citizens were growing desperate.

The Black Hawk sliced through rays of evening light and hovered above the landing. Brody could make out the faces of men in helmets and battle fatigues as they descended. The whole thing seemed unreal. Young soldiers, ready to subdue their own countrymen if necessary, were at the ready.

Fifty yards away, men boarded the Huey to await liftoff.

The blades wound down, a hatch opened on the Black Hawk, and a man emerged. "Are you Brody Hays?"

"Yes."

The man reached out and briskly shook his hand. "I'm Colonel Meese. I'd like to go over the details of our assignment." He slipped a laptop from his pack and booted it up. A map appeared on the screen, showing I-66. He pointed to a spot on the map. "This is the cell tower that picked up your wife's last call attempt."

Colonel Meese typed on the keyboard, and a circle appeared on the screen. "This is our perimeter, assuming that traffic hasn't moved since that call, which I highly doubt. Our objective is to get in, locate and retrieve our targets, and then retreat with minimal civilian disturbance."

"Of course." Brody tugged at his collar.

The colonel swept his hand toward the craft. "Okay then, Mr. Hays. Daylight's burning!"

Brody climbed aboard, strapped on a headset, and nodded at the soldiers seated around him in rows. The whine of the engine grew shrill, and the foom-foom-foom sound of the blades melded into one sound.

A moment later they were in air, cutting across the massive Thunder Ridge facility. From this viewpoint, Brody noticed snipers positioned on the rooflines. Along the fence-line were turrets housing machine guns. Up ahead at the north gate, trouble was brewing.

The road just outside the twelve-foot-high chain link fence was clogged with civilian vehicles.

A crowd had gathered—their faces angry, their fists raised.

Suddenly, a shot rang out. A bullet deflected across the Black Hawk's window. "Cripes, we've been fired upon!" the pilot cried out, putting more power to the throttle.

The Huey took a less direct route to avoid the fray. More shots followed. Brody looked back to see the civilian crowd scattering. One American lay dead on the roadway with a pistol at his side.

"You ain't seen nothing yet," one of the flight crew said. "We just came from surveying the inner cities. It's like a bad Hollywood movie."

Over the ridge, Brody spotted the tiny village of Paris, Virginia. It looked like a circus. Just beyond that, US 50 snaked across the valley, every inch jammed with cars.

As the aircraft passed overhead, people spilled from their vehicles, waving frantic arms.

"There's a bit of a logistical problem down there," the colonel said. "We're trying to line up a relief effort, but they can't get in with supplies until the road is cleared. If we drop supplements in the middle of this mess, riots could break out."

The mood in the helicopter was tense. The soldiers' eyes were downcast, their faces pensive. The message, though unspoken, was clear. These people could be neighbors, family, even friends. Brody wondered how many of these young men were worried about their own loved ones.

"So, it's your wife and kid we're going after?" one of the soldiers asked.

"That's right." Brody rubbed at a knot in his neck.

A couple of silent minutes later, they flew over another rise and spotted Interstate 66.

The colonel barked the coordinates to a member of the crew and pulled out his field glasses. "Land Rover, you say?"

"Yes. It's silver."

Onboard, a communications specialist leaned forward. "Sir, I'm going to patch something in that you'll be interested in hearing."

Brody raised an eyebrow at the young specialist. "What am I listening to?"

"Your wife, sir. Basically, cell phones are radios that can also be used as listening devices, even when they're turned off."

Holding his hands over the headphones, Brody strained to hear over the rotors chopping at the air. He heard a horn honk, muffled shouts, and the rustling of paper. Then the sound of soft but steady breathing met his ear. "Mom, I'm hungry." A lump caught in Brody's throat. *Connor's voice!*

"I know, sweetie," Paige soothed. "We'll get something to eat just as soon as we can."

Brody stared from the window of the helicopter, scanning the cars for any sign of his family. "There it is!"

"We'll make a pass over the Land Rover and try to prompt her by hand," the colonel said.

Below, a crowd of stranded motorists gathered as the helicopter hovered.

"We need to get our targets to an open area. Try and direct your family to that field."

Paige stepped from the Land Rover, shading her eyes against the dusky sky.

The craft swept lower, and Paige's face lit with surprise when she saw Brody.

The aircraft's radio device came to life, and they heard Paige say, "Daddy's here! He came to get us."

Paige waived her arms, but she stopped when Brody held a finger to his lips. He pointed to the field on the south side of the road.

The crowed surged forward, swallowing Paige and the Land Rover.

People screamed for help.

Brody again pointed to the field and mouthed the words, "We'll be back." The helicopter banked over the tree-lined ridge to give Paige a chance to respond to instructions.

"You think she understood?"

"I hope so," Brody said.

Colonel Meese pressed the headset to his ear. "Roger that." He tapped the Black Hawk pilot, who turned back toward the interstate. "The decoy is ready, and our targets are in place. It's now or never, boys."

On the north side of Interstate 66, the Huey descended as a decoy. Motorists scrambled toward the aircraft like moths to a flame.

The diversion worked. On the opposite side of the interstate, in a field, Paige and Connor awaited their evacuation.

On the north side, people scratched and clawed their way toward the decoy, but the Huey lifted back into the air. The people went wild. It was now a mob.

Yards away from Paige, the Black Hawk descended. Doors opened, and armed soldiers spilled from its belly.

"Come on!" Brody yelled.

Paige scooped their son into her arms and raced for the aircraft.

The crowd was now wise to their tactic, and the soldiers,

with guns at the ready, formed a perimeter.

Paige reached the Black Hawk as the mob pressed in.

"Stay back!" the colonel ordered through a loudspeaker. "We are prepared to use deadly force if necessary."

"I'm an American!" someone screamed.

"We have rights!" another shrieked.

Brody heard the sound of warning shots as Paige fell into his arms. The rotors picked up speed. The soldiers quickly boarded, and they lifted off.

Without warning, one man leapt onto the helicopter's skid and hung on. Undaunted, the pilot flew over the hill and then hovered low until the exhausted civilian dropped safely onto a clearing.

Paige's eyes filled with grateful tears. "How did you know?"

"David let me know you were in Shenandoah, and these guys did the rest." Brody pulled her and Connor close and held them in a tight embrace. "Everything is going to be okay now."

It was a short flight back to Thunder Ridge. Brody breathed a sigh of relief when his family disembarked on protected ground

The president and a handful of other personnel were waiting near the helipad. "An organization has claimed responsibility for the attack," Atwood announced.

Spence Carlyle took it from there. "A group made up of frustrated G-20 nations." He shot Brody an icy look. "This will play out as a huge diplomatic blunder. I hope you realize that this tosses our political opponent a huge bone! Weeks away from the election, and we've got a nation in chaos.

Ground transportation has halted. Just think about the implications—grocery stores and pharmacies with shelves stripped bare! People will be looking for someone to blame."

The president held up his hand to silence his chief political advisor. "The election is the least of my concerns right now. Moreover, no 'diplomatic blunder,' as you say, warrants a surprise attack!" He turned to Brody. "I'm glad your family is safe. They must be exhausted. I'll have an aide show them to your quarters."

Suddenly, Connor rushed forward and tugged on the president's jacket. "I'm supposed to tell you something."

"Connor!" Paige admonished.

"It's all right." Atwood stooped to ruffle the boy's hair. "What's on your mind, little man?"

"It's a secret—I can't tell anybody but you."

Atwood smiled. "Your son's got the makings of a future CIA agent," he said, kneeling beside the child.

Connor cupped his hands around his mouth and whispered into the president's ear.

The nation's commander-in-chief drew back and stared at the boy. "Who told you this?"

"A man."

"What did he look like?"

Connor thought for a moment. "Kinda like our yard gnome."

"Old—with a white beard?"

"The child nodded."

The president stood slowly, turned a pale face to his staff, and said, "Ladies and gentlemen, we've got a wounded nation to mend."

Epilogue

North Dakota

Friday, November 2nd

At the Bargain Bin, Nora took inventory of God's provisions: a roof over her head, the generosity of neighbors, and her best friend, Abigail, who had joined the growing helps ministry. But, above all, Nora thanked the Lord for bringing her son back into her life.

She thought anxiously about Joel's future. The locals all knew who he was, yet they chose to keep it to themselves. Still, it was only a matter of time before someone would turn him in to the authorities. Today, however, she set her worries aside. *This is to be a day of celebration—my son's birthday.*

In the kitchen, one of Gertie's famous German chocolate cakes was waiting with sixteen candles on top. It was an occasion Nora thought she would never see. *If only his father could share the moment.*

The election was days away, and things did not look good for Thomas Atwood. His personal past was the least of his political worries. The president's opponent found ample fodder in his quest for the White House. He blamed Atwood for economic and diplomatic blunders that led to one of the most devastating attacks ever perpetrated against the United States of America.

J. J. O'Shay pushed open the front door. "Hey, everybody, it looks like rain!" Behind him, Joel's arms were loaded with boxes.

"Do I smell chocolate?" J. J. asked, sniffing the air. "Sure beats the smell of Gertie's cabbage stew."

"I heard that, you big huckleberry!" the old woman bellowed.

Joel peeked around the stacked cardboard. "Where do you want these?"

The telephone rang as Nora pointed to the storage room. She watched her son navigate around racks of used clothing. She plucked the phone from the cradle and said, "Bargain Bin."

"White House switchboard calling. Please hold for the President of the United States."

It was the call Nora had been dreading. The fact that she'd kept Joel's whereabouts a secret from Thomas Atwood brought on a wave of guilt.

The president began with an apology. "I hope you understand why I've been remiss in calling."

"I assume you've been a little busy lately," she returned.

The president laughed. "Nora, I have some new information about Joel. The FBI has made an arrest. His sister has confessed to the murder of both their parents."

"What? I don't understand! I thought Joel's sister was dead."

"The FBI found some postcards in Joel's room in

Florida. These led them to New Orleans where she was living. I'll spare you all the details. Bottom line: Joel is innocent, and Florida's State Attorney is moving to have the governor pardon Joel." The president paused. "Nora, I'd like to wish my son a happy birthday. Will you put him on the phone?"

"What? But I—"

"I've known for a while now that he was with you," Atwood said. "You don't need to explain anything."

Nora spotted Joel as he emerged from the storage room. She motioned him over and handed him the phone, whispering, "It's the president—your father."

The teenager's eyes widened.

"It's okay," Nora assured him.

Rain pattered softy on the porch roof as Joel talked to the man who had given him life. "Yes, sir, I'd like that very much." Joel hung up and bucked like a calf bursting from a stall. "I've been cleared!"

Gertie had slipped into the kitchen and returned with the cake, lit with candles. Everyone joined in song and shared in the celebration.

Outside, the skies opened up to quench the drought-baked soil. *God has heard our prayers!* Nora thought as tears of gratitude fell with the rain.

Arizona

Saturday, November 3rd

It was a beautiful morning at Hope Springs. Blue sky reflected in the fresh pools that flowed from the spring.

David pulled Paige's letter from his jacket pocket along with some enclosed photos. He passed them to his wife. "My sister is planning to come out to see us."

"I can't wait!" Elita eagerly thumbed through the pictures. "Connor looks like a little cutie!"

In the distance, a long line of vehicles caravanned over the recently graded road. "It seems like the whole town of Arroyo Seco is turning out," David observed.

"Who can blame them?" Elita squeezed her husband's hand. "It's not every community that can claim so many heroes."

"We only did what we had to do," David said. "That's hardly worthy of all this fuss."

The ragtag bikers were the last to arrive. News cameras followed the Freedom Riders' slow amble to their designated seats beneath the pavilion and panned the crowd as an Arizona congressman stepped to the podium and began the ceremony.

"We have assembled here today to honor our local heroes with our nation's highest civilian honor: the Presidential Medal of Freedom," he said. "These men and women bravely faced mortal danger in aid to their fellow man and also to our country." One at a time, the congressman called their names, and the recipients came forward to receive their medals. Among them were David Filmore, several border patrol agents, members of the Civic Border Guard, the leather-clad Freedom Riders, key residents of Hope Springs, and a group of brave Mexicans, who would be fast tracked to US citizenship if they so desired.

The US representative concluded the formal procedure

by reading a letter from the President of the United States, "Your selflessness and courage remind us of everything that is right with America. In the heartbeat of citizens such as you, the lifeblood of our freedom flows."

The people of Arroyo Seco launched to their feet and thundered their applause. There wasn't a dry eye in the pavilion.

"Would you look at this?" David said, noting the bikers and barflies picnicking with church ladies from neighboring communities.

"Everybody needs to feel loved." Elita cast her husband an anxious look and added, "David, there's something I need to tell you."

He draped his arm over her shoulder. "I'm all ears."

"Not here," she said, watching a cluster of children playing near the spring-fed pool. "Would you walk with me?"

On the hill behind Hope Springs, David helped his bride climb atop the rock—the same rock where Rupert Sims had once stood as a boy.

"Look!" Elita pointed to a rainbow that arched over the new town. "It's a sign!" They watched until the colors faded.

"What did you want to tell me?" David asked.

Elita looked at him with worried eyes. "I'm pregnant."

He took her in his arms, but she pulled away.

Her eyes met his, confused. "But you didn't want children."

David held a finger to his lips. "That's all changed. Love like ours can only bring forth joy!"

"If it's a girl, that's what we'll call her!" Elita's face glowed.

From atop the rock, David turned toward the gathering at Hope Springs. “Hey, everyone,” he yelled. “I’m going to be a father!”

Washington, DC

Friday, November 9th

Brody Hays escorted his wife and son into the East Room, still reeling from the recent turn of events. He could still see the headlines in his mind: ATWOOD LOSES WHITEHOUSE 57-43.

He did his best to put the defeat aside. They were there to say goodbye to other West Wing staffers and their families.

He leaned over and spoke softly in Paige’s ear. “Did I tell you how lovely you look?”

“Yes, several times.” She smiled and squeezed her husband’s hand as Connor hurried over to look at the ice carving on the hors d’oeuvres table.

A servant moved about the gathering with a silver tray loaded with champagne flutes, originally planned to toast the president’s reelection.

Everyone was mildly surprised when the staff dinner remained on the schedule despite the opponent’s landslide victory on Tuesday.

It was just politics, but to Brody and the rest of his West Wing comrades, it was also deeply personal.

The cocktail hour dwindled, and everyone found their places around linen-covered tables with elegant settings.

Brody and his family sat across from White House Press

Secretary Irene Moyer and a few members of the legal team. The mood was subdued and the conversation stilted—there was nothing left to say.

The chaplain asked a blessing as the wait staff served the first course: lasagna swimming in plum vinaigrette. The main course would be a thyme-roasted sea bass and three-bean succotash.

Paige leaned over to her husband, holding her menu. "The chef has outdone himself."

"Herself," Brody corrected. Then he whispered, "She doesn't hold a candle to my own personal gourmet."

After dinner, the servants removed the plates and served dessert and coffee.

President Atwood rose to speak. He paused to look at each familiar face. "We were all stunned by the sudden and deep wounds inflicted upon our country. Never in my lifetime did I anticipate such an invasion, and certainly not on my watch. There will be no second chance for us to shore up our country's breeches—no time to rebuild a stronger America. For this, I grieve."

Thomas Atwood gazed up at the crystal chandelier, his face reflecting sorrow. "The future of the United States of America is tenuous. I fear she now stands upon sinking sand."

The president clasped his hands upon the podium and continued. "The vision and tenets of faith held dear by our nation's founding fathers are being usurped by a new global culture. Why is this happening in our time?" he asked.

"General George Washington once said, '. . . it is the duty of all Nations to acknowledge the providence of Almighty God, to obey his will. . . .'" Atwood paused and then added reflectively, "Could it be that we have fallen short and reaped divine consequences?"

The president's gaze swept across the room. "I want to share a strange but remarkable tale—one that has changed my perspective and given me a deep sense of peace."

All eyes, many moist with tears, were fixed upon their commander-in-chief.

"This story began with a reoccurring dream I have had. The contents and details of this disturbing nightmare, I have shared with no one—not even my dear wife, Heddy."

Atwood took a moment to steady his shaking hands. "In the dream, I am dressed in a suit, sitting in a fancy chair, and reading financial reports. Something disturbs me, and I look up to find that I am in the midst of a burned-out field. In the distance, I see a city burning." The president drew in a sharp breath and continued. "My heart is racing and my fears are aflame! Then, as if from nowhere, a strange little man with a white beard appears. He places a single red rose in a combat boot, as though it were a vase, and turns to speak to me."

The president stepped from the podium and moved to Brody's table. He laid a hand on Connor's head. "On one of the darkest days of my life, this child spoke those very same words to me—the exact message given by the bearded man in my dreams."

The East Room fell to unearthly silence. No silver spoon or china cup was raised. It was so quiet that it seemed as if no one dared to breathe.

"'It was never in your hands,' the old man said to me." Thomas Atwood rubbed his chin. "Such a simple statement, yet it carried the power to set me free from hopelessness and despair."

Brody felt overcome by humility as he watched his little son smiling up at the President of the United States.

Thomas Atwood returned to the podium. "Friends, it has been both an honor and a privilege to serve with you. I leave you with the wisdom of George Washington who spoke of a destiny that cannot be resisted by the strongest efforts of human nature. As you work to rebuild your individual lives, consider that a sovereign hand still moves among us."

Be on the lookout for
Books Two and Three of the Trilogy –
The Third Woe and The Third Day

ABOUT THE AUTHOR

From her Grandfather's tales about Buffalo Bill to the mystique of the West, L. P. Hoffman's imagination was primed at an early age. In her transient childhood, she experienced the dark side of Caribbean culture and survived war in the Middle East. As an adult, the author has traveled the world and moved among Washington insiders. L. P. Hoffman values unique perspectives and believes that culturally relevant stories born of experience are the ones best told.

Read more about
L.P. Hoffman

LPHoffman.com

Visit and "Like" L.P. Hoffman,
Author on Facebook

L. P. Hoffman Author on Facebook

OTHER NOVELS BY L.P. HOFFMAN

Murder in Maine, wolves in Wyoming, and a fugitive—one life-changing summer for wolf biologist, Anna O'Neil. She needs answers. Who shot her father and why? Then, the arrival of a mysterious document forces Anna to examine her own beliefs and gives her the key to restore a divided community. But, first, she must find the courage to confront a hidden evil and catch her father's killer.

The Pied Piper still plays his tune, and in his shadow, many fall.

When a disturbed teenager arrives at the Pittsburgh Rescue Mission, Cali turns things upside down by claiming to know "secrets" about a young evangelist's shadowy past. The deranged girl lures Jesse Berry across the country only to slip away after they reach their destination. Hamlin, Montana, is not the quaint mining town it appears to be. Something sinister moves below the surface—the youth are at risk—and someone there wants Jesse dead.

L. P. Hoffman books are available in paperback and eBook at:
Your Local Bookstore
www.HopeSpringsMedia.com — 1 (434) 574-2031
www.Amazon.com
www.BarnesandNoble.com

HopeSpringsMedia.com